She journeyed into the wilderness to find a kidnapped relative. She stayed to build a new life filled with adventure, danger, and passion.

Spring, 1768. The Southern frontier is a treacherous wilderness inhabited by the powerful Cherokee people. In Charlestown, twenty-five- year-old Quincy MacFadden receives news from beyond the grave: her cousin, a man she'd believed long dead, is alive—held captive by the Shawnee Indians. Unmarried, bookish, and plagued by visions of the future, Quinn is a woman out of place . . . and this is the opportunity for which she's been longing.

Determined to save two lives, her cousin's and her own, Quinn travels the rugged Cherokee Path into the South Carolina Blue Ridge. Defying her furious grandfather and colonial law, she barters for leverage against the Shawnee with a notorious Cherokee chief—and begins building a daring new home in the Keowee River Valley, a fiercely beautiful place.

But in order to rescue her cousin, Quinn must trust an enigmatic half-Cherokee tracker whose loyalties may lie elsewhere. As translator to the British army, Jack Wolf walks a perilous line between a King he hates and a homeland he loves.

Together they journey across the Appalachian Mountains and into the heart of Cherokee country. They encounter wily trappers, warring Indians, British soldiers, desperate settlers, and a contested backcountry on the brink of changing forever.

When Jack is ordered to negotiate for Indian loyalty in the Revolution to come, the pair must decide: obey the Crown, or commit treason . . .

Praise for *Keowee Valley*

"Keowee Valley is a terrific first novel by Katherine Scott Crawford—a name that should be remembered. She has a lovely prose style, a great sense of both humor and history, and she tells about a time in South Carolina that I never even imagined."
—Pat Conroy, author of *The Prince of Tides* and *South of Broad*

"Keowee Valley is Katherine Scott Crawford's stunning debut novel. You will savor her artful prose and storytelling. She writes of American south, in particular, the mountains with awe and wonder. South Carolina has never been more evocative or beautiful. The story of Quincy and Jack is compelling and real. A glorious debut from a gifted author."
—Adriana Trigiani, bestselling author of *Big Stone Gap* and *The Shoemaker's Wife*

"Katherine Scott Crawford has merged history and drama in this compelling story of one woman's boldness and courage. Crawford is a fresh and valuable new voice in Southern Literature."
—Ron Rash, author of *Serena* and *Saints at the River*

"In Quincy MacFadden, Crawford creates a feisty, gutsy heroine who survives those fraught years before the American Revolution in Appalachian Indian country, finding love even as she defines the spirit that will create a nation. The frontier equivalent to Abigail Adams in Boston or Dolley Madison in Philadelphia. I read it in one eager, page-turning sitting."
—Beverly Swerling, bestselling author of *City of Promise* and *Shadowbrook*

"Keowee Valley is a wonderful story, and Katherine Scott Crawford is a powerful witness to the lost world of the Southern frontier when much of it was Cherokee land. Her understanding of the complex history of the times and her obvious love (and intimate knowledge of) the landscape make this

book a treasure, especially to those of us who knew the gorgeous Keowee Valley in South Carolina before it was destroyed by a power company lake. Above all, though, this is the story of a strong woman, Quincy MacFadden, and her equally strong half-Cherokee soul mate, Jack Wolf. Their passion in this doomed world is the lens through which one can once again touch and be touched by a place that was once so beautiful, so historically important, and which has now so tragically vanished."
—Philip Lee Williams, author of *A Distant Flame*, winner of the Michael Shaara Prize for Civil War fiction

"Adventure and romance abound in Katherine Scott Crawford's rich and evocative debut novel. From the bustling streets of colonial Charleston to the beauty and savagery of the untamed Carolina wilderness, the reader is swept up in the tale of one woman's quest for independence on the American frontier, and of the extraordinary man she meets along the way who finally tames her heart. Keowee Valley is a story of the courage and passion it takes to follow a dream, and of the sacrifices often required in order to hold on to it."
—Darci Hannah, author of *The Exile of Sara Stevenson* and *The Angel of Blythe Hall*

"With a distinctive voice and fine eye for the details that shape character, Katherine Scott Crawford richly depicts a fascinating time and place. Her themes are not only southern but human."
—Elise Blackwell, author of *The Unnatural History of Cypress Parish*

To the stellar list of Appalachian fiction writers we can now add Katherine Scott Crawford for her impressive *Keowee Valley*. Crawford manages to interweave the historical and the personal in this novel, and, perhaps more important, give voice to the landscape in which this story takes place. Well-grounded and well-narrated, this novel will take its place in the library of any reader who cares about Appalachian literature.
—Kathryn Stripling Byer, author of *Wildwood Flower* and *Black Shawl*,
   2005-2009 Poet Laureate of North Carolina

Keowee Valley

CHOTA

Cherokee Lands

NORTH CAROLINA

Keowee Valley

Ft. Prince George

Saluda River

Ninety Six

SOUTH CAROLINA

GEORGIA

Savannah River

Santee River

Creek Lands

Charlestown

ATLANTIC OCEAN

Keowee Valley

by

Katherine Scott Crawford

Bell Bridge Books

Bell Bridge Books
PO BOX 300921
Memphis, TN 38130

Print ISBN: 978-1-61194-172-2

Bell Bridge Books is an Imprint of BelleBooks, Inc.

We at BelleBooks enjoy hearing from readers.
Visit our websites – www.BelleBooks.com and www.BellBridgeBooks.com.

10 9 8 7 6 5 4 3 2 1
Cover design: Debra Dixon
Interior design: Hank Smith
Cover Art: M.C. Krauss
Keowee Valley Map: James Pharr
Interior art: James Pharr
Black Bear: Sergei Galushko@dreamstime.com
Feather: Artcp5@dreamstime.com
:Lvkx:01:

For my family, who always believed

(especially for Stuart)

Prologue

My story begins before the fall, in that Indian summer time when the hills are tipped with oncoming gold, and the light hangs just above the trees, dotting the Blue Ridge with gilded freckles. The mornings and the evenings are cool, but it is the mornings I remember most: waking before the men, wrapping a shawl around my shoulders and slipping out through the fields, the dry grass crunching beneath my boots. Drifting down from Tomassee Knob the mist would spread over the Keowee Valley in a great, rivering pool of gray, the sun rising in the east flecking the horses' breath—suspended in the air before their nostrils—with slivers of shine. It was then the whole world was quiet, no crows eating my corn, the peacefulness not even broken by the bay of some wolf on the ridge, calling to the still-lit moon in the western sky. The whole world was silent then, and the Blue Ridge breathed beneath the deep purple earth. I thought I could feel it, a great heart beating in the wilderness.

He came to me in the morning. I had crossed the north fields and made my way to the creek at the edge of the forest to check on the last of the Solomon's Seals I'd watched cling to the embankment in the final days of summer. Ferns reaching the height of my elbows billowed out from the ground, spreading for what looked like miles. The smell of sap emanated from fallen pines where woodpeckers searched for tiny bugs and snakes lay still in the cool undergrowth. Every once in a while a squirrel or rabbit leapt from its camouflaged hiding place, skirting the path I walked.

Coals from a recent fire smoldered black in a pile a few yards from a bend in the creek, and I looked up and farther into the woods, wondering if a Cherokee scout or perhaps a trapper had decided to take his rest on our land. But the woods were eerily still, and not a bird sang nor cricket chirped. There was no movement except for the creek itself, bubbling up against a tiny dam made by runaway branches, cane and weeds. My eyes came to rest across the creek on shadows at the bottom of an enormous oak. Suddenly, the shadows shifted, and the shape of a man stepped forward, seeming to emerge seamlessly from the trunk, his feet making no sound in the leaves.

The breath caught in a knot in my throat, and I placed a hand there, the other fumbling in my skirts for the lady's flintlock I'd been given. He walked closer, still without sound, and stood watching me from the edge of the creek bed. I pulled the pistol from its hold, pointing it unsteadily at the stranger.

"Come no closer," I ordered, the words tumbling awkwardly off my tongue and echoing softly in the small dip of valley.

He raised his head, eyes emerging from beneath the brim of a battered farmer's hat. Across that creek they looked as green to me as moss growing on boulders in the water. His hair was long, the fawn color of a well-worn leather saddle, and the ends were tipped with the same pale blond that streaked through the rest, like he'd dipped his head in white paint. He looked like a white man turned savage, with his moccasin-laced boots and dirty, fringed deerskin shirt, a beaded strap crossing his chest, holding a hatchet and musket on his back. He did not speak, just looked at me from under that hat, shadows cast high on his cheekbones and the solid line of his jaw. The creek gurgling and my breathing were the only sounds. Soon, I knew, the settlement would awake, and the animals would need to be fed, the horses let to pasture.

Surely someone would notice I was missing.

It was the first time he had come to me, but it would not be the last. And though my story ends with him, he did not cause it to begin. I did that, on a midsummer day in the year of our Lord 1768, in the twenty-fifth year of my youth.

Part I

Backcountry

"Enter these enchanted woods, You who dare."
—*George Meredith*

"Boldness be my friend!"
—*William Shakespeare*

Chapter 1

Charlestown
Spring, 1768

I was an unlikely adventurer, at least by all appearances. I knew what the people of Charlestown saw when they looked at me: a wealthy woman clad in the new fashions, small of stature but possessed of an unruly mane of yellow hair that made me seem taller—a bluestocking with a well-worn volume forever in hand, one who looked out at the world from a pair of disconcertingly direct blue eyes. The ladies, especially, would whisper "orphan," and allow that the early demise of my parents could be reason enough for a man such as my grandfather to keep me a spinster at age twenty-five. The gentlemen viewed my person with vague calculation, surely wondering just how much—as the sole granddaughter of Campbell MacFadden, Esquire, heir by marriage to a profitable rice plantation—I was worth. And so when the trapper arrived in the hour before dawn, smelling of wood smoke and the sweat of a hard ride, I was ready: ready to abandon Charlestown and my life there, to shutter permanently those judging, prying eyes.

It was the banging on the door that woke me, more than the shouting. On the peninsula, banging on doors in the wee hours nearly always meant one of two things: a slave uprising, or a fire. On Tradd Street alone there had been three devastating fires the past year, conflagrations that destroyed entire blocks, and I threw off the covers and rounded my bed in moments, pulling a stout case from beneath my desk and dumping the contents of my drawers—papers, pamphlets, quills, stoppered inkpot—as quickly as I could. I heard Grandfather's footfall on the stairs outside my bedroom door, his step bounding and spry.

"Hallo, the MacFadden house!" a man was shouting from the street. "Hallo the house!"

With one arm I swept as many of my books as I could into the case, then latched it with twin *thunk*s. I dragged it to the armoire, eschewing fragile slippers for my second-hand riding boots and yanking them on beneath my dressing gown. I caught the case up in my arms and rushed into the hall. Candles were lit in the foyer below, the open doorway casting edging dawn light and a wash of spring fragrance into the wide, high room. At the landing I halted, stunned by the sight of the man with my grandfather. He wore muddy boots, deerskin leggings and a yellowed linen shirt, a knife at his waist and a rifle on his back, caught by a series of beaded leather straps. Hearing me, Grandfather turned and looked up, his broad Scots face ablaze with more than the excitement of the hour, and the stranger removed a grubby farmer's hat, revealing a painfully freckled face and matted auburn hair caught back in a tail.

"Is there a fire?" I asked breathlessly, and Grandfather shook his head, more as if to clear it than in denial. Between his large, gnarled hands he was wringing something, and I squinted for a better look. Outside, the world was swiftly brightening, and through the transom window I caught sight of the lamplighter dousing the light across the street. So concentrated was I on my grandfather's expression that I almost didn't catch the expected shout: "Six of the clock, and all's well!"

"Grandfather?" I asked, confused, and that was when he opened his hands like an offering, and candlelight glinted on the object there: a thick, silver man's ring embedded with a fat emerald, hung on a piece of rough leather.

"It's Owen," he said, a catch in his throat. He cleared it, louder now. "Quincy, he's alive."

In the eighteen years I'd known my cousin Owen, I'd lost him four times. The first was only months after he'd moved into the Tradd Street house with Grandfather and me. I was six years old then, and had been warded to Campbell MacFadden myself only a year, sent to him after my parents—my father having been his only son—died on the crossing from Scotland. It was a tragic stretch of time for my Grandfather, because naught but a year later we were delivered of Owen. His parents—his mother having been Grandfather's firstborn—had perished in a house fire in Philadelphia. Owen arrived lanky and sullen, but found the South Carolina environs endlessly exotic, and within weeks he brightened into a serious boy with a streak of the trickster. On his tenth birthday he sank a dinghy on the Santee River only feet from the dock of the du Pont rice plantation, the smaller of the many plantations along that river, belonging to my dead grandmother's Huguenot family. We felt certain he'd been eaten by alligators until he'd stumbled through the azalea bushes on the water-side lawn hours later, dripping with muck and spotted to the knees with leeches.

The second was when he left Charlestown at sixteen to attend Harvard College in Massachusetts, and I was sure he would become so learned he'd outpace me by bounds, want nothing to do with his younger female cousin and return completely unlike the unpretentious Owen I'd known. Each Christmas, though, he'd emerge from the stage, luggage brimming with presents of books—books most men would deem too erudite to gift a mere girl.

The third time we lost him was in the spring of 1757, when he abandoned Cambridge and Harvard after only two years to join with the British army in the war against the French. But he'd proved us wrong yet again, returning five years later from the Pennsylvania frontier, scarred but whole, and looking out from much older eyes. I, and Grandfather, too, I think, believed Owen would settle in Charlestown then, marry into one of the appropriate families in our insular circle and join Grandfather's practice. He'd been studying law, after all, before the War, and was possessed of a keen eye and an artful tongue; returning home a hero would only bolster the already stalwart MacFadden reputation.

But Owen had other ideas. He'd been exposed to the great frontier during the War, and to the land and adventure to be got there, and sitting at a desk inside a brick building on the Charlestown harbor—drawing up tedious legal notes for cotton and rice merchants—was not something he considered desirable life's work. Being a war hero and speaking passable Iroquois, he was offered a position as a land speculator for the Transylvania Company on the frontier west of the Appalachian Mountains. We'd received letters, and parcels containing small treasures like porcupine quills, Indian beads, and the occasional bear claw, but he did not come home again.

On a bitter day in February, only a year and a half ago, an aide to the Royal Governor brought a letter to our door that upended my sheltered little world. By way of the web of colonial politics, Governor Bull had got word of a South Carolinian of reputable family involved in a tragedy on the Kentucky frontier. And so Owen was finally lost to us forever, killed by a band of Shawnee raiding across the Ohio Valley. He, two other speculators and their Cherokee scout had been murdered at their encampment, their bodies burned.

Six months later we were brought Owen's saddlebags—or what remained of them, charred as they were—by a sad-eyed young emissary of the Transylvania Company. I spent days simply staring at the scorched leather, then finally fingering its contents: a wool bullet pouch containing three lead balls, a singed blue ribbon, and a dog-eared copy of *Robinson Crusoe*, the initials *O.M.S.* etched awkwardly in the binding. I mourned for Owen like a sister, and Grandfather retreated to his study for weeks on end, upon eventual emergence appearing an aged, empty copy of himself. It had been only in the last six months that we'd found happiness in each other's company again. *We knew he lived dangerously*, Grandfather had said when he spoke finally of Owen's death, his warm hand lightly cupping my bare head in benediction. *We must get on with it.*

I dropped the case on the landing and raced gracelessly down the stairs, my boots clomping against the wood and my uncovered hair flying scandalously round my face. The trapper cleared his throat and averted his eyes, showing him to be a man of conscience, for all his rangy appearance. I put a hand to my chest where my heart beat madly, and one to Grandfather's forearm. "Is it true?" I demanded.

"He was taken captive by the Shawnee. They spared his life." Grandfather's voice was hollow, his eyes unnaturally bright. He took my hand, turned it palm up and dropped the ring into it. I stared at it momentarily, the tail of leather it had been looped through draped rather elegantly over my wrist.

"Sir, you'll want to know more," the trapper said, his rural accent unbearably slow.

"Yes, of course. Let us go to my study." Grandfather turned so quickly and marched down the hall that the trapper looked to me, and I shook my head woodenly. He'd started after the old man, a hand reaching up to play with the strap on his left shoulder, the one attached to his rifle, when Grandfather spun and stepped around him, eyes narrowing. "What are ye waiting for, girl? Come on!"

Grandfather's study was dark, and it smelled of books: of dust and leather, of old pages thumbed by generations of hands. He stepped to the unusual desk made especially for him by a friend of his, the famous cabinetmaker Thomas Elfe, a desk for a tall man, with thick, claw-footed legs, far removed from the current style. He lit an oil lamp there, gesturing at me without looking up at the trapper, who hovered uneasily beside one of a pair of ancient, wing-backed chairs. The man continued to rub a hand on the strap at his shoulder—assuring himself of his rifle, I thought.

"Tell her," Grandfather ordered, his Highland Scotch burr thickening in his excitement. "Tell my granddaughter what ye know."

Too stupid with shock to demand a proper introduction, I held out the ring like a question, my mouth agape.

"Miss, my name is Clemens. I'm recently down from the Cherokee country—I'm a deerskin trapper, see. It was at Fort Ninety-Six I saw the advertisement Mr. MacFadden here posted, for word of his grandson." He stopped, glancing back and forth between Grandfather and me, bewildered at what must have seemed our lack of propriety, or for that matter, our silence. He could not have known how much we'd loved Owen, how desperately we'd mourned . . . how unbelievable it was to think him alive. "Well, I knew the face on the advertisement soon as I saw it."

"The face? Forgive me, but I don't understand." I walked to the desk, folding my hands as if in prayer and raising them to my lips, blowing air through my clasped fingers. The ring on its leather strap hung from my pinky like a loop of rein. "Grandfather, what does he mean? Whose ring is this?"

When the old man didn't answer, only stared off into the dark corner as if in a trance, I clapped my hands together loudly. "Grandfather!"

The stunned look vanished, and he smiled suddenly, the old humor spreading warmly across his whiskered face, his blue eyes flashing with it. He wore no wig, just his own dark hair, powdered with white talcum and peppered by gray age. "It's Owen's ring, left to him by my Adelaide—by his mother." He reached out, snatched the ring and held it beneath the lamp.

"See here, Quinn? The initials *A.M.S*: Adelaide MacFadden Scott, Reginald Scott being Owen's father, your uncle." Mr. Clemens and I leaned forward to observe the spidery letters engraved in the silver, and when Grandfather stood straight and set the ring down on the desktop with a *clap* we both started. "It's proof, child—proof he's alive."

"But where is he? Why hasn't he come home?" I turned to the trapper again, my hands pressed against my waist as if anchoring myself to the spot. "Mr. Clemens, please."

"He's with the Shawnee. Alive still, when I last saw him near Virginia and he gave me the ring." The man shifted his feet, clearly uncomfortable indoors. "Begging your pardon, miss—he'll not last long with the savages. You'd best send someone to make a trade."

It was the opportunity for which I'd been recklessly longing: a chance at new life, at breaking free from the rigid confines of Charlestown society and from all that was expected of me. For twenty years I had been like a swimmer caught in a dangerous undertow, scarcely able to keep my head above the swells as I'd been swept further into the sea of my own predestiny. Since childhood I'd felt that I was different—that I did not belong anywhere except in my Grandfather's library pouring over books, enveloping myself in other worlds; or, out on the Santee—free to ride my horse at a wild gallop down lonely sand roads, Owen atop his own mount at my side, my sole companion.

But in the backcountry, I could be free. After rescuing Owen—for rescue him I must—I could make a home there. It was done nearly every day: settlers of all class and creed moving to the frontier, making new lives. Why should I not take part in such an exodus?

And so this was how I found myself standing on the promenade at White Point Park—a not-so-young woman who for all purpose should have been married and with children at her side long before—waiting and hoping that this man I loved like no other would give me the improbable leave to live my life.

"Child, ye will marry," Grandfather said, standing ramrod straight, his face to the harbor. The gulls swooped behind the stone wall facing the sea, sending crabs scuttering about in the pluff mud. Their screeches were lost in the dull roar of the wind, but I could hear my grandfather above it all, his deep barrister's voice resolute and unyielding.

"I will not," I answered, surprising myself. Grandfather flinched ever-so-slightly, yet his gaze remained on the sea. "I love no man, and will not marry one only to satisfy the requirements of your will. I have reached the legal age. The dowry is mine to do with as I wish. You said so yourself—"

"I said nothing of the sort!" He spun away from the wall, shoving big hands into the pockets of his greatcoat. His cheeks were red with rage, his silver-blue eyes making angry slits at the corners.

"You did," I protested, unwilling to give up on a promise I knew he could not help but keep, no matter how long ago he'd made it. "When I was eleven years old Malcolm Pinckney tied a knot in my hair and stuffed it with cotton, and I was furious. I told you I hated boys and would never marry, even though I'd end up a spinster like Aunt Eloise. And you promised that I'd never end up a destitute old woman because you'd give me a dowry whether I married or not." I reached out, grabbed the wide cuff of his coat and tugged. "I know you remember, sir."

"I'll not have ye sacrifice your inheritance, Quincy. Not even for Owen—and certainly not for land in some godforsaken wilderness." He rubbed a hand over his head, wigless as usual. He blew air out through his long nose. "Aye, I remember. But ye were a child."

"I know. But you are a MacFadden, and you'll not betray your bond, even to a child."

Carriages clacked on the cobblestones behind us as residents of the peninsula hurried to market before it closed for the evening. A slave and her charge, a small boy with a spinning wheel, played on the lawn of the park. The boy was laughing, refusing her will, and the woman admonished him—but I couldn't hear a word either said. I could hear nothing but the rush of the ocean wind and the slap of waves against the seawall.

9

It all came to this: could Grandfather send me to trade for Owen, surely a man's job, dangerous and uncertain? He could not leave Charlestown, for there was none he'd trust to conduct his business in his stead, and we could be at search in the wilderness an unforeseeable amount of time—months, certainly, perchance even years. Even the fact we'd enlisted the aid of one of his dearest friends, a traveling minister with knowledge of backcountry geography, did not seem to mollify his fears. Indeed, the Reverend Archibald McDonough was to chaperone me and keep me safe for as long and as far as he could.

I watched Grandfather with my hands clutched in the fabric of my skirts, wondering if he'd answer with reason or rage. Though he undoubtedly loved me, sending me into the inhospitable frontier without him, even with money he'd given—and lacking a husband—might be more than he could bear.

The tidal bell clanged in the harbor, and the wind shifted, flipping the weathervane on the Brewster mansion in the opposite direction. It seemed as if all the mighty wheels in Campbell MacFadden's brain were turning at once. He pulled on his mottled, red-gray beard and then whirled on his heel, snatching his tricorn from the park bench nearby and yanking it onto his head.

"Lass, if I made ye a bond I shall not break it. God help Owen should ye find him." He stalked to the four-in-hand where his coachman, Naji, waited patiently, tapping the crop on his liveried thigh. When he climbed inside he dropped heavily onto the bench, folding large-knuckled hands in his lap. I stood in disbelief, unable to move my feet. He turned and blew out his cheeks, slapping his hands on his knees. "By God, Quinn, I gave ye what ye wanted. Get in this carriage!"

My feet snapped from their spell, and I hurried to the carriage, stumbling on broken cobblestones. I grasped Naji's outstretched glove, and he leaned down, whispering into my ear as he helped me up. "You may want to remove that smile, miss."

"The two of ye quit your yapping and let's be off. I've had enough of the harbor today," Grandfather ordered, refusing to meet my eyes.

I looked out over the water as we started up Bay Street, opening my eyes wide to the sting of the wind. A wave bashed against a loading dock as we passed, droplets spraying my face. It was a benediction, a blessing for the new life I'd soon begin and a most favorable omen: I *would* find Owen, alive and whole.

I stretched my neck to get a last view of the sea before it disappeared behind the Exchange Building.

That night I dreamed of the Cherokee. The vision was ruthlessly quick, and I sat abruptly upright, pulling the neck of my dressing gown from my chest and flapping it. It was soaked where I'd sweated through the linen. Had I called out, I wondered?

I pressed the pads of my fingers into the hollow beneath each eyebrow, pushing hard against bone. The visions always ended in headache. I closed my eyes, seeking a shard of truth in the dark melee of my mind—if I could only remember, piece the dream together, it might help me. Against the black of my eyelids I focused on a single point of white, watching as it spread, inking into shapes and then shattering. *Don't go*, I begged silently, and light bloomed.

There were two men like shadows, a fire burning on the dirt between them, half-lighting their faces. Smoke snaked up through the branches of bare trees—it was bitterly cold.

One of the men spoke, guttural and strange. He poked the fire with a tree branch, sending sparks shooting skyward in a quick burst of red that faded instantly against the black. He turned to his companion, and his face was lost.

"The woman claims he lives," the other said, in English.

"Quincy, are ye well?"

I blinked, my focus momentarily blurring on the foot of my bed: there, the scalloped edge of the white lace quilt, the twin finial posts, and across the room in the large mirror above my desk, me, my blond hair a disheveled mess, matching the pale of my face. I felt as I always did after a vision, as if I'd been hovering underwater, eyes open, awaiting something sinister to emerge from the brine.

There was a banging at my door, and the knob rattled. "Answer me, girl. Are ye well?"

"I am," I called out, forcing my voice to calm and slipping out of the bed. I padded to the door and stood before it, rubbing my face, hard. "I'm fine, Grandfather."

"Did ye dream?" His voice was a soft rumble.

"Yes."

"Did ye see Owen, lass?"

I heard the wishing, and I pressed an open palm to the thick oak between us. The house was making its night sounds: palmetto fronds brushing the piazza roof in high wind, a creak of movement on the first floor, air whistling down the chimneys and the shutters rattling against their iron hinges. Soon, hurricane season would be upon us.

"Quincy?"

I longed to say yes. Instead, I made a promise I could not keep. "Not yet."

Chapter 2

The Cherokee Path

The coach lurched beneath my feet, sending my stomach to swirling and the well-dressed man on my left almost into my lap, his hand steadying itself on my shoulder. I clutched the stout wood of the windowpane, offered the stranger a strained smile and kept my eyes on the forest outside the window. It was my first excursion west of the High Hills of Santee, and I did not want to miss a single moment, despite the impetus for the journey. I knew Owen lived. I felt it in my bones, in the pit of my stomach—a place Grandfather called "the gut." If Owen died, I'd know that too, and I'd feel the emptiness take cold hold of my throat. I rolled my shoulders beneath the stiff, restrictive sleeves of my riding jacket, ridding myself of the notion.

I could feel Reverend McDonough watching me. He'd been doing so ever since we left Charlestown, his bushy white eyebrows made wild by wind whipping through the fabric flaps drawn to keep dust from spraying inside the coach. A wheel hit another rock, and the vehicle lurched, sending my dexterous neighbor once again into my side, his hand in my lap. I gave him my best disgusted-schoolmarm face, complete with the eyebrow lift I'd been practicing in the mirror back home. He ignored me and took his time moving away.

Reverend McDonough cleared his throat and wobbled across the coach, planting himself between the stranger and me. The man shifted and regarded us with a bored snort.

"Thank you, my kind protector." I leaned into the Reverend as I spoke, glaring worthily at the man across the way. He glanced at us, frowning, then turned his attention to the handle of his garment bag.

Just outside of Charlestown, the Cherokee Path cut up and over the peninsula into the mainland, took a rutted turn northwest until it reached the Santee River, then followed along fertile bottomlands until it melded into the Saluda. If it had just been a horse and me, and not the coach making its dilatory way along the sand and dirt trail widened by time and the influx of settlers to the backcountry, we could have made it to Fort Ninety-Six in about a week. Traveling slow as we were would have us arriving at that frontier town in over a fortnight.

I'd learned that Ninety-Six, the farthest most courthouse town in the colony of South Carolina, consisted of one other governmental building, a jail, a trading post and a few houses owned by the judge, his family, and the trade post operator. Mail from Saxe-Gotha, Charlestown and Savannah stopped there at that remote gateway to the seemingly never-ending frontier. Already the land had changed from bustling savannah to the plantation countryside around the Santee. As we rode west alongside the Saluda River and nearer to Ninety-Six it was as if the trees themselves had crept closer to the road, the forest a darker, wilder thing than it had been along the coastal plain.

It had taken Grandfather and me over a fortnight to prepare for the journey west, and on advice from the Reverend we had acquired a bevy of items to trade for Owen's release, including blankets, tools, whiskey and rum—in addition to my own things, which had been secured to the accompanying wagon. Bookworm that I admittedly was, I'd done my research. In Ninety-Six we should have no problem hiring a guide to take the Reverend and me further into the frontier. During the past several years hordes of poor European immigrants had arrived in Charlestown and immediately headed west, seeking cheap land and freedom from both overlord and bishop.

Unfortunately, after Mr. Clemens's startling appearance at our door and the announcement of Owen's inconceivable return from the grave, not to mention a subsequent reward of heavy coin from Grandfather, the man had disappeared without a word. But since money was not a hindrance—my dowry had been substantial—I was confident that with or without the mysterious trapper, I'd have no trouble securing a willing soul to help us navigate the wilderness.

"You're a brave lass, Quinn, my dear," the good Reverend said simply, folding and unfolding his felt black hat in broad, callused hands as the coach bumped along the Path.

"To you, perhaps," I answered. "But to my grandfather, I'm a willful chit lacking any concern for my own welfare. I thought he might disown me when I told him of my plans to settle in the wilderness—after finding Owen, of course. I believe he called them 'preposterous, dim-witted and inane.'"

The old man laughed, releasing the hat and slapping his tremendous kneecaps with both hands. "That sounds exactly like your grandfather. Campbell never has learned to temper his speech."

Resting my head against the coach and peering out at the brushy undergrowth in the spring-green forest, I couldn't help but think of the life I was leaving behind—and the way in which I'd left it. I knew I'd done the right thing, knew that if I'd stayed I would have become someone else entirely, someone I did not want to be. And despite his protests, I think Grandfather knew it, too.

When I was a child in Charlestown, my grandfather told me the best of the world was waiting just outside our door, and that all I needed to do in order to seek a life of purpose and adventure was to step out that door and into a life of my choosing. I suppose he forgot that one day I'd grow from the urchin who used to bounce on his shoulders into a young woman of the certain breeding and social standards he himself extolled, and that it might not be proper for me to take the world as my stage, refusing to settle into the life society had provided.

What Campbell MacFadden had refused to acknowledge was that I, too, came from a long line of mercurial, granite-willed Scots, and that his fiery blood pulsed just as staunchly through my veins as it did through those of the male members of our family. Closing my eyes, I saw him as clearly as though he stood before me in splendid reality, the buttons on his coat on the verge of bursting over his belly, one hand on his hip, the other gripping the curved end of a silver-tipped cane. The scene as I'd left the Lowcountry had not been a pleasant one. My Grandfather had not sent me off with best wishes or a kiss to my cheek. Instead, he'd stormed like the Celt he was, cursing in Gaelic—words I had yet to understand—and raged at me as though I was one of the young law clerks he so often let sup at our table.

"You'll be killed!" he'd shouted. "Murdered by savages or worse—captured and made to be one of their wives. The frontier is no place for a woman. You'll be scalped in less than a month or molested by roving outlaws. This notion of staying is ludicrous! If you find Owen, you must return to Charlestown."

Though I knew his anger stemmed from fear, and from the helplessness he must have felt at not being able to make the journey himself, my own Scots temper—something I usually attempted to quell—flared instantly. I'd shouted right back at him, said I was going no matter what he told me: "If you can't give me your blessing, I'll pray for your vengeful soul and hope to the Lord above that you learn patience and trust in the girl you've called your own for twenty years!"

As I'd packed my bags in silence, he'd brooded in his library, the curl of smoke from his cigar dispersing among the rafters.

"Quinn, answer me this," the good Reverend said suddenly, crossing his arms over his black-coated chest. "If you are successful in liberating Owen from the savages—which would be God's own miracle, my dear—do you truly think to make a life for yourself in the mountains? It is so far from home and all you hold dear."

By now the stranger sitting across from us had grown bored with my inattention and was asleep, his head stuffed into the corner of the coach, fleshy chin resting in a lacy jabot. Maybe he would exit the coach at Ninety-Six, I hoped. I tore my eyes away from the flipping motion of his mustache hairs, flittering about each time he exhaled.

"I do, Reverend," I said. "I have grown weary of the stringent rules governing Charlestown society. I feel stifled there. I want to walk through green fields with my feet bare as the day I was born." This I said with a grin as I pulled back the flap at the window, knowing it would shock the good Reverend.

"These windows are simply too small. One can barely see the landscape," I continued, before he could find the words to chide me. "And we will find Owen, with or without the Lord's help—though I pray for the former. Perhaps he'll want to settle with me, betroth himself to a country girl and beget prodigiously."

The muscles in Reverend McDonough's red face worked in silence as he attempted to form a proper response. Finally, seeming to relent, he pulled his hat down on top of his head, covering his eyes. He leaned back in the seat, feigning sleep, and I smiled at him half-heartedly. I was determined to remain stalwart when it came to thinking on Owen. In fact, what he was most certainly enduring at the hands of the Shawnee was such a terrifying prospect that I refused to allow it entry into my subconscious. If I did, I'd be consumed by darkness, unable to press on—and that was not an option.

I breathed deeply and cleanly, returning my attention to the world outside the window. The coach passed a short train of three wagons, kicking up dust from the road and causing the rider at the front of the entourage to fan his hat in front of his face as he glared at us. A young boy walked beside the wagon, a musket slung over his shoulder. The knees of his breeches were split and stained, but he gave me a snaggle-toothed grin when I lifted a hand in greeting.

I wondered where their train was going, if it was headed as far into Cherokee lands as I, or if the family planned to stop short of the mountains and take the Dividing Paths to the Long Canes, make a homestead there. I wondered if they'd read the same books I had, and knew of the white, bell-shaped flowers, peregrine falcons, black bears and mountain lions that waited in the woods.

We'd been several days on the road, and by the time we'd stopped on this day I was weary, already missing Grandfather and the ease of his familiar presence. Nights on the Path were long, and as the lone female in the company of four men—the drivers of both the stage and accompanying wagon, Rev. McDonough, and the only other passenger a courier by the name of Whitfield, charged with taking court documents to the Fort judge—I found myself oddly removed. We always pulled off the road well before dark, usually in a glade or some sort of resting area utilized by other travelers, so that the drivers could make camp. They were brothers: taciturn, fair-haired, stocky young men with nearly indecipherable accents I could only place as Dutch, and I'd not managed to learn either one of their names until we were at least three days into our journey.

"It's Willem Van Dijk, madam, but most call me Wim. *Mijn broer* is Claes," the younger of the two said shyly as he watered the horses. I ran a bare hand—I'd abandoned my damp gloves after the first day on the Path as they were utterly useless—along one of the horse's flanks. *How I'd love to be riding, instead of cramped inside the coach, forced to make conversation with the leering Mr. Whitfield,* I thought briefly. I smiled reassuringly at Wim.

"I am Quincy MacFadden," I said. "Very pleased to meet you." He blushed violently, and I hurried on, pretending to pick a burr from the horse's coat. "How did you and your brother come to be stagecoach drivers, Mr. Van Dijk—Wim?" I said his surname slowly, stumbling over the Dutch but wanting to make an attempt.

"We ran *paarden*—horses—in *Nederland*, Claes and me. So when we get to Carolina we do same." He glanced around, clearly wishing for an escape. "We keep the stage clean, *ja?*"

"Oh, yes." I nodded assuringly, then backed away, leaving the poor man in peace. "Quite clean, thank you. I will let you to your work."

Rev. McDonough was gathering downed branches and kindling for a fire, a task that had become his, Mr. Whitfield having attached himself to Claes, who was in charge of hunting small game for our nightly meals. I wandered across the camp to the much-used fire pit, tucking flyaway hairs into my bonnet as I went, swiping a hand across my face. The mosquitoes were becoming quite relentless, buzzing round each of us like mad little flies. The Reverend heard my approach and stood, brushing his hands on his breeches.

"Ah, how goes it, my dear? Did you get a life story from young Willem?"

"Not quite," I said ruefully. "I believe I frighten him, which makes no sense at all."

"Of course it does." He swiped his minister's hat from his bald head, rubbing it with a handkerchief he'd had in the other. "Look at you."

I glanced down at myself, shrugging inelegantly. My blue cotton riding dress with its silk flounces was simple but fine, my riding boots—a pair of Owen's he'd outgrown years before—scuffed yet serviceable. I was petite of stature, plagued by a slightly more womanly than average curve of hip and bosom, something I'd attempted to camouflage since the age of thirteen, when a drunken client of my grandfather's had called me "distractingly lush." He'd looked over his shoulder and then leaned into me as he'd whispered it, fingering the lace at my neckline.

Disgusted with the memory, I waved a hand before my face again, dislodging a fly from the tip of my hat. "I see only that I require a bath," I said.

"Well, Wim does not see the dirt, I promise you that. He sees a Diana. Fair, lovely, determined to rescue her beloved kinsman—and in possession of striking blue eyes, unbound by the custom that would dictate she never speak directly to a man of lower class." Rev. McDonough stuffed his kerchief into his pocket and adjusted his hat on his head.

Flabbergasted, I could only manage a short laugh. "You are kind, sir. But certainly in possession of a healthy imagination."

He reached out a hand, lightly tapping the tip of my nose as if I was a schoolgirl. "We rarely see ourselves for what we are, my dear. And you, shamelessly educated, are no exception."

He started back to his work, and I looked to my options: preparing the night's supper, which would inevitably embarrass either of the Van Dijk brothers, or steering clear of Mr. Whitfield and retiring to the coach—my makeshift night quarters, the men having taken to sleeping on pallets on the ground round the fire. I had to do something. My mind at rest was a maelstrom of worry and fear for Owen's safety, and without concrete purpose would shift to nightmarish imagery, usually involving fire and savagery. And with my capricious gift of Sight, I had enough of that sort of thing.

I picked my way to the coach, avoiding Wim, who still cared for the horses and who watched me from the corners of his eyes as if I'd been inflicted by some sort of rare disease. I hefted my skirts in one arm and opened the door before gentlemanly instinct could arise in any of my companions, and propelled myself awkwardly into the cab. The leather seats were sticky with the heat of the day, and Mr. Whitfield had left his cane—surely an affectation—leaning against the far door. I shuffled to it and moved it out the open window, hooking it over the side of the door. I didn't want him returning for it while I slept. I fell heavily into the seat and tugged off my bonnet. I was hot, miserable, lonely for Grandfather and Owen and more than a bit terrified of night in the forest, with all its sounds I couldn't identify. I felt an instant ardor for the country inn we'd visited the night before, and the rope bed in which I'd slept without waking—despite the fact it was likely infested with bedbugs.

One of the horses whinnied, and I looked out the window. The elder Van Dijk and Mr. Whitfield had emerged from the trees, the former holding a flopping trio of skinned rabbits by their hind legs. I closed my eyes and breathed deeply.

"An inn, an inn—my kingdom for an inn," I muttered.

At night I willed the vision to return. I lay awake, desperately aware of the sounds outside my awkward little haven—the snort of horses, crickets and frogs loud as an orchestra, the low wind in the tall pines and the unsettling crack of a branch under foot—attempting with all my might to concentrate on the memory of my dream. Fleeting though it may have been, I was certain it was in some manner related to Owen's capture. But it never returned wholly formed, and I should not have been surprised. The visions rarely revisited once I'd had them, and I'd been having them since I was a child.

As far as I knew, most of the MacFadden women had the Sight, and so did some of the men—Owen included. It was not information we shared with those other than family for fear of being ridiculed, and at worst jailed for witchcraft. *In the Hielands*, Grandfather had told me once, *ye would've been an Auld One, or a Seer—respected but feared. Here you're a witch, and mind ye don't forget it.*

The day I learned Owen shared my capricious gift, he'd been living with us for a few months and we'd not spoken much, only kept a respectful distance, eyeing each other like circling cats. I had been in the carriage house with Naji, sitting atop the driver's box playing with a spinning top as he worked on one of the horse's hooves. He was stooped over the horse's bent knee, the hoof upturned, and he set the pick he'd been using on a stool nearby. It was when he reached for a hammer, a pair of nails held lightly between his brown lips, that my mind went white and I saw it happen: a wagon breaking an axle on the street outside, the horse jerking, and the hammer bouncing back, its metal edge catching Naji in the eye. *Blind*, a voice had whispered, *he'll be blind.*

When I regained my sense of the present, Naji was poised to hammer the first nail, but Owen came tearing through the side door, dark red hair loose from its tail, his thin chest heaving. He skidded to a halt when he saw the horse shift, the whites of its eyes showing. "Don't do it," he whispered hoarsely. "Please, sir, lay down the hammer."

With a raised eyebrow—either at the strange request or Owen's use of the title "sir" in addressing a slave—Naji began to set the horse's hoof gently to the ground, and it happened: a loud crack came from the street outside, and the horse reared, missing Naji and the hammer he still held by mere inches. Owen slipped swiftly around the wall near the stalls, avoiding the horse's back legs, and took hold of its bridle, talking to the beast lowly. When it calmed, Naji looked between us, knowledge blooming in his dark, intelligent eyes.

"So he's one, too," he said. He stepped to Owen, taking the horse's bridle and inclining his head: a humble acknowledgement from an African king. "I thank you."

Chapter 3

Fort Ninety-Six

The first place we stopped after bumping along into Ninety-Six was the courthouse, a rough log structure standing in the town's center. Beside it sat a half-erected brick building—the new courthouse, I supposed. Rev. McDonough and I unfolded ourselves from the stifling coach, bid Mr. Whitfield an appropriately polite farewell, and gave coins to Wim to procure fresh beverages from the trade post operator.

"Here, lass," the Reverend said, offering his arm. "Let's see who's about."

We made our way through bright midday sunlight to the rude courthouse, managing to dodge a wagon loaded with boxes and animal skins that went barreling down the main street, heading out of town. The driver tipped his hat in a courteous rush, not meeting our eyes.

"It's empty," I said, surprised after a knock on the door offered no human return.

"Who you lookin' fer?"

Seated to the side of the door, his back against the wooden logs of the building, was a man in crumpled country breeches and a ragged deerskin shirt, a dusty tankard at his side. The Reverend took my arm to lead me away, but I pulled against it.

"We're seeking a guide to take us into the Cherokee country," I answered. "Do you know where we may find one?"

"Quinn," the Reverend admonished, his lips a frown, "I don't think—"

"Might try Gowdey's trading post," the bedraggled man interrupted, giving me a wink. "Ask fer Clemens, he's crazy enough."

"Our thanks," Rev. McDonough offered, pulling me firmly but gently off the porch and once again into the street. He raised an eyebrow. "That ruffian has no idea where we could find a reputable guide—he's obviously inebriated."

I grinned, excitement slipping into my blood like a cooling serum. "How fortunate if Mr. Clemens is here. We might as well try the trading post. Where else are we to look?"

He harrumphed, looking around at the rustic town and shaking his head. "I'd thought there would at least be a church. We could've made inquiries there. Seeing as there's nothing of the sort . . . lead on, my dear."

The trading post was a rude log cabin located near a creek-like tributary of the Saluda River, just across the rustic town square. Outside, a lanky man—his back to us—unloaded some of the same skins we'd seen fly past on the other wagon and drop them onto a covered porch. Just inside the open serving window stood another man, this one older and bearded, leaning up against the frame, his hands draped over the side.

"Name's Robert Gowdey, post operator. Can I help you folks?" he asked, chewing on the inside of his cheek. "Clemens here just brought a new batch of deerskins down from Indian country—you sure look like a lady who'd want a nice new set of gloves, if you don't mind me saying so."

I turned quickly to the other man, surprised. "Mr. Clemens, how are you, sir? I'm so glad we've found you again. We are in need of your help."

He glanced back and forth between the Reverend and me, offering a hand to the clergyman. "Fine to see you again, too, miss," he said. "Hello, sir." He looked at me with a mix of open curiosity and bashfulness, and I vowed to obtain his services then and there.

"My good fellow, I am the Reverend Seamus McDonough. I'm friend to Campbell MacFadden, and so I know of the circumstances under which you met. We seek a guide to take us to Fort Prince George: someone who can help us in locating Miss MacFadden's cousin." The Reverend took a quick glance at me, leaned in conspiratorially. "We offer good coin and meals for the journey."

The trapper's eyes went wide in his freckled face. He looked me up and down without guile, his eyes taking in the fine silk flounces of my hoopskirt, the opal brooch pinned near the fall of my lace shawl. "You mean to take a lady into Cherokee country, do you?"

Irritated, I sought patience. "I mean to take myself," I said, causing both men to turn. "I intend to trade with the Shawnee for Owen's life. And afterwards, to settle on the frontier, to purchase a large tract of land past the Boundary Line. I've read it's the most beautiful place on earth."

"Sir," Clemens shook his head at Rev. McDonough, ignoring my words, and his boyish face turned suddenly serious. "I know you're a man of God, but you can't mean to take your young wife into the wilderness? She won't last a day in the hills."

"Mister Clemens," I ground out, "the Reverend is not my husband. I am unmarried, which means I may purchase land as I please. But enough of land. We must find my cousin—that is our most vital purpose. If you cannot offer us your services as guide, perhaps you can offer the name of someone who can?"

"My dear, please don't fret." The Reverend put a staying hand on my shoulder. I smiled politely but turned slowly to the trade post operator, who still stood at the window, watching our exchange with an open mouth that revealed a bottom row of missing teeth.

"Mr. Gowdey, perhaps *you* can give us the name of a guide?"

"Just a moment, miss." Clemens swiped a hand through his hair, expelling a long sigh. "The frontier is a lawless place—no white settlers are allowed beyond the Boundary Line." I started to turn back to the proprietor again, and Clemens spoke quickly. "I do know of a man at Keowee Town, name's Jack Wolf. If anyone could get your kinsman back from the savages, he could." He scratched his chin. "For that matter, he'd know best how to go about buying land from Little Carpenter. The Cherokees can be stingy."

"We'll be sure to seek him out, then," I said, folding my hands primly at my waist.

Rev. McDonough rolled his eyes, clapping a hand on the shorter man's thin shoulder. "Dear sir, though I feel for the lass as my own granddaughter, she is stubborn as any man and will continue into the frontier with another guide, if not yourself. My opinion on the subject's no matter. Will you help us, then?"

Clemens looked at me again, and I could almost be certain that a faint smile curved the corners of his lips. "I'll take you as far as Fort George," he said. "I'm delivering supplies to the garrison there as is. We'll need make contact with Wolf soon enough, if you're to bring your cousin home alive. Could be, too, the Shawnee have already taken him over the Ohio River Valley, or traded him north to the Iroquois." He looked over his shoulder, nodding at his own wagon. "We'll be taking that, though—a coach won't make it up the Path."

"We took the Cherokee Path from Charlestown and made our way as well as could be expected," I said numbly, still shaken from his casually spoken, *traded him to the Iroquois.*

Clemens looked down at me, and this time his face split in a wide, tobacco-stained grin. "The Path from here into the mountains is mere trail, miss, just wide enough for a couple of passing wagons. From here on, everything's different."

The air quickened into coolness as we journeyed into the frontier, past the blazed trees that marked the border of Cherokee lands, past the great boundary into the west, and the dark unknown of the Blue Ridge. As we made our way toward the British outpost at Fort Prince George, the tall, slender pines that thicketed midland forests changed to short-leaf pines, hickory, and towering oaks whose leaves spread the beginnings of an umber carpet upon the ground. As we rode, the wagon frightened dozens of deer from the brush. I counted them along the way, fascinated by their graceful sprightliness of spirit, their lightly-tread dance on dainty long legs as they leapt across the path in front of us.

Clemens looked over his shoulder, resting the reins lightly in his hands. "Out here there's thousands of 'em," he said after another doe bounded across the pitted trail. "Not so many as there used to be—trappers and settlers took care of that. But still more'n anyone could count."

"If I may ask, how long have you been traveling this path?" I braced myself against the rough bench when we hit a rut, then brushed a hand delicately across my forehead, wiping away sweat.

"Oh, about twelve years now. Back then the Boundary Line came almost to Ninety-Six itself, but with so many folks wanting a piece of their own, the red Indians just couldn't hold on to so much of the frontier." He turned back to the horses. "I started out trapping, beaver and deer mostly. Spent a bit of time over at Keowee Town with the Cherokee, picked up the language pretty quick. Settlers out here need someone who can talk to the savages, else they'll find themselves with burnt out cabins and stolen horses."

"Keowee Town—that's their capitol city, is it not?"

"Of the Lower Towns," he answered. "The Cherokee are a powerful people—granted, not so powerful as before the Wars of '60 and '61, though Lord knows Bull and his legislature still fear their might. But there's still a great many of 'em. Their lands stretch west across the Blue Ridge into places none's explored yet, some say all the way to the sea of China."

He gave one rein a pop, urging the horses over a rocky culvert. "They got hunting grounds farther than you can imagine, but mostly their land's divided. There's the Lower Towns here in South Carolina, the Middle Towns up in North Carolina, and the Overhill Towns heading all the way west into the wilderness. Each one has a capitol city. The one in the Lower Towns is Keowee. Sits right on the Keowee River, just across from Fort George."

Behind me Rev. McDonough perked up, shifting from his reclining position among the trunks and supplies. "Lad, I remember when the Indian chief came to Charlestown demanding Fort Prince George be built to help ward off enemies. I wasn't much older than you then, but I can still recall the little red man riding into town with dozens of his tribesmen, going to meet with Governor Lyttleton. Caused quite a ruckus, he did."

"Little Carpenter," Clemens said. "Or Attakullakulla, that's what the savages call him. Chief of the Lower Towns. He's an old man now."

"Aren't we all." The Reverend turned back around, settling his formidable weight into the sacks of cornmeal. Clemens and I smiled at one another.

"You must think I'm mad to want to settle in the mountains," I said quietly, feeling a sort of traveler's kinship with the guide. He glanced up and met my eyes for a heartbeat, then looked back to the trail. "Or perhaps it's my grandfather you think mad, for sending a woman on a man's errand?"

"I don't know as I'd say mad," he said. "But I do wonder if you know what you're getting yourself into, miss—if you'll pardon me saying so. Life's hard in the hills, nothing like Charlestown. And the Shawnee, well, I'd not send my dog to trade with them."

I swallowed. "I do know a little of the Blue Ridge, from reading. I do not expect it to be easy. I'm certain I'll be quite out of sorts for a while, in the beginning." I folded my hands in my lap to keep from drumming my fingers. "I am at least determined to try. And thankfully there's the fort—having an entire British garrison nearby is a blessing. I know that my grandfather would never have given me leave to search for Owen, and certainly not leave to settle there, without them."

"Well, even if they are redcoats, at least they're soldiers. You've got to think that most of 'em can shoot."

I had a barrage of questions to ask the guide, things about the Cherokee country that I knew I could never learn on my own, despite the many weeks of nights I'd spent pouring over books by waning lamplight. As we continued up the trail and into the night I made no move to stifle my own curiosity. Thankfully, Clemens seemed eager to talk. *Perhaps long years of lonesome travel made a man eager for polite conversation*, I considered.

At night we made camp much like before, away from the trail and a short distance into the woods. As on the Path from Charlestown to Ninety-Six, there were cleared spaces where others before us had done the same. Not having the luxury of a closed carriage as cabin, we used their abandoned supplies and downed branches to make shelter. On clear nights I slept in the back of the wagon, wedged between the sacks of cornmeal and trunks filled to stretching with my clothes, saddle, books and bedding, and the few pieces of furniture I'd managed to bring. The men slept near the fire in the open air, as men are free to do.

Until this venture into the wilderness I'd never once slept outside, and despite the biting insects and fear of snakes I rather liked it. The first night on the trail, before we'd even reached Fort Ninety-Six, I'd spent the majority of the evening terrified, unable to sleep, thinking that we'd be set upon by thieves. But by this point in the journey I'd become almost easy with the utter dark, willingly staying awake to listen to the croak of frogs and soft hoot of owls, and watch the millions of stars waver before my eyes in the huge sky above my head.

In the first few days after leaving Ninety-Six, we encountered others on the trail, most on horseback, some walking. We saw very few women, the last a mother and daughter heading with their German family southwest of our destination, toward the Long Canes. We were not to see another soul—white or red—until reaching the Keowee River.

Chapter 4

The Keowee River

Blue water curved slowly, cupping riverbanks green with new summer. The sun shone fiercely from its position high in the early afternoon sky—flashing off the Keowee, forcing us to shade our eyes. We'd ridden north along the wide river that was the northernmost tributary of the mighty Savannah. But in these blue hills, with purple mountains guarding the distance, the river became something else . . . something wild, pure, and Cherokee.

The horses drank frequently, heat from a cloudless sky making them slurp with abandon, water running down the sides of their necks as they flung back big heads, shaking off horseflies. Though it was not nearly as unbearable as a Charlestown summer, it was hot, and I was eager to reach Fort Prince George. We hit a rut, and I caught the side of the bench with one hand, grasping the brim of my planter's hat—another item pilfered from Owen—with the other: my bonnet had been as useless as my gloves. Clemens looked over his shoulder sheepishly, yanking down on the lead when the horse jerked back a bit. He walked beside the beast with the ease of a man used to the bumps of trail travel.

"You all right, Miss MacFadden? Sure you wouldn't be more comfortable in the back?"

I wiped a hand across my forehead beneath the brim of my hat, flinging away sweat. I looked back at Rev. McDonough, who was settled comfortably with his back against my saddle, his feet propped on a sack of cornmeal. His hat covered his face as he snored peacefully, his formidable belly rising and falling with each breath. "I believe there's only room for one," I smiled, indicating the sleeping man with a crook of my head. "And I prefer to sit here and watch."

Clemens chuckled and turned back to the path, his boots making soft indentions in the damp grass. "I don't know how a body can sleep in this heat."

Across the river, small, leather-covered huts were emerging from the camouflage of poplar and pine, and an Indian woman walked along the riverbank, stopping to fill a skin with water. She looked up, and her eyes met mine, unwavering. I lifted a hand tentatively; she was the first Native woman I'd seen, and I thought her beautiful.

She stood and clutched the neck of the skin with both hands, black braids—shot through with gray—hanging to her waist. She wore a calico shirt and a deerskin skirt that hung from her body without adornment. I held my breath until she moved away from the river, stepping carefully among the sand and rocks.

Interspersed with the huts were several rough cabins, open on the sides, and finally a huge round building with a thin line of smoke emerging from the top, shifting in the breeze. Here the river widened, and I could no longer make out the faces of the people who moved among the cabins and huts, filtering in and out of that rotund building that I thought could be the Council House—meeting place of Keowee Town, capitol of the Lower Towns of the Cherokee.

"We're here, miss," Clemens said. "Time to wake the Reverend."

Up ahead, on the eastern side of the river was the British outpost of Fort Prince George, built fourteen years ago by order of then-Governor Glen to protect the Lower Towns along the Keowee from invasion by the Creeks—or so Clemens had explained on our exit from Ninety-Six. The fort had a dark history. It had been attacked during the Cherokee Wars by the same people it had claimed to protect, and the mood about the place was one of urgency, not leisure. But still, the fort was a large, square building surrounded by a wall high as a tall man, fixed with sixteen stockades and two large cannons. Outside, soldiers milled about, loading supplies onto wagons, which sat around the side of the fort beyond a long ditch.

"What are they doing?" I asked Clemens as he hitched the lead horse to a post about twenty yards from the fort. He walked back and offered me a hand. I took it, jumping down and tipping the wagon precariously to one side. Rev. McDonough sat abruptly upright, his hat still stuck on his face. He yanked it off and blinked into the sunlight, working his mouth silently. Clemens and I exchanged looks.

"They may be taking supplies to Fort Loudon," he replied. "Some say food's scarce around the Little Tennessee these days. Soldiers are too scared of the red Indians to go hunt game." He took a swig from a skin of water hooked alongside one of the horses' saddles, wiping his mouth with the back of his hand. "I'll see about finding Jack Wolf."

He walked away before I could insist on accompanying him, and I watched him stop and speak with one of two soldiers guarding the opening at the side of the fort. The soldier could not have been more than seventeen years old, with a ruddy face that must have once been pale, his English skin burnt brown by the frontier sun. At Clemens's gesturing he looked over at me, and I smiled, lifting a hand. His face darkened into an immediate blush. The other soldier, a bit older by the filled-out look of him, gave his comrade a shove and pointed towards our wagon. Then the older fellow walked back into the fort, and Clemens and the young man walked towards me.

At this point, I would have given away a tankard of my precious rum for a clean cloth and a private dunk in the river. Sweat was beading between my breasts, dampening the fabric of my dress. I pulled the now-grungy rag I'd carried since Ninety-Six from a pocket in my skirts and held it lightly against my chest, hiding the spot.

"Miss MacFadden, this is Lieutenant Carroll."

I inclined my head. "Hello, Lieutenant. How goes it on the frontier these long days?"

He seemed a bit taken aback by my question, but recovered enough to cough into his fist. "Busy, miss. Governor Bull wants us back to Charlestown by summer's end, so we're a tired lot."

I blinked, confused. "Back to Charlestown?"

"Yes, miss. We're to quit the fort and take all supplies to Ninety-Six." He glanced at Clemens, realizing he'd said something amiss. "Do you have a man here, then? Or will you settle at the Long Canes with Patrick Calhoun and the rest?"

Clemens cleared his throat and answered before I could find my voice. "Miss MacFadden plans to settle here. Does the entire garrison leave, then?"

The sun was unrelenting, beating down on us as we stood there in the dirt, watching soldiers empty supplies from the fort. At his answer I saw white spots swim before my eyes, and my knees went soft.

"Fort George's being abandoned, mister. We're for home."

"Quinn, my dear, open your eyes. She's coming to, lads—there's a good girl."

Light cracked beneath the dark curtain of my closed eyelids, and I opened them to find Rev. McDonough crouched over me, his hands braced on his knees. I was seated beneath a huge oak tree, my back against the trunk. Before me were half a dozen sets of legs, an expanse of grass and dirt, then the bright Keowee. The Reverend came into focus, then the soldiers around him, circled like boys around a tortured frog. Clemens bent from the waist and held out a rough wooden mug. "Drink this, miss. It's the commander's best brandy."

As soon as the smell hit my nostrils I reared back and pushed the mug away. "Might I have water, please?" I asked, feeling red take to the crowns of my cheeks. I looked up at Rev. McDonough. "I don't know what happened. I've never fainted in my life."

The Reverend took his hat from his head and rubbed a hand over the shiny bald spot, grimacing. His face was abnormally flushed; I realized that he was angry. "'Twas the shock of it, lass," he said gruffly. "Damned English—abandoning their posts like dogs. Making a lady travel these miles for naught, the cads."

"I beg yer pardon, sir," one of the soldiers, a man with a Cockney accent and yellow teeth, bristled. "We've orders, now. 'Tis Bull who sends us away—we got no say in the matter!"

My throat went dry, as much with fear as with thirst. I knew now why I'd come to with a hollow feeling in the pit of my stomach. "So there will be no outpost here? What about the Creeks, or the settlers nearby? I was told that this place offered protection for the Cherokee—"

"Lady, there ain't settlers anywhere near these parts," another soldier answered, getting an elbow in the ribs from the young man Clemens had spoken with earlier. He shoved at the younger soldier and looked at the others, indignant. "Well, there ain't! Closest white person—besides trappers—is them homesteaders up near Estatoe, or maybe even down at Long Canes."

"Naw," another soldier shook his head, scratching his chin at the same time. "The folk at Estatoe were run off by some braves . . . got their horses stolen. Don't think they ever found the sons of bitches." He ducked his head, "Beg pardon, miss."

There was silence, the only sound the buzz of a persistent mosquito and Clemens clearing his throat. I pulled my knees to my chest and began to rise, reaching back for the crutch of the tree. The Reverend leaned down and took my elbows, pulling me upright with a huff. The look in his kind brown eyes was a mixture of anger and pity. He, too, knew what this meant for me and for Owen.

"You are all leaving," I muttered stiltedly, pressing the heel of my palm to the ache spreading between my eyes.

A few of the soldiers shifted and looked away. Even Rev. McDonough seemed at a loss for words. My eyes followed the line of the river behind them, and the expanse of mountains in the distance blurred with tears in a moment of weakness. I blinked and focused on the crowd of men before me. One of the soldiers in the back was absentmindedly digging a finger in his nose. He lifted his hand close to his face, examining the specimen he'd found, then wiped it haphazardly on his breeches.

I laughed then, deep from the pit of my belly. I laughed so that I doubled over, clutching my stomach. Rev. McDonough stepped towards me, but I held up a hand to stay him and straightened, wiping tears from my eyes. The soldiers stared at me as though I'd gone mad.

"All will be well, miss, half of us are to settle at Ninety-Six—you'll be safe," Lieutenant Carroll sputtered, removing his hat with one hand and running the other through his red hair.

I covered my mouth quickly, stifling a giggle. "Oh, I appreciate that, Lieutenant," I said, smiling inanely, "but if I'm to be scalped by a roving band of Indians I should think they'd have done with me before you all could make it the week's journey to my rescue.

"I believe I'll stay," I continued with more control, brushing off the back of my skirts with one hand, shading my eyes with the other. "I'll speak with your commanding officer, however. Where is he?"

Lieutenant Carroll, obviously the only man brave enough to speak to the crazy woman, scuffed a boot in the dirt and looked around for help. He shrugged. "He's left too, miss."

"Quinn, you can't—" Rev. McDonough began, but I cut him off by brushing past him through the crowd of men and walking towards the river.

"Of course I can," I said. "I will not abandon Owen. And I refuse to retreat merely because I won't have at my disposal a large band of adolescents for protection."

He followed me to the river's edge, wringing his big hands as I bent and scooped cool water, splashing my face. "Your grandfather won't allow it. Without the garrison here as buffer to the Indians, you'll be a sitting duck for any rotten soul. This is the wilderness, not the Santee," he pleaded. "One wrong turn and you're off a cliff, or worse—taken by the savages, forced to endure unknown terror. Please, you must reconsider."

Across the river a Cherokee girl, maybe six years old, splashed in knee-deep water. She slapped at the river with her hands, sending the spray above her head and laughing as it fell onto her upturned face. She was naked; her brown body glowed like an acorn in the early afternoon sun. I could hear Rev. McDonough beside me, still speaking, but his words were muffled as though he whispered through cloth.

The child stopped suddenly and looked directly at me, placing her hands impertinently on her hips. Then she let herself sink down into the river so that she was covered just below the nose. With a splash, she threw up her hands and dunked, emerging fearlessly in a spray of water. When she flipped dark hair from her eyes I waved to her, and her mouth stretched in an uninhibited grin.

I wanted that, I thought suddenly. I wanted that freedom enough to risk everything.

"Quinn!" the Reverend admonished, either at my lack of listening or the gesture, I knew not which. I put a hand on his forearm and smiled.

"I'm staying."

Chapter 5

Fort Prince George

A horsefly lighted on my upper arm, and I slapped at it, impatient. Clemens stood across the dirt lawn in the fanning shade beneath a large oak, gesturing at two Cherokee men. Both looked to be familiar with the trapper; the older Indian clapped a hand on Clemens's shoulder and wagged a finger at him. The battered soldier's tricorn that sat atop his gray head looked an anomaly, though he also wore English breeches. Both men were shirtless, but the younger—in his middle age, perhaps—looked somehow wilder in his deerskin leggings, a dangerously long knife tied with a leather strap to his waist. His black hair was shorn into a single, spiky line that became a long tail at his nape.

I stood transfixed as they argued. I'd never in my life seen men who looked as they did. I'd heard tales of Indian savagery in Charlestown, and had seen sketches on pamphlets and posters around town, but the sight in person was a startling thing. Their skin looked the color of burnt cedar that gleamed in the sunlight. They were tall and leanly muscled, and for the most part, strikingly handsome.

The old man turned, and his gaze met mine, then he turned back to Clemens, shaking his head. The two Cherokee seemed to say their goodbyes, for they brushed past the shorter man, heading into the fort. Clemens started for me, and I met him halfway, shading my eyes against the blinding brutality of the afternoon sun. He already looked apologetic, and my heart sank.

"Miss MacFadden, they say they don't know where Wolf is."

"But—" I began.

"And," he cut me off, wiping his brow with a handkerchief, "they say as you're a crazy woman for seeking out the Shawnee, and even crazier for wanting to settle here. I'm sorry, miss."

I looked over his shoulder and watched the Indians walk back out of the fort towards the river, where a huge canoe—at least twenty feet long—sat bobbing on the water. I took off towards them, running unsteadily across the rocks. "Wait!" I yelled, waving my arms.

They looked at me blankly, but stopped loading bags into the skinny boat. It occurred to me then that they'd probably never seen a white woman running before, much less running towards them. I slowed as I neared and gave my best smile, clasping my hands. "Please," I said, "do either of you speak English?"

They looked at each other, and the younger man muttered something beneath his breath at the older. He gestured at me and barked something at the younger man, who seemed reluctant. I turned towards him when he spoke.

"Why should we make talk with you, lady?"

Even from several feet away the Cherokee man was formidable, and I found myself fumbling for words. "I seek a man named Jackson Wolf," I said. "My intentions are honorable—I'm not here to do you harm."

"You are one of Wolf's ladies, yes?"

"Certainly not—I've never even met the man." I felt frustration rise to the surface, then saw laughter in the old man's eyes. "My kinsman has been taken captive by the Shawnee, and I need Mr. Wolf's help in finding him. I would also like for him to help me ask Little Carpenter if I may trade for land, to settle on. I have rum and cooking irons."

At this the younger man's face darkened, and his eyes narrowed. He would've stepped towards me if not for his companion's staying hand. "Just like the Virginians—land is all the *un'ega* wants," he said.

The old man put a hand on his arm, and the two seemed to argue for a moment. I felt a tap on my shoulder as Clemens came to stand beside me. He spoke under his breath as we watched the younger Cherokee gesture sharply, the older man shaking his head. "The old one's Kicking Horse," Clemens whispered. "He's a friend of Wolf's. The other's called Laughing Crow. Don't know much about him, except that he's an angry one—lost his wife and daughter when Colonel Montgomery and his troops raided the backcountry in '61."

"They killed them—British soldiers?" I asked, horrified.

"They killed most everyone," Clemens said quietly. "Burned villages, corn—anything they could get their hands on."

"You, lady," Laughing Crow said suddenly. He stepped forward, and I stepped back involuntarily, Clemens steadying me with a hand to my elbow.

"Yes?"

"We will bring you to Attakullakulla this night," he said, pointing to the riverbank between us. "Be here with the trade and we take you across *Yun'wi Gunahi'ta.*"

"Tonight?" I fumbled, my mind a whirl. "But what of Mister Wolf?"

The two men simply turned from me and finished loading their canoe. They did not look back as they pushed off and began to paddle for home. In a heartbeat they were outlined against the green trees lining the far bank, and I watched them stroke on opposite sides in perfect synchronicity, their paddles barely rippling the water as the current took them downstream towards Keowee Town.

Clemens rocked on his heels and wiped the sweat from the back of his neck. "Well," he said, "looks like you won't need Jack Wolf after all."

What did it mean, what they said before they left?" I asked Clemens.

We stood by the Keowee in the light of a waxing moon, the fingernail-shaped orb casting a silver sheen on the broad river. Insects buzzed in the humid air, and we swatted at them, wary of stinging. Beside us on the bank sat a trunk full of iron cooking utensils, several wool blankets, and two casks of rum.

"It means 'the Long Man.' That's what they call the river—or any river, I suppose. They say that the Long Man's head starts in the mountains and his feet run into the sea."

"The Long Man," I whispered to myself, scanning the dark vastness before us for a sign of life.

Across and down the river orange fires glowed from different spots between townhouses, and shapes moved across the flames, indistinguishable. Tonight, in this wild place with wolves, night owls and crickets filling the forest with a primal cacophony of sound, the river could come alive, I believed. I imagined the Long Man a dark shape just beneath the surface, sliding his hand around our canoe and pulling us under.

My nostrils twitched at the smell of smoke, and I fingered the druid rock I kept in my pocket for luck. I was terrified.

"I see someone," Clemens said. "Now Miss MacFadden, you just keep your wits about you and you might not have to say much. You sure you want to do this?"

I nodded in the darkness, not caring whether he saw me or not. A huge canoe slipped smoothly through the water and onto a shallow spot at the bank, the curved poplar bow scraping across the sand to a stop. Laughing Crow stepped out and walked towards us, his mouth an impenetrable line. Faint light from the opposing shore backlit his face, shadowing the hollows beneath his cheekbones. "This is the trade?" He motioned toward the trunk.

I nodded, finding my voice. "Yes."

"We go, then."

I walked to the boat and felt suddenly awkward, unsure how to get my skirts over the side, or even about where I should sit. I glanced at Laughing Crow, who refused to meet my eyes. "Would you—" I began tentatively, thinking to ask for assistance.

"Here you go, miss," Clemens took my arm and helped me into the wobbly boat, settling me in an undignified crouch in the middle. Laughing Crow motioned for him to take a seat in the bow, mumbled a few words in Cherokee, then pushed us off. He waded into the shallow water, caught the stern and hoisted himself aboard without rocking the boat.

I'd never sat so close to the water, and it felt as if we were on the precarious edge of another world. A second canoe, piloted by two Cherokee I hadn't seen, pulled alongside us, the trunk its booty. I looked over my shoulder at the Indian behind me. He was kneeling, stroking only on the left, his paddle dripping with each move—and he looked past me as if I wasn't even there. I turned back to the front, forcing my eyes away from the solid line of Clemens's back and toward Keowee Town, where the outline of the Council house glowed and drums beat a rhythm that echoed off the hills.

I took a deep breath and closed my eyes. Then I pulled the sleeve of my dress up to the elbow and let cool water from Laughing Crow's paddle drip a Cherokee tattoo on my white skin.

Keowee Town pulsed with voices, the wild beat of Indian drums, and the smell of burning meat. I followed Laughing Crow through the village, my eyes ahead, avoiding the stares of the Cherokee who'd come to watch me make my entrance. The two men from the other canoe shuffled behind us, carrying the trunk. Clemens had been ordered to stay with the boats, and I watched him over my shoulder as we left the riverbank until he faded into darkness.

A man with a half-painted face emerged from the shadows to my right and shouted something at me, close enough for me to smell his mealy breath. I recoiled and inched closer to Laughing Crow's back. Though he was certainly no protector of mine, he carried a blazing torch through the dark village, and he was the only remotely familiar thing in this frightening place.

A group of Indian men, loudly arguing, stood outside the entrance to the Council House. At our arrival they parted, and we ducked inside; I felt their eyes burn into the back of my head. There, at the other side of the room behind a small fire, sat a surprisingly slight man in nothing but a breechclout, his sweat-glistened chest adorned with strands of pearls and blue beads. His hair was shaved to the middle of his head, where a long, thick white strand hung down the side of his face. He wore one eagle feather as a headdress. He was flanked by two others: a woman, equally aged, with twin white braids and heavy-lidded eyes, and a middle-aged man, his expression hidden in the shadows cast by the fire.

The old man looked at me and said something in Cherokee to Laughing Crow, who responded by glancing back over his shoulder and making a sweeping motion with his hand. "Come, sit," he ordered.

I walked forward and sat awkwardly in front of Little Carpenter—called Attakullakulla by his people—chief of the Lower Towns. I attempted to spread my skirts about me in the most graceful way possible, though it seemed an impossible feat on the dirt-packed floor, and in the irrepressible heat. I knew not whether I was to speak first. I kept my head down respectfully, studying the man through my lashes.

"Welcome to Keowee," Little Carpenter said, his voice deep and surprisingly friendly. I felt relief rush through me at the disjointed sound of my native tongue. The men behind me dropped the trunk with a thud and disappeared back through the opening. At their exit the torches along the curved wall flickered, settled. The woman raised her gaze, eyeing me through the sheen of smoke.

"Thank you, sir. I'm grateful that you will see me this night," I managed.

"When a *un'ega* woman comes to my home asking for something others take, I think I should see this woman. What is your name?"

I cleared my throat and glanced around for Laughing Crow, who had taken a seat on a bench at the concaved wall behind me. "My name is Quincy MacFadden. I come from Charlestown, but the mountains will be my home now."

"You want land that belongs to the *Yun'wiya*," he continued, pointing a finger at me, "and we do not have much land to give. These mountains can be bad for a woman, especially a *un'ega* woman." There was a long pause as I searched for an answer: *What could I possibly say that would convince him to help me? How does one barter with a Cherokee chief?*

"Why do you come to this place with no man?" The old woman asked softly, and I was so stunned that she spoke in English—or even spoke at all—I blinked, my eyes watering at the smoke.

"I want to be free," I heard myself blurt before I could stop the words, the heat in the room and my own rashness sending a hot flush to my cheeks. "I have a dual purpose. I come in search of my kinsman, who I believe is a captive of the Shawnee. But I also want to trade for land. I don't need much. I'll take whatever you can give."

Little Carpenter took a long pipe—its stem made of wood and the mouthpiece clay, leather straps hanging from it like hair—from the bench next to him, placing it in between the logs of the fire, puffing quickly. He offered it to Laughing Crow, who stood and took it between his lips before handing it to the woman and settling back into his seat. I watched, transfixed, as she inhaled before passing it to the other man.

Little Carpenter crossed his arms over his chest and studied me intently, dark eyes narrowing. "I have tried for many years, since before the Wars, to make peace between the *Yun'wiya* and the English. There are many men who come to me for land. Most marry a *Yun'wiya* woman, and then I must give their sons land because they, too, are now *Yun'wiya*." He paused, ran a hand over his smooth chin. "I thought this would make peace, but it does not. What have you to trade?"

I swallowed, afraid to move, though I wanted desperately to wipe my brow. "I have iron tools, and spices, and four wool blankets."

"You have rum, yes?"

"Yes." My heart beat erratically against my chest, and I felt the silence compress my lungs. I knew from my research that John Stuart, long time friend of the Cherokee and the Superintendent of the Southern Department of Indian Affairs, had made the barter of rum illegal. But I was too afraid, and too selfishly stubborn to let anything stay me from my course.

Little Carpenter sighed, two deep lines furrowing his brow. He seemed suddenly elderly, his energy dampened. I knew he'd been one of several Indian delegates to sail to England more than thirty years earlier, to stand in the hall of King George II, and I wondered at the person that he was. He and Grandfather were of an age, yet no two men could've been more disparate.

The beat of drums outside the Council House seemed muffled and far away. His eyes met mine, his brow clearing. "Your people are coming, will keep coming—proclamations or no, with or without treaty. Perhaps if I show friendship to you they will see there is opportunity to live together in peace.

"I will trade goods for land—four hundred acres," he continued, and I felt the air leave my lungs. "A day's ride northwest from here, into the mountains. There is water there, and good growing land left by the *Yun'wiya* after the English killed many at a town there during the Wars." He looked over my shoulder, eyeing the man behind me. "Laughing Crow will take you there at sunrise."

"Thank you—oh, thank you," I broke in, a flood of relief loosening my tongue.

He cocked his head. "You are a strange woman, even for a *un'ega*. The English must think this."

I nodded mutely. He dropped his hands on his knees, rubbed them thoughtfully as he continued to consider me. My legs were tingling with the want to leap up and spin round the room in joy. I'd have my land, and Owen safely home too, God willing.

"We have women like you." He shrugged. "I will get word to Jack Wolf"—here he shaped the name slowly on his tongue, as if unused to saying it—"that you are in need of a tracker. He will find your kinsman."

"When?" I blurted. I could almost feel the blood beat beneath my skin, a melding of fear and excitement. Though I thrilled at the thought of a place of my own, I was afraid any delay could result in Owen slipping further away.

He held up a hand. "It will take time. Do not fear, lady. The *Shawano* will not kill your kinsman—a *un'ega* of his stature is too valuable . . . at worst they trade him. Listen now: You must promise to allow safe passage for any *Yun'wiya* who passes through your land, and also hunting rights—but only to *Yun'wiya* and to traders who are friend to us. And, you must be careful who you choose to settle with you. They must be friend to the *Yun'wiya*. You must be friend to the *Yun'wiya* always, and remember the good deed I have done you."

Little Carpenter stood without sound, the old woman and the younger man followed, and I scrambled to my feet, dirty skirts and all. A stream of sweat poured down my face, but I ignored it, eyes on my host. He walked closer, and I stood my ground as he leaned forward. "There, what is that?" he asked, pointing at my chest.

I put a hand there, startled, and felt the opal brooch of my grandmother's beneath my fingertips. My heart sank. "It is nothing," I muttered.

The old woman leaned in and lifted the brooch, and I had to fight the urge to jump backwards. Her dry fingers were warm against the thin cotton of my dress, even through the chemise beneath. She said something in Cherokee to Little Carpenter, and he responded: a quick back and forth of foreign syllables and arching stresses.

"I will take this nothing, to seal our promise," Little Carpenter said, holding out an open palm, black eyes unblinking.

I closed my eyes, then quickly unpinned the brooch and placed it in his palm. He took it and studied it momentarily, holding it up to the firelight. He looked at me again. "Your kinsman, he is tall? With hair like dying fire?" At my whispered "yes" he pursed his lips, nodded. "I have seen him."

With this he walked past me and ducked through the low door, disappearing. The old woman followed, the middle-aged man lending a hand to help her bend through the door, and I held a hand to my mouth, the questions desperate on my tongue. Behind me, Laughing Crow got to his feet.

"*Hwi'lahi*," he said sharply, and I turned and looked up at him blankly. "Come, you must go," he said in English, holding open the flap of the hut. I stood shakily and followed him back out into the night.

Part II

Homestead

"It is a bad plan that admits of no modification."
—*Publilius Syrus*

"Push on—keep moving."
—*Thomas Morton*

Chapter 6

The Keowee Valley

The long, steady, winding creek that lazed and rippled its way down the middle of the land cut an ancient swathe through meadow and forest. The trail leading us to this place was a footpath that moved up into the hills from Keowee Town, broke west from the main thoroughfare and swelled with the land towards the South Carolina Blue Ridge, that purple-shadowed range the Cherokee called "the Great Blue Hills of God."

As we hiked along the lonely path we passed by the foot of a small, singular mountain, and the remains of an Indian village that had been burnt during the Cherokee Wars. Tomassee, it had been called, and according to Laughing Crow—who had spoken only once before on the morning trek, insisting I carry a skin of water—had at one time housed more than forty people. Now the village sat in small heaps of stones and wood, and broken fence lines and rotting corn still reeked, six years later, with the faint, choking tinge of smoke.

We left the village and the shadow of Tomassee Knob and followed the creek deeper into the forest. I swatted at mosquitoes, wiping specks of blood onto my skirts and refusing the bear grease Laughing Crow wore. That the nasty stuff worked was undeniable—I never saw him scratch a single inch of skin—but the smell was awful, and I couldn't shake from my mind theories about how it had been rendered from the fat of dead bears.

In the depths the forest, when Tomassee Creek turned rocky and the path became unrecognizable to anyone but Laughing Crow, and the sun was entirely blocked by a layered canopy of hickory and elm that populated the sky above our heads, leaving us in darkness, I'd had a moment of sheer panic. What if my land was like this: an infinity of trees, black and endless and just as wicked as the Germanic woods I'd read about in the Grimm

41

brothers' fairy tales? It suddenly seemed a medieval dungeon, dank with the unknown. Like a fool, I'd expected beautiful, rolling fields dotted with enchanting groves, much like the land along the Santee.

But then we'd come to this place. My place.

I looked out over the dividing mountain creek and green hills rolling to rest at the foot of blue mountains, and I felt like a hawk who had instinctively flown her way home.

Laughing Crow waved an impatient arm out in front of his chest, encompassing the valley below us. "Your land is here," he pointed to our feet, "to the foot of the mountains. It is good land."

I looked up at him, wiping a sweaty strand of hair from my cheek. "And you wonder why it was given me."

Laughing Crow said nothing, simply walked over to Rev. McDonough and dropped his skin of water into the older man's lap. The Reverend sat upon the ground, chest heaving from the hike. "Drink," the Indian ordered, stalking away to unload the packhorse.

I walked to my old friend and lay a hand on his shoulder. "I'm going to walk along the creek," I said, noticing his sudden widened eyes. "Just a little ways."

He placed his bigger hand warmly over mine and nodded. "Get on with you then. I'll watch from here."

I glanced at Laughing Crow. He was bent over the small wagon filled to brimming with my things, unlatching it from the horse. I turned quickly and started down the hill into the valley, careful not to stumble on the slippery carpet of brown pine needles. My eyes stayed focused and sure on the green beyond the trees where the land—my land—opened up into meadow, and farther still the swift little creek. The urge to run out into the open meadow, shouting with delight, was so strong that I cupped a hand over my mouth, squeezing.

I felt an unbearable guilt at my elation—at my freedom—when Owen surely suffered. It was as if my heart was rent in two, a transcendent joy alongside the fear. But I could not deny that this was the loveliest place I'd ever seen. I stopped just outside the thicketed woods, in grass to my knees, and with my eyes devoured the lay of the land: the meadows rolling up into higher meadows, the flashing creek curling through it all, and the Blue Ridge, reigning like an azure crown.

"Finally," I whispered. And from mere feet away, a tremendous deer went barreling out of the forest and across the valley, huge antlers bobbing above the grass.

Behind me, Laughing Crow let out a shout. I spun to find him with musket raised and sighted. I screamed and dropped to a crouch, hands clasped over my ears. He fired and sprinted forward. I saw his moccasins pass inches before my nose.

Rev. McDonough puffed his way down the hill and helped me to stand, a huge smile splitting his reddened face. He pointed off in the direction Laughing Crow had taken. "Did you see that, Quinn? What a shot! We'll eat for weeks if he offers us any of it."

"Any of what?" I said, brushing off my skirts, my heart thumping so loudly I could hear it in my ears.

He grabbed my wrist and pulled me forward. "Venison, girl. A bit gamey but delicious all the same. And we haven't had red meat for days."

Stunned, I let him drag me along through the grass to the place where Laughing Crow knelt beside the downed buck, his hand on its neck. Blood poured out onto the dirt from a wound in its massive chest. Laughing Crow held his other hand over the wound, muttering words in his guttural language, blood gushing through his fingers.

"You killed it," I muttered, and the Indian lifted dark eyes to mine. The Reverend took his hands from me and clapped in delight.

"Aye, man—and what a shot. If we might share in the bounty, I'll help you skin it."

Laughing Crow, his eyes still on my face, nodded. Then the deer moved beneath his hand, and he whipped a long-bladed knife from the leather sheath at his side, slicing it across the brown fur at the throat. Black-red blood spurted out, and I closed my eyes, holding up a hand.

"I think I may be ill," I said.

"Ah, venison. Fit for King Geordie himself!" Rev. McDonough patted his robust belly and smacked his gums.

I stumbled away and braced a hand against a lovely little poplar, hurling the remains of my breakfast into the grass.

"Here, I think," I said, hands on hips, my elbows crooked out like wings. We stood, Rev. McDonough and I, at the crest of the highest meadow, long afternoon shadows from a nearby grove of hickory and pine shading our faces.

"A good spot for a cabin," the Reverend said, rubbing pointer finger and thumb against his bristly chin. "You've a nice lookout, in case of danger, and you won't be caught by the creek flooding or rain run-off in a big storm. The trees will help keep you cool in summer, too."

I turned, my back to the Blue Ridge, and pointed down the gently sloping valley. "I want the barn there, in that flat space, where there's room enough for a large pen. A dairy house could be dug nearby, closer to the creek, and maybe the meat house several yards away. The homesteaders' cabins should be placed intermittently throughout the middle meadows, leaving the lower and upper pastures for farming."

"Looks as if the savages cleared the land already. You won't have as much work as otherwise, to plant crops."

Viewing the valley with the sun to my back, I could almost see the faint outlines of the small cabins that I hoped would one day stand there, trails of smoke puffing from chimneys up into the air. "Owen can live with me, or have his own home, should he choose, but heaven knows he'll be back adventuring soon. I want to be close to the homesteaders, but not so close that I make them uncomfortable, like some lord on the hill," I said, turning and shading my eyes against the midday sun, face lifted to the spot where my new home would stand. "But I will have this hill."

"You sound like your grandfather, my dear." Rev. McDonough smiled at me, and I knew it to be a compliment. "I believe you'll have your settlement. Though it will take much hard work, and a good many strong backs to build what you wish."

I walked to him, and we turned together to make our way across the wide series of meadow, overgrown pasture and trees that was the cupped palm of the Keowee Valley. For over a fortnight we'd made camp at the edge of the forest, using the wagon as shelter. Laughing Crow had stayed with us that first night—whether by command or choice I'd never know—and had helped us construct a hardy lean-to with pine boughs and rocks. And I was certain that the Reverend would make his way northward as soon as we'd made arrangements with Jack Wolf—and when he felt I was settled and well protected.

I'd been forced to accept that finding Owen could take quite some time. I felt as if the waiting—waiting to find a guide, waiting to meet Mr. Wolf, waiting to see in what condition we'd find my cousin—was going to drive me slowly mad. So before leaving Fort Prince George I'd done the one thing I could: I'd sent Clemens on a task to gather homesteaders for my settlement—families, in particular, who'd help it to grow and prosper. He seemed confident it would not take long, and had promised to travel to outlying settlements. Me being white, and a woman of name, he said, and most importantly having a legal claim to Cherokee land—unlike most backcountry squatters, who'd crossed the Boundary in spite of Crown law—should make my land all the more valuable, more attractive to potential settlers.

"Clemens should be back soon," I said, giving voice to my own thoughts as if doing so would make action out of air. "Perhaps he'll have word of homesteaders."

"That would surely be a blessing. I'd rest easier knowing you'll have good people by your side, Quinn. These mountains are no place for a lady alone, though the past weeks have been quiet, haven't they?"

"They have," I agreed, sitting on the edge of the wagon and unlacing my boot. I slipped it off and tipped it over; a stone tumbled to the ground. Rev. McDonough wandered to the wagon, his hands in the pockets of his breeches.

"I think I may lay my head for a bit," he said. "My old bones are weary. You won't wander off, will you?"

I smiled, slipping off the other boot and cradling both in my lap. "No. In fact, I may do the same. I don't know that I've ever felt this tired."

He put a hand on the edge of the wagon, heaved himself up. "It's the start of a new life, my dear," he said, settling against a barrel of rum and folding his hands over his belly. "You get weary from the work you've done, and weary just thinking of what's to come. It's natural."

I eyed a patch of pine needles and walked to them, tucking my skirts beneath me and sitting. The hem of my dress was already the color of mud; I'd been tramping about the overgrown pastures all morning, studying the lay of the land. The sheer freedom of it—the fact that I could do such a thing, could sit upon the ground barefoot, without being frowned over or whispered about—was enough to make me breathe a long, contented sigh, stretch out bare feet and lay back. The pine needles were soft beneath my head and cool from the shade, and soon the quiet lulled my anxious brain, and all thought ceased.

Later—I didn't know how long—a hand grasped my shoulder, shaking me gently. I opened my eyes. Rev. McDonough stood above me, and I focused blearily on the red indention of the wood barrel on his left cheek. Above him the sky through the green canopy was the mellowed orange of late afternoon. "Time to wake, my dear," he said. "We've visitors."

I ran a quick hand over my face, rubbing puffy eyes. Nearby, the packhorse snorted and pawed at the dirt, and I looked up to find Clemens and two strange men making their way down the pine embankment.

"Ahoy, the settlement," Clemens called.

"Isn't much of a settlement yet," Rev. McDonough said, hurrying across the glen and reaching out to clasp the trail guide's hand, "but it will be. Who do you have for us, Mr. Clemens? Good Christian gentlemen eager for a piece of pretty land such as this, aye?"

I tugged my boots back on and hurriedly tied the laces, stood quickly, smoothing my hair into place and brushing off my skirts with a swift hand.

The two men standing at Clemens's side were a study in contrasts. The taller one was well dressed, aristocratic. He wore fawn breeches, the knees dirty from the hike, and a pristine tricorn atop his blond head. Despite the heat, his shirt collar was tied primly at the neck. He had pale skin, and above a thin, sunburnt nose his blue eyes were solemnly formal.

"Madam MacFadden, I presume," he said, removing his hat and bowing. His accent was startlingly upper-crust English: he could have just as easily been speaking to the queen at Buckingham Palace. He rose, releasing my hand.

"Miss, actually," I said quickly, folding my hands at my stomach.

The man faltered, clearing his throat. "Miss MacFadden, I am Benjamin Harris."

"*Lord* Benjamin Harris," Clemens interjected with a wicked twinkle in his eyes. Harris took a breath and began again.

"Yes, I am Lord Harris, but I do not prefer the title, seeing as how I've abdicated it and moved to the wild frontier," he said, a bit self-deprecatingly. "I am formerly of Virginia, and was traveling to Charlestown to seek word of land for sale when I met your man here at Fort Prince George. He said that you are building a settlement, with plots for potential homesteaders?"

"Yes, this is true," I answered, but paused to smile at the other man, who was doing his best to fade into the background. "Hello, sir. And you are?"

He stepped forward and nodded jerkily at me, pulling a battered farmer's hat from his head and swiping a rough hand through his speckled brown hair. "Samuel Simons, madam—miss," he said quickly, in a soft continental accent. "My wife and I come from Savannah. My two sons, too . . . they're waiting for word at the Fort." His breeches were stained and worn, and though he was most likely near the same age as Harris—perhaps in his middle thirties—criss-crossing wrinkles fanned out from his hazel eyes, making him seem much older.

I took a deep breath and considered my potential neighbors. "Well, gentlemen, why don't we walk the land a bit, and I shall try to explain what I hope to build here."

Obviously stunned at a woman taking charge, they stood with mouths agape until Rev. McDonough came up behind them and clapped a hand on each of their shoulders. "I know it's unconventional, lads," he said, winking at me, "but 'tis true Miss MacFadden is the landholder here, and what she says stands solid as iron. Let's have a walk-about."

We took the matted path that the Reverend and I had made through the meadow, heading toward the upper end of the valley. We stepped high in the long grass. The sun had begun its quick descent behind the Blue Ridge, turning the mountains a deep, ethereal purple—some otherworldly shade cast from the spell of a mountain wizard. Both men drew in breath behind me, and I felt relief spread through my veins, cooling and sweet.

"I have four hundred acres of land, which I was given by Chief Little

Carpenter, of the Lower Cherokee," I told them. "I'm settling here, and will oversee the valley and its production, most of which will hopefully be enough to allow us to sustain ourselves without outside help. I'm opening up six parcels of land to be cultivated by homesteaders and their families." I swept out a hand, hoping to encompass the central section of the valley. "There will be room along the middle of the valley for six cabins. We'll also work the same communal fields, and we will decide together what is to be grown and harvested. Some of the forest can be cleared for more farming, but I do plan on keeping most of the land as it is, for hunting and trapping."

Pausing, I looked directly at each man. This was what worried me most, and the words came quickly. "I must soon leave this place, and for how long I don't know. My kinsman—my cousin—has been taken by the Shawnee Indians, and I only wait now for a guide to take me to him. I'm hoping to trade for his release." I cleared my throat, gulping back the knot there. "So you see, I need men here whom I can trust. We are well beyond the Boundary Line, and will rarely see white settlers of any kind, except for each other. When I purchased this land I promised Little Carpenter that any Cherokee would be free to hunt and trap on it, and that if need be they should pass through without harm. I can't have anyone who does not presume to keep to that promise settling here."

Rev. McDonough crossed his hands over his chest, resting them on his belly as he studied each man. After a moment, Lord Harris nodded curtly, and surprisingly, Samuel Simons stuffed his hands in the pockets of his breeches and lifted an eyebrow.

"I don't claim to understand the red men, but I got no problem with 'em," he said. "I figure out here, we'd best get along."

Clemens continued to prove to be a man of his word. By the Sunday of the second week I'd had two more potential settlers come to Keowee Valley. They came on foot, not a horse to their names. And yet, when they made the walk with me to the highest pasture, their eyes lit just as mine had on the first day I'd seen the Blue Ridge. They must have thought me unbelievably rich, being able to purchase such an expanse of prime farming land from the Indians who wanted us anywhere but here. But for the most part, when I told them of my plan to build a settlement that functioned as community they nodded, eager to start digging into dirt they could call their own.

Late one night as I sat by the fire—my thoughts, as usual, on Owen—a young man named Ezekial O'Hare approached me in the dark, clutching his hat in his hands. "Miz MacFadden," he choked out. "Did I hear you right? You're giving us our land parcels—they're free?"

I nodded and smiled up at him, this angelic-looking boy of sixteen who had traveled the Great Wagon Road from Virginia, and whose wife was still in Ninety-Six, and would be joining him within the next week or so. "Yes, Mr. O'Hare, they are free. But in return I expect to have good, hard-working people living here, and that's rare. Most are afraid, with us being so deep in Cherokee country."

"Me and Eliza, we're hard workers," he said earnestly. "We'll do anything to homestead in a place pretty as this. It is wild, ain't it?" he continued, looking into the dark. "But it sure is pretty. And, truthfully speaking, we can't afford nothing else."

I stood and brushed down my skirts, then held out a hand. "Well, then, I think we've come to an agreement, sir."

He looked at my hand for a moment, then grabbed it and shook it heartily. "Thank you, Miz MacFadden, ma'am."

After he disappeared back into the dark, heading I supposed towards his own shelter for the evening, another of my new homesteaders stepped out of the shadows and took at seat on one of the barrels nearby. Jehosaphat Brown was black as the Southern night, and all I discerned as I focused on his broad face were the striking whites of his eyes. He'd come with Ezekial from Virginia, where he'd recently been given his manumission papers by a dying master. Apparently, he and the boy had known each other since Ezekial was a child.

"You sure you wan' be takin' on some slave?" he asked quietly, his deep voice thick with the cadence of the Caribe islands.

"You're a free man, Mr. Brown." I lifted my chin and looked at the stars above the meadow in the clear summer night, and knew there to be thousands more than I could ever count. "Here life is not as we know it. We will literally be living among a people most consider savage, heathen, and strange. I can't think of a better place for a free man to make a new beginning, can you?"

He made a noise in his throat, and the whites of his eyes flashed in the firelight. "I don' know 'bout no red men. But I'm thinkin' they may be worried more 'bout some white face than mine."

"Will you settle here, then?"

"Yeah, I be stayin'."

I found him again in the darkness, hoping he would look me in the eye. "I'm glad."

Chapter 7

Late Summer, 1768

In my dream I knew that the voice came from the forest on the wooded side of the creek, shrouded now in a damp, heavy mist. I walked towards it, sloughing through the water, the hem of my sleeping gown soaked to my shins.

Save him, child, it whispered, and the voice was my mother's.

The cold struck my ankles, and I woke, clutching at my skirts. My eyes blurred and cleared, and I stumbled through the water away from the silver forest, pushing my way through the cane growing at the edge of the creek.

"I am *awake,*" I said forcefully, my voice harsh in the quiet as I walked quickly through the tall grass.

The Valley was still sleeping. Fog hung low in the trees, sneaking around the bottom of the barn and hovering near the rough wooden frames of the cabins-in-progress. I shook my head to clear it, stung with the knowledge that I'd somehow made it all the way down the sloping fields, through the new construction, across the lower pastures, and into the middle of Tomassee Creek—asleep. I ran then, and didn't stop until I reached the top of the highest meadow and my own cabin.

Still here, I told myself, the hand around my heart easing its bony grip. I spun a quick circle, just to be certain, and halted with my gaze toward the low-hanging clouds that hid the Blue Ridge from view. The entire valley was saturated in fog, and there was no sign of it lifting, at least for the moment. Even the sun seemed to be hiding, unable to slip pale fingers of light between cracks in the gray.

My cabin, though larger than the others, was still a humble one-story frontier home built of logs and clay, with a covered, wood-planked front porch and four windows, two for each side, now covered in burlap cloth. It sat at a slant, facing West, and the mountains. I'd wanted it that way, so that I'd wake and sleep to the sight of my freedom: those big, blue hills promised a life all my own whenever I looked upon them. I walked to the one step leading up to the short porch and sat, tucking my wet gown beneath dirty bare feet and resting my chin on my knees.

They'd built it for me, this cabin: Rev. McDonough, Lord Harris, Ezekial, Hosa, and even Clemens. With huge trunks of oak and hickory, taken from my own land, they'd fashioned a home—and I loved it, more than any grand mansion in Charlestown. The cold space in my chest warmed as I remembered how they'd argued with me, insisting that they build the "big house" first, that it was what should be done, seeing as how their land had been freely given.

But despite the people whom I knew slept hundreds of yards away in makeshift shelters throughout the middle pasture, I felt alone. We'd had no word yet of Mr. Wolf, no communication with Keowee Town—and because of this, I still did not know when I'd find Owen. Fear for his safety had become a solid lump in my chest, a cancer that would grow if I did not assuage it with work. And though we'd been here for almost a season, the barn built and the homesteaders' cabins coming together at a steadier rate than I'd ever imagined, I still felt as though we were nothing but a small haven carved from the wilderness. And that maybe, if we halted even for a day, the forest would swallow us up.

"Pardon me, Miss MacFadden."

I covered my chest with a hand and looked up. Eliza O'Hare stood shyly a few yards away, fingering the hem of her muslin apron. She was much taller than me, and gangly with it, though at fifteen she surely had more years to fill out. In the morning light her hair seemed gray as a mole's skin, but I knew it to be light brown. She looked at the ground near my feet.

"Eliza, good morning," I said, embarrassed to be found in my shift, even if I did sit upon my own doorstep.

"And to you," she said quietly. "We've got coffee on at the fire pit, if you care for some. Lord Harris brought it from London and's willing to share."

"Thank you, I'll be down soon."

She nodded quickly and slipped away, a skinny brown pigeon disappearing into the fog. I stood and reluctantly went into my cabin, relinquishing the small hold I'd had on the solitary morning. Inside, I stopped in my tracks before the cold hearth, looking down at my sopping hem. I'd no real notion about the purpose of the vision, why it had led me to the creek. *Save him*, the voice had said—and the "he" to whom it was referring could only mean Owen. It infuriated me that I remained at the

mercy of Jackson Wolf, a man I didn't know and was beginning to doubt I'd
ever meet. If there was ever a time for patience—certainly no talent of
mine—this was it.

Though the season should have been heading towards a crisp, mountain
fall, the air still sat humid with summer, the sky heavy with the haze of
sweltering days and languid nights. I longed for a time when I could push
back the rude curtains covering my windows and feel the chill of autumn,
but to do so now would risk moths in the oil lamp and mosquitoes in my
bed. I woke hot in the mornings, the sheet wrapped round my feet, and I
shifted constantly through the night on the rough mattress, unable to sleep.

This morning I'd gone early to the barn to check on the progress of the
stalls. Though the settlement claimed only a few horses, I was hopeful that
with time and the success of the first harvest most of the homesteaders
would be able purchase more. I walked quietly through the long run that
followed the middle of the structure, my boots sinking slightly into the red
clay floor. In my mind's eye I could see the now makeshift stalls as stalwart
as a Scottish earl's, the horses inside each well-fed and hardy.

I missed my horse, missed Grandfather as I thought of the cobbled
floors in his pristine stables in Charlestown. His horses were a matter of
pride for my grandfather. Most were shipped from Ireland and Scotland,
and were tall and well-mannered, bred for show and strength. The last time
I'd seen Campbell MacFadden had been in his stables. I'd had to hunt him
down on the morning I was to leave for the trek to Ninety-Six, and he'd
been nowhere to be found in the house on Tradd Street. I'd slipped out the
back door and through the gardens and into the carriage house: he'd been
standing in the stall with Ninian, the horse he had given me the year I'd
come to live with him.

*There stood the Scotsman, one big hand on the mare's blazed nose, talking to her in
a low voice. "She's leaving you too, lassie," he muttered, shifting his booted feet in the straw.
"And God knows if I'll live through it, knowing my girl's among the heathen savages and
ne'er do wells."*

*"Grandfather." I cleared my throat. "The coach is here. We're to fetch Reverend
McDonough on the way out of town."*

*"I've been telling your horse how you're deserting her for the wild frontier," he said,
giving Ninian's nose a rub and turning to me. His blue eyes met mine, the crinkles webbing
out from the sides as he frowned. "Ye mean to go, then—and damn what I think of it,
though I've naught but raised ye as my dearest own."*

*"And I love you for it," I said brokenly. "But Owen may still be alive, and I must
make any effort I can to find him. Here I'll never be more than an oddity—the old maid
bluestocking who rides horses as a man does, shaming the MacFadden's good name. I don't*

want to leave you," I rubbed the back of my hand roughly across my eyes, "but if I stay I'll simply wither away. I'll always wonder if I could've been different."

There was silence, and through my tears I saw Grandfather draw his chin in towards his chest and take a deep breath. He gave the mare a hard pat on the neck and walked to the stall door, putting his weathered hand over mine. "I want more for ye than dirty huts and an early grave," he muttered, his Scotch burr deepening. "But I'd rather ye be scalped a maid than lose your fire, hole yourself up in the library here."

I choked on a half-laugh. "What a fine sentiment."

We stared at each other, the old man and I, and suddenly I could not bear the thought of leaving him, this man who had shown me the world.

Without thinking, I lay my head on his hand, his craggy knuckles pushing up against my cheek. A tear dripped from one of my eyes, and I watched it pool at the dry dip of skin between his pinky and ring fingers. Ninian whinnied softly, upsetting the quiet, and I felt his other hand come to rest on my hair, cupping the back of my skull.

"Well, I think you've got yourself a settlement, Miss Quinn."

Jolted, I rubbed a harsh hand against my cheek and saw Clemens standing in the open barn doors, bathed in light from the outside. He lifted a saddlebag onto his shoulder, his freckled face lit in a smile. "You're not leaving us?" I asked.

"I've stayed long as I could," he said. "Got to get back to Ninety-Six, and see to my family. There's plenty there who'd wish to be back in Charlestown or Savannah, couldn't stand the wilderness. I'm thinking you might not be one of those, though I'd have wagered differently at first."

I inclined my head at what I knew was the trapper's gesture of compliment and stepped forward, clearing my throat. "You see, Mr. Clemens, I was hoping you'd stay and take on one of the plots of land. I could use someone with your knowledge of the frontier, and your language skills, to stand as overseer when I am away." I threw up a woeful hand. "Whenever that should occur," I added.

He shook his head, hefting the bag higher on his shoulder. "No'm, but I thank you. The sedentary life's not for me. I'd rather be headed up and down the Path with no plans to stop. But I'll check in on you in the new year, see how the crops'er doing." He inclined his head, a frontier gentleman, and started toward the opening of the barn. At the doorframe he turned.

"Almost forgot, and don't know how because I know you've been waiting, but Wolf should be here within a fortnight. He's been in the Middle Towns, just down from hunting the Kentucky territory, so Little Carpenter couldn't get word any quicker, or so Kicking Horse said last I saw him at Fort George. He's a different sort, Wolf is. But don't be afraid to trust him—he's a good man."

Before I could get a word in he hitched the bag again, tapped his hat with a finger. "Other than that, remember to keep a musket by the door, and keep an eye out for midnight raids. You can mostly trust the Cherokee, but I don't hold stock with no white war parties in these hills—they're only out for trouble." He smiled shyly. "You take care, miss."

"And you," I answered, more than a little surprised at the regret I felt at seeing him go.

By afternoon the Simons's roof had been completed, and little Micah Simons and his younger brother raced in and out of the wall-less cabin, war-whooping in delight. Watching the men pat Samuel on the back, and seeing his shyly prideful grin, I wondered when the family had last had a home. That they were poor was no mystery. Abigail's face held the story of a good many more years than she'd lived. And Lord Harris had revealed one day during the morning meal that the pair had been indentured to a wealthy family in Savannah for seven years before traveling to the frontier, though the Simonses never spoke of it.

"Miss MacFadden," Micah hollered, skidding to a stop in the dirt in front of me, his breeches torn at the knee. "It's up, our cabin's up!"

"Yes, it is," I said, giving into the urge and ruffling a hand through his bronze-colored hair. "Won't it be lovely to sleep off the ground? No more bugs in your ears."

He shifted impatiently. "Oh, I don't mind bugs, but Mamma gets cock-eyed when she talks about havin' a bed. You got a bed, Miss MacFadden?"

"Yep, I got a bed." I grinned, and he took off like an arrow towards the creek, where Eliza and Abigail were scraping clothes against one of the larger granite boulders.

The boy splashed into the water and wrapped his arms around his mother's knees. She placed a hand on his shoulder and listened to his excited garble, then looked up and past me at her new home. At the sight of the nearly-finished cabin she dropped the quilt she'd been cleaning and hugged Micah tightly, her face hidden beneath a checkered bonnet. I watched as the quilt rippled and moved slowly with the current, catching on a fallen tree limb downstream.

Suddenly Samuel Simons stood before me, hat in hand, much like the day we'd met. And I knew he'd thank me, good man that he was, and I couldn't take it. So I reached out blindly and grasped his hand, shaking it energetically.

"I'm so happy for you, Mr. Simons," I said. "You've a fine home now."

He opened his mouth to speak, but I slipped from his work-roughened grip and spun on my heel, hurrying past the other makeshift cabins towards freedom.

Chapter 8

Autumn, 1768

Wake, Quincy, said the voice.

I opened my eyes and stared at the dark ceiling, focusing on a spot between the logs where the clay had dried to a mud color. I wiped eyes gone stagnant with sleep and rolled to the edge of the bed, slowly sitting up. Lazily, I reached out a hand, brushing back the burlap curtain, and yawned wide as a whale. Outside the world had turned to rose: the soft, pink-gold light pieced its way through morning mist and lit on the mountains, carving out rounded ridges against a sky just beginning to crisp with autumn.

Blessed silence. I padded across the rudely planked floor and found my boots, and slipped them on hurriedly minus the stockings. In a rush I drew a gown from the bottom of the chest I'd brought from my room in Charlestown, pulled it over my head and yanked the laces as tightly as I could from the back. I took my grandmother's flintlock pistol from the drawer in the side table and slipped it between the folds of my skirts, into the pocket I'd sewn there. On my way out the door I grabbed the indigo shawl I kept draped over the oak dressing table and hooked it around my shoulders as I slipped into the morning.

I reveled in mornings like this, when the whole valley sat still as a painting, and I was the first in the settlement to wake—a rare occurrence since the cabins had been built and filled with homesteaders. I headed to the western edge of the high meadows, picking up speed at the sight of sunlight in the woods, glinting off a bare boulder in Tomassee Creek.

Though I passed the pen in a wide arc, the few horses there caught my smell and whinnied softly, air from their nostrils puffing out in tiny clouds. I ran then, cutting a path through a small crop of picked corn, the drying stalks crackling at my passing. I wanted the creek to myself, the whole valley to myself, the world—before life began again and the day wasn't wholly mine anymore. I wanted to think of my cousin, to pray for his safety, and to walk, and keep walking, until I could think on it no more.

I crossed the creek at the rock path and followed the water up toward the hills and deeper into the forest. It gurgled as it splashed against rocks and boulders, and a rabbit cut across the pine-strewn bank before me, disappearing into the underbrush. Ferns high as my elbows coated the forest floor in a texture of rippling green. I breathed in deeply, inhaling pine and sweet sap and cool water.

At the widest crook in the creek I caught the smell of fire. A pile of coals smoldered black several yards from the water, and I wondered if some trapper or Cherokee scout had perhaps taken refuge there for the night. I walked to the dying embers and kicked them lightly with my boot. Suddenly it seemed that the forest was silent—no birds called, nor any crickets chirped, normally cheerful constants in the mountains.

Movement from the other side of the creek had me spinning, and I watched the shadows shift at the bottom of an enormous old oak. A man stepped forth. *Danger,* the voice in my head said solidly. I drew the pistol from my skirts and held it shakily, all my breath caught in a knot at the base of my throat.

He walked to the edge of the creek, still without sound.

"Come no closer, sir," I said, and heard my words escape the woods and echo across the still waking valley.

He raised his head then, and I could see beneath the battered hat he wore that his eyes were green as the moss growing on the boulders in the creek. Shadows cast his high cheekbones in stark relief, and as he nodded at me the tips of his long hair fell across his shoulders. It was startling to see light-colored hair on such a man, for despite that and the eyes he seemed quite savage: he wore a dirty, fringed deerskin shirt, booted moccasins, and he carried a musket and hatchet attached to his back with a beaded strap. He shifted to remove his hat, and my eyes went again to that arresting face, with its long, aquiline nose and hooded eyes. Surely he was Indian, I thought, though his hair was the color of a well-worn leather saddle, the tips dipped in white paint.

He watched me solemnly. "My guess is you'll shoot that thing, and it'll backfire in your face," he said with a surprising Irish lilt.

"It will not," I said, lifting the pistol, my arm thankfully steady. "Who are you?" I asked boldly, and the question hung in the air. My mind raced. The settlement would be waking soon, and the horses would need be let to pasture.

Surely someone would notice I was missing.

He took his time answering, and I kept my grip hard on the pistol. As he studied me I shifted my feet in the pine needles, noticing for the first time just how tall he was. Taller even than Owen, I thought, seeing my cousin in my mind—and Owen had a full foot on me. But Owen, stalwartly Anglo-Saxon, looked nothing like this man. This man looked like none I'd ever seen, with his unusual height, swarthy skin, broad, rangy build, and an Indian's face beneath a white man's hair and eyes.

"You'd be Miss MacFadden," he said, mouth crooking up. "My given name's Jack."

Jackson Wolf . . . finally. I lowered the pistol, slipping it back into my pocket. "Mr. Wolf, I presume," I said, irked even as my heart picked up beat—*at last, to find Owen!* "You, sir, are a difficult man to locate. I'm in need of your services as a tracker, though I suppose you already know why. Nearly a year ago my cousin was taken by the Shawnee. We must be off soon—I fear that in being forced to wait for you I have let far too much precious time pass."

He cocked his tawny head, the beaded feather at the tip of a skinny braid bumping his shoulder. If he heard the accusation in my tone, he ignored it. "Hard to get word up in *Kentahteh*. I came soon as I heard." He narrowed his eyes, studying me with an impertinence that prickled along my back. "I wanted a look at the fearless white woman who bartered with Attakullakulla. Not much to you, is there?"

Bristling, I turned rudely and started back down the path, heading for the opening in the woods that led to the north fields. "There's no time for banter, sir. I won't wait another week to find my kinsman."

I crossed the rock path, and he was at my side, his long stride irritatingly silent. "I mean no offense, lass," he said, shifting the weapons on his back as he walked. "But you're a little one, despite all that pretty yellow hair. I'd thought to find some Amazon tall enough to look a man in the eye, and built like one of those fancy brick privies."

"A privy?" I choked. I swallowed back ire and gripped my skirts so hard I knew my knuckles went white. "Kindly tell me what we'll need for the journey—you can do this as we walk, I assume." Then despite myself, I stopped in full stride and turned. "One doesn't need to be a giant to look a man in the eye, figuratively speaking."

I started forward again, swung back. "And where does a backwoodsman like you learn of Greek mythology?" Thoroughly annoyed at myself and the wide grin that split across his face, I stalked away. Surely the man would follow.

He caught up with me, laughing. "A bluestocking, that's what you are. Kicking Horse said you'd brought a trunk load of books with you. I told him he was crazy—what does an Amazon need with books in the backcountry?"

"I'm not an Amazon," I said indignantly. "I am a woman who wants to find her cousin and bring him home, that is all."

We reached the edge of camp; nearby Abigail stood with Samuel beside a newly-started fire, bending to set a kettle in the coals. Up a ways I could see Hosa in the pen, shaking a bucket at old Plato, the gentle stallion I'd used as packhorse. The other horse, Mutt, was a sloop-backed gelding the Simons family had brought with them from Savannah. He wandered over and nosed at the black man.

"You started a settlement, miss. I don't think that is all," the tracker said softly, taking my elbow. I jerked it away, rubbing it.

"We are not familiar," I said sharply, and I could feel the eyes of the settlement on me as I backed away from the man. "You have a horse, I assume? You may board it in the barn. Then, please, come to my cabin so we may speak of tracking Owen—my cousin. I assume we'll need to discuss supplies, routes? It's the largest one, there," I added, pointing up towards the high pasture toward my new home.

I folded my hands together at my waist, more to calm myself than anything else. The man watched me silently, and for some reason this irritated me, for surely he had much to tell me. I licked dry lips, pressed them together. "Obviously we aren't hindered by social mores here, so I will meet you on the porch." When he did not speak, again, I sucked in air through my teeth. "Does that suit you, Mr. Wolf?"

"*Tadeya'statakuhi'*," he answered, and I could almost hear the grin in his voice as I gave him my back.

When Jack Wolf walked up from the barn through the high pasture towards my cabin, he made no sound in the wet grass. I stood from my seat on the porch where I'd been waiting, setting my inkpot and quill on the railing and tucking the papers I'd gathered beneath one arm. I was anxious to make plans, though still irked by his earlier behavior. But something in me simply stilled at the sight of him: he moved gracefully, confidently, his knees breaking the morning mist as it swirled behind him like the tails of a translucent gray cloak. He'd left his hat in the barn, and he wore his hair loose.

He is the one, said the voice in my head. *Trust him.*

My heart thumped violently in my chest, and I sucked in air through my nose, pressing a hand against my breastbone to quiet it. "No," I whispered harshly under my breath.

He stopped in the dirt below the step, so tall he met my eyes. We stood there for moments, not speaking. When he simply cocked his head, making a careful study of my face, I shook myself as if exiting a trance. "Mr. Wolf, thank you for coming. Shall we begin?"

One sun-bleached brow rose, and he propped a foot on the step. "Were you a schoolmarm?" he asked.

"What? No. I gave riding lessons." Exasperated, and failing at keeping my tone light, I turned abruptly and sat in my chair. "Mr. Wolf, please."

He grinned so quickly it was startling, and stepped up onto the porch, moving to lean against the railing nearby. "It's only that you've the sound of one," he said. "Not that you look like one." He folded his arms over his chest, lifting his chin at my papers. "Making lists, are you?"

"I am." I sat, adjusted the papers, reached for the quill and dipped it into the inkpot. "Tell me, what provisions are needed?"

"First, miss, you need to know just how dangerous a journey this will be. We'll be traveling through enemy lands, and the going is sure to be slow and difficult. The days will be long, and the nights short. You'll not sleep much. And the truth is, we may never find your kinsman." Though the man spoke succinctly, there was an underlying kindness in his words, a solemnity in opposition to his earlier teasing. He braced his hands on his thighs, leaning forward, and spoke gently. "He may already be dead, Miss MacFadden."

"He's not," I said sharply.

"How do you know?"

I pressed a hand to my breastbone again, rubbing at the spot. "Because I'd feel it, Mr. Wolf."

Surprisingly, he nodded. "All right, then. You'll need a strong horse, young enough to travel miles—mountain miles—at a time without trouble, but old enough not to spook easily. You'll need clothes that aren't fit for the drawing room"—at this he glanced pointedly at my flounced dress—"sturdy shoes, and a bedroll. Are you getting all this down with your wee pen there?"

I'd been scribbling furiously, and I looked up at the smile in his voice. "I am," I responded stiffly. When he didn't speak I waved a hand. "Do go on, please."

"You need things to barter. You need a knife. You need a gun. And you need know how to use them."

I raised my head again, fighting to keep the bite from my voice. "Isn't that what I've you for, Mr. Wolf? Certainly you know I've no knowledge of how to handle a knife."

"No? You pointed that pistol at me fair convincingly down at the creek. I figured you'd likely surprise me."

I laughed shortly, I couldn't help it. "At some point, Mr. Wolf, I am sure I will. It's my nature."

His smile widened, and his green eyes flashed with appreciation. He stepped forward and I gulped, but he turned to the step, leaning a shoulder against the post there and looking out over the Valley. It was a moment before he spoke again. "Do you believe in Fate, Miss MacFadden?" he asked without looking at me.

I set the papers down on the floor beside the chair, the quill and inkpot on the railing again. I felt strangely antsy and hot, though the morning was cool. I needed to move. "Fate, Mr. Wolf?" I stepped to the railing, gripping the rounded wood.

"Aye," he turned his head, looked at me with a gaze so strong I could not break it. "Fate. Do you believe that there are people chosen to find each other?"

I wetted my dry lips with my tongue, and when his eyes moved to my mouth I took an involuntary step backwards, and the spell was broken. "I believe I am meant to find my cousin," I said. "I'll do whatever it takes to bring him home safely."

"Do you love him, then?" He spoke the words with his gaze still on my mouth, and at my answer lifted his eyes to mine.

"Of course I do."

"Ah."

At the knowing tone I frowned. "He is my cousin. We were raised together as children. I feel for him like a brother."

Though I'd never have thought the man anything close to tense, at this something in him relaxed, and he stepped lightly off the porch and turned back to me. The sun was at the tops of the trees now, and it backlit him with a yellow glow. I shaded a hand over my eyes. "Where are you going, sir?" I asked, indignant again. "There's much to be done."

"A last question," he said, and I threw my hand up in frustration, resisting the urge to growl.

"What is it, Mr. Wolf?"

"Do you dream? And if you do, do you think the dreams true?"

At his words, uttered so easily, I froze. I felt as if I'd lost all sense of gravity, and I had to brace both hands on the railing to keep myself from crumpling. *How does he know?* I thought frantically. *How can he know that I have the Sight?*

"Are you well, miss?" he asked, making a move forward, but I held out a hand, finding my feet again.

He can't know, I told myself. *It's naught but a silly question.* "Fine. But your questions seem pointless, sir. Our imperative should be planning for the journey ahead, finding my cousin. Why do you ask me such things?"

One corner of his mouth crooked up, and though he didn't smile the hard planes of his exotic face softened. "When I journey with someone, I like to know a thing of them."

I blew out air through my nose. "Yes, I dream."

"And do you believe them true?"

I lifted my shoulders, honest. "I don't know."

"Thank you." He dipped his head in acknowledgement and turned, walking away.

Stunned, I found myself shouting at him. "Mr. Wolf, where on earth are you going?"

"To the barn, Miss MacFadden," he called over his shoulder, not slowing. "I need to lay eyes on your horse. You'll not be going anywhere without a good horse."

Who is this man? I wondered, watching his back, certain the way he moved was more animal than human. He was infuriating and strange, and around him I felt strikingly unsettled—in a way I did not believe I'd ever felt before. I ran a hand through my hair and gripped my topknot in frustration.

When he disappeared over the crest of the hill I took a deep breath, picked up my skirts and followed.

"Quinn, I must leave you." The Reverend stood at the bottom of my porch, his felt preacher's hat clasped in big hands. He'd followed me to my cabin after a supper of roasted trout, hard bread and cheese. On our walk up to the crest of the highest meadow we'd talked of the settlement, of the new homesteaders, but mostly of Mr. Wolf, and of the journey I was to take with him—a journey that defied all convention. The sun sat at its six o'clock position in the sky, still bright and bold with yellow light.

At his words I sighed, seeking inner strength. "I know you fear for my reputation. But the situation warrants it. Owen's life warrants it. Clemens feels we can trust this man."

"Aye." He looked around. "We are so far removed, are we not? You are correct, I'm afraid—and I admire your determination. I will pray for you, and for Mr. Wolf."

"What will I do without you, my kind protector?"

"Well, now, my dear—most you've done all yourself," he said, indicating the settlement with a nod. "I've naught but been a guardian of sorts, though to my own bafflement you needed no such thing. And now I must be off to do the Lord's work, for the frontier is fraught with nay-sayers and non-believers. Makes me feel better knowing you will have people with you now, when you return. I don't think I could leave you in this desolate wilderness otherwise."

"We have carved a wee niche in it, though, haven't we," I said, copying his Scottish burr. "You'll keep in touch, won't you?"

"Of course, my dear. Though the post-rider hasn't made it to the MacFadden Settlement yet, has he?"

"The MacFadden Settlement," I repeated, liking the sound of it.

The Reverend stepped onto the stoop, and his eyes met mine. He took my hands in his and held them warmly. "Be wary, Quinn. Do not lose yourself from Mr. Wolf—whether you find Owen or not. And don't you be wandering off with the savages, else Campbell will scalp me himself."

I laughed, imagining my austere grandfather wielding a tomahawk. "Have you enough food and supplies? Where will you go?"

"I've a pack of dried venison and plenty of water," he said. "I'll go to Fort George first, try to buy a good trail horse. Then I'm headed through North Carolina—there's some of my Campbell cousins there—and on to the Great Wagon Road, up through the Shenandoah Valley. Though young Zeke tells me it's as much a wilderness as here, he says there's plenty a frontier family to minister to. Mayhap I'll even try to convert the natives, but 'tis no secret I'd as soon stay far from them as I can."

I leaned up and kissed his peppered cheek, bringing a brilliant flush to his face. "Be careful, dear friend."

"Yes, and you too, dear girl. I'll send word to Campbell as soon as I'm able." He gave my hands a hard squeeze and stepped off the porch. As he turned to go he yanked his hat upon his head and headed away through the meadows. I watched him walk down into the middle of settlement, stopping to speak with each person and bidding them farewell.

I stood on my porch until he disappeared up the pine embankment at the south edge of the valley and onto the trail to Keowee Town, the dark woods swallowing him whole. I sighed deeply, painfully aware that with him went my last connection to Charlestown, and the lovely Scots accent that had given me a piece of Grandfather every day.

I pulled the shawl more tightly about my shoulders and walked to sit in a chair I'd left out earlier—one I moved from inside to out, depending on my mood. I picked up the book I'd placed on the floor by its back legs and sat, more than willing to watch the Blue Ridge go cobalt with dusk as I navigated through one of my favorite tales. Though my ragged copy of *Sejanus* did not seem the kind of literature to watch a sunset by, I enjoyed its biting wit and unapologetically horrid main character. Ben Johnson's plays could always take me into a whole new world, and wasn't that the purpose of reading?

It must have been late; the world mellowed behind my sinking lids. I curled my knees into my chest as best I could and pulled the shawl closer, unwilling to retreat inside.

"Ah, lass, 'tis true you're a bluestocking. But where are the trunks? Inside with your spectacles and scholar's robe, I'd say . . . if I had to guess."

The low, golden voice, tinged with a mix of Ireland and something else I could not name, brought me back to the waking world. It had gone completely dark; the moon rose in the east in a clear night sky. I blinked like an owl, setting my feet on the floor.

The man was mere feet from me, leaned up against a post on my porch just as he'd been that morning, his back to the mountains now outlined in the dark. I jumped out of the chair, and he held out a staying hand, palm down. "Steady, now," he said. "You're skittish as a spooked colt."

"What are you doing here?" I asked indignantly, cool night air permeating my thin daytime clothing. "Is something the matter with your quarters?"

"The barn is fine. I thought I'd come for a visit."

Something about him—about his voice—was nicking at me. "Are you Irish, Mr. Wolf? Your accent sounds it at times, but there's something different about it, and you sound almost Scottish. It's been bothering me."

"Oh, aye?" he asked, amused, one eyebrow crooking. "Mayhap it's because my own dear mother is Irish, but I was educated by a Scotch priest from the age of five. So in my mind it's all bungled, and what comes out I've no control over. That answer suit you?"

"Where do you live?" I asked rudely, ignoring the friendly teasing in his voice. "Or do you just lurk about the countryside, frightening women?"

As he folded his arms over his chest moonlight lit the hair above his forehead in a silver crown, and in the dark his eyes looked a shade of blackest green, the color I imagined the bottom of the sea to be. "Sometimes I live among the Cherokee. And sometimes I make camp in these hills, depending on my disposition for the day. My disposition usually never turns to frightening women, though. It's sorry I am if I've worried you."

"You don't worry me, Mr. Wolf," I muttered, wanting to go inside to the sanctuary of a warm bed but willing to endure his company in order to find Owen. "I am afraid for my cousin. Reading simply keeps my imagination at bay until we can leave."

"Miss, *we* won't be going anywhere. I've pondered long and hard on it since we spoke this morning, and though it's sure you're a braw lass, I can't in good conscience allow you to accompany me on such a journey. I am sorry. I can see how afraid you are for your kinsman, how far you're willing to go to assure his safety. But I can't take you—I told as much to the holy man before he left."

It was said with such low kindness that the words almost didn't register. When they did I stepped toward him. "But you must—we've no other way. Please, Mr. Wolf, I know my cousin is alive." I found myself perilously close to begging, close to tears, and I looked up into the man's eyes. "I've waited, done everything I said I would. You must believe me, it wasn't solely for land—"

"I know that," he interrupted, shifting his stance so that he was somehow closer, even in the dark.

I hurried on, desperate to convince him of the honor in my intention, "Owen is alive, Mr. Wolf. I have given up a comfortable life and betrayed my Grandfather's wishes—most assuredly broken his heart—in order to find him. Please, you must—" The echo of his words halted my stream of thought, and I stopped, sputtering. "The holy man? Rev. McDonough knew you would not aid us? You spoke with him?" I took a step toward the railing, releasing one end of the shawl and grasping the plait of my hair firmly in hand, disconsolate. "I cannot believe this—he would never agree to such a thing!"

"A moment, lass—I never said I'd not follow through on the task myself, merely that I wouldn't have you go with me. I won't take you to the *Shawano*, not for all the Crown's gold. But I'll certainly search out your kinsman, bring him home to you if I can." He stepped toward me then, took my elbow in his warm hand, and I was too bewildered to protest. He led me to the chair, helped me to sit and then sat in the one beside it, scraping its legs against the porch as he faced me.

"You've just to trust me," he began again. "Can you do that?"

I blinked, raising my face from a study of his broad hands where they cupped the caps of his deerskin-clad knees. "I don't know you," I said woodenly. "You could take my goods—all the things I'd brought to trade for Owen's life—and disappear into the wilderness. And Owen would be left to die."

"But I won't. What I will do is travel swift and hard, use what I know and who I know to find where he may have been taken or traded, and unless I am killed, I'll bring him back to you, alive or dead. I'll do all in my power to assure the former."

When I met his gaze at that haunting assurance—*alive or dead*—he stood and bent closer so that I could see his eyes. His presence there in the dark was a heated thing, and when he spoke again I startled. "If I am killed before I find your cousin, someone from Keowee Town will bring word. Give them this." He reached up then, untied the eagle's feather from the one skinny braid in his long hair and held it out to me. I took it, shivering. "I've had the feather since I was a boy, and my father will know its significance on sight. They will take it, and you, to him. And he'll find Owen, no matter the cost. This is my pledge to you."

I folded my fingers around the feather. It felt, more than anything, like a talisman. A strong wind had begun to blow through the hollow of the valley, rustling leaves and moaning in the trees along the smudged edge of the meadow. Despite the chill that promised rain, despite logic insisting I take heed, I felt an unquestionable pull to believe this strange man—for surely, surely he was the only one who could save Owen. I did not need voice or vision, this time, to tell me as much.

I let out a shaky breath, licked dry lips. "I think," I said softly, "if I am kept waiting, as I have been, wondering whether he is dead or alive, I shall go mad."

"Then I'll send word when I'm able," he said, and I jerked my chin toward him in shock. "I can write a fair hand," he added on a hidden laugh.

"But how? The post-rider stops at Ninety-Six. Any letters that enter the backcountry are delivered by passing travelers." I smiled grimly. "Mr. Wolf, we have no passing travelers."

This time he did laugh, and it was a deep, bounding sound as he stood. "You've plenty, you just don't see them." At my blank look he cocked his head toward the outline of the Blue Ridge, indigo against the black. "You gave your word the *Yun'wiya* could pass through this land unharmed, and they have. I'll send word. And if you've a mind to, you can write in return. It may take some time, or may not, depending on what hand gets hold of the letters when. But it may help to ease your mind. I'd think," he continued as he stepped off my porch, "there's a chance we could have your Owen returned to you by the second snow. Mayhap the third."

Alive or dead, he'd said with brutal honesty.

"When will you go?" I asked, and just like that I let it be known that I trusted him.

"You showed me earlier, in the barn, where you'd gathered the goods for trade. I can be off with first light, and it suits you."

"It suits me," I said quickly, so quickly and with such relief that I nearly stumbled on the words.

"I'll bid you goodnight, then."

The shawl slipped from my shoulder and I looked over, reaching the hand that still held the feather to right it—to cover the cold spot. When I looked back, he was gone, and the night had made no sound at his passing.

Chapter 9

8 October, 1768

Tuckaseegee

Dear Miss Quincy MacFadden,

There has been word of your cousin in the Middle Towns. A hunting party recently returned from the Ohio Valley brought with them a Catholic priest they found alone and near starved. He claims his name is Francois de Charlevoix, and that he saved the souls of the Illinois for a decade before the Shawano raided the village where he lived. If we're to believe the good Father, he went to hiding with a few surviving members of the village before he was cast out for being slew-foot (fact is, the man's long in the tooth and most like couldn't keep pace).

Charlevoix says that a few weeks before he was outcast, he spoke with a man who called himself Owen Scott at a stickball game on the Upper Holsten River. How the Frenchman got so far east, I'm uncertain, but I've no reason to doubt him. He said Scott was educated, tall of stature and auburn haired, and that he spoke of family in South Carolina. Charlevoix also said that Scott looked worse for the wear, and was not allowed to play in the ball game, but was kept captive by a covey of Shawano women nearby, though he wasn't bound. It looked to the priest as though they were using him as translator.

Now, before you start to pacing that porch of yours like

*an English soldier, think on this: they've kept him alive, so
he's valuable to someone of high clan. They won't starve
him out, and seems to me as though they're not thinking on
trading him north, either—else they may have looked to do
that on the Holsten, where there were most likely stickball
players from a bevy of different tribes in the area.*

*That being said, my brother and I are off in swift
pursuit, so say your* un'ega *prayers that we're able to catch
their trail before they disappear into the Ohio Valley. If they
do, we'll keep at it, but the going gets a fair bit more
treacherous. I'd appreciate being kept in your thoughts,
too, for I imagine you store those up nice and tight in that
bluestocking head of yours.*

Your servant,

Jack Wolf, of the Ani'Waya

Also called Silent Wolf or Walks-Between

Autumn was a riot of color over the Blue Ridge, so gorgeous it hurt the
eyes to look upon hill and mountain. This—this patchwork of russets and
reds, oranges and golds, all the colors of a long-burning fire—was nothing
I'd seen before in nature. In Charlestown our autumn lasted but a week or
more, and often arrived in the last days of November. Tree-lined streets
would suffer a quick change—my favorite tree on the whole of the
peninsula was a gold poplar in the dooryard of St. Philips Church—and
then the leaves would fall, a carpet of brown that crackled beneath horses'
hooves and carriage wheels. But here in the mountains October was a
month for the gods, and I found myself waking to each day with a renewed
energy, a new hope for Owen's safe return and for the continued
productivity of the settlement.

In spite of myself, I also hoped for increased news from Jack Wolf—if
I was to be completely honest, a valiant attempt I was determined to make
in this new world and in my new life—and hoped that in his letters I'd find
not only good news of Owen, but also insight into the tracker himself. He
intrigued me, and there'd been no man who'd caught my interest and my
intellect in equal parts in all my twenty-five years. Though his easy tone
seeped through his letters—so much so that I could hear the man's voice as
I read, his unique accent lilting and far-too familiar—it was becoming
increasingly difficult to remain irritated at the man's impertinence. In my
cabin, alone, I called him charming.

And so we began a correspondence, and he sent word of his search for

Owen as promised. Letters arrived in the hands of an interesting array of Cherokee: crumpled and removed from the pouch of one of a trio of Cherokee boys hunting in the Valley, the tallest of the three casually carrying a deer across his shoulders like a tawny Acteaon; from an old woman on horseback who arrived at the foot of the Keowee Path as though she'd been birthed from the green undergrowth; from one of two warrior-aged men who'd stood like statues at the edge of the high meadow, rifles held menacingly cross their chests until Lord Harris approached them tentatively, hat in hand; and even from Kicking Horse, who'd come bearing a pair of deerskin leggings he pantomimed were a gift from Little Carpenter himself.

The letters, few and far-between as they were, became like lamps lighting the edges of a dark, dangerous alleyway. I studied them while a cold wind beat at the walls of my cabin, held them until they softened under my hands.

29 October, 1768

The Nolichucky

Dear Miss Quincy MacFadden,

I beg your forgiveness for the muddle of my script, as I am bone tired. We rode hard on the priest's word and are now at an outlying village on the Nolichucky River. We took our rest here one night to wait out a devil of a storm, and will stay but another to refresh our horses and our supplies before continuing north into the hunting grounds. There is no good word yet of your Owen, but I have precious paper and quill and I find myself itching to write to you, despite my weary hand.

As I sit my saddle I find myself thinking on you, and wondering just how a fine lady of Charlestown, obviously of some means given the barter I know you made, came to seek out the wilderness. Surely you were warned of the Indians, of backcountry dangers and ill will? Yet there you remain, overseer of a valley and a gaggle of settlers on whom you bestowed land free of coin. I imagine your face is flushing now, and you probably pace that porch in those man's boots, swearing beneath your breath in your queen's manner at my overstepping. But I must know—why did you do it? Perhaps you'll give me an answer upon our return.

I am no wordsmith, but I do like the talk, especially

with a yellow-haired woman. I will send word when I'm able.

Your servant,

Jack Wolf, of the Ani'Waya

Also called Silent Wolf or Walks-Between

* * *

14 November, 1768

Fort Patrick Henry, the Kantuckee territory

Dear Miss Quincy MacFadden,

We are encamped tonight with the English soldiers at Ft. Henry, who have generously offered us lodging in the hog house. I write to you now with the hot breath of a sow in my ear; she has taken residence in the stall beside us and is curled against the wood planks at my back.

My brother and I would not stay in this place (to him, especially, it stinks of foul-smelling un'ega *and their Indian fears) but we have got word on the trail that there was a trader here who makes frequent business with the Shawano. Tomorrow we will seek him out and see what he can tell us about your cousin.*

The going was slow through the mountains from the Nolichucky to this place. There is an unsettled crack in the air, a feeling more from the humans here than the storms blowing through. When the animals go underground, this is a time to wait. My dear mother would say that the little folk are about their wicked business, and to tarry too long in one spot would be to risk being spirited beneath a faerie raft and lost for two hundred years. My father, a pragmatic soul, would if within hearing shake his head at her fancifulness—but he has his own little people to fear. And so sitting in this hay, weary as an ox after plowing fields, I am plagued by the old fears of both the Celts and the Cherokee. I will likely dream tonight of an army of dwarves.

I am sending this letter with a load of supplies headed to Fort George. It may not be possible to get word to the Lower Towns for some time after, as we will be likely headed farther northwest into fearful territory prized by

69

both the Shawano and the Cherokee for its salt licks. But if you've a mind to write to me as I have done to you, send post to the fort here, and give it the next scout or hunter comes through the settlement . It should get to me, and we will pick it up on our return south.

There was a dusting snow last night, and I wonder if the Keowee Valley has seen its first this season. I have not forgotten my promise.

Your servant,

Jack Wolf, of the Ani'Waya

Also called Silent Wolf or Walks-Between

In the night I dreamed, and in my dreams I saw a man with Jack—a man who was not Owen. The dream came as if the viewing of it was a painting, a large rectangular canvas set upon a wooden easel. The stranger stood tall and well-made, but his face was hidden from my view, the entirety of his shoulders, neck and head cast in darkness as though an angry child had gotten into the artist's palette, rubbed the black in a smudge over the top halves of all the people.

Jack's letters sparked something dangerous in me, and though I hated to admit it, I was scared of being burned. I did not write to him, though something very strong in me went wishing for it.

* * *

7 December, 1768

Fort William Henry, the Kantuckee territory

My dear Miss MacFadden,

We have Owen. When he is recovered enough to travel, we will begin the journey south. This post may reach you after we do, if all goes well.

You are no doubt in question of his health, and of his experience—the former I can tell of, but the latter I'll leave to him upon your reunion. He is of fair good health, most especially considering what he could have endured at the hands of the Shawano had he not been such a valuable captive. He has had a reset leg, which he says was broken at the hands of his captors when he made an early attempt at escape, and because of this now walks with a hitch. His hands and arms have been burned but are healed. You'll be relieved to know he has not been tattooed, which can only mean the Shawano were not yet prepared to adopt him into the tribe. It may be just our luck we found him when we did.

Your Owen has a fair wicked sense of humor, which my brother and I can both appreciate, especially seeing as none would hold it against him had he lost it these months in the wilderness. He went with us willingly, and at the sound of your name a light came into his eyes which makes me think he'll not be long recovering. He is not able to write, but asks me to share his affection and his thanks. There is a memory he begs me to relate: something about a Madam Brewton and your grandsire's cigar? Well, your kinsman is set to snoring, so that will have to do. That's a tale I'd like to hear you tell, perhaps sitting on your porch of a winter afternoon.

Pitch your prayers to the stars, lass, and to whatever gods you choose. We're for the Cherokee hills.

Your servant,

Jack Wolf, of the Ani'waya

Also called Silent Wolf or Walks-Between and Quinn's Wolf by Owen Scott

Chapter 10

The MacFadden Settlement
Christmas, 1768

I pulled back the curtain, stiff with cold, eager to see whether it had snowed the night before. It hadn't—brown grass peaked up through frost—but the Blue Ridge held the sheen of ice, and tree branches creaked with the weight of frozen rain. Today, I knew, would be a much different holiday from those I'd spent in Charlestown.

The first Christmas morning I can recall emerges only from hazy memory, and surely is marked by the capricious tinge of time, which often changes events in the mind. It has a mother lifting a hand to smooth back the hair of a daughter, when she might very well have been taking the child's hand, or patting her head.

I was four years old. It was before the crossing, when we still lived in Scotland. In my childish memory I can see the tiny house, festooned on the dark inside with berry boughs and greenery. A fire burned steadily in the stone fireplace; my father bent to tend to it between bouts of playing with me on the rug. Though the images are filmy, and tend to flee into the recesses of my mind whenever I try hardest to get them in my grasp, I know that my mother cooked that day, and that the smells were of roasted duck and plum pudding. She put a hand to my cheek—she did—and when she brushed the white-gold down at the back of my ear I looked into eyes that were hazel, but fringed with black lashes, big and round like my own.

I know only that the house was small because it was on land leased by my grandfather. He'd told me years later, when I was in my teens, that my father had refused to live in the manor house. Instead, he'd insisted on paying Grandfather—his father—a yearly fee for the use of the caretaker's quarters. Though I certainly had my mother's wide-lipped smile and diminutive size, I did most resemble my father, a lean Scotsman of average height and flashing blue eyes, whose yellow hair was surely descendent from some marauding Norseman, and whose stubbornness came undoubtedly from his own protean sire.

My father was a writer, a trade my grandfather certainly appreciated—what with his own love of the written word made flesh by his immense library of scholarly works—but abhorred in his own son. Instead of becoming a barrister and master of the MacFadden land holdings, Ian Jonathan MacFadden had insisted on being a poet and essayist. And since he could not deny the occupation that had helped him woo my mother, and would not put it aside to take on the duties of the MacFadden house, he refused to accept anything from his father save rental fees, use of the library and the dairy cow, and weekly visits for supper at the manse. Because my mother was a Christie, and the daughter of another prominent Edinburgh family, my grandfather and Maxwell Christie argued out concerns for their wayward offspring over whiskey, cheroots, and cards.

And so this is all I remember of my mother: that one sweep of soft hand against my cheek, a fall of brown hair as she bent over me, full lips curved and stained with red, and the feel of a kiss against the top of my head. I know that my father turned from the fire to watch, that his blond hair was tied back at his neck, and with the flames behind him his eyes seemed deepened with gray solemnity. This is my only memory of them both: of the long crossing of the Atlantic, and the sickness aboard that claimed both their lives, I remember nothing.

This Christmas morning was twenty-one long years from that one, and I was rooted now in a place that my poor, lovely parents could have never dreamt. I walked back to my bed, took stock of the things lying there. Though I knew that the homesteaders would not expect gifts from me, and certainly had no means to give any themselves, I could not imagine Christmas day passing without doing so. The gifts I meant to offer were modest: a pair of leather gloves for Hosa, a corncob pipe for Lord Harris, a feather pillow for the Simonses and a wood flute for the boys, and a tea pot for Zeke and Eliza. Most of the things I'd bartered for on the last trip I'd made to Fort Prince George, but the tea pot was made of china, and that and the flute I'd brought from Charlestown.

I wrapped the tea pot and the pillow in a blanket and tucked the pipe and flute in the pocket of my dress. In a moment of pure narcissism I pulled open the drawer of the cherry side table, holding up a small, silver mirror. Once ruddy with the sun, my face had gone pale in winter, but an excited flush colored my cheeks and forehead and the tip of my nose. My eyes shone like a child's, clear and directly blue. I touched a finger to my lips, wishing they'd lose the puffiness of sleep but not willing to wait. I smiled, remembering the perfect, tiny, Cupid's bow lips of Henrietta du Gaul, a classmate of mine at Miss Picard's in Charlestown, and how at thirteen I'd longed for mine to look just like hers. Instead, the wide mouth that had long been the bane of my girlhood had followed me into adulthood, and there was nothing that I could do about it.

I set the mirror back in the drawer and shut it gently, then straightened my skirts with a tug. Though I had decided to dress a lady despite the chilling weather, I was certain no one would be able to see the boy's breeches I wore beneath. Over the years I'd become a thief of sorts, scavenging Owen's cast offs and taking them for my own use. I draped the blanket over my shoulders, hooking the edges together with the loop and button I'd sewn at the corners, and reluctantly took a bonnet dyed indigo-blue from the chest, securing it beneath my chin. I tugged the hair I'd tied back in a tail out from under the cotton bonnet, and flipped it over my shoulder so that it hung down in a stream of yellow over my chest: my one womanly vanity.

The fire still burned steadily. I walked to it, taking the broom beside the hearth and sweeping ashes over the flames so that the coals would stay hot but the chance of sparks would lessen considerably. I backed away from the smoke, thinking fleetingly that I'd become quite good at building fires since I'd settled in the mountains.

As I gathered the blanket of presents in my arms I thought I felt a hand brush my cheek. Then the smell of the dampered fire lit my nose, and I remembered my grandfather, wondered how he would be celebrating Christmas this day, if he would spend the day as we'd done since I was a child, gorging on candies and playing chess. It was the one day of the year that Grandfather sent his slaves off on their own to join friends and family where they could, their pockets filled with illegal coin.

I balanced the awkward parcel in my arms, pushing open the heavy door. The chill hit me at once; outside the world was ice-covered and gray. I looked back into my cabin as I shut the door. For a moment my vision blurred, and I saw there in front of the hearth my father kneeling, the yellow crown of his head glowing with firelight. Then suddenly the world shifted, and I was faced with my first American memory: standing on a Charlestown wharf with my five year-old hand clasped in the ship captain's, and being suddenly swept into my grandfather's strong arms, my face pressed against his beard. My memory, after all, begins with him.

I blinked, eyes watering from the cold, and took my hand from where I'd pressed it against the closed door. Tremendous gray clouds ballooned over the Blue Ridge, threatening snow. I wondered of Owen, and Jack Wolf, and hoped they'd find good shelter if it stormed. When I turned to the Valley I saw the cabins sitting like stones in fields of glittering ice, and from each chimney lines of hearth smoke whispered up into the winter sky.

Light ringed the bonfire, warming cold faces in a nebulous glow. And in the darkness outside the ring, something ancient hovered, breathed, and watched the families gathered there. Though the night was black, and clouds covered the half-moon with a midnight hood, I did not feel threatened by the forest, and whatever lived within.

Zeke bent down and brushed a strand of hair back into Eliza's bonnet. She sat before him on a long log, a steaming mug in her grip. She turned up her face for a kiss, and before his face covered hers I thought she looked almost beautiful there in the firelight, her cheeks flushed with love. I cleared my throat and turned away.

On the other side of the fire pit the men toasted each other with rude flasks of whiskey—no doubt another treasure brought by our resident nobleman. They laughed and talked, and as Samuel Simons uncharacteristically swung an arm around Harris's shoulders, I considered the possibility they were all quite drunk. I smiled to myself, staring down into my own mug and watching the black coffee swish as I tipped it back and forth, catching an inky flash of red in the depths.

Abigail stood and snagged young Micah by the collar of his coat, just as he was about to drop a pine cone down the back of his brother's breeches. Little Sam sat unknowing on the log before him, leaned over, drawing pictures in the dirt with a stick. He whipped around at the sound of Micah's protests, and in mere seconds Abigail was herding them off to bed. I watched her lips move as she bent her head to the boys.

"Not on Christmas," she told them.

Passing Samuel, she put a hand on his arm, and he halted in the hilarity for a moment, clasping his wife by the elbows and kissing her full on the mouth. The men hooted, and she blushed, but then gave him a playful pop on the shoulder. As she and the boys disappeared into the dark, I watched the normally shy Simons bid the men a hearty "Happy Christmas," and follow.

I looked up the hill through the dark, searching for my cabin. The moon caught a break in the clouds, and I caught the upside-down vee of a roofline against the backdrop of the coal-black Blue Ridge. The candle I'd left burning sat on the porch step, a tiny beacon in the wilderness. I felt its subtle call and stood, blowing breath out in a tiny puff of white smoke before my face. Morning would come quickly to the Valley, and I had a small Christmas day celebration planned: a *ceilidh*, Grandfather would call it.

At my movement Zeke and Eliza raised red-cheeked faces, smiling in unison. "Oh, goodnight Miz MacFadden," Zeke said, his arm around his bride's skinny shoulders.

"Goodnight," I smiled back, taking my homemade torch—a birch stick with knotted end wrapped in an oil-soaked rag—and dipping it into the fire. "Happy Christmas."

I made my way carefully around the fire, stepping over a pile of kindling and waving a hand at the rest of the men, still carousing with their own holiday spirits. "Goodnight, gentlemen," I called, grinning. "I shall hope to see you all hearty and hale tomorrow. Do try and avoid the fire."

"Ah, Miss MacFadden," Lord Harris waved back, his face flushed with drink and merriment. "May Father Christmas be kind to you, dear lady."

Hosa, who stood nearby warming his hands, rolled his eyes at me, the whites brilliant in the dark. I chuckled, leaving the circle of warmth and human companionship and stepping into the pitch, my torch a flaming guide.

My boots crunched in frozen grass as I felt my way up through the meadows and past clusters of trees, the night held back by the light. At the crest the cloud lifted from the moon, and immediately Keowee Valley was bathed in a veil of silver. I stopped in my tracks, catching my breath as the mountains loomed up before me like the undulations of a great black sea.

A December wind came whipping through the trees, and I tucked my chin into my chest, bracing myself against the chill that had already chapped my lips and cheeks. The candle on my porch flickered and went out. But with the moon as my guide I stepped easily through the grass, and when my feet touched the stoop I breathed out through my nose: home. Turning, I took one last look at that mysterious Christmas sky, the branches of pines stretched out against it like black lace, and started inside.

Movement came from the dark end of my porch, and I halted, a hand at my mouth to stifle an involuntary scream. A man sat on my porch and in my chair, wrapped in a hulk of black bearskin with his legs stretched out before him. A worn farmer's hat tipped low to hide his face—a hat I recognized. "Jack?" I breathed, before I could help myself. "Mr. Wolf?"

When I took a step forward he raised his head, and the sight was like a fist in my belly. "Owen!" I yelped, and launched myself into his arms. "You're alive. You're well, you're safe," I repeated as if to make it true, and breathed against the fur at his neck as his arms came around my back and banded tight. When he laughed it shook us both.

"I am all of that." He squeezed me tightly, then took my upper arms in hand, holding me firmly away from him. "Thanks to you. My God, Quinn. Look at you, just look at you." His eyes, so blue like our grandfather's, had the beginnings of faint lines winging out from the corners when he smiled. His face above a full dark beard was tanned brown as a berry, his auburn hair a shaggy mess that hung to his shoulders, and his nose had an odd bump on the bridge and crooked a wee bit to the right—but he was still my Owen. And he was beautiful.

"Look at me? Look at you," I gushed, reaching out despite his grip and tugging at the beard, then giving in to the urge and smoothing my palm against his cheek. The tears came unbidden: how I loved this dear man, in all rights my brother—how I'd mourned him. And now he was here. "We thought you were dead," I managed, my voice cracking. "We thought we'd never see you again. Grandfather. Grandfather will—" Giving in, I collapsed against his chest and wept.

He rubbed my back in circles. "Come now, coz. All will be well. You rescued me, lass. You and your Wolf." He squeezed once more, clearing the hitch that had snuck into his voice. "I'd likely be dead if not for the two of you."

I sniffled into the fur, noticing for the first time the odd smell that came with it. "My wolf?" I sat upright, sliding from his lap and brushing the front of my skirts. But I reached out again, kept a hand on his shoulder as he looked up at me. "Where is Mr. Wolf? Did he leave you here alone, and you battered and used? Why are you not inside, Owen?"

"He and his brother were wary of interrupting the reunion, I think," he said. "I've the notion they'd rather sleep in the woods. He's a rare one, your Wolf. God thank him."

"He's not my wolf," I muttered, hiding the bite of disappointment with indignation. "Did he leave a message for me?" I added innocently.

Owen moved gingerly to his feet, and I reached out to take his arm. Through the layers of deerskin and rough cloth I could feel the bone of his forearm, and my heart skipped a beat. He was not recovered, no matter how he teased me. "He left no message," he said. "But as they didn't say where they were off to next, I've a notion he'll be back. Let's have a sit by the fire, shall we? And perhaps you'll read to me from one of your books? I heard a rumor you brought to the frontier the whole of Grandfather's library."

"I'll read you anything you like," I murmured, concentrating as we shuffled to the door. I pretended not to notice the way he seemed to lightly drag his left foot—the way his face shuttered when he thought I couldn't see. But when we pulled the thick door closed behind us and I led him to the crackling hearth, light banished momentarily the fear, and warmth from the fire settled in like a promise.

Late that night I woke at a *thump* outside my door. I slid from the warm bed and into the chill, in my curiosity not bothering to cover myself with shawl or blanket. I stepped quietly past Owen's pallet, relieved to hear the sound of even breathing, and to know that he still slept as he had as a boy, with an arm thrown overhead, the other cross his chest. At the heavy door I hesitated, glanced back at him, but then pulled, wincing as it creaked open.

My stocking feet bumped something hard. Just outside the door sat a parcel. I picked it up and gave a quick sweep of the darkness—nothing—before stepping backwards, pulling the door to. I tucked the parcel beneath my arm and hurriedly lit the lamp by my bed, and it was then that I saw it was a gift, wrapped carefully in supple, white deerskin. I sat on the edge of the bed with the gift in my lap, running thawing fingers over the gorgeous fabric. Then I slipped them beneath the hemp chord tying it together like a ribbon and tugged. It was a book, rough with handling but firm and small in my hands as I lifted it, studying the cover.

"*The Turkish Embassy Letters*, by Lady Mary Wortley Montagu," I whispered, turning back the front cover with the care of one handling a rare gem. Inside, an inscription had been written in a rough hand, the words embedded in the starchy linen with an unusual blue ink: "For another braw, wee traveler ~ Merry Christmas."

I folded the deerskin quickly over the book and stood sharply, setting it on the bed. Then I ran to the door, regardless of Owen, and flung it open, racing to the edge of the porch and peering out into the darkness. My breath fogged in front of my face in quick clouds, and I desperately searched the night, utterly uncertain of what I'd say if I saw him, and too reckless to care.

A horse snorted to my right, and I whipped my head around, unable to make out anything but the ghostly movement of tulip poplars in the wind. It was like peering into the blue-black of a bottomless pond: drop a pebble and the water ripples, and spreading out from it shapes form on their own, disappear. I caught my breath as the moving darkness of the trees morphed into a man on a horse.

"I thought that was you," I said quietly, tucking wild hair behind my ears as he urged the horse forward into the weak light, cast from the still-open door like a path. "Silent Wolf, indeed."

Hatless, he slid from the horse, landing lightly on his feet. He walked to the edge of the light and smiled up at me, the corners of his eyes crinkling. He stood easily, hands hanging at his sides. A huge blanket, furry with bear hide, draped his shoulders, tied at his chest with a leather loop. He looked the itinerant mountain man, his cheekbones hollow and his hair a burnt umber in the dark, and I knew then that even with my own boundless imagination, I could have never dreamt of anything even remotely like him.

Without thinking, I stepped off the porch and walked to him, stopping close enough to see the green in his eyes. He dipped his chin. "It's hoping I am that you don't already have the wee book," he said.

"No, I don't. But I have nothing for you."

"Now that's a lie," he said. He made a move to turn but I reached out and laid a hand on his forearm, feeling the hard muscle beneath. Stepping up on tiptoe, I pressed my lips to the bottom of his jaw.

"Thank you, Mr. Wolf. For Owen, and for the gift. Happy Christmas," I whispered. I turned, hurried up the step to my home, and did not look back. I could not help the grin that stretched from ear to ear with the hot, growing thrill of my exit, the heat from his body still warm on my lips.

Chapter 11

The MacFadden Settlement

Someone was inside my cabin.

It had to be the middle of the night; the room was dark as pitch, and through the burlap curtain at the far window I could see a thin sheen of moonlight cast a line along the edge of my quilt. I swallowed and breathed in slowly through my nose, all instincts urging me to stay still as a mouse hunted by a falcon. *Why in God's name did I allow Owen to move to the barn?*

He stood like a ghost at the foot of my bed. I could make out the dark outline of a man's body in the gray light, unmoving. Desperately, I pushed back against psyche, against the need to pull the covers up over my eyes like a child.

A whistle came from outside, and the figure moved swiftly to the doorway—opening and closing it in an instant—and was gone.

I sucked air in a ragged gulp and slid from the bed, kicking off the quilt in a rush. I grabbed my overcoat, planted my old hat on my head and flung open the door. I ran barefoot across the upper pasture, incognizant of rocks and frosted grass, towards the glow of torchlight and rising voices.

There were strange men—six or seven, I thought—mounted on horseback, their backs to the mountains. Two others stood on the ground before them, both holding torches. And before them, his broad back to me, was Jack. A tall Indian stood at his side, and in the flickering orange light I watched one of the strangers step forward to shout in Jack's face, so close I could see spittle in the air between them. "Wolf, you know as well as I do she's got one here!"

The man's accent, though ignoble, was not uneducated, which

surprised me. Hadn't Grandfather railed about the lawless men of the backcountry, rough and dumb, riding in groups over the hills? I crept closer as the other torch-wielder nodded a head at the Indian at Jack's side, sneering.

"One day you'll have to decide what you are, Wolf," he said, his face shadowed. "You can't keep hiding out with the savages and niggers."

Jack said something in Cherokee to the Indian, and he turned in the darkness, heading away from the light and straight towards me. I crouched behind what I thought was a mulberry bush, pulling the scratchy wool coat closer to my chest. The Indian stopped just before the bush and turned back to the mountains as if guarding me where I hid.

"What she has is a freedman, McCrady, though I don't see how it's the business of the Regulators to be hunting down slaves. Working for some Lowcountry planter now, are you?" Jack's voice came out clear, and the horses shifted uneasily in the dark.

"We work for none but the people of the backcountry," another said from atop his mount. "But by law, if she is sheltering a runaway she'll be tried for it in Ninety-Six."

Jack reached over his shoulder, and the two men on the ground stepped back, bracing. He swung his musket gracefully in front of him and planted the stock in the dirt, leaning on the tip of the barrel. "What are you doing so far west, lads?" he asked politely. "This is Cherokee land, there are few settlers here—none who are beholden to colonial law. Why don't you make your way back to Camden, or the Waxhaws, and have at the criminals there. 'Tis true you're not needed here."

The man he'd called McCrady slapped a hand on an impressive belly, giving a nasty chuckle. "What is this MacFadden woman, your squaw?"

In an instant, Jack swung the musket out like a line of rope, knocking the big man's legs from under him. He fell in a heap, cursing as he lumbered back to his feet, and in the torchlight I saw his mouth work angrily.

One of the mounted men jumped from his horse and rushed forward, gripping his friend's arm, pulling him back. "William, enough—that's enough!" He looked back over his shoulder at the riders. "We're leaving. There's naught for us here. But Miss MacFadden must have the black's manumission papers sent to Ninety-Six within a fortnight, or we're coming back." He pulled the man back toward the posse and nodded at Jack. "Wolf."

"Laurens." Jack inclined his head, lifted a hand in farewell to the other men. "Watch your backs tonight, lads, there's a Creek war party on the move. I'd get out of Cherokee country quick as possible if I were you."

The horses moved then, and the men headed for the woods. I started from my hiding place, meaning to confront them before they left. What right had they to accost a man—any man—on my land?

The Indian turned at my movement and held out a staying hand, saying something in his language in a low voice. I looked up at him in surprise; his black eyes blinked in the moonlight. "Let me pass," I said, but he stood still and formidable as a slab of granite, and I knew suddenly that it was he who'd been the ghost in my cabin.

"Miss MacFadden," Jack said, materializing out of the dark. "Allow me to introduce my brother, Ridge Runner, a *Yun'wiya* of the Wolf clan."

"Your brother?" I repeated, clutching the folds of the coat and shaking my head. "What's going on, Mr. Wolf? Who were those men?"

He looked suddenly at my feet and grinned, his teeth white in the dark. He said something in Cherokee to Ridge Runner, and the other man laughed softly, answering in kind. "You've lost your shoes, lass." He looked at me, his cat eyes direct. "Shall I give you a piggyback to your cabin?"

The three of us sat in the only chairs I owned, before a fire Jack had started. The cabin, though dark, was filled now with firelight that flickered across the ceiling, flashing around the edges of the hearth. I set a kettle on the spit and went to my own chair to sit, folding my hands in my lap and praying for fortitude. "Were they truly Regulators?" I asked, unable to begin with polite conversation.

"Aye, they were," Jack answered, stretching out moccasined feet toward the stone hearth.

The two of them seemed an anomaly sitting there in my cabin. Jack's hair hung long and sun-streaked, and a silver stud winked in his left ear, with a bent sliver of the metal hanging from it. Ridge Runner sat calmly beside him, his face a stoic mask. He looked a painting, with his black ponytail and shuttered eyes, and the section of brown, smooth chest that showed beneath a half-open trade shirt, despite the cold. I looked back and forth between the two men. If what Jack had said was true, and they were brothers, then what they shared was unusual height, high, sharp cheekbones, and hooded, impenetrable eyes. They shifted at about the same time, and Jack twisted in his chair, stretching. Ah, I thought—and breadth of shoulders.

"I thought that the Regulators were a group of landed backcountrymen, that they'd formed to prevent thieves and vagrants from upsetting the frontier." I stood, needing to pace, and went to the cabinet for teacups.

"There's truth to that, of a sort. Up until about a year ago, many vigilante bands roamed the countryside—though never quite this far into the frontier," Jack said. "For the most part, they are good, God-fearing men of high repute who simply want the Commons House of Assembly to answer their missives."

"Missives?" I asked. "What do they want?"

"A frontier militia to protect them from the Indians and ruffians. Schools, courts . . . a say in the colonial government, I suppose," he answered. "Being from Charlestown yourself you'd be knowing where the power lies. The planters there might as well be royalty—some of them surely hold land blessed by King George himself. How can hardscrabble farmers compete with that, such as it is?" He ran a hand through his long hair absently.

I reached for the kettle, poured water in a cup and offered it to Jack. He shook his head, and I turned to Ridge Runner. "Does he speak English?"

Jack looked at the big Cherokee and cocked his head. "What say you, *agina'ii*? Sure, and can you speak English then?"

The men grinned at each other, and I rolled my eyes. "You mock me."

"Ah, lass, 'tis naught but a bit of teasing, is all."

I gave up on offering tea to Ridge Runner and took the cup myself, sprinkling leaves in the steam and swirling it with my wrist. "I heard you ask them why they'd come this far west," I said. "What are they doing in Cherokee country? They've no rule of law here, do they?"

Jack pulled his feet back and set his elbows on big knees, letting his hands hang between. "They've no call to be here. This is the only white settlement for miles, what with the garrison at Fort George heading east. But I think they were seeking yon black man, Mr. Brown."

"But he's a freedman," I protested.

"Aye, but to some he's still just a poor Negro, better off in chains." He looked up, waiting until I met his eyes. "You'll need to send a rider down to Ninety-Six with his papers on the morrow. It'll sate the Regulators for a while, and keeping them far from here's a good thing. No need to stir up the young *Tsa'lagi* braves, make them want a fight."

Ridge Runner said something in Cherokee, and Jack smiled at him. "I do not relish a good fight, you red devil," he answered affectionately. "Haven't since I was much shorter."

I sipped the hot tea slowly, rolling it around on my cold tongue. "How can they demand something like that? Have they such power, then?"

"Well, the Assembly finally grew weary of their constant complaints and made them colonial rangers," he said. "They've now the legal right to hang outlaws as they please, or brand them, send them to Charlestown. They call it the 'Plan of Regulation.'"

"It sounds very much like piracy to me, whether they do good or not," I said, brushing a stray strand back off my forehead. "With the king's law at its strongest in Charlestown, the colonial government has no way of knowing what's being done here. These men could run rampant, killing as they wish."

"I'm not much for men in a mob," Jack said slowly, scratching behind his ear. "Men tend to do horror in a mob, oftimes in the name of deity or monarch. But here, you do as you must, because surely there are no king's soldiers to help you, should you need use of them. In the wilderness you fend for your own, try to be as true to who you are as the land will let you."

There was silence, and I cleared my throat, the realization that I had welcomed two strange men into my home in the early morning hours an itch at the back of my throat. "You are welcome to stay in the settlement as long as you wish," I said, and Ridge Runner raised his head and looked at me, his gaze unflinching.

"Both of you," I added, staring back.

Jack shifted, and the two men got to their feet, shadows giant in the firelight. "We thank you, Miss MacFadden, but we'll take our shelter on the Knob for the night."

I walked them to the door, waited until they'd reached for the weapons left there and held it open, following them out onto the porch. They loped down the step and started out into the night side by side, and I cleared my throat again. "Thank you for your kind deed tonight," I called out. "Please know you're more than welcome in the Valley, should you choose to return."

They stopped, and Jack turned, and I could almost feel his warm gaze in the dark. "Not to worry, lass," he called. "We'll return soon enough."

Before I could utter another word they'd disappeared into the shadows. I leaned forward and searched the dark meadow, straining my eyes, but could not make out a thing. I looked up, watched a filmy cloud roll past the half-moon, and let out a yawn, not bothering to cover my mouth. Then I headed inside, latched the door behind me and doused the fire.

At the foot of the bed I tugged off my boots and tossed them toward the hearth. As I slipped beneath the quilt, working my chilly feet deep into the blankets, a wolf called out on the mountain and another answered, the howl echoing across a ridgeline.

I turned my head into the pillow and smiled.

Chapter 12

January, 1769

Music drifted down through the Valley, hovering in low clouds that had descended over our settlement for the night. I grabbed a wool blanket and wrapped it round my shoulders, stepping out into the evening. The chill stung my cheeks, and I pulled the blanket close, following the mournful sound of a fiddle through the fog, careful not to step into the smoldering embers of the fire pit.

There was a man's voice, low, singing along with the fiddle. He sang words in a language I did not understand, but which sounded faintly like the Gaelic I'd heard from my grandfather. For a moment, the urge to know what he was singing was so strong I began to quicken my pace in the darkness, desperate to know the meaning behind such a pure, killing tune.

The pen materialized out of the gray film of fog, and the bays were there, broad necks curved over the fence, the air from their nostrils forming clouds of smoke before their noses. The music was strong here. I glanced toward the barn and saw the light, passing a hand gently over Plato's muzzle as I made my way around the fence line.

We'd had visitors the night before. Three Scotch-Irishmen, hungry and on foot, had lost the main trail and happened upon the settlement on their way to claim land in Georgia. They were much like the rest of my homesteaders: poor, work-weary and hopeful, sure they'd eke a home out of the wilderness.

I stopped at the barn doors and peeked through the crack between the planks, unsure still of my place here, with these people . . . wondering if I'd be welcome at all. Inside, the trio of men sat a few feet from each other, one on the hard-packed ground littered with hay, his hat pulled so low over his eyes that his face was shadowed, the other two on overturned milk pails.

One of the men seated on the pails—owner of a red beard that brushed his lap—tapped on an ancient-looking drum covered with an animal skin. The last, young enough to be a boy, held a battered violin to his chin, eyes narrowed in concentration on the strings. But it was the man with the hidden face who sang, the words now in thickly accented English, crooning an Irishman's ballad:

And lonesome among strangers
I sleep among the bushes
Or mountain caves alone,
Either I'll find some quiet
To live as best contents me
Or leave them all behind me
For other men to own

No, I did not belong here, I thought, turning from the light and the song.

"Weary yet of 'John O'Dwyer of the Glen,' coz?"

Owen's voice came from the pen. I startled, seeking the dark. The fog had dissipated, and the clouds broke momentarily, casting a pale silver light over the man sitting atop a hay bale. Plato was nuzzling his trouser leg, but Owen shoved him gently away with the side of his foot. I walked closer, unable to make out his face.

"No, not weary of it. I simply do not wish to disturb the musicians," I said. "Is there something the matter, Owen? You've been . . . quiet lately." And he had. Though he'd attempted the work of ten men, carpentering with Hosa in the barn, hunting with Jack and Ridge Runner, or building a meat house with Samuel and Lord Harris—there was an air of sadness about him.

He ran a hand through his shaggy hair, pulling idly at the cropped tail. He seemed to pause for a moment, then slid to the ground, wincing at landing on his left foot. "Besides the damned leg I'm well."

"Owen—"

"A moment, Quinn. Listen." At his upheld hand I stopped, shifting from foot to foot impatiently in the cold. The music had melded into something a bit more primal. There was a slow beat of the drum along with the low moan of the violin. "He's a hand with the *bohdran*," he murmured. "All they miss are the pipes."

"It's lovely," I allowed.

"Come, I'll escort you safely to your cabin." He took my hand and slipped it easily through the crook of his elbow as we turned and made our way through the grass in the darkness. A fog had settled in, and we brushed through it as we walked. "I'm going home, to Charlestown," he said matter-of-factly, and I stopped. "No, come, we'll talk as we walk. It's too cold to stand like statues."

"But you've not recovered," I said, trying to keep the pleading from my voice. I wasn't ready. "You need more time to heal, Owen. You can't sit a horse yet. Besides, you'll die of boredom in Charlestown—you know you will. Nothing has changed since you left it. It's still the same routines, the same spirit-numbing society. You'll go mad within minutes."

"I've healed much as I'm able. And I can sit a horse. It's you who needs more time." I watched him sidelong as we walked, traced with an invisible brush the familiar line of his forehead, his long nose, the stubborn set of his MacFadden jaw. "The God's truth of it is I'm ready for boredom, Quinn. I'm looking forward with joy to sitting safe behind a desk, to dealing with bewigged planters and harried merchants. I've had enough adventure for five men's lifetimes."

"You're right, I'm not ready. I don't want you to go. I need you here with me."

"Quincy," he said, this time halting and putting his other hand to the forearm I'd tucked in his, squeezing gently. His tone was admonishing. "You've never needed me, and you don't need me now. You've built a settlement, by God. You've a home here, friends. And certainly a man who'd like to call you his own, should you allow it, though I'd have some thoughts on it."

"You would, would you?" I narrowed my eyes. "I see. And just what would those be?"

"Quinn, you are a blind woman if you can't see what the man feels for you."

"Oh, he enjoys laughing at me, yes," I said, stepping forward and tugging him along with me—mostly out of sheer embarrassment. "I am but an amusement to him, I think."

"Then you are not thinking," he said shortly. "He stands by you like some savage protector, some Celtic charger. And though he may offer that charming smile of his, there is more going on in his head than he offers—I'm sure of it."

At my porch step I stopped, feeling a freedom in the moment and knowing that if there was anyone to whom I could reveal my innermost thoughts—erratic as they might be—it was Owen. "He overwhelms me," I admitted. "He is so unlike the men in Charlestown. Do you know he actually likes the fact that I can ride astride—seems proud of it, even? And he never berates me for talking of politics, or philosophy. I'd never imagined I'd meet a man like him, especially not here. I'd always assumed that I'd live the life of an annoying old maid, free to do as I pleased."

I paused, staring up into the sky, a smattering of stars revealing themselves in the black spaces between clouds. "The confounding bit of it is, I do believe he understands me."

"I am glad of it, Quincy," Owen's words came soft out of the darkness beside me, "for he seems to be a good man. But he has a wildness in him, make no mistake of it. And though you live far from civilization, and may choose never to return, if you continue the path that I believe this relationship is headed you will at some point be detrimented by his Cherokee blood."

"Owen—" I started, angry.

"No, I am no hotheaded intolerant—I've lived and worked with the Indians enough to know what they're about. But the fact is, Jack Wolf is half Indian. He is of these mountains, and there are parts of him that will never be accepted by English society. It's easy to ignore this, because of your isolation here . . . but you will not be able to avoid the continual hardship that will befall you, should you choose to pursue a marriage to this man."

At this I stepped up onto the porch, glaring at him at eye level. "Marriage has not been discussed, so I suggest you keep your concerns to yourself, cousin."

We were silent for a long moment, and I breathed deeply, stewing with anger and the hot rush that was a mixture of shame and fear, shame because Owen spoke of things I'd thought on myself but had not wanted to admit. "You may feel that you know Jack, from your time on the trail together," I said, breaking the humid silence. "I don't discount that. But I know him, too."

"Yes, you are right. And you have never been one to let another choose for you."

He cleared his throat, and I crossed my arms over my chest to ward off the chill. He was staring out at the fog where it curled across the meadow floor like an incoming tide. As I watched, his chest rose and fell deeply before he spoke again. "Your Mister Wolf has fought in wars we've only half heard of, whose names we cannot pronounce. I just wonder if you've considered that by trusting this man, you are taking on two lives: one white, one savage. Can you live in that in-between world, Quincy? More so, can you live with what he tells you, if you ask him of his darkest secrets—of the lives that may have been taken with the tomahawk he wears on his back?

"I love you Quincy, I always have. Promise me you'll keep safe." He reached out then, cupped my cheek in his dry hand and smiled. "Write to me once I'm home, won't you?"

"Of course." I pressed my own hand against his, closed my eyes briefly. Though I'd imagined him making a home here, perhaps he needed the bustle of Charlestown and what was sure to be a daily battle with Grandfather to make himself right again. To allow himself to forget.

To make it all better, I smiled. "The Lord only knows why I'll miss you," I said.

He leaned in, pulled me close and let me go just as briefly. "I'll leave for Keowee Town after the morning meal. If you've anything you want sent to Grandfather, have it ready then." He turned, stepped into the grass and then stopped. "I had you with me, you know. I had you with me every day," he said softly, not looking back.

Safe in my bed, the visions came in a fervor, harshly colored. I saw Owen thrashing through a wood, his face mottled and bloody. Then Owen again, this time dressed the gentleman, walking a wharf with a friend, talking of politics. And as I tossed beneath sheets damp with my own sweat, I dreamed of a man with two faces—one white, one red—dancing around a midnight fire, howling out to a moonless sky.

Chapter 13

Early Winter, 1769

Somewhere, in the back of my skull, I heard a sound.

I sat up and wiped the crackle of sleep from my lashes, pushing long hair from my face. The light filtering in from the windows was pale. I wondered if it was moonlight.

"Miz MacFadden!" There was banging at the door. "We got us a situation, ma'am."

"One moment!" I called, sliding from the bed and shimmying into my gown, the air touching my bare skin like a freezing fire. I did up the laces in the back as best I could, and splashed water from the wood basin onto my face, drying it hurriedly with the edge of my quilt. I flung open the door before I realized that I'd forgotten to tie back my hair.

Zeke stood at the bottom of the steps with hat in hand, scratching the youthful beginnings of a beard. He blushed at the sight of my bare head, ducking his. He could not seem to find his words, and I cleared my throat, feeling as though I was old enough to be his mother.

"Mr. O'Hare," I started.

"Oh, do call me Zeke, ma'am. It's surely been long enough we've been neighbors," he interrupted, still looking at the dirt in front of his boots.

"Zeke." I couldn't help but smile. The dawn lit up the camp with a lemon light, and though it was almost blinding to my waking eyes, it made a halo around the young man's head as though he was a lesser angel from a Botticelli painting. "What is the matter?"

He brightened at this and took his hat in both hands. "There's an Indian horse what got into the fence with Plato and Mutt. He's kickin' something fierce—knocked over the feed buckets but didn't eat nothin', just keeps prancin' around makin' trouble."

"Well, has one of the men let him out?"

He balked, looking at me as though I had grown a third eyeball. "No, ma'am. Nobody can get close enough, and Mr. Wolf's out on the mountain with that big Cherokee. We thought to lock up the pen and wait for Mr. Wolf to get back, seein' as how maybe he'd want it."

I rolled my eyes, exasperated at the respect some of the men gave the Irishman. Though most considered him quite savage—a mysterious half-breed—when it came to matters of frontier life they likened him to a god. "There are others capable of miracle work besides Jack Wolf," I said shortly. "But I do need a horse."

Zeke must have seen the gleam in my eyes, because he scratched his head with dirty fingers, looking perplexed. "Oh no, ma'am, this horse ain't for lady ridin'. It's an Indian pony, 'cause of its shorn mane and all. But it's a biggun and it's mean . . . must'a been mixed with some English horse."

"Zeke," I said, stepping down onto the dirt and brushing past him, walking purposely toward the pen. "The horse I rode in Charlestown was sixteen and a half hands high. This one will do just fine."

At the pen chaos lit the air. The homesteaders gathered to watch like children at a puppet show. No one got close to the fence, though little Micah Simons lay on his stomach, watching from beneath a bottom slat.

"Miss MacFadden," he called excitedly upon spotting me. "Ain't it the grandest horse you ever saw!"

"It certainly is," I answered, watching the beast in awe as it pawed the ground like a lion, the whites of its eyes gleaming through the steam rising from its warm body. Every snort of air from its nostrils ballooned in front of its nose like white smoke from a cannon. Lord Harris and Samuel stood near the break in the fence among the splinters, Harris with a shorn rope in his hands. He saw me coming and held up a hand.

"Stay where you are, Miss MacFadden. He could bolt at any moment."

The cultured English tone nicked at something prideful in me, and I skirted the back of the pen and headed into the barn, lifting my chin at the men. Micah leapt up and scurried after me, brushing the dirt from his shirt. "Where ya' goin', Miss MacFadden? Are you gonna shoot the horse? Can I watch?"

I stopped inside the barn, snatched a rope bridle from a nail and turned, bending to the boy's eye level. "Micah, I thought I instructed you to call me Quinn."

He grinned, cocking his head to one side. "I forgot." He eyed the bridle, and his eyes widened. "You gonna ride that horse, Quinn?"

I tousled his hair and headed out the barn doors, reaching up on my tip-toes to take an almost rotted apple from the ledge where I kept them. "I intend to make an attempt."

Lord Harris met me at the pen, Samuel on his heels. "I cannot let you near the beast, miss. He's huge—he could take your life with one strike of his hoof."

"Miss MacFadden, please, this ain't no place for a lady," Micah's father pleaded, and I saw real concern in his eyes.

I hesitated, leaning around the men to watch the stallion trot over to the fence where Plato and Mutt stood on the other side, too domesticated to make any move toward freedom. Zeke was right: the horse was too large to be a full-blooded Indian pony, but the curve of its neck and its unusually long legs on such a muscled body led me to believe it could not be English, either.

Suddenly the rogue horse turned from the others and made a sweep of the pen, kicking up dirt in its wake. The sun had risen so that it lit the Blue Ridge with pink light, the one time of the day when it seemed the mountains were a true green. In this warming light the horse was gold, its black shorn mane and tail reminding me of the drawings in my grandfather's *A History of the Roman Empire*, and I wanted that horse for my own with a gut feel of possession that chased away any trace of fear.

"Gentlemen," I said, drawing myself up to my paltry full height and looking them both in the eyes. "I am a MacFadden, and I was raised with a Scotsman's stable of horses, all big, all stubborn. I realize that I may appear delicate, but when it comes to horsemanship I believe I am equipped with a different sort of experience from Mr. Wolf, though just as useful. Step aside, please."

Lord Harris looked as though he wanted to speak, but I held out a hand to quiet him, something I'm certain no one had done to him since he was a boy. Samuel stood with mouth agape, and so I left them there and slipped into the pen between the fence posts. The horse caught sight of me and reared up, whinnying loudly. One of the women gasped.

"Watch out, Quinn, he's a devil, that one," Micah yelled, earning a quick pop from his mother.

I took a calming breath, inhaling cold mountain air tinged with a smell I'd come to associate with the South Carolina frontier: pine, wood smoke, and something wild and inexplicable, something I had yet to put a name to. The world disappeared around me as I approached the horse in the brightening morning, and I felt myself come alive quietly, tiny pin-pricks dancing along my skin.

"Hello, bonny lad," I said softly, calling on Dougal MacFadden with all of my being. The kindly Dougal was Grandfather's cousin, and had been the Master of Horse at the clan keep back in Scotland. As a child he'd taught me, secretly, to ride astride one summer. "You're a wild one, aren't you?" I held the apple out to my side, my arms outstretched, away from my body. I muttered the words I'd heard Dougal use to calm an injured horse: "Step softly, love. You willna be harmed."

The animal stopped its pawing and stood still, watching me. I backed away slowly until I felt the fence behind me. I placed a booted foot on the fence post and pushed myself up until I was sitting atop the rail. "Come, friend. The apple waits."

The horse—though a stallion it truly was, with its muscled chest and tremendous knees— came toward me at a loping walk, stopping before me, close enough that I could feel the warmth of its breath on my thighs. "You are gorgeous," I whispered, as if it were just the horse and me, there alone in the waking valley. I let my hand rest upturned on my knee, the apple waiting. I brought my other hand up along one thigh, the bridle held loosely in my cold fingers.

Finally the horse leaned in, taking the apple with its teeth and dipping its head to chew, but not moving away. I reached out a hand and smoothed it down the horse's neck, just beneath the tuft of mane. The animal stilled, but kept munching. I drew the bridle up slowly, and it was as if the horse eyed it and knew it to be his capture, yet stayed still long enough for me to pull it along his nose and settle it over his ears. I kept the rope, connected to one side of the cavesson, held in my right hand. Then I stood from my perch, running a soft hand down the horse's back, and repeated a phrase of Naji's—one he used to calm my grandfather's bays in the midst of town traffic. "Be still, lion."

I took the long bit of mane nearest the withers in my left fist and held tight, lifting myself lightly onto his back. He jerked at the weight of me and lifted his front hooves from the ground in a bit of a jump, testing. Then he trotted around the pen in circles, slinging his head back and grunting.

A yell went up from someone outside the pen, and the outer world came into focus with a thunderclap. I saw Lord Harris smiling, and Samuel clutching the railing with a whitened grip, and Abigail looking at me with something akin to horror in her eyes. Suddenly I wished them all gone, and I cursed beneath my breath, a thing I only did away from anyone within hearing. And the horse came out of my spell and headed for freedom, leaping the broken rails and galloping down toward the lower pastures.

The air stung my face, and I held on to the mane with both hands, sure that I could keep steady until the animal stopped. We leapt Tomassee Creek, and I started to slide, righting myself and leaning down to grasp tightly around its neck. Scotland came back to me, a whisper of memory in the wind.

The storm was growing, and the moors moved like a living thing in the wind. I could feel the saddle beneath me and I grinned wide, knowing how Grandfather would rage if he knew I rode astride. I could hear Owen behind me, riding Robert the Bruce into a lather, but he couldn't catch me—not while I rode a horse like Wallace, and not when we were so close to the barn.

"Lightning!" Owen shouted, and a flash caught the corner of my eye. I leaned into Wallace and watched the buildings emerge from the heather ahead. The horses took their heads and thundered into the barn. Dougal stepped out from a stall and snatched me from the saddle, setting me on my feet with a thud.

"You're a horsewoman to be sure," he said, keeping his hands on my shoulders, his lips a thin line in the gap in his beard. "But ye ride my horses into a lather again, lassie, and I'll burn yer bottom myself."

Mortified, I moved from his grip and raced out the door, wanting to run from the disappointment in his eyes. Owen was at my side, and he took my hand as we felt the first drops of rain.

"Next time remember to ride side-saddle when ye get within sight of the hoos!" I heard Dougal bellow from the barn door as we ran dripping into the keep.

The horse lit up the trail into the woods, and I pulled back on its mane, shouting "whoa" with all my might. It wasn't until we reached the wider, deeper place in the crook of the creek that the animal finally stopped, its sides heaving, and bent its head to slurp from the water. I slid from its back, the rope in my grasp, and bent to splash water on my face. I needed it—the ride had frightened me, for all my bravado. But the horse was mine, and I reached up and scratched beneath its chin as though it was a dog, laughing aloud.

Men's voices came down the path, and Jack rounded the bend with Ridge Runner, both running lightly and quick, long hair—black braided and blond wild—flying out behind them. They stopped at the sight of me, and Ridge Runner turned to Jack, saying something in Cherokee. Jack's face split in a grin, and he put a hand on the Indian's shoulder, answering him in the same tongue. I stood, wiping wet hands on my skirts.

"What did he say?" I asked without pretense. Ridge Runner watched me with an unreadable expression, though I could swear that there was laughter in his eyes.

"He said you have rightly claimed the horse," Jack said. He walked down to the edge of the creek, nodding at Ridge Runner over his shoulder. The other man said something else I could not understand, then walked silently back up the path into the forest. Jack stepped across the creek, hiking easily over the large gray boulders there. He held out an open palm to the horse, and it ran its nose over his knuckles, nostrils quivering.

"This was someone else's horse once, but it's yours now." He looked down at me, his hooded green eyes lit from beneath with such a light I caught my breath. No man had ever looked at me like he did, and it frightened me, though I'd too much pride to show it.

"How do you know?" I asked, bothered. "Are you mystic as well as savage?"

"Ridge Runner says this horse is the get of a Spanish herd that belonged to the Creek," he answered, ignoring the insult. "What will you name him?"

The stream bubbled up over the bottoms of the boulders, and an eagle called somewhere up in the mountains. I looked at Jack Wolf full in the face because I could not look away. "I don't know. I'll have to research a deserving title."

He reached out and ran his hand over my unbound hair, brushing against the top of my breast. I did not breathe.

"You look like a runaway queen," he said. Then he seemed to right himself and took away his hand, and I felt bereft of its warmth, flushed with a feeling I refused to name. "Research, aye? Well, don't wait too long. Though I'm sure you'll come up with a good one." He walked past me, back toward the break in the trees and the pasture, his footfalls silent on the pine needles.

"Mr. Wolf," I called after him, the rope in my hand and the horse at my side, unmoving. Jack turned and lifted an eyebrow at me. "What did your brother say, before he left?"

"He said you ride like an Indian," Jack grinned. "So he gave you a Cherokee name: Rides-Like-a-Man."

I harrumphed, wanting to be compared to no man. "I do ride well, but riding well is certainly not a trait garnered solely by the male sex."

"No, apparently it isn't," he said, his big body seeming to take up the entire trail. I felt myself drawn to him, and suddenly I knew that if I were to come any closer to the man I might lose sight of all I had planned.

"Mac—that's it," he spoke again, his grin widening.

"Mac?" I asked, bewildered. "What on earth are you talking about?"

"I've been thinking of a name for you," he said, turning to leave. As I watched his back I felt infuriation rise within me, the way it inevitably did with this impossible stranger.

"What is it with names? And what does Mac have to do with anything?" I called, impatient.

He stopped at the edge of the forest and turned again, and I could see the creases at the corners of his eyes deepen with amusement. "It's for MacFadden. You ride like a man, Mac. You need a man's name."

Stunned, I couldn't form words. I wanted to find a very large rock and throw it at him. "I have a perfectly good name, Jack Wolf, and I suggest you use it," I shouted.

He grinned and tossed up a hand, heading out across the field.

"Rides-Like-a-Man," Micah said, tilting his head as he considered it. "It's a good name."

We were seated on logs placed in a circle around the fire pit, watching the coals grow orange. People milled about the settlement, men putting horses to stable and cleaning up the last of the broken fence, women preparing the evening meal. I had attempted to help, asking Abigail and Eliza what could be done. But they'd shooed me away, I suppose presuming that a wealthy, unmarried woman from the Lowcountry knew nothing of a kitchen. I did not want to admit that they were right. I'd never had to cook in Charlestown. We'd had slaves to do that work. And I hated the feeling of being the only woman of privilege in the Valley. I could translate Socrates, but could not make cornbread. I looked to the heavens, but there were no answers in the stars, despite the promises of the philosophers.

"You shouldn't sigh, Quinn," Micah looked at me in consternation. "I'd give anything to have a Cherokee name. I bet Ridge Runner knows lotsa good names. I bet he could scalp a hundred men without 'em even knowing he's there."

Micah, though he barely knew the man, hero-worshipped Jack, and with him, Ridge Runner. He would talk of the enigmatic Cherokee all night if I let him.

"Why don't you ask him," I said. Micah looked up in surprise, and I had the sudden urge to wipe the dirt from his forehead. "Though I would not mention the scalping—he might not want to speak of such pursuits."

"Aw, he don't even speak English," Micah muttered. "And I don't know no Cherokee yet. But I'm gonna learn. Jack'll teach me."

"Jack's Cherokee is mediocre at best," a strange voice said behind us. We whirled, and Micah slipped off the log onto the ground. Ridge Runner bent and helped him up, brushing his backside with a swift hand. He seemed to pause, then bent to Micah's eye level. "I'll teach you, boy."

Micah scampered off into the darkness, barely avoiding a collision with Jack, who was leading Plato towards the barn. He looked after the boy and back at Ridge Runner and me, lifting a hand in greeting.

Ridge Runner was almost as tall as Jack, but a bit leaner through the chest and shoulders. He still seemed utterly powerful; the muscles in his neck gleamed in the firelight as he looked down at me, unsmiling. He wore his black hair long and braided, and his eyebrows, dark as a raven's wing, crooked up in question. Like Jack, he wore thin deerskin leggings and a simple linen shirt, his tomahawk strapped across his back with a piece of leather, the hilt of a knife revealing itself at the top of his boot. He watched me, and it was almost as if he was willing me to speak.

"You speak English," I said inanely.

"The same Catholic missionary that taught Silent Wolf of his *un'ega* religion taught me English," he said. "I prefer Cherokee."

"Why do you call him Silent Wolf?"

"His is of the Wolf clan, and he moves without sound—better than any Cherokee scout. He said you seek to learn more of your horse. Shall we walk?"

I looked up and into the darkness for Jack, who had disappeared into the barn. I could hear Abigail calling the men to supper, but suddenly I felt no need for food. "Would you like to sit?" I asked him.

He inclined his head toward the crowd gathering at the fire pit. "I am not welcome here," he said simply.

"It is my land, sir. I shall determine who is or is not welcome," I said, perturbed. But he only watched me, unanswering.

I felt no unease when looking at Ridge Runner. Though he was so very foreign to me, I knew nothing but quiet comfort from him. The things I'd been told in Charlestown, of the savageries and drunkenness of the Natives, were still unproven. And while I was sure that Ridge Runner, and Jack for that matter, had done things I'd rather not ascertain, I wanted to hear what he had to say. I stood, straightened my skirts, and walked with him away from the fire.

"Your horse is of Spanish descent," he began, matching his longer step to my shorter. "When the Spanish quit Georgia for land to the south, they left behind a number of horses. Most had been stolen by the Creek and the Cheraw. These were mighty horses, taller than what any of the *Yun'wiya* had seen, and they were excellent in battle, good war horses.

"Yours belonged to Mankiller of the bear clan, who died three moons ago in the woods. The horse had been a gift from his good-son. But Mankiller was too old to train the horse, and when he died it found its way to you. He's a stubborn mount, strong-willed and mighty, and he has traveled far," Ridge Runner said as we walked down to the edge of the pasture, far enough from the firelight so that we could no longer hear the others, but close enough to have the light to make our way. "He suits you. But he needs a name, Rides-Like-a-Man. What will you call him?"

"My name is Quinn," I muttered, unwilling to give in. I looked up at Ridge Runner, who regarded me with an arched brow. Finally I relented, unable to deal with his silence. "Fine, to you I will be Rides-Like-a-Man. As if I had any choice in the matter." I sighed. "I do not know what to name him."

"You have done research?" The Cherokee smiled without revealing his teeth.

I ignored him, folding my hands in my skirts to keep warm. "Yes, as a matter of fact I have. I feel as though I should seek his Spanish roots, but no name seems to suit me."

"He is more *Yun'wiya* than Spanish, by now," Ridge Runner said, pausing. "He is orange-gold and dangerous, and he would come to no one but you. He ate from your hand."

"He did, did he not," I said to myself, unable to hide the smile. "The men would not touch him."

"If you would allow me, I believe I have a proper name," Ridge Runner said quietly, his face to the sky. He did not look at me, yet I could feel all his concentration centered on my answer as he rounded the English words on his tongue.

"Please," I said, deciding then and there, quite unlike myself, that I would allow this exotic stranger to name my horse for me.

"Fire Eater," he said. "It is a good name."

Then, as if I had given him leave, he bent at the waist like an English gentleman, turned, and walked into the field until the darkness swallowed him whole.

Chapter 14

February 1769

Mid-day the sun sat high in the gray sky, casting the kind of light that warned of a winter storm. I stood at the top of the orchard, praying silently for a soft rain, one without the hail that could kill our still dormant apple trees. Hosa and Zeke had left their shears against a tree, and I wondered if they'd remember to collect them before the downpour began. The wind blew, stronger now, casting strands of flyaway hair out of my topknot and into my face. I held a hand there at the top of my head, holding the hair back as I looked out over my land.

My land. I still felt a bit faint when I considered it—that I had actually purchased four hundred acres in the South Carolina wilderness, a thing my grandfather had warned me against for years. I had a sudden vision of him in his library in Charlestown, pipe sticking out of the side of his mouth as he perused his Aristotle. Thinking of him made my heart ache.

Trees rustled, and a couple of crows took to the sky, cawing angrily at something. I looked down the rutted path between the apple trees and saw two Cherokee youths step out, one with a deer over his shoulders, antlers bobbing as he walked. They saw me and stopped, still as a painting, the blue mountains in the distance their backdrop. I raised a hand in greeting and nodded, smiling. They nodded back and walked on through the rows of the trees until I could no longer see the backs of their dark heads.

As far as I could see the land was mine, the dirt path winding through the middle of it, curling around the outskirts of my pastures and tapering off into a trail, not yet wide enough for a coach, that cut a skinny swath through the forest towards Keowee Town. Not a human soul had come up the trail in weeks. The last had been the post-rider, with a letter from Owen.

I pulled it from the pocket where I had folded and left it since that day—a silent reminder of the life I had left behind. The words, written with an invaluable quill pen, I was sure, had begun to fade from handling.

The first of February, 1769

Tradd Street, Charlestown

My dear Cousin,

> *Word of you and your continued venture in the frontier has come slow to us on the peninsula. You should know that our Grandfather believes your wits to be carried off by the savages, so nonsensical he seems to see this new life of yours. I have comforted him with the thought that perhaps you had instead taken up with a Regulator, and were presently ravaging the countryside with an infant on your hip. But I have been working hard in my role as Junior partner, and I am assured of a place in the auld man's good graces.*

> *I know that when I was there, the American Argument had not reached the frontier. The discontent here in the city rages at all hours, as British taxes are heaped upon merchant and aristocrat alike. There are those who believe that War is not far. I fear it and all it brings, but we are Scots, and so I cannot claim to be wholly averse to separation from England.*

> *I find I don't abhor sharing an office on the Harbour with Grandfather. Your favourite scholar, Mr. Wragg of the Library Society, often stops at the corner here to philosophize with whomever he can repeal to meet with him. Mayhap you will come to visit us after the summer, so that you can ask him to be quiet, allay Grandfather's worries, and scold me for bandying about with the ladies.*

> *I do think of you often, as you are the reason I live. Please pass on my good wishes to Jack Wolf and to his brother, and do ease Grandfather's heart by avoiding undue danger.*

With affection, Your Cousin,

Owen Scott, Esquire

I smoothed out the creases at the corner of the letter and tucked it back into the extra pocket I'd stitched in my skirt, giving it a light pat. Dark clouds had continued to build over the Blue Ridge while I had been too focused on the letter to notice. I picked up my skirts and headed back up the path, thinking fretfully of my fruit trees. We would need those apples in the coming fall. We certainly could not afford for their growth to be stunted.

I crested the hill just as a fork of lightning lit the ridgeline, an enormous boom sounding so loudly I hurried my pace, hoping to beat the rain back to my cabin. I was rushing past the pen when the heavens let loose and the downpour came, and I watched Zeke trying to lead Fire Eater into the barn. The big horse reared up over him.

"I'll bring him, Zeke," I called, a hand over my eyes. I crouched and stepped through the fence slats, my boots sliding in the mud. Zeke cupped his hands around his mouth, shouting to be heard over the thunder.

"You sure, Miz MacFadden?" His unspoken fear of Fire Eater overtook any shame at giving up the task to a woman.

"Yes—go see to the rest of the animals!"

Fire Eater saw me coming and visibly settled, his great head bent in supplication. I grabbed his lead and gave a quick tug, my boots sucking down into the red mountain clay that surrounded the barn. After seeing the horse safely to a stall, I made a run for my cabin, rain beating down on my shoulders, the wind a wall against my back.

I flung open the door and reached down, unlacing my boots as water pooled at my feet. My teeth chattered so violently I could hear myself in the empty room, and so I rushed about, lighting the oil lamp on the dining table and adding a log to the fire, which was low from lack of tending. I'd peeled off the shoulder of my dress when there was banging at the door.

"Mac!" Jack shouted, "Are you there?"

Startled, I shoved my arm back into the sleeve and took a quilt from the spindly-backed chair by the hearth, tossing it about my shoulders. Jack and Ridge Runner had left for Keowee Town days ago, to meet with Cherokee leaders there and talk of still more trade negotiations with the British government. I'd no idea he was back already.

I pulled open the door, and Jack and two strange men entered, the rain blowing in from outside in a torrent, splattering across the cabin floor.

Jack hooked his sopping hat over a chair and motioned to the men, the look in his eyes searing. His words entered my mind, succinct and unbidden: *Be calm, follow my lead.* "Miss Quincy MacFadden, may I present General Elliot Southerby and Lieutenant Andrew Pickens, of the South Carolina Militia."

"Gentlemen." I buttoned my collar swiftly and started toward Southerby, offering my hand. He looked down at it as though it were a bug of particular ugliness, and so I jerked it back, embarrassed, tucking it into the fold of my skirts.

Pickens cast a sidelong look at Southerby, removing his tricorn with one hand and offering the other, his face expressionless. "Mistress MacFadden, our thanks for the shelter."

I took his hand, studying him. He was a man of average height, dark hair held back in a queue, his entire personage seemingly dominated by a long, hooking nose. His speech held none of the refinery of England, but instead made him sound as though he were a man of the upcountry. "Please warm yourselves by the fire, gentlemen." I rounded the rocking chair and hooked a kettle over the iron spit, then brushed the rust from my hands. "May I offer you a cup of tea?"

"No, thank you—" Pickens began, before he was interrupted by Southerby, whose English voice came out clipped and high.

"Yes, thank you, tea would be appreciated."

Southerby ignored Pickens and removed his coat, shaking it out by the fire. I watched the water soak my grandmother's hand-woven rug and grimaced, but I held my tongue.

"Well, Mr. Wolf, how do you find the Cherokee at present?" Southerby rubbed his hands by the fire, looking at Jack over his shoulder. "Still resistant to English expansion, or have they realized the inevitability of colonial rule?"

Jack walked to the fireplace and leaned a shoulder against the mantel, propping one boot on the stone hearth. He folded his arms across his chest, his expression unreadable. "I find the Cherokee a strong people who've been promised much and given little, whose lands have been taken as though they were nothing but the spoils of war. The Boundary Line has been pushed farther back, twice in the past twenty years—the last no more than six years ago, despite a proclamation from the English King.

"Their game is stolen by the Creek from the South and the Chickasaw from the West, and the white man comes without invitation to take their women and their deer." He bent and stoked the fire with my poking stick. "How do you find the Cherokee, General?"

Affronted, Southerby sent a shocked look at Pickens and puffed up like a peacock. He fingered a gold button on his shirt cuff. "As you are half Cherokee, I see that you are biased in your views of the savage nation. I should have thought your experience at their mercy would have tempered your loyalties."

He walked to the window, pulling back the burlap and peering out into the darkness of the storm. "You saw, firsthand I assume, what they did during the Cherokee Wars. You served as translator for Captain Demere at Fort Prince George, did you not?"

Jack nodded, unmoving from his position at the hearth.

"Then you are paid in British currency for your work. The Crown assumed you would be of more help, sir."

Pickens spoke then, breaking the tension in the room. "We seek an audience with Little Carpenter," he said. "A trading post on the Tugaloo has been raided, the trader there killed and his wife disappeared. Governor Bull wishes the good friendship between the Lower Towns and Charlestown to be restored."

Jack cocked an eyebrow. "The royal governor wishes the deerskin trade uninterrupted. What would the gentlemen and ladies of Charlestown do without their leather gloves?"

"Mr. Wolf," Southerby strode forward, red-faced. "You, sir, are a subject of the Crown, and a servant to the colonial government. We seek a friendly meeting with your people." At this his lip curled, and I could see the insult forming in his mind as he looked at Jack: *half-breed.* "If you will not assist us, as officers of the Crown, we shall be forced to take you into custody."

I coughed delicately, moved to the fire and took the poking stick to stoke the flames. I then took a rag from the mantel and gripped the kettle handle, carried it with me to the cabinet. I took two precious china cups from the top shelf—Jack would not drink English tea—and poured steaming water into each.

"There will be no need for such action," Pickens said, quite forcefully. "I am certain Mr. Wolf will assist us in any way that he can."

At this, Jack pushed off from the mantel with one shoulder and came to me, taking the cups. Though his voice held Irish charm, his green eyes were hard. He handed a cup to each man, smiling without showing his teeth. "I'll do what I'm able, officers. I won't let you go to Attakullakulla unguided. The Cherokee have long memories, aye? They do not forget easily, and you'll not be seen as friend."

Pickens's chin jerked up at this, his eyes narrowing at Jack. I spooned tea leaves into their gently held cups, knowing without doubt there was much more to this exchange than what had been said during the storm. After it cleared, I would ask Jack to explain what had been unsaid.

"The storm has abated." Jack smiled at the other men, but it did not reach his eyes. "Drink your tea, gentlemen, then I'll show you to the barn. You can take your rest for the evening there. We'll leave for Keowee Town before dawn."

When Jack returned to the Valley after a three-day absence, he came bearing gifts of bearskin pelts, pottery, and a pair of moccasins. He dropped them onto my porch as I stood in the doorway watching, rolled his broad shoulders and bent his head to each side, cracking the vertebrae in his neck and exhaling a pleasurable sigh.

"Ah, Mac," he said, reaching back to rub the place where neck met shoulder, "I've brought you presents from Keowee Town, so you must greet me properly, aye?"

I reached out, fingering the corner of the pelt he'd draped over the railing. Its inside was smooth and soft as feather down; some Keowee woman must have spent hours scraping the hair from the hide. "Welcome," I said. "Did you have success with the British officers? Were they able to speak with Little Carpenter?"

He started toward me, grinning, and I backed up, running into the solid oak of my front door. "Just what are you about?"

"I'll give you no answers 'til I'm properly welcomed," he said, placing a hand on the door near my left cheek, uncomfortably close.

I rolled my eyes and made a move to skirt past him on the left, but he put up his other arm, blocking my escape. "Jack, really," I said, crossing my arms over my chest and blushing violently.

He reached out and tucked a wayward strand of my hair back behind my ear, closing his fingers softly over my earlobe before taking away his hand. I met him eye for eye despite the mortifying red that I was sure covered my face, and I glared at him, refusing to budge. "Have you been seeing another man in my absence, then?" he asked quietly.

"No!" The denial came automatically, and I shifted uncomfortably. "Not that I'm 'seeing' you," I sputtered. "We're in the wilderness, for heaven's sake—it's not as if I've a row of suitors waiting to call."

"There's the nobleman. And it's sure he's not objecting to the way you look in those fine petticoats of yours."

"Be quiet," I hissed, casting a furtive glance to the left and right. "You don't know what you're talking about."

"So it's only me you yearn for." He smiled, his green eyes gleaming as merrily as sunlight on a summer lake.

"If you're done accosting me I'd like to see what you've brought." I moved before thinking, shoving a hand at his chest. He caught it in both his hands, bent and pressed a quick, formal kiss against my knuckles, then let me go. I stood unmoving, my eyes wide. He caught my look and laughed at me, the dolt, then bent to the chair and picked two pottery bowls from the blankets, setting them gently on the ground.

"Kicking Horse's wife sent these," he said. He pulled a pair of moccasins from the trove. "These *ulasu'la* too—I tried to tell her the shape of your feet, so it's hoping I am that they'll fit. They may seem an oddity to you, you being a well-born Charlestown lady, but you'll get more good use of them than those silly slippers." He nodded at my delicate but serviceable shoes and grimaced.

"You kissed me," I accused, but reached out and snatched the moccasins from him. "You've no right to touch me like that, Mr. Wolf."

"Oh, it's Mr. Wolf now, is it? And after I've brought you these fine things. You could be a wee bit more gracious, I'm thinking."

I held the moccasins to my chest and swallowed my ire, a bit embarrassed. "I am grateful," I said slowly, "but you can't just kiss me whenever you want, Jack. The homesteaders will talk, and I don't want them thinking I've become consort to the resident mountain man."

"Fine," he said softly, backing off the porch. "The fancy man may be more for you, anyway, lass. And maybe it's you don't want a half-breed coming to your door."

"Now just a moment," I said angrily, struck at his cold tone. I stepped down from the porch and walked to stand before him, still clutching the moccasins to my dress front. "I've never said that—I don't feel that way. You've no cause to put words in my mouth, Jack Wolf."

I watched his face cautiously, deeply afraid I'd damaged the friendship I'd reluctantly come to cherish, and furious with him for making me want more. "Come back to the porch and have something to drink. I do want to hear of Little Carpenter."

The corner of his mouth twitched. "I'll have a greeting, lass," he said solemnly.

I rolled my eyes, exasperated, and held out my hand. "I am glad you're back," I admitted.

He smiled down at me with such a look that I jerked my hand from his and went back to the porch. He followed me and took a seat on the stoop. "Just water for me, lass, and thank you."

"Be happy you don't get mud," I muttered, shoving open the door.

"What was that, now?"

"Nothing," I called, moving to the table and pouring water from the china pitcher into a rough, wooden mug. I walked back out, handed it to him and sat gracefully beside him on the stoop, a proper distance away, spreading my skirts to cover my feet.

Jack drank the entire contents of the mug with one big gulp, his Adam's apple working. Then he set the mug on the planked floor between us and draped his hands between his knees.

"He wasn't there," he said, looking off toward the mountains.

"Who?"

"Attakullakulla. He wasn't at Keowee Town. I tried to tell the *un'ega* soldiers that the morning we left, but they wouldn't listen, stubborn fools." He cracked big knuckles, wrapping his left hand in the right, and I wondered suddenly if he were imagining his hands around Southerby's pale, British neck.

"Where was he?" I asked. "I thought he lived there."

"No, he lives at Chota, farther back in the mountains on the Little Tennessee River. 'Tis the capitol town of all the *Yun'wiya*, lass. He's a regular diplomat now, Little Carpenter is. Travels between villages mostly, encouraging peace between the white settlers and the royal government. But he's an old man, and the young would rather fight than lose their lands—even his son, Dragging Canoe. That one's got a fire in his belly for war."

"You said that to the Lieutenants, didn't you—that the Cherokee Boundary Line had been pushed back?" I played with the folds of my skirt, watching him closely.

"Aye. One day the Line will be past the mountains, and then where will the *Yun'wiya* go? No, lass, your people won't be sated 'til mine are driven from their lands, and they're populated by white farmers and loyal subjects to the Crown instead."

"But the Cherokee lands stretch so far back into the wilderness," I said, bewildered. "Surely they'll always be theirs?"

"Mayhap," he said, with a half-smile. "But there are more of you, Mac. And you'll keep coming."

I eyed him hesitantly, stung by his words. "I didn't ask for so much land," I said stiltedly. "I only wanted a bit, but Little Carpenter offered me more than I'd ever imagined. How was I to turn it down? You've no idea what my life was like in Charlestown. I had to leave, to find something of my own."

"Oh, it's not you I'm thinking of," he said gently, "though you are one of many. I'm thinking of the people who come without asking, who settle in on Cherokee land and kill more deer than they could eat, and shoot without warning, scared to death of those they've stolen from.

"You . . . now, you're a different tale. You welcomed Ridge Runner and me to your home, savage as we are—though 'tis true you put up a bit of a fight with me at the first." He grinned, enjoying my annoyance. "You are the most unusual *un'ega* woman I've ever known. It's a rare, fine pleasure now, just to see what you'll do next."

"Lovely to be of service," I said sarcastically. "But where *is* Little Carpenter?"

"I don't know," he said. "Perhaps up in the Middle Towns, or maybe even back to Chota by now. I went to Tugaloo myself. And I sent a runner to the Middle Towns, to see if the trader's wife had been taken there. It was all I could do for the Lieutenants."

"That was good of you," I said. "I hope they appreciated it."

He chuckled, lifting his chin in amusement. "Oh, aye. They gave the half-breed a few coins, sent me on my way. Ordered me to report to them as soon as the woman was found."

"Pickens didn't seem such a bad sort," I said quickly.

"Maybe not," he said. "But had I been all Indian, I doubt he'd have treated me with as much measure as he did, and little that. These backcountry whites travel the mountains frightened and trigger happy, thinking they'll be scalped around each bend in the trail. Not to say that's not the case, for they do come unwelcomed." He looked at me solemnly. "But it seems to me that there's no service in hating a man before you know a thing of him. Let him fail in your eyes first, then doubt him—but not before, aye?"

"Aye," I said smartly, smiling at his speech.

We sat in comfortable silence for a few minutes, and I realized that it was the first time I'd felt that way in his presence since meeting him so many months before. The sun had begun the first curve of its descent behind the Blue Ridge, and as I started to speak I heard Hosa clang the cow bell down at the middle pasture. "Supper," I said quietly.

He stood and offered me a hand. I took it to rise and then crossed my arms again, the quiet comfort of our meeting fading rapidly. I thought to invite him to eat with us, but before I could say anything he made a motion at the moccasins, which sat on the ground at my feet.

"Wear them, Mac," he said. "Your feet will thank you for it."

Chapter 15

March, 1769

Winter delivered a wicked blast over the backcountry, two weeks of cold that crept over hills, up waterfalls and into the mountains' granite heart, chilling and freezing the land like a gust of breath from the Ice Man—a malicious snow monster feared by the Cherokee. The trees iced over and glistened like glass when caught in the sun; icicles hung in scythes from the falls, forming beneath rocks in parts of the creek where the water grew stagnant. In the creeks and rivers trout that had so recently emerged with the thought of spring now tucked themselves up against boulders, avoiding whitewater. Each morning the fields were encrusted with frost, and the sounds of someone walking could be heard hundreds of yards away by the crack of grass and dirt.

I was cold all the time, and I dressed as a man would, abandoning hoop skirts and delicate linen for a pair of rough breeches I'd sewn from a wool blanket. Whenever I rode Fire Eater, or worked in the barn, I wore them and an old greatcoat of my grandfather's—much to the dismay of Hosa, who gave me a glinty-eyed look and shook his head in disgust whenever he saw me.

"You are mad," he said this morning as I stood with my backside high in the air, holding Fire Eater's bent foreleg in my arms and digging at a stone in his hoof. "You'd be took to jail, we be in Charlestown."

"Well, it's a good thing we're not in Charlestown," I said, working the wooden pick. Fire Eater swung his big head around, snorting.

"I know," I told the horse. "But it'll soon be over with."

"Dressed a man, talkin' to beasts," Hosa grumbled, his lyrical voice lightening the complaint. He broke the ice in the water trough with an ax.

"You too fine a lady for dis, now—you be temptin' de devil wid dat look."

The stone flew out and hit the stall door. I straightened, looked down at myself, and frowned. I did look a boy, with the fitted gray breeches and black greatcoat of Grandfather's that hung past my knees, the hugely cuffed sleeves flapping with each move. But in this frigid weather, I honestly didn't care. There were no society ladies to frown at and gossip over my improper garb, no Grandfather to send me back to my dressing rooms, insisting I change. "I'd rather be ugly as a toad than freeze to death," I said. "On a morning like this I'd be out the door two steps and have the hem of my skirts dripping—by noon they'd be frozen."

Hosa rolled his eyes and hung the ax on a nail.

"Besides," I grumbled, hanging the pick on the nail beside it and walking to take Fire Eater's lead, "hoop skirts are nonsensical on the frontier. The air gets underneath, and it's literally freezing."

Hosa held both hands in the air and backed away, and I could swear I saw his dark cheeks turn a shade of deep berry. "Dat's it," he said. "I don' wan' be hearin' no more 'bout what's up no skirts." He turned and headed to the other end of the barn, shaking his curly head. "Madwoman," I heard him mutter as he left.

"Some days I believe I am crazy," I said aloud to myself, leading Fire Eater back into his stall. I took a rough brush from the wall, running it hard over the stallion's rump. Dust puffed out, and I blinked, kept at it.

"I miss it," I whispered to the horse, and the stall felt suddenly small and lonely. "I miss Ninian, and my pupils. Little Sarah Gadsden was just learning to canter, and Naji's nephew had almost conquered his fear enough to trot." I set the brush down on the ledge of the wall separating it from the next stall, picked a few burrs from Fire Eater's long, black tail.

"Miss MacFadden," a voice called from the end of the barn.

"In here," I answered, walking to the stall door. "Oh, good morning, Lord Harris. How did you fare the night?"

"Well, though a mite cold," he answered, halting at the sight of my mannish outfit. He recovered quickly and removed the hat from his head, ever the gentleman. "You still give me a start, every time," he said, his mouth crooking up at the corners. "Before you the only lady I'd seen dressed as a man was on the London stage."

I sniffed, feeling a trite embarrassed. "I do apologize, sir. I know my appearance offends, but I can't seem to rationalize wearing a dress in this cold. In fact, it seems idiocy, no matter the scandal."

He coughed, hiding a full-fledged grin behind his fist. "Well said, though your appearance could never offend."

I started at the compliment, turning back to shut and latch Fire Eater's door. "Have you had word of your friends yet? I know you received a letter in the last post, but it's been several months since, hasn't it?"

His face immediately brightened. I knew how worried he'd been. After settling here in the Valley, Harris had come to me requesting to write friends of his in Savannah about possibly taking on one of the plots of land still left open. They were an intriguing pair, an Anglican priest and his daughter, a girl of twelve. They were English, Harris had said.

"They should be here by Easter," Harris said, happiness warming his normally formal speech. "They've followed the Savannah River and are garnering supplies in Tugaloo. They'll stay with a family there for the last snow before starting with a guide back up the path. A friend of Mister Wolf's apparently saw them and sent word."

I took a bucket from Fire Eater's stall and bent to dip it in the icy trough, thinking that Jack Wolf must know the whole of the frontier.

"Let me, Miss MacFadden." Harris reached out, taking the bucket before I could protest, and eying the big stallion warily before hanging it over the side of the stall. I brushed my hands on the long expanse of the old greatcoat, sliding them down into the pockets. We walked together to Plato's stall at the other end of the barn.

"You're looking forward to your friends' arrival, aren't you?"

"Quite. Joseph Wheeler served my family's church in London before making the crossing," he said, wrinkling his nose at the smell of manure wafting out from the old horse's stall. "You'll enjoy his daughter, I believe. Wheeler had the raising of her after his wife died in childbirth, so she's a unique urchin. He's given her leave to learn a bevy of scandalous subjects for a young girl, and I'm afraid she lacks much ladylike poise. Quite similar to your upbringing in Charlestown, I presume."

My head snapped up from the study I'd been making of the cracked board at the base of Plato's door, and before I could retort Lord Harris's pale cheeks went red, and he coughed to cover embarrassment. "My dear lady, I do apologize. I did not mean that as it sounded."

I pulled a hand from my pocket and covered my mouth, unable to suppress a chuckle. As he started to make what I knew would be an unbearably maundering and aristocratic apology, I held out a staying hand. "I am not offended, sir. In fact, I view it as an odd sort of compliment."

I waded into the steaming manure and took a crude shovel from the wall, meaning to muck out Plato's stall. Lord Harris gasped in dismay and snatched the shovel from me, his nose twitching.

"I'll do it, Miss MacFadden, really. You should not be out in this cold—this is a job for the stableman."

"Honestly, Lord Harris. Do you really think that one need be a man to shovel shit sufficiently?"

Watching his face, I immediately bemoaned my quick tongue and slower brain. When would I ever learn to temper my speech?

He dropped the tool and went white, planting his gloved hands on his hips. His breath coursed out in long white puffs, and for a moment I thought I'd be getting a tongue-lashing in the self-righteous tradition of my great aunt Eloise. But then he laughed, a honking guffaw that had no business coming out of the mouth of a displaced English lord. "You just said 'shit,'" he managed, eyes streaming. "I'd have never thought—"

"I'm sorry," I choked back, wiping my nose and grinning foolishly. "I do believe that my tongue does get away with me sometimes."

At this Harris doubled over with mirth, clutching his stomach. He swiped the now-battered tricorn from his head and looked me in the eyes. "Oh really, do you think?" he asked with just the slightest hint of sarcasm, bracing his hands on his knees.

Hosa found us there later, still standing in the manure, laughing like lunatics. He snatched the shovel from the ground and shook his head at both of us. "An English lord an' a Charlestown lady, standin' in de shit pile," he muttered, sending manure flying toward the door. "All you people mad as bats."

I looked up at Harris, and he grinned at me, and I snorted.

* * *

The eleventh of March, 1769
Keowee Valley
Dearest Owen,

> *I take up my quill to write to you, Cousin, for the first time in the new year. I can hardly believe that this is so—it seems as though we were but children yesterday, together as always, arguing over the first carving of duck at Grandfather's table. I pray that you are well and warm during these bitter days. May they soon break and bring warmth to us all.*

> *The settlement continues to grow. Soon we'll add an Anglican priest and his daughter. I wonder will he want to hold service here? Perhaps I'll let him, and may our Scottish Catholic ancestors on Grandfather's side and the French Huguenots on Grandmother's vie to see who can roll heavier in their graves.*

> *I wonder, has Grandfather said anything of me? He has not written, and I fear that he still opposes my new life. I*

am certain that he is kept busy by his work, and that you and Naji keep him in good health, but I cannot speak falsely—I do wish to have word of him. Though I do not regret taking permanent leave of the Lowcountry, I had hoped Grandfather would understand.

I am eager for news of your life as a lawyer, and if you've a mind to finally tell me of your time with the Shawnee, I'd know that, too. You may find it relieving to write it all down. And I would know of it, because it's part now of who you are, Owen. And I am, after all, your family.

With Love,

Quincy

I rode Fire Eater with a vengeance, racing him across Tomassee Creek and through the lowest pasture, jumping a set of broken wagon wheels I'd had Hosa and Zeke plant in the dirt. We caught air, and I crouched over the big stallion's back, lifting my backside from the saddle like a racer. The leather of the saddle felt smooth and familiar beneath my thighs. I was thankful I'd brought it to the frontier, despite the hassle of its bulk. I held tight to the tuft of hair at his withers, clutching the reins and mane together in both hands. We hit the ground at full gallop and kept going, rumbling straight for the next obstacle, a pile of stumps left from building the settlers' cabins.

The wind was chilled, hitting my face with icy slaps, but I tucked my head into Fire Eater's neck as we neared the jump. The hot thrill that always came with riding rushed violently through my bloodstream, pooling in my gut like lava. We took the jump from too far back and Fire Eater's back legs brushed a stump, sending it tumbling to the ground. As his hooves touched earth he faltered but kept his legs, and I pulled back lightly on the reins, squeezing his heaving sides with the heels of my boots.

"Whoa, boy," I said softly, keeping my voice calm and deep. "That's it, you did well." I reached down, patting the side of his sweat-wet neck companionably, and slid easily from my mount, grinning like a child.

"Rides-Like-a-Man, *a' stu' tsiki'.*"

I whipped around, startled, to find Laughing Crow, whom I hadn't seen in nearly a year, standing several yards away in the brown grass. He watched me, expressionless, and if it had not been for the fact that he'd spoken in Cherokee, I would not have thought he'd spoken at all. He held the lead rope of a horse attached to a wagon. Behind him stood two white people: a tall, stooping, crane-like man in a faded black coat and breeches, and a girl, skinny with the height of her father, but without the bent back. She stood straight as a young tree, two chestnut braids emerging from a yellowed bonnet to hang down onto her dress.

I smiled at them hesitantly, mortified that I'd been caught riding roughshod over my land like a wild woman. Laughing Crow cleared his throat, and my eyes jerked back to his face. Something flashed in his black eyes, and he made a gesture at Fire Eater. "You do ride like a man. *A' stu' tsiki*—very good."

I cocked an eyebrow at him, still shocked he'd actually spoken to me, much less given me a compliment. "*Wado*," I said dryly.

The tall man stepped forward, removing a well-kept, black tricorn from his head and tucking it between his elbow and side. "I am Father Joseph Wheeler, and this is my daughter, Margaret. You are Mistress MacFadden, are you not?"

He said it with such kindly disbelief that I glanced down at myself, realizing belatedly that I wore the wool breeches and Grandfather's oversized greatcoat, and that my head was scandalously bare, my hair a wild tangle that hung down my back. "Yes, I am." I coughed delicately, moving forward to offer my hand. He took it gently, bowed gracefully over it and then stepped back, replacing the hat.

"Welcome to Keowee Valley," I said, smiling warmly, keeping my eyes on the girl. "Lord Harris has been anxiously awaiting your arrival. He'll be so happy to know you've reached us safely. Are these your things?" I asked, making a motion at the wagon.

"Yes, miss, as much as we could carry. I'm afraid we had to leave most of our fine things, our furniture, in Savannah."

The girl turned away, and I caught a glimmer of tears in her eyes. Apparently not everyone had wanted to make the trip west. "Then it's a good thing we've a fine carpenter here," I said. "His name is Jehosaphat, and he can build anything if you can sketch it. He made me a rocking chair." I looked directly at the child. "Which cannot be easy, if you've ever seen one."

"I have," she said quickly, swiping at her eyes with the edge of her sleeve. "My schoolmaster had one, in Georgia."

I put a hand out to her, and her eyes widened, but she took it, letting me shake it gently. "Well, that's good then," I said softly. "Now you'll know what to tell Hosa."

"Rides-Like-a-Man," Laughing Crow said curtly. "You will take them now."

"Yes, of course." I walked to him, taking the horse's lead that he held out to me. He nodded and walked away.

"Should he not take us at least to your stables?" Father Wheeler asked, disturbed. "We paid good coin for the trip."

The Indian turned silently, sending us a cold look and waving a hand. "You are here, priest. Be satisfied."

"Travel safely, *Ka'gu*," I said quickly, and he jerked around, studied me momentarily, then headed for the forest.

"What did you say, Miss MacFadden?" Margaret Wheeler took my hand without a thought and tugged, and my heart was lost to her.

"Meg," her father scolded, but I shook my head at him.

I smiled down at her, pulling lightly on one of her scraggly braids. "I called him 'crow,' in Cherokee, because that's his name."

"What's *wado?*"

"It means 'thank you,'" I answered, delighting in her curiosity. I kept her hand in mine and pulled down on the lead, and the horse and wagon lurched forward. "Well, let's go pick a spot for your cabin, shall we?"

Meg kicked a rock with her laced-up leather boot, scruffy with wear, and looked up at me again. "I'm going to want to know more," she said simply, tears abandoned.

I chuckled, looking up into the middle pasture, where Lord Harris was hurrying past the fire pit, his face split in an unabashed grin. "I'm sure that you will," I said solemnly.

Chapter 16

Early April, 1769

The sky was deepening into dusk, and I was lost. In the distance I could see Tomassee Knob rising through the trees, still bare but budding with the red of early spring. It was cold enough that when the scarf came loose from my neck as I walked, the skin there stung as though bitten. I turned again and tried to recount my tracks, but they led, I knew, in a circle. I'd been to this spot twice already. The rare midnight snowfall had left fallen trees and underbrush hidden by a layer of white thick enough to make the world unreal. I'd thought it magical when I had awoken early this morning to Hosa knocking on my door, shouting that the dairy cow had broken out of her stall and disappeared into the forest along with Mutt, who'd apparently followed.

Were it summer, and only the old horse, such an event wouldn't be quite so worrisome. But in the snow an animal could become entangled in downed tree branches or break a leg in a hidden gully, and freeze to death before we could find it. The affection we all felt for these two creatures notwithstanding, they were vital to our lives on the frontier. After the search party had been hastily formed I'd broken from the group, insisting on going alone—I was not about to stay back at the settlement, and I did not want to be paired with Samuel or Hosa, much as I cared for them. One would stay painfully silent, the other lecturing. But I informed them all of my route. I planned to walk for a half hour down the trail towards Tomassee Knob, and turn round long before I got there. I figured Mutt, especially, knew that trail, and might not have roamed far from it. I hoped, too, that I'd find some evidence of tracks, though I knew it was likely they'd been covered with new snow overnight.

Despite the impetus for the hike, the valley in snow was utterly magical. It was the silence that mystified me: nothing moved, or sang, or even crept. The snow engulfed my whole world, and I had been intent on enjoying it. To a Charlestonian, who had never once witnessed a snowfall, it meant nothing of hardship, and was instead as luring as the piper's tune to a small child.

But now it was late afternoon, and the sun was setting quickly, the last red of it lighting the top of Tomassee Knob like a fire. The cold seeped through my clothes and into my bones, and I felt fear tingling at the soles of my wet feet. I rubbed my gloved hands together, blowing warm breath into my palms. Perhaps if I walked up the crest of this ridge, I could see well enough to spot the settlement. Surely someone would have a fire burning in at least one of the chimneys, I thought, and I'd see the smoke.

I ploughed through the snow farther into the woods, coming to a slow halt at a huge fallen oak, blocking what looked to me to be the best path to any lookout. I'd managed to pull myself up onto the trunk when voices came from the other side, deep and foreign. I squinted, seeing nothing in the trees. Then the woods came alive, and a band of six men, all Indian, walked out of the darkness. One saw me and yelled something, and I was so startled that I lost my footing and fell, my ankle twisting painfully beneath me.

Two of the men rushed forward, speaking angrily. Their faces were painted half black, their heads shaved bare but for a swath of spiky dark hair that reached down onto their napes. My first thought was that they were not like Ridge Runner; there was nothing of anything recognizable in their eyes. I dug my fingers into the snow and tried to pull myself away from these strangers, these men with the biting voices who barked rapidly at one another. I'd crawl if I had to.

Suddenly hands gripped my bad ankle and yanked, my skirts dragging up to my chest, snow cold against my shift. I cried out, in pain and fear, and some part anger. "Leave me be," I yelled, slapping at their hands.

They dragged me across the ground, my back scraping against branches and rocks beneath the snow, my hair coming unbound from its wrap. I was dumped at the feet of an Indian, smaller than the others, with a pockmarked face and lazy eye. He spit on the ground near me and said something in sharp, staccato syllables, his words piercing the quiet woods. I tried to stand, but was pushed down by the foot of another man. The two snapped at one another for a several minutes as I lay there, freezing, my wet hair numbing the back of my head, the cold seeping painfully into the sockets behind my eyes.

"Let me go," I said, hoping one of them spoke English. "You have no use for me."

The small man motioned to one of the others, and he came forward, a rope in hand. He tied it around my neck as though I was a dog, the fibers cutting into my numbed skin. The woods had gone almost dark, the light in the sky now low and pale blue, and with it the cold sharpened, and my fear grew. They meant to take me, I thought, realization like a knife in my belly.

"Please, let me go," I begged. "You have no quarrel with me."

One of the men yanked up on the rope, motioning for me to walk. The group started forward, and I limped along as best I could, my mind running wild as a mountain stream, wondering what—if anything—I could do to escape. My hair was jerked back, and a face filled my vision, dark eyes glimmering with a look that had my stomach turning.

"Yellow," the man said in English, yanking again on my hair.

Walking ahead, the leader turned and uttered something unintelligible over his shoulder. The man gripping my hair dragged me close to him and pressed his face into my neck, sniffing. The shock of it tore at me, and I screamed, the sound catching a ridge and splintering out.

The leader started to the back of the group, the whites of his eyes showing in the poor light. I stepped back, terrified. He stopped before reaching me and held out a hand, palm down, fingers spread. The others stopped in unison, turning in slow circles, searching the woods. The small man called out something in his language, and an amazingly familiar voice answered in the same language from the darkness of the trees to our right. Relief washed over me, biting and welcome, like warmth from a fire to frostbitten toes. I wanted to shout to him, but kept silent. The group's leader spoke again, and Jack walked out of the trees. He made high steps in the snow, a musket in his left hand. In his right he held a basket, with what looked like an animal tail flapping over the side.

Jack did not look at me, but spoke calmly to the Indian leader. The pockmarked man responded, gesturing sharply at me. He came to me and grabbed the hair at the back of my head, yanking my head back as he talked, jerking it from side to side. The pain was so sharp that my eyes filled; I gritted my teeth.

Jack spoke again, lifting the basket and dropping it at his feet. The Indian who had touched my neck came forward, arguing with the leader. I stared at Jack, willing him to look at me. But his eyes did not waver from the other men. The Indians quieted and were silent for what seemed like an eternity. A large pile of snow fell from a tree bough farther in the forest, hitting the ground with a soft thud.

Finally Jack said something else to the leader, and I felt hands on my backside, feeling roughly down my thighs. I shuddered, holding my breath. Then the leader laughed, and the rest joined in, the sound cracking the quiet woods. One of the Indians walked up to Jack and took the basket. The pockmarked leader took the rope and threw it towards Jack, shoving me forward. I stumbled but kept my feet. The pain in my ankle was immense, and I knew I'd collapse in the snow if I had to walk farther. I could hear the men moving behind me, talking amongst themselves, and it was then that Jack looked me in the face, his lips forming words.

"Don't move," he mouthed.

We stood there, staring at each other, long after the sounds of their voices faded into the gathering dark. Jack was no more than fifteen feet from me, but his face was shadowed in the last vestiges of dusk. The sky had grown deep purple in the spaces between clouds. I could not stop it—a salty tear stung the corner of my eye and slid down my cheek into the side of my mouth. I felt hollow, as if I were on the edge of a great ravine, with nothing to do but leap. "Jack," I whispered, my throat raw.

He moved then, and I realized that he'd been standing so still that the snow had settled back in over his moccasins. He kicked it up into the air as he came toward me, his face expressionless, but closer, and his eyes were bright. He clutched my shoulders violently; I sucked in breath.

Then his lips were on mine, unrelenting, and we kissed like we'd been lovers parted by death. His tongue wrapped around mine, and I lost feeling in my legs, but I reached out and clutched his elbows. We stood together for a long time, our mouths on each other, breath commingling. Then he bit my bottom lip, hard enough to draw blood.

"Are you hurt?" he asked. I could only stare at his mouth like a mute. "Dammit—did they touch you?"

"No," I managed. "No, not like that."

"Can you walk?"

I shook my head, strands of wet hair slithering down into the top of my dress. I had not worn my coat. It was still sitting on my chair in the cabin, forgotten in the rush to find the animals before they'd wandered dangerously far from the settlement. Goosebumps covered my chest. I realized that the top of my dress was torn, my shawl lost.

Jack slung me up into his arms and tucked my head into his shoulder. The ends of his hair brushed my face as he walked into the woods in the opposite direction of the Indians. It was so dark that I wondered how he could see to place his feet, but he walked surely and silently, and did not speak to me. At some point he bent to pick up a burlap satchel tucked in the nook of a fallen pine tree. By then the pain in my ankle was so great that when he dipped to grab it my stomach churned, and I felt my gorge rise.

"Put me down," I said.

He held me across his arm and I emptied my belly into the snow, wanting to weep. It was all coming to me now: the merciless realization that my carelessness could have ended in death, or worse. I saw the Indian leader's lazy eye in my mind as if he were still standing before me, his rotten breath on my face. I wiped my mouth on my sleeve.

"I'm sorry," I said.

Jack reached down with his free hand and picked up snow, handing it to me. "Wash out your mouth, lass."

He swung me up again as though I was a child, walking farther into the forest. I shut my eyes against the cold and turned my face into his deerskin coat, the smell somehow comforting and familiar.

He carried me across a small creek cutting a line through the snow, and minutes later we stopped at what he told me was an abandoned trapper's cabin. Inside, the cabin was as musty and dark as a cave, but Jack soon got a fire started in the fireplace, and warmth and light lit the room, womb-like and safe. He pulled a thick quilt from the satchel, making a pallet on the floor near the fire with it and a coat that looked strangely like my own. He helped me stand and brace myself against an old chair, one of two pieces of furniture in the room. The other, a tall cracked mirror, stood at the back of the room, firelight flickering in its depths.

"You'll freeze if you're not out of those clothes soon," he said, placing his hand at my collarbone. It was so warm that I was sure he would leave an imprint there on my pale skin. He lifted an eyebrow and smiled. "Care for help?"

"I can suffice," I said, still hollow with shock, and even more so, unsure of this uncertain new place in which we found ourselves. I had never in my life kissed a man like I'd kissed Jack Wolf, and I think he knew it. "Kindly turn your back."

He moved his hand and the chill hit my skin, bereft. I braced my hand against the chair back and reached to pull out my laces, almost completely undone from being dragged along the uneven ground. I pushed my skirts down onto the floor and stepped back.

"I need a blanket," I said quietly, unable to strengthen my voice.

"Shift too, lass," he said, his back to me, arms crossed. "You'll catch the chill if you don't."

"Really, I could stand before the fire and dry," I countered, feeling unnaturally helpless.

I watched him shift his weight and sigh, the firelight gilding his long hair, casting his broad back in relief.

"Mac," he said simply.

I pulled the shift over my head with a huff, flinging it towards him. It hit the back of his head and landed softly on the ground. "I need a blanket," I repeated.

He walked to the bag and pulled a blanket from it, tossing it to me as he kept his eyes on the opposite wall. I caught it and wrapped it around myself as well as I could with one hand, then sat down in the chair. I curled my good foot underneath, tucking it beneath the bottom rung for balance. He took my clothes and laid them before the fire, straightening my skirts carefully along the wooden floor. I felt suddenly and irrationally angry with him—this man I still barely knew, who had undoubtedly saved my life.

"How did you know?" I asked sharply.

He looked up, and his eyes followed me from my toes to the top of my head, and in the shadows cast from the fire his cheekbones looked high and stark. "Hosa found me, told me how long you'd been gone. That's a man who doesn't scare easily. And Ridge Runner saw Creek prints on the southwest side of the Knob. He figured they were tracking over tribal boundaries, looking for game."

I lifted a hand to my mouth, the reality of the situation a chill in my bones. "They were Creek," I repeated dumbly. "What would they have done with me?"

He walked to the fire and bent to toss in another branch he'd collected, dead leaves crackling and disappearing in the flames. "Kept you for a slave, mayhap. Or sold you to the Chickasaw for rum, or horses." He looked up at me, unsmiling now. "Know this, lass. They would not have treated you well."

I pulled the blanket tightly around my shoulders, the wool scratching the naked skin beneath. I had almost forgotten that there was only thin fabric between us. "How did you persuade them to release me?"

At this he smiled again, and he looked like the Jack that I knew from the civilized world.

"I offered a basket of beaver pelts, and told them that you had too broad a rump for their liking."

"Too broad a—" I stuttered, placing my feet on the floor and starting to stand before the pain rushed up my left ankle. "You pig-headed imbecile," I ground out. "If I were a man I'd throttle you."

He stood and walked over to crouch before me, comfortable as a frog. "It helped, did it not, lass?" His hands dangled between big knees. "They didn't want you enough to take you. And you do have a lovely, round rump."

I kicked out my good leg as hard as I could but he caught it, pulling me toward him so that the chair fell out from under me and I found myself in his arms, my back inches from the floor. "Leave me be," I said succinctly, his nearness bringing color to my cheeks. He stood easily and carried me to the pallet, setting me there with my back against the wall, settling himself beside me.

"I canna," he said, the Irish in his voice emerging, softening his tone. He reached out and tugged on my hair so that it fell straight, brushing my lap. "You are as prickly as a riled porcupine, and when you're angry you click your teeth together like a mule."

I looked up at him in disbelief, my eyes filling. "Now you insult me." I wiped my nose on the corner of the blanket, looking away before he could see the ridiculous tears. "First I have a large backside, and now I look like two of the most unattractive animals in the frontier."

"Mac." He leaned over me, reached out and took my chin, turning my face toward his. "When I saw you at the creek that day, you were the most beautiful thing I'd ever laid eyes on. It hurt to look at you, there with that yellow hair done up like a priestess, and those big blue eyes looking at me like you knew all my secrets."

He moved his hand up my cheek, tracing the line of my jaw with his fingers. He ran his hand along my neck, soft, then settled again on my jaw, rubbing his thumb across my bottom lip, back and forth. I did not move. "The Cherokee say that you dream of your mate before you meet her. Mac, I dreamt of you. A fortnight before Attakullakulla sent for me, I dreamt of a woman with long, yellow hair carrying a king's load of books. And when I saw you that day by the water, I knew."

The tears came now, spilling down my cheeks and pooling against the top of the blanket, where I held it to my chest like a shield. He paused, his green eyes somber. "Of course, lass, it was only after I watched you walk back across the pasture, and I saw that fine, round rump of yours, that I truly knew—"

I could not stop it, the laugh bubbled up from my throat, and I covered my face in my hands, choking on tears, almost losing my breath. I knew I should be berating him, or wounding him in any way possible, but it wasn't in me—not this night, when my world had turned inside out, when I had been bartered over by savages and dragged by my hair, when I had kissed an infuriating man in the snow, a man so much still a stranger.

The tears flowed freely through my fingers, and I hiccupped uncontrollably. Jack simply sat there, silent beside me, grinning like a pirate, his long legs stretched out in front of him. In the firelight he seemed something of a Viking marauder, his gilt hair in all its various shades of copper and gold, his braid with the tiny white feather, the silver stud winking in his ear. The muscles in his neck convulsed in a chuckle, and I stopped laughing and reached out my hand, tracing the sinews there with my fingertips.

The grin disappeared as he let me touch him, his chest rising and falling steadily beneath his trade shirt, open slightly at the neck. I smoothed his unruly eyebrows, then let my hand fall away, bringing the other to my mouth, my teeth gripping a thumbnail, heart thumping so loudly I was certain he could hear it.

"You are beautiful," I said, moving my hand from my mouth, before I could take it back.

Then I let the smile come, pressing away memories of the night. "Incorrigible, and utterly pompous, but beautiful all the same." I looked off toward the mirror, watching the flashes of orange and gold light reflected there, and took a chance. "When I saw you that day by the creek, I was frightened. Frightened, I think, because I wanted you then."

He leaned forward, and I knew he would kiss me again. But he reached around my side and settled the quilt over the two of us, pulling me against him. My body, for so long nothing to me but a vehicle for simply walking, and riding, and moving about, was suddenly warm and alive and flush against him, all my soft places seeming to melt into his hard ones. Beneath the quilt he loosed his own shirt, opening it completely. Then he tugged the blanket from my chest, baring my breasts in the dark. He tucked me into his side, and where my body touched his it felt as though we burned. "Quinn," he started, then cleared his throat, his voice gruff and deep. "I won't compromise you. Just lay your head, and we'll sleep."

I curled a hand up over the ridges of his stomach, resting it lightly against the soft down of hair there. The cabin, darker now with the dying fire, should have been cold and unwelcoming. Instead, the room glowed with a quiet light, and I shut my eyes and let it play over my eyelids, certain that I'd never again be the same.

"You said that you dreamt of me."

Through gradually thinning, still-bare poplars we could make out the nearing Valley, and the outline of the cabins in the middle pasture. We walked quietly, had been for the most part silent since leaving the old trapper's cabin at dawn. He kept a slow pace as I limped along beside him, testing weight on my sore ankle. Though I loathed to upset the comfort I felt walking with Jack through the thawing forest, I needed to hear his voice, to know if what had happened on Tomassee Knob was nothing but the momentary effect of a near-death experience.

"Aye," he answered, catching my elbow as we hiked up and over a fallen oak. "Watch your feet, lass."

I took the soft flesh at the side of my mouth in my teeth and bit down gently, taking a short, cold breath in through my nose. "Do you have the Sight, then?" I asked quickly.

"No. Not in the Celtic sense of it, if that's what you're asking. The Cherokee believe in dreams, and when dreams come they're taken as powerful omens, messages from God—whether they come true or not. To be honest, lass, when I dreamt of you I woke the next morning thinking I'd been hit in the skull during the last game of *anesta*."

I smiled. "Who convinced you otherwise?"

"You," he said, stopping and reaching out for my hands. He took them in both of his, held them cupped between and brought them to his mouth, blowing warm air through the knitted gloves I wore. "At the river, I thought you were a vision. But then you pointed that pistol at my head, and I thought, by God, she's real."

I took my hands from his, pushing them deep into the pockets of the coat he'd brought me. I'd told him before, but I needed to make sure he understood. "I have it," I said, focusing on his dark pupils, flashing in a sea of green. "The Sight, that is. I've had it since I was a child. I see things in my dreams, and I hear voices, and I know that they come from some place in a time before or after my own." I stepped back, my boots crunching down through the sheet of ice layered over hardening snow, and covered my face in my hands, rubbing my forehead violently.

"I sound a madwoman. And if anyone were telling me something like this I'd think they belonged in an asylum, but since it's me—and I'm practical as they come—I know it's true. I can't choose the visions, or make them cease. I wish I could—there are some things I'd rather not know."

Jack reached a hand over his shoulder, shifting the musket on his back. "Mac," he said softly, "quit your pacing. Do you think I'll haul you off to Ninety-Six, see you hung for a witch? My people see visions as gifts. When a beloved woman speaks of what she's seen in her dreams, men listen well. I don't think you a madwoman, lass. A wee bit contrary, aye, but not mad."

"Well, that's a good thing, then," I said, smiling again.

He stepped suddenly, closing the space between us. He brushed a lock of hair away from my face, the tender gesture from such a large man surprising. "You have no cause to fear me, Mac. But know this—we are meant, whether you like it or not."

I put a hand to the cheek where he'd touched me. Want of him—utter relief that he'd accepted my most alarming secret without reservation, and anxiety at the thought of what being bound to him could do to the free life I'd so carefully constructed—warred with the need for him to touch me again. He'd said we were meant. That we belonged together. But was it enough?

"How can you say such a thing?" I was weary of the war that had waged between my head and heart since the morning I'd met him. "We know so little of each other. What is it that you want from me, Jack?" My voice grew hoarse, and my cheeks flamed. "It isn't enough to want to lie with me."

"Aye, it isn't," he said sharply, his cat eyes narrowing dangerously. "I do want you, make no mistake of it. I want to take you into that cabin of yours and run my hands down the length of you until you curve like a bow, and I watch your blue eyes go black. But for some godforsaken reason I want to wake with you, too, hear you read aloud from your books and talk with you of the day's plans.

"What do I want from you?" he growled, his voice rising. "I want everything."

There was a roar in my ears, and I took off at a limping run, stumbling through the snow, heading for the opening in the trees. Just inside the clearing I fell, my knees sinking, hitting the frozen earth beneath. Jack scooped me up by the armpits and held me above the ground, shaking me roughly and shouting in a broken mix of English and Cherokee. "What is the matter with you?" he yelled, his cheeks and the tips of his ears going bright red. "A man tells you a thing like that, and you run like a rabbit! *Ha!* Will you stop acting the lunatic and talk to me?"

"Put me down," I spit out.

"You won't run?"

"I won't," I said, and he dropped me, steadying me at the elbows. The scar at his temple had gone white, and he kept hold of my arms, his grip an iron clamp through the wool. I felt something inside my chest click, the opening of a floodgate.

"Don't you see?" I asked awkwardly. "I'm afraid. This wasn't supposed to happen. I've finally a life of my own, with land of my own and no one to tell me what I can or can't make of it. I want you," I said, gulping against the painful knot in my throat. "But I can't lose my freedom, not now."

"And you think I'd ask you to give it up? From what you know of me, lass, do you truly believe I'd take the Valley from you?"

"I don't know. The only thing I know is how you make me feel, and what if it's a lie? What if I believe that what I feel for you is true, and still I lose everything?"

Jack pulled me to him, holding me tightly against his chest, my face pressed into his throat. "We are meant," I heard him say above me, his chin on the top of my head. "I'll not pressure you, lass—at least I'll try. Look at me," he said, backing away, and I looked up into his face. "The *Yun'wiya* believe that people come together for more than love, for connection and clan and to bring sons and daughters into the world. But I've enough Irish in me to know a bit about destiny, and no matter what we know of each other, there's no fighting it."

"But if I were to marry you, I'd lose all control of the Valley—of my land holdings. I'll be another wife ruled by her husband, like a serf or slave with no power to be anything other than what he proclaims."

Jack threw back his head, looking to the sky and laughing roughly.

"She thinks I'd have her a slave." Then his eyes pinned mine. "You surely know less of me than I of you, Mac. The *Yun'wiya* hold women in much higher esteem than the English, though the knowing of that shouldn't matter. I want nothing of your land, lass. I've plenty of me own."

He released me suddenly and turned sharply, striding back towards the woods.

"Wait, Jack," I called, fear rushing through my bloodstream, a snowball gathering speed. "Can we not be together, without marriage?"

He stopped, his back to me, the broad line of his shoulders stiffening. Suddenly I was grateful not to see his face. Beneath the hanging pine boughs that marked the entrance to the forest he looked like a marble statue: permanent, unyielding and cold. "You'd have me treat you the whore?"

"Certainly not!" I said sharply, but then it occurred to me that in any sort of society, polite or otherwise, that is what he'd be doing. My grandfather's face came swiftly to my mind, and I blanched, imagining his fury and shame, should he find I'd been with a man before marriage.

"Will you court me?" I asked, holding my breath.

His shoulders loosened, and he took the tomahawk from his back, holding it in a soft grip, his hand hanging at his side as he moved the weapon loosely in his palm. "Aye," he said, so softly that I could barely hear the word.

As I stepped forward to go to him he moved suddenly, throwing back his arm and sending the tomahawk hurtling violently towards the forest. It lodged with a *thunk* in the trunk of a young oak. He glanced back over his shoulder, shooting me a narrowed, animal look that sent a chill to the base of my spine.

"You lie to yourself," he growled.

Then he jogged silently into the woods, ripped the tomahawk from the tree and faded into the melting Blue Ridge.

Chapter 17

Spring, 1769

Ridge Runner lifted his musket and turned in one fluid motion, his mark a blur of black movement that lumbered forward through the trees, smashing into the dirt and underbrush. Three crows cawed angrily, splintering out from the woods and into the sky. Suddenly, a fourth crow came crying out of the trees, joining the others. Ridge Runner turned and looked at Jack, speaking in Cherokee. Jack answered, laying a hand on his brother's shoulder and gesturing at the crows, who had settled across the clearing in the grass, ruffling offended feathers.

"What is it?" I asked, whispering. The men looked at me at the same time, almost as if they were just remembering I was there. I cocked an eyebrow, annoyed.

"Four *ka'gu*," Ridge Runner said simply, sliding his musket into the leather sheath on his back and taking his tomahawk in hand. I waited for the explanation, but it didn't come.

"And?" I asked, pursing my lips impatiently. I'd come with them on the hunt because I'd wished to see more of the mountains. Another day of mucking stalls and baking bread with dear but simple Eliza, and I thought I'd lose my mind. Trying to make conversation with the girl was like prying open the locked jaw of an alligator.

But I'd also come on the hunt because they'd arrived at my door at dawn and asked, and because I wanted—damn his eyes—to be with Jack.

"Well, Mac, four is a number sacred to the *Ani-Yun'wiya*. For there are four cardinal points to the earth, four directions in which to go. 'Tis an omen to see birds flying in four."

Ridge Runner studied me, lifting his hairless chin and looking down his long, straight nose. "At first there were three *ka'gu* only, but before we could make some Catholic nonsense of that grouping, the fourth arrived. It proves that in these hills, the gods are *Yun'wiya*."

I couldn't help but smile at him, standing frightfully fierce and handsome, with polite English emerging from his foreign lips. "Ah, I see," I said. "And what if there had been five crows—what then?"

He cocked his head at Jack. "Nothing."

"Then, lass, they'd be but birds—and angry ones at that. We'd best see to the *ya'nu*, brother."

They crossed the clearing, and as they walked the two men began singing, their voices deep and natural, the words guttural and strange to me. I hurried to catch up, completely intrigued—my bookworm's brain thrilling.

> *He! Hayuya'haniwa, hayuya'haniwa, hayuya'haniwa, hayuya'haniwa.*
>
> *Tsistuyi' nehandu'yanu, Tsistuyi nehandu'yanu—Yoho!*
>
> *He! Hayuya'haniwa, hayuya'haniwa, hayuyahaniwa, hayuya'haniwa.*
>
> *Kuwahi nehandu'yanu, Kuwahi nehandu'yanu—Yoho!*
>
> *He! Hayuya'haniwa, hayuya'haniwa, hayuya'haniwa, hayuya'haniwa.*
>
> *Uyaye' nehandu'yanu, Uyaye' nehandu'yanu—Yoho!*
>
> *He! Hayuya'haniwa, hayuya'haniwa, hayuya'haniwa, hayuya'haniwa.*
>
> *Gatekwa' nehandu'yanu, Gatekwa' nehandu'yanu—Yoho!*
>
> *Ule-nu' asehi' tadeya'statakuhi' gu' nage astu'tsiki'.*

They stopped at the downed bear, and Ridge Runner bent at the knees. He shook his head, changing his mind, and slid his tomahawk back into its sheath at his back. When he lifted his legging and reached for the knife there I turned away quickly, the memory of Laughing Crow and the deer flashing behind my eyelids.

But when I heard Ridge Runner speak softly in his language I couldn't help but look back, keeping a hand beneath my nostrils to quell the smell of blood. He had a palm on the bear's head, his fingers disappearing in the black tuft between the ears. Jack stood then, murmuring in Cherokee, and crossed himself. I blinked, startled at what most would consider the unholy melding of the sacred and the pagan.

During a spring dusk in the foothills, when the last of the winter leaves have left the budding trees for the soft death of molted earth and the sun begins to set, it lights the sky like a fire, moving along the ridgelines and down among the naked, black trees as if engulfing all of it in an orange, living glow. At times, it looks to the unknowing traveler like the mountains have caught fire—save for the absence of smoke.

It looked like this now, as we hiked back to the Valley in the coming dark, leading our horses over fallen branches, through shallow creeks and up into the hills. We talked softly as the light faded and the woods began to encircle us like a great, hovering bird.

"Next time, you will shoot," Ridge Runner said to me. He held the lead of his horse, a mare covered in black and white splotches, carefully; the dark shape of the bear made the equine seem an Egyptian camel with an overgrown hump.

"I don't know about that," I said, raising my eyebrows and tugging on Fire Eater's lead, urging him up a slippery spot in the icy leaves. "I think I'd have a difficult time killing anything, much less a defenseless creature."

Jack laughed. "Defenseless?" He shook his head in denial. "Then it's sure you've never had to get around a sow and her cubs. Besides, lass—who's to bring the meat to the table for you, should you choose never to lift a musket of your own?"

"You are, *Wa'ya*," Ridge Runner interjected. "Surely you know that."

I broke from his gaze, looking back up at Ridge Runner. It was like walking between two small, steadily moving mountains. "What was that the two of you were singing, back in the meadow near the river?"

"Ah, well, we were a bit late about it, the bear having revealed himself a mite suddenly, but it's a song the *Yun'wiya'* hunter sings to urge the bears to him. You call to them in their dens in the four mountains: *Tsistu'yi*, *Kuwa'hi*, *Uya'ye*, and *Gate'kwahi*. So that's what we were about, see."

"I see," I said, and though it seemed a bit strange, I couldn't shake from myself the feeling that when these men had stood over the dead animal murmuring words in a language I could not understand, they were apologizing.

Tomassee Knob hulked in the distance, just visible in the dark. We followed the creek from the south up into the Valley, entering from the Keowee Path at the bottom of the settlement. Small fires burned out in front of two of the cabins. At times, some of my homesteaders wished for familial solitude, instead of the roaring of the community fire pit that lay in the center of the middle pasture. It was a notion I completely understood, being a bit of a hermit myself.

As we passed the skeleton of the Wheeler cabin I looked around, wondering where Joseph and Meg had decided to take the night.

"The holy man and his daughter—they're with the Englishman," Jack said, in that uncanny way he had of reading my thoughts. "It's sorry I am for the two gentlemen, stuck all night in a cabin with that girl. She'll talk until your ears shrivel up from the sound."

Ridge Runner grunted in agreement. I chuckled, remembering how Meg had pestered the two men that morning as we'd made our way down the valley, with a thousand different questions about Cherokee life. It wasn't until we'd reached the head of the path that she'd stopped, given us a jaunty wave, and turned back.

"She's a good girl," I said. "Children are wonderful, aren't they—free of all prejudice and misapprehension."

"I'm beginning to wish she were afraid of me, like most *un'ega*," Ridge Runner murmured.

"Aye, but she's fearless." Jack patted his brother on the shoulder in companionable male support.

We led the horses to the meat house, and Jack and Ridge Runner hefted the huge bear onto the ground, dragging it into the small building for cleaning. I'd have to be sure they didn't give me the whole of it, I thought. They were a generous pair, and usually brought whole elks, deer and turkeys down to the valley if they'd been hunting. This generosity was something I'd come to expect among the Cherokee: whenever a hunting party or scout traveled through the Valley they always came with gifts of meat, fruit or grain.

But Jack and Ridge Runner would surely need some of the bear for themselves—the beast was so huge it could feed the Valley for weeks. And at this time of year, red meat could still be hard to come by. According to the two men, it was great luck to have found a bear wandering the woods today, when normally sows stayed close to their dens, nursing cubs to waking after a winter's sleep.

I dropped Fire Eater's lead and scratched his neck beneath the short, black mane. "Stay a moment, friend," I whispered, then went to the doorway of the meat house, meaning to tell Jack and Ridge Runner to come up to my cabin for coffee or supper before leaving, if that's what they planned to do.

At the rough doorframe I caught again the iron whiff of blood, and saw in front of me—instead of meat hanging to dry from the rafters—a Lowcountry field awash in red.

There were hundreds of them, some dressed in homespun cotton and others in the bold red and white of British Regulars, lying strewn across the marshy field. A cannon boomed, and a wicked ball from it went tumbling into a sea of limbs. The screaming—there was no end to it. And the boy who picked up the flag, tattered but bearing stars and crudely sewn stripes, watched a mounted officer lean down before him, the deadly end of a bayonet entering his eye socket.

I covered my right eye, screaming. Hands gripped my arms, shaking me. I pushed at them, rolling in the dirt. Through cracked eyelids I watched a man bend over me. It seemed to be Jack, but the vision wavered, and instead it was a raven-haired man in a crooked wig and an officer's green and gold-trimmed coat, his eyes murderously blank.

I sucked in air and crawled backwards like a crab. My boots slipped in the blood on the floor. As I brought myself to a crouch the hands were there again, and I flung myself from them, cracking my head into something solid.

The world went black.

I opened my eyes to see Jack and Ridge Runner at the foot of the bed, arguing in Cherokee. Ridge Runner gesticulated wildly, his black eyes narrowed. Jack ran a hand through his hair, responding curtly and passing his other hand through the air as if he were cutting it, then crossing his arms over his chest. The door of the cabin flew open and light from outside filled the room, the sight searing my pupils like a branding iron. I closed my eyes tightly, covering them with a clammy hand. "For God's sake," I said, my voice scratchy, propriety out the window.

"Oh, now, Miss Quinn, you shouldn't be taking the Lord's name in vain, no matter how poorly you feel."

I squinted warily, and since the killing light had ceased I opened them entirely. Abigail Simons stood beside me with a cup of steaming tea in her hands. "There now, let's have you sit up and drink."

It was the most she'd ever spoken to me. I acquiesced without thinking and sat up against the wall behind me, the bottom edge of the window frame digging into my back. "Thank you," I murmured, taking the mug and sipping cautiously. Jack and Ridge Runner had stopped talking, and they watched me warily. I cleared my throat, but before I could speak Abigail turned politely to them.

"Thank you for carrying Miss MacFadden up the hill," she said quietly. "I do think she needs her rest, though."

Jack's eyes met mine, and I could tell he was concerned, and that he wanted to ask about the episode and what I'd seen. But he nodded politely at Abigail, and he and Ridge Runner turned, exiting swiftly out onto the porch. As the door opened and closed I grimaced at the light, but set the cup on the bedside table, studying the one person in the settlement that I knew least.

"Thank you, Abigail. I appreciate your help, but I'll be fine in a moment. I know you may need to get back to your family."

"Samuel can surely handle the boys for one night," she answered, pulling the quilt up from my feet and settling it around my waist like a nursemaid.

"One night!" I swung my feet to the side of the bed, flinging back the quilt. Stars danced in front of my eyes, and I pressed my hands into the bed to steady myself.

"You must lie back, dear," she said, coming and lifting the quilt, helping me get my legs back beneath it. "You hit your head yesterday evening, when you came back from hunting with those men. They stayed outside on the porch all night long. I just couldn't let them in, you being unmarried and them not being kin and Indians to boot."

"I can't believe that I was unconscious all night," I murmured.

"You tossed and turned like you were plagued by demons," she answered, just as softly, and went to stoke the fire. "I hope you're not troubled."

I resisted the urge to snort, not wanting this kind woman to think I was laughing at her. The truth was, I'd been plagued by the Sight my entire life, and it was nothing if not troublesome. A memory of the time I'd been nine, and had told Miss Picard that her husband had been visiting a bawdy house on the harbor, flitted through my mind. The old woman had taken a strap to my hand; it had stung ferociously and for days. Naji's wife, Elsa, had been one of our house slaves at the time, and she'd sat at my bedside for several nights, pressing a cool cloth to my blistered palm.

"I'm not troubled, no," I lied, examining Abigail's back as she tended to the fire. She was frightfully skinny, like most frontier women, and her hair was hidden beneath a tight cotton bonnet, although I'd seen tendrils of it around her face and knew it to be red, just a shade duller than her eldest son's. "I must have tripped and hit my head. I'm sorry for taking you from your family, madam."

She turned from the crackling hearth, folding her hands at her waist. "You'd do the same for me," she said simply, picking a blanket from the back of a chair and wrapping it around her shoulders. "You rest now, and I'll sit here a bit longer, just to be sure." She sat gracefully in the rickety chair, her back to me.

A thought came to me then, and I hesitated, but spoke: "Abigail, why did you let Jack and Ridge Runner come inside the cabin? I know how you feel about the Cherokee."

She didn't turn to look at me, keeping her face focused on the glowing coals. "He's a good man, Mr. Wolf. And I can see the way he looks at you. The other—well, there's been a rabbit or a deer sometimes at our doorstep this winter, and I know he brought it." She paused, clearing her throat. "He's kind to Micah."

We sat in silence for the rest of the afternoon. She brought me broth at dinner, watching me closely to be sure that my hands were steady as I held the spoon to my lips. As she bent over me, straightening the covers or putting a hand to my forehead to check for fever, I studied the deep lines that spidered out from the corners of her eyes and considered the many miles this woman had traveled.

"What have you seen, lass?"

Jack turned from the hearth, keeping one hand braced on the rough-hewn mantle. His voice was flat and serious. Ridge Runner sat upon the floor, his legs crossed and his back to my door, studying me with dark, expressionless eyes as he repeatedly sheathed and unsheathed the knife that lay across his lap.

I considered feigning exhaustion, knowing that if I did they would leave off questioning until tomorrow, however reluctantly. But they'd risked Abigail's ire and the disapproval of the settlement to be here with me now. I pulled the blanket closer to my chin, crossing my arms beneath the fabric and clutching my elbows for warmth. "I suppose you know now, about the visions," I said quietly, my eyes on Ridge Runner. He nodded.

"Aye, I told him. Mayhap I shouldna," Jack muttered, his accent thickening, "but you called out a name in your fit, one we both knew. It shocked us."

"A name?"

"Tarleton," Ridge Runner said softly, moving silently to his feet. He slid the knife into the top of his left boot.

I shook my head to clear it. "I don't know who that is. But I say things sometimes, when I see things. It could very well mean nothing." They glanced at each other, and I cleared my throat. "Who is this Tarleton?"

Ridge Runner moved to the window, brushed back the burlap and peered outside. "Banastre Tarleton. He's an Englishman of the first blood, an officer of the Crown. We knew him at Fort Wilderness, met him there and in Charlestown once, before the Cherokee Wars."

"He's a right bastard, that one," Jack said. "We just wondered what you might know of him, and why you would've called his name like that when you were out o' sorts. If he means nothing to you, then all right."

Perplexed, I made a move to speak, but Jack cut me off, crossing the room and squatting beside my bed, his hands hanging comfortably from his knees. "Are you well then, Mac?"

"I'm fine, really."

"Then can you tell us about what you've seen?"

I described the scene in as much detail as I could, recalling the battle between British regulars and what looked to be continental troops—men in plain, country dress, wearing no uniforms of any one sort. I told them of the tattered flag bearing stars and stripes, and of the boy who'd been wounded, and who may have been killed by the man they called Tarleton's bayonet.

"Can you tell when this battle will take place?" Ridge Runner asked.

I shook my head. "No, I never can—not unless someone speaks of the date in the vision. But that rarely happens. I can only guess that what I saw will happen as war begins with England, when those loyal to the King and those rebelling against him finally take up arms." I cleared my throat. "What are you really seeking, both of you? Because it seems to me I'm not telling you anything you want to hear."

Jack stretched out a hand from his frog-like position next to my bed, fingered the crochet edge of my quilt. His mouth quirked up at one corner. "Aye, well. The *Ani'Yun'wiya* must decide who to trust."

"Which devil to take," Ridge Runner said softly, so much so I almost didn't hear him.

It came to me suddenly. "You are employed by the Crown," I said to Jack.

"Aye, when I want to be. They've no hold on my loyalties, lass." When I breathed a sigh of relief he stood, looking down at me darkly, his eyes slanting at the corners. "But don't you be thinking I'm eager to side with land-hungry colonists, either." He ran a hand through mussed hair, tugging at the braid there. "Did you see the Cherokee in your dream, Mac? Any red men at all?"

"No."

"It is an omen," Ridge Runner said, dropping the curtain and turning from the window. He took his musket from the doorway and slid it into the sheath on his back. "If you see anything of us, of our people, we should know." He dipped his chin curtly at Jack and me, said something in quick Cherokee.

"I'll be but a moment," Jack responded in English, and Ridge Runner pulled the door shut behind him. When we were alone he went to the hearth and kicked coals over the fire with his boot. Then he, too, went to the door, taking his own long musket—longer than Ridge Runner's, I'd noticed—and sliding it onto his back. "I'm glad you're well," he said.

I moved my arms from beneath the quilt, resting my hands in my lap and clasping my hands nervously. "I haven't run your brother off, have I?"

Jack shook his head, a slow smile forming. "No, he's *Yun'wiya*. He believes when a woman sees. You've got us both thinking, is all—and truth be told, worried of what's to come."

"I'm for liberty, Jack."

He cocked his head, pulled open the heavy door easily. A cold wind blew in from the dark, fanning the coals and starting a spark. I shivered beneath my shift.

"I know," he said.

I woke with a start, clipping my forehead on the underside of the windowsill behind my head. Thunder boomed and rolled across the ridges, echoing down into the valley like some parting epithet from an angry god. The cabin was shaking with the tremors, I realized as I rubbed the tender spot.

May was a capricious month in the mountains, or so I'd learned. We'd had days warm with the promise of summer, and I'd noticed upshoots of new green beneath the dark winter overcoat that the Blue Ridge seemed so intent on shedding. This was but one of the many big storms we'd had since the middle of February, and Keowee Valley was flooded with rain, Tomassee Creek swelling and overflowing its banks, making a soppy marsh out of the lower pastures.

I relished a good storm. Even in Charlestown, before we left the peninsula for summer on the Santee, I'd reveled in the lusty danger of it whilst others had battened down their homes, boarding up windows and cursing over the flooding on King Street that damaged the shopkeepers' goods.

Grandfather took to calling me a "wee stramash" during those wind-tossed weeks, but he left the top floor window near my room unboarded as long as possible, so that I could sit there and watch the tips of the ships' masts careen wildly in the harbor. Though the storms themselves held real danger and oftimes great destruction, I could not fight the hot urge in my belly to at least watch—if not rush out into their midsts.

I turned, clutching the quilt to my chest as the cold air reached into my sleeping gown, and pulled back the burlap curtain covering the window. Lightning flashed, and I could see through the downpour the faint, gray outline of the Blue Ridge. The storm had settled into our valley, I thought, snuggling back down into the bed, a bit guilty about the rush of pleasure I felt at not having to wake so early to tend to the animals.

The cabin was cold, for spring mornings and evenings here still held the surprising chill of late winter, though the days were increasingly warm. I looked longingly at the fireplace, arching an eyebrow at the splat of rain on the stones. So much for a morning fire, I thought. Instead, I sat up again and wrapped the quilt about me, fumbling at the cherry bedside table until I was able to light my lamp there.

The lamp lit the room with a soft, buttery glow, edging out the darkness. I lugged one of my precious copies of *Plays by William Shakespeare* from beneath the bed and onto my lap, smoothing a hand over the worn cover. Grandfather had given me the volumes before I left—all six of them—and I treasured them as though they were the Queen's own jewels. I traced my fingers over the words on the cover: *Alexander Pope, editor, London, 1625*. I considered choosing another volume, for certainly it was a morning for the windswept magic of *The Tempest*. But I'd begun *Hamlet* again only a few nights before, and was unable to part with the prince's tortured soul just yet. I imagined him pacing among the shelves of his dead father's library, muttering beneath his breath, more wild with knowledge than madness.

I flipped open the book and ran a gentle hand along the weathered leather binding, slipping the sliver of birch I used as marker from its place and setting it on the other pillow. I found where I'd left off, at the end of Act One, and began to read, whispering the words aloud:

> *Horatio: These are but wild and whirling words, my lord.*
>
> *Hamlet: I am sorry they offend you, heartily; Yes, faith, heartily.*
>
> *Horatio: There's no offense, my lord.*
>
> *Hamlet: Yes, by Saint Patrick, but there is, Horatio, And much offense too. Touching this vision here, It is an honest ghost, that let me tell you. For your desire to know what is between us, O'ermaster 't as you may. And now, good friends, As you are friends, scholars, and soldiers, Give me one poor request.*
>
> *Horatio: What is 't, my lord? We will.*
>
> *Hamlet: Never make known what you have seen tonight.*

Something triggered in the back of my mind, and I shut the book over my hand, cocking my head to listen. There it was—a faint knock at my door. I reached for the piece of birch bark and slipped it between the pages, setting the old book aside. Then I slid from the bed, smoothing back my hair as I walked to the door, lifting the greatcoat from the back of the rocking chair and pulling it around me.

"A moment," I called, releasing the latch.

I cracked the door and peered out, careful not to show anything but my face in case one of the men had come with a concern. The rain pelted the porch roof, pouring down over the sides and onto the stoop in sheets. Meg Wheeler stood before me, sopping wet.

"Good morning, miss," she shouted cheerily above the din.

"Good heavens, you're soaked," I said, reaching out for the cuff of her sleeve and pulling her inside. I heaved the door shut with my hip and whipped the coat from my shoulders, settling it around her. "Let's get you out of these clothes."

"May I visit with you, Miss MacFadden? Papa said I must be sure you answer truthfully, because you're an importantly busy lady."

I reached out and snatched the bonnet from her head, draping it over the back of a chair.

"Oh, I'm frightfully busy this morning, can't you see?" I answered, chuckling. "I've not even started a fire yet." I rubbed her arms briskly and bent to look her in the eyes. She watched me guilelessly, brown eyes blinking above freckled cheeks.

"Sit here, and I'll try to light one," I said. "And please, Meg, you may call me Quinn."

"Quinn," she murmured, testing it.

I walked to the hearth and took the poker, pushing fruitlessly at the coals. They were hopelessly wet, and I could not remember if I'd asked Micah to leave fresh kindling on the porch. I stood and turned to the girl, shrugging. "Well, it looks like we're out of luck, as my grandfather would say. I guess we're just going to have to snuggle up in the bed, and you're going to have to listen to me read."

Her eyes went wide, and she grinned broadly. "You have books?"

"Do I have books?" I said in mock disbelief. "I have more books than I know what to do with. And I hear from Lord Harris that you're quite the reader yourself, so come now—let's get you into dry clothes."

I shuffled through the chest of drawers, pulling out one of my old sleeping gowns. Together, we tugged the wet dress over her head. I handed her the dry gown and hung the other on a hat hook by the door. Thunder boomed overhead, shaking the cabin in its violence. Both of us jumped, and Meg—for all her childish confidence—looked frightened. I lay a hand on her shoulder and turned her toward the bed.

"That's it," I said, "into bed."

She grinned wide, then ran to the bed, leaping onto it and scooting over to the far side. I climbed in beside her and took the book in hand, settling back against the pillow. Rain pattered against the burlap drawn over the window behind our heads, and I bent down, pulling the quilt up around us.

"What are you reading?" She asked, folding her hands in her lap like a schoolgirl.

"It's a play about a man who must avenge his father's murder. And it's set in snowy Denmark, amidst castles and graveyards and armed guards."

"Lovely," she said succinctly. "Will you read aloud?"

"Certainly," I answered. But something in her expression had me curious. Another boom sounded, this time from farther away. The lamplight flickered faintly. "Meg, do you know about William Shakespeare?"

She nodded solemnly. "Oh, yes, my father knows him."

"Do you know of *Hamlet*, too?"

With her answer I was once again taken aback by the intelligence in her eyes, and knew with complete certainty that we'd begun a wonderful friendship.

"'Words, words, words,'" she quoted, grinning.

Chapter 18

The MacFadden Settlement
May, 1769

Quincy, the voice whispered.

Smoke and fog hovered in a grassy vale between two walls of tall trees, an otherworldly glow lighting molecules in the air. There was the muffled pop of a musket and a round of grapeshot, then a shout from the eastern line of oaks and pines. A young man, no older than fourteen, lifted his bloodied forehead from behind the safety of a felled oak.

Had he hit him? Had he killed the dark man, the one who wore blue paint like a gash across his face—like some ancient devil?

The boy sucked in breath, and along with it the smell of rotten leaves and undergrowth, and the halting tang of blood. He raised his wounded head higher, but the morning had silenced after his shot, and the smoke and fog sat languidly in the air. He felt a sudden prickle at his nape and looked up. Above him stood the painted man, his dark eyes bright above the blue slashed across his cheekbones. The blunt stock of a musket filled the boy's vision, and all went black.

I sat abruptly in bed, hands gripping the sheets at my sides. I was sweating—I'd flung the muslin blanket to the foot of the bed. I swung myself around the side so that my bare feet brushed the wooden floor. There, I thought: permanence. I steadied myself enough to pour water from the china pitcher to cup. But as I lifted it to my mouth I felt a name on my lips—Jack!

The cup splintered on the wooden floor, and I sank back onto the bed, lifting my feet and curling my toes around the frame. My entire body chilled, as if the season had lifted in no more than a moment, and all was winter.

It was Jack, I was sure of it. Though surely he was hunting in the mountains, safe with Ridge Runner. Yet I knew those wild eyes as if they were my own.

"Where was he?" I murmured aloud, hugging my knees, my chin digging into the bone. A forest near the city? Some wooded countryside? And painted like a warrior—albeit, an ancient Celtic warrior.

I slid from the bed and took a step across the floor, intent on my quill and parchment. Pain shot up through my left foot, and I hopped gingerly, grimacing as I picked a china shard from the pad of my big toe. I hobbled to the chest and ripped a small strip from the old blanket I kept there, tying it tightly around the wound. But the pain was only a pulsing reminder of the task at hand: I had to find out what was happening in Charlestown. I had to know if the war I'd been dreaming of had begun.

My eyes lit on the desk beside the curtainless window, and as I watched fingers of pink light reach up from behind the Blue Ridge I limped toward my parchment, and Grandfather.

Spring had burst upon the Blue Ridge like a verdant autumn. Instead of the warm hues of fall, every shade of green imaginable filled the forests and valleys in a testament to new life. The trees seemed to beam with the palest, purest of the color. And sometimes, but only in direct sunlight, the mountains shed their mystical blue coat, opting for patchworked shades of emerald. Deep in the woods, dogwood trees bloomed in quiet, the white petals with their blooded hearts opening to the dark.

I walked along Tomassee Creek, setting one foot carefully in front of the other, toe to heel, as Ridge Runner had taught me. I picked my way gingerly through a row of cane, stopping to tie my skirts before hiking up through the woods.

I loved following the creek—even more so, I luxuriated in being alone, in tracking the water up into the hills without a soul to guide me or speak to me. Truth be told, I felt a quiet kinship to the forest, and though oft times I still felt fear at the remembrance of my run-in with the Creek on the Knob, I was comfortable among the trees. Besides, I'd learned my lesson then, and it was not one I'd soon forget. I'd left word of where I'd be walking with Hosa.

At a rocky island in the creek I stopped on the far bank and refilled my skin with water, staying crouched to relace grungy boots. At that moment, the underbrush on the island rustled, and three deer leapt across to the other side, sprinting off through the woods. Startled, I stayed low to catch my breath.

The tiny hairs rose on my arms, and I lifted my eyes again to the fork in the creek. There, in the shadows between mountain laurel, was a wolf. It stood with preternatural stillness, black and sleek, its dark gaze centered on the brush where the deer had fled. I braced my hands on my knees and prayed that it would slip back into the woods without noticing me. *Please*, I thought silently, *go away. I'd be a foul-tasting meal.*

The wolf lowered its burly head and sniffed the ground, then turned and looked directly at me. My heart beat so loudly against my chest that I was sure the wolf could see it thudding through the fabric of my dress. It opened its jaws.

Owen, it said.

I blinked, and the wolf took a flying leap off across the creek, disappearing into the trees.

It wasn't until I was running back down the path towards the settlement that I realized it had been the voice in my head, and not the wolf, that had called my cousin's name.

The north fields were empty. I raced across them, sprinting through rows of planted strawberries. The fields were empty—something was wrong. Breathing heavily, I skirted the back end of the barn and hurried past the pen and up the hill to my cabin, untying the rope that held my skirts. They flapped against my legs in the rush.

There, standing in the dirt before my cabin were Jack, Ridge Runner, Lord Harris, and a stranger, his back to me. Hovering at a distance was everyone from our settlement: the O'Hares, the Simonses, Hosa, and the Wheelers. They were a blur of faces as I waved my arms ridiculously, fear lighting my voice. "Jack!"

He turned, as did the other men. The stranger wore a travel-worn gentleman's suit: fawn breeches and shirt opened to the neck, tricorn atop his auburn head. His face lit in a grin at the sight of me, and I felt the air leave my chest. "Owen!" I shouted, flinging myself into his open arms. He lifted me off the ground, spinning me in a circle.

"Quincy," he said gruffly against my hair. "You haven't changed." He set me down, and I cupped his face in my hands, surprised to find tears filling my eyes.

"You look wonderful," I said. "I can't believe you're here. Why are you here so soon? Grandfather—is there something the matter?"

Owen laughed, taking my hand in his. "Slow down, coz. I'll answer you straightaway," he said, bending to whisper in my ear. "But I'd rather do it without the whole of the settlement to hear my business."

"Of course." I turned to those closest, meeting Jack's green eyes. "You all remember my cousin, Owen Scott, Esquire, of Charlestown."

Lord Harris stepped forward, extending a hand to Owen, who grasped it. "Welcome back, Scott. Do you have news of the discontent in New

England, then?"

"Is it true the British navy's anchored in New York harbor?" Father Wheeler said.

I lay a hand on Owen's arm, and gave him time to speak with the homesteaders he'd come to know in his earlier convalescence here. Jack watched me silently, and I wondered what he was thinking.

"Enough," I finally said, hooking my arm through Owen's. "You must be exhausted—come into the cabin, and I'll fetch you something to drink."

As we turned, Owen stopped, looking back at Jack. "Wolf, would you join us?"

Jack inclined his head, said something in Cherokee to Ridge Runner, and followed us into the cabin. I walked immediately to the cabinet and took three cups from the top shelf. I poured the men water, myself a cup of cool tea. Owen watched, amused, as I handed them their cups. "You don't take the tea either, Wolf?"

Jack leaned against the windowsill on the far side of the room, shook his head. "No, wouldn't drink anything English if they offered gold bullion. You?"

"No—I'm no friend of the English, though I practice law in a colony much ruled by the practice. Quinn." He took my hand in his, leading me to a chair and taking the rocker across from me. "How are you, then? You seem ruddy with the sun, and your hair has lightened so. It suits you. Have you been riding?" he asked, taking off his hat and hooking it over the back of the rocking chair.

Jack cleared his throat, and we turned to him. Finally, he was smiling. "She rides," he said, looking at Owen, his green eyes direct. "She rides like a hellion. Though I assume you might be the cause of that, aye?"

"No, 'twas always Quincy," Owen answered. "She's been a mighty horsewoman since we were children. Do you remember racing the Middleton twins at midnight down Meeting Street? You wore that old hat of mine, with your hair tucked up so they thought it was I. Zounds, they were angry when they found they'd been bested by a girl!"

"Irving broke his crop against one of the columns at Saint Michael's." I shook my head at the memory. "He was forbidden to ride his horse for the whole of the summer."

Owen and I laughed together, quieting comfortably. Jack watched us over the rim of his cup. Finally, I asked, "Owen, why are you here?"

My cousin rocked back in the chair and rubbed a hand across his forehead, sending up an unruly cowlick. His gray eyes grew serious. He glanced between Jack and me. "I wanted to see you."

"Owen," I laughed, baffled, love for him softening my words. "I wanted to see you, too. But that is not why you've traveled these hundreds of miles so soon after having left us in the first place. Tell me."

"Wolf, I asked you to sit with us because I know you've become important to Quinn," he said to Jack, off-putting my request. "I can see that she trusts you."

Jack shifted, and I looked out the window, uncomfortable. No matter how entangled I'd become with the man, I wasn't quite ready to give voice to feeling.

"War is coming, *mo ghradh*," Owen said quietly, the Gaelic endearment bringing a knot to my throat. "It may not be for months, or for years—but it will happen. I have seen it, and I know you have as well. I am for America, for a united country free from England. And I will fight, if it comes to that . . . when it comes to that."

I stood quickly, the memory of my dreams a flash of pain behind my eyes: dreams I now knew he must have been having too, of revolution and war. I walked to the window and looked out, knowing what Owen would say, unwilling to consider the dreaded possibility of his words.

"Quincy, look at me, please."

"Mac, all will be well, lass." It was Jack's golden voice, low and comforting, that gave me the strength to turn from the safety of the outer world.

"Quincy," Owen said again, and his voice was thick with the years we'd shared. "I need to send a woman to you, someone for whom I care deeply. I'm asking you to watch over her after the war begins."

I knew what he was telling me, that this was a woman he loved, a woman he planned to marry. But what frightened me more than talk of war was the solemn acceptance in Owen's eyes—as if he'd seen his own fate, his own death, and too readily believed it. "You know I'll keep safe what's yours," I told Owen, crossing to take his hands in mine. "I'll love her like she's my own flesh and blood, no matter what." I bent and kissed his hair. "But it won't come to that. The dreams could be wrong. They have been before."

"And what if they're not? You know as well as I do that there will one day be war between the Colonies and England," he said, squeezing my hands. "And the fight will continue here, in South Carolina. For she is a rich colony, much beloved by England. The slave trade alone brings wealth to King George, and to all the aristocracy—keeps them clothed in fine linens and cotton. I see it in my work every day. You do not know how the Cherokee will side, Quinn. The frontier could be more chaotic than it already is."

"Why would you send her here if you believe this place to be so dangerous?"

"Because I think it will be a long while before the fight reaches the frontier. And until then, this may be the safest place for the both of you."

"Pardon me," Jack said politely, his eyes on Owen, the unique lilt in his voice always stronger when frustrated, "but I'm lost, and the two of you seem to be speaking in code. What is it you're asking of the lass?"

Owen and I looked at each other and he nodded imperceptibly. I focused on Jack, clearing my throat. "Owen wants me to watch over his wife, should war begin. He wants her to come here to live, because he believes that he will die."

Jack looked at us both as if we'd each sprouted another head. "His wife? You never mentioned a wife, man. You mean to say you've gone and married in the months since you left us?"

"I've met someone in Charlestown. She's visiting friends, and we're courting. But she's from Boston, originally, and soon she'll be return there." Owen said. "We've not married yet." But when he looked back to me I saw it in his eyes.

"Not yet," I murmured. "But you will."

"What is she like, Owen, this woman you love?" I asked. We walked through the highest pasture and stopped at the crest. A warm wind blew in from the south, and new spring grass brushed the backs of our knees. In the distance, two vultures followed an updraft high above the Blue Ridge.

"It's beautiful as I remember," he said, patting the arm I'd wound companionably through the crook of his elbow. "Did you think it would be like this?"

"Owen," I grumbled, wanting to know more about my new cousin to be, irritated at the change of subject. He turned to me and searched my eyes.

"Did you? Did you know that the mountains would be as blue, or the rivers as clear?"

"No," I said, giving in, cocking my head thoughtfully. "I'd read that the frontier was wild, and had been told repeatedly by Grandfather just how dangerous. But this—this was nothing I could have conjured from my books. It's the solitude that surprises me most. Waking to the sound of insects, knowing that a traveler may not cross our Valley for months on end . . . it's just so different. But I suppose I don't have to tell you that."

"I honestly don't know if I could do it again," he said, looking back at the mountains. "Every day the *South Carolina Gazette* tells of some horrific Indian uprising in the backcountry, here or in New England, and it nearly brings me to my knees. The memory of it all, I mean." He took a breath, his eyes clearing. "With all you know, aren't you frightened? You know little of the Cherokee, nor they you."

"I have been frightened, you know that," I said. "Asking for land from

Little Carpenter was absolutely terrifying. And still I'm worried every time one of the horses makes a sound at night that we're being raided by the Creek, though it's usually just an opossum, or a bear foraging in the grain."

"A bear!" Owen laughed, dropping my arm. "Listen to you, so calm as if it were an everyday occurrence."

I grinned up at him, enjoying the moment. "Have you forgotten? Some days it is. But really, coz, I think I'd much prefer being frightened some nights on the frontier than bored and dull in Charlestown. Present company notwithstanding." I paused, bending to pick up a rock and toss it towards the woods. "I am wholly myself here, Owen. 'Tis an incredible blessing not to be harrumphed over by the grand dames when I walk about barefoot, or looked at as though I were a leper when I reveal that I'm able to read Greek."

"No one has looked askance when you've read your Greek?" He lifted an eyebrow at me.

"All right," I admitted, brushing my hands off on my skirts. "So I haven't had the chance to reveal that particular talent yet, between the caring for my wounded oaf of a cousin, the harvesting of apples and strawberries, and the milking and fishing. But I think I could, if I wanted to."

"I couldn't risk writing you," he said. "I've seen in my dreams that when war comes, any missive considered suspicious could be captured by the Crown. The penalty for this will be treason. The dreams—they're maddeningly jumbled, and I don't know when the revolution will start. That's why I came myself."

"I know." I paused, studying him. There wasn't much else to be said. War would come no matter what we wanted, or what we saw in our peripatetic dreams. "You look well, you know. City life agrees with you, and I never thought it would again."

We stood in the comfortable silence of long friends, watching the afternoon sun begin its slow descent behind the hills. Two deer walked out of the forest at the corner of the pasture, took a look around, then vanished into the trees.

"She's taller than you," he said suddenly. "And she has brown hair. Her eyes are brown, too, like walnuts. And there's a dash of freckles that runs right 'cross her nose, and she doesn't care to cover them." He looked at me again. "She's no bluestocking like you, but she reads well and loves the theatre. And I am going to marry her, though she doesn't know it yet."

"She sounds lovely," I said. "But you've not told me her name."

"Rebekah—Rebekah Bradstreet. Scott soon, of course."

"Rebekah," I repeated softly, reaching for his arm. "I'll love her, Owen, I know it."

144

Part III

The Cherokee Country

"I am more and more convinced that man is a dangerous creature."
—*Abigail Adams*

"The will to do, the soul to dare."
—*Sir Walter Scott*

Chapter 19

Keowee Town
Late May, 1769

Shouts echoed out against the hillside, the crack of sticks and the thud of bodies knocking into one another filling the morning air. I stood with Micah and his younger brother, Sam, before a field of half-naked men—mostly Cherokee—who were tossing about a small ball and chasing after it, tackling each other in the process.

Jack, Lord Harris, and Owen were the only white men in the group; the two Englishmen's pale skin stood out like a beacon among the brown. Jack, who was as tawny as the Indians, would have melded into the crowd if not for his flash of yellow hair. I could not take my eyes from the slick play of muscles in his back, bunching as he leapt into the air, flinging his racket with the ball flying toward Ridge Runner. His arms and legs held long scratches, like most of the other men, made by Keowee Town's medicine man before that village's team had approached the playing field.

"I've never seen a game like this," Micah said, his eleven year-old eyes wide with awe. "What's it called, Quinn?"

"Well, I'm unsure if I'm pronouncing it correctly, but according to Ridge Runner it's *anesta*—the Cherokee call it 'little brother of war.'"

Shouts came from the field as Ridge Runner charged between two posts about ten feet apart at the far end of the field, the ball tucked in the small, hemp-woven cup at the end of a long birch stick. He raised his arms and yelled, chest gleaming with red paint. The man who had been chasing him trotted back towards his team, tossing an insult over his shoulder.

"Looks better than war," Micah muttered, scuffing a boot in the grass.

I rubbed a hand over his chestnut-colored hair, making it stand on end.

He put a hand on his hair in childish annoyance, casting a look at his tow-headed little brother to make sure he hadn't seen. I grinned. "Go on," I said. "Go to the river. But only up to your ankles—your mother would have my head if you were swept down to Keowee Town. The people there might mistake you for strange fish and fry you both for dinner."

He smiled widely and took off through the crowd of Cherokee who had gathered to watch the game. Suddenly, I heard screams. I looked back at the action to find an Indian with a shaved head tearing towards me, his racket held high above him. A hand jerked me aside, and I watched as a group of players tumbled upon each other in a pile where I'd been standing. Finally, one scrambled out, ball in hand, and they raced back to the field.

Beside me stood a stout old Cherokee woman, dressed in a simple calico shirt and skirt and moccasins, clothing I'd come to recognize as popular among the Indian women. Blinding white hair hung to her waist; her face was deeply lined. She shook her head at me and gestured to the game, saying something unintelligible.

"Oh, it was you. Thank you. *Wado*," I said.

She smiled then, showing her teeth, and handed me a piece of cooked pheasant wrapped in a small cloth. I took it and nodded, biting gently into the meat.

We stood together for the rest of the game, the old woman and I. By the time the sun hung low over the trees and the mosquitoes buzzed incessantly, we'd discovered each other's name. She was Stands Alone, and from her harried pointing at the team of men from Estatoe, I figured a citizen of that upriver village. She spoke continually in Cherokee, and as she did I'd hold out my hands in confusion, completely lost. But she was good company, there in that crowd of strangers who watched me from afar.

At the end of the game the teams moved in unison to the river, where the medicine men from Keowee Town and Estatoe said prayers over the game and the players. Then the men "went to the water," as the Cherokee called it, and cleansed themselves.

I turned away from the sight of water sluicing over the hard curves of Jack's chest and into the opening of his breechclout, sliding down his big thighs. Seeing him there, half-naked and beautiful, sent heat into the pit of my belly. When I turned back I saw that he was staring straight at me in the coming dark, his eyes flashing like a panther's in the sinking sun.

Owen left us for the second time not two weeks later. With a full skin of water from Tomassee Creek, two deer pelts for bartering, bread and cheese, an eagle's feather for Naji and several letters to Grandfather, he headed down the dirt trail toward Keowee Town. I stood at the top of the south pasture and watched him until he disappeared into the thick forest, a tiny figure atop a toy horse. By leaving, he'd carved a small hole in the area of my chest that protected my heart. As we'd parted I felt air whistle through the space, cold with the fear that he would never return.

Jack stepped up beside me, hands in the pockets of his thin deerskin leggings. A cool wind that promised rain funneled down through the valley, blowing long hair around his shoulders. I turned my eyes from the dark opening of the forest where Owen no longer was and studied the strong line of Jack's face, my fingers itching to touch the thin scar that ran from the outer corner of his right eye into his tawny hair.

"Tomorrow I'm heading out for the Overhill Towns, to visit my family," he said. "Ridge Runner has gone ahead and will be there waiting, with new horses and guns." He turned his head, the corners of his mouth quirking up in a half-smile. "Would you go with me, then?"

"Go with you?" I repeated, stunned. "Will it not take weeks?"

"Longer. My family lives at Chota, on the Little Tennessee. But I owe a friend a favor, first, at a village in the Middle Towns, in North Carolina. We'll take the path from here towards Jocassee, but cut up the trail before and make our way over the mountains until we reach a river called the Cullasaja. We'll travel upriver from there."

The wind grew stronger, and my mind whirled like a dervish at full spin. I pressed a hand to the top of my head, holding the flyaway strands there.

"I trust that Harris and the rest can handle the valley until you return," he continued, still watching me, his deep eyes giving the constant appearance of languidness, something I knew well to ignore. If anything, he was more alert than ever.

"We'll be in Indian territory the entire time. Will we be safe? There are bears, are there not? And wolves. And what of crossing the mountains?"

"Mac, I've made the journey since I was a boy," he said, green eyes narrowing. He stepped forward suddenly and grasped the back of my head, pressing his lips hard against mine. Then he released my mouth and rested his forehead to mine, and his hand slid to circle my neck.

"If you'll not go with me, then say it. But by God don't fashion excuses."

He stepped back as sharply as he'd come to me, turned on his heel and stalked away through the spring green grass.

"Miss Quinn, you sure you wan' be goin' wid dat man?" Hosa asked as he lifted Fire Eater's saddle gently onto the big horse's back. I stood holding the reins, soothing my mount by rubbing my knuckles across the soft skin between his nostrils.

Hosa reached under to tighten the girth and Fire Eater shifted, snorting. The wiry black man stepped back and shook his head, his Caribe accent lyrically thick. "It's gotta be you, Miss Quinn. Dat horse won' tolerate no one else."

I crouched and latched the girth, giving the horse's belly a pat. "Yes, I'm going with him. And if you don't mind, I'd like for you to keep an eye on the other horses while we're gone," I said. "Don't let Samuel give you any trouble—he may be a smithy, but you know the animals better than anyone in the valley."

Undaunted, Hosa crossed his arms over his chest and raised his eyebrows, direct brown eyes skeptical. "I just don' see's how you should be on de trail wid dat man alone for so long. Dere's no tellin' what's in dem woods, now. Dey might catch you and turn you Indian—den what'll you do?"

"Jehosaphat," I said curtly, hooking the saddlebags tight. "What wrong has Jack Wolf ever done you?"

"He ain't done nothin'," he answered. "But I seen him call a hawk in de woods, an' it landed right on his arm. He got de witchcraft in him, I think. You be careful, now, you promise."

I laid a hand on Hosa's forearm and squeezed gently. It had taken months of me making similar small gestures for him to not flinch from my touch, nor to look down at his feet when we spoke. Though he was a freedman, Jehosaphat Brown knew well what would have happened to him in any place other than the frontier, had he touched a white woman. "I promise. But he is a good man, you know."

He patted my hand quickly and stepped away, throwing up an arm in a half-hearted wave as he left the barn. "He may be, but dem cat eyes tell different."

I shook my head, smiling to myself. Granted, there were parts of Jack that lay in some darker, primitive realm of himself that I might never be able to touch. But there was one thing I knew of him, and that was that he was an honorable soul, and a man undaunted by custom or social conform. If anything, Jackson Wolf was a charming saboteur of civilized thinking. And I liked him for it.

I took a long, sweeping look at the Keowee Valley, following the curving smoke-line of the Blue Ridge. We'd be traveling right into those mountains I'd come to think of as my own, but we would do it by taking an old hunting path out of the northwest end of the Valley, up and over the South Carolina Blue Ridge into the steep mountains of Western North Carolina, and following a river trail out of that colony into the deepest part of the Cherokee country. It was a path the Cherokee had taken for centuries, long before white men had come offering small charms of modernity for pelts, skins, and sacred lands.

Summer was coming. I could feel its heat in the air, hidden beneath the mildness of spring. The May wind was cool, but when it stilled the sun seemed to contract and expand imperceptibly, in gleeful anticipation of July. Would we return before the fall, I wondered? According to Clemens, who'd patiently answered my many questions about frontier travel on our trip up from Ninety-Six last year, the trail to the Middle and Overhill Towns was treacherous and slow, made even more so by steep cliffs, almost impassible rivers with giant waterfalls, and wandering Chickasaw made mad by the French.

I hooked my foot into the stirrup and swung myself up onto Fire Eater's back, settling into my saddle. For the journey I'd fashioned myself a pair of riding breeches from an old pair of Owen's, stitching an extra seam in the seat for comfort—though I'd never admit it. It felt incredibly freeing to wear them, to ride astride without having to tie my skirts beneath my calves. I'd also tucked my hair into a topknot and stuffed one of Zeke's farmer's hats down onto my head, hoping to disguise my sex in case of any other run-in with enemy parties.

At the crest of the south pasture I halted Fire Eater, sitting back in the saddle and breathing deeply. Up ahead of me Jack crouched on the ground, bent at the knee, one hand in the dirt. I watched as he stood with a fistful of dry earth, blew parts of it north, south, east, and west. At each he called out something in Cherokee, words chanted like music gone mad, the rhythm like nothing I'd ever heard. After he did this he knelt and held out his arms to the heavens, his face upturned, and I could no longer hear him calling to his god.

Chapter 20

Cullasaja River Gorge
The North Carolina wilderness

I slid my hand along the wall of granite, feeling the wet stone like a blind woman touching the face of her lover. Behind me Fire Eater pulled against the rope, teeth bared, the whites of his eyes bright with fear in the dusk-light.

After traveling steadily over the past several days we'd followed one of many trails up and over the South Carolina mountains and into North Carolina. There was no telling where one colony ended and the other began. The mountains grew together like a great blue sea, and I realized that this ruthlessly wild land was nothing the English could claim, but belonged only to the Cherokee. Very few white people had ever stepped foot where I now walked, towing my horse behind me like an unyielding child.

If I reached out a hand I could touch the solid rump of Jack's horse. I followed him closely, hoping that Fire Eater would sense Murdoch's calm. The big paint had obviously traveled this path many times. He stepped surely along the dirt trail, oblivious to the torrent of deadly whitewater rushing below us. The spray hit my face, and I blinked, unwilling to take my hand from the rock wall. But even the touch of solid earth did nothing to allay the hollow feeling in my gut—the wall, permanent though it was, had been steadily chiseled away by the river itself since time eternal.

"Ruthless bastard," I whispered in unladylike irritation, glaring down at the swirling white mess. Across the river and through the spray I could make out the other side, which was no better than this one: merely the sheer half of a mountain, covered in bushy pines, wild rhododendron and rock outcroppings.

"It won't help, lass," Jack shouted over the rush of water. He stood on the trail before me, sweaty and shirtless, one hand on Murdoch's rump.

"What?" I shouted back, irritated at his easy stance so close to the edge of the cliff. Though we'd been walking beside the river for hours, with every step I lived in fear of the ground giving way, or one of the horses taking a tumble.

"Cursing the river—it won't help," he answered, grinning as he wiped long hair back from his face, tying it in a quick tail. "Water's up. Will be all summer, with the storms coming through each day."

"How far are we to flatter ground?"

"We'll rest ahead. The rock ends, and we hit trees again. We'll camp there." He nodded at Fire Eater. "Do you need help?"

"He won't move," I shouted over the roar of water.

Jack walked back to Murdoch's side, pulling something from his pack. It was a long piece of cloth, which he folded twice and used to cover Fire Eater's eyes before the big horse could react. Then he grinned at me, his eyes moss-green in the dusk, and headed back to the front. After a moment Murdoch moved forward slowly, his hooves cutting into the muddy ground and flinging back patches of it. I tugged once more on the lead and Fire Eater walked, no longer struck dumb by the threat of imminent death.

The thought of making camp once again sent a jump to my stomach, one having nothing to do with the raging Cullasaja. For the past five nights we had set up camp together in quiet companionship. Jack had laughed at me as I'd shared fireside stories of my childish escapades—the one female in a house of men. Jack, of course, shared nothing, and he'd not made the slightest movement towards me. Every night he built for me a lean-to shelter from downed limbs and leaves, then settled by the fire with a blanket, his arms crossed over his chest. And every night I'd lain there in excruciating silence, want of him making me squeeze my eyes and mouth tightly shut, afraid I'd explode in a thousand tiny pieces.

Darkness fell quickly. Soon I could barely see the outline of his body as he led Murdoch along the path. The river was much calmer now. I could no longer hear only the gush of the water, but now the sounds of night in the forest: crickets, insects, and the odd, hushed quiet of sheer wilderness.

Suddenly Jack was at my side. I jumped, covering my mouth with a hand. "You move like a ghost," I hissed, more frightened than angry. "What are you doing?"

"It's too dark," he said. "There's a cave here—we can't go farther like this." I felt his hand take mine, and my first instinct was to yank back, but his grip was sure. "Drop the lead, lass. The horses will be fine."

I dropped the rope reluctantly, patting Fire Eater on the neck as I skirted around him, my hand still tightly ensconced in Jack's. I stretched my other hand out behind me, brushing the granite wall, just to be sure it was still there. We walked until the sound of the river grew once again increasingly louder; he stopped, placing my hand on something, and moved behind me. It was a rough ladder, attached to the wall beside us and overgrown with ivy and brambles; the wood was worn and old.

"*Hi'lahi*," he said loudly, jerking his chin toward the ladder, and I wondered if he knew he'd spoken in Cherokee.

"You want me to climb?" I asked in disbelief, shouting to be heard above the roar of water. We were nearing the Cullasaja Gorge; the sounds were of the river screaming over the falls and onto the rocks below. I wiped sweat and dirt from my forehead, felt the welt of a mosquito bite at the crook of my left eyebrow. "Will it hold?"

"Aye, lass. I'm behind you, not to fret."

I turned into the ladder, gripping one of the rungs above my head and hoisting myself up, thankful I'd chosen to wear man's breeches on the trail. A dress could quite literally have been the death of me. I felt Jack's hand at my back, steady. "Keep going, Mac," he shouted.

My fingers felt dirt, and I hauled myself up and over the top of the rocky embankment, crawling to the foot of an elm and waiting, my chest heaving. Jack's head popped up over the side, and he grinned at me, his teeth a flash of white in the dark. He tossed his pack over the ledge, pulling himself up. "Come on," he said, taking my hand and tugging. "This way."

"This way" was apparently a short hike through the thick underbrush along a small creek—a tributary of the Cullasaja that eventually emptied into the river down near the Gorge. My moccasins slipped in the mouldy leaves beneath my feet, and I clung to his hand, unable to see a thing in the dark forest. When he stopped I ran into his back, my nose smashing into the wet muscle along his spine. I rubbed it gingerly, the musky smell of his skin burning my nostrils.

A waterfall, tall as a Charlestown church and steeple, poured out from the slope of the hillside before us, spilling in a wide sheet into a shallow pool. The water from the pool fed the creek; it rushed past our feet and into the endless forest, surely meeting its doom down in the Gorge.

"We're going behind," Jack said loudly.

Though not as deafening as the Cullasaja, the falls still blocked out most sound. I nodded, and he dropped his hand, following the edge of the rocky pool and slipping around the back of the falls. I stayed close to his back as we skirted the rock. In an instant the world went dark, the rushing water to our left and sheer blackness to our right its transient boundaries.

"Stay there, Mac," he said, the words reverberating hollowly against cavern walls. I heard him digging through his pack. There was a scrape of blade against rock, and a spark flashed, and in an instant he'd lit a torch.

"Where did that come from?" I asked, rubbing my upper arms for warmth. Though the outside world was muggy with heat, here inside the cave the air was wet and cold, and a slow wind seemed to be coming from the deepest dark, wherever it lead.

The torch cast a faint circle of light around us, and I could see that the cave was obviously a resting spot for Cherokee travelers. Tree limbs and dried kindling were stacked beside the wall, and a rusty tea kettle sat in a pile of burnt-out coals. Jack held the torch aloft in one hand, dumped the pack on end and shook it with the other, and a large, folded quilt and small tin fell out. The tin clinked when it landed, rolling to the edge of the coals.

"Coffee," he said. He shoved the torch at me, and I took it without thought. "You know, lass, the Cherokee believe that the *Nunnehi*, the Immortals, live behind falls like this. The places behind are sacred, entrances into the otherworld," he said conversationally. "I'm going back for the food, to check on the horses." Then he turned without sound, disappearing into the waterfall.

I went to the wall and leaned against it, the stone a shock of cold against my back. A rush of chilly air moved past me from the back of the cave. I felt it brush my nose and cheeks, unsettlingly human. I slid slowly down the wall into a crouch, clutching the torch in front of me like a sword—King Arthur at the stone—and waited for Jack.

I'd felt things before in the woods—quiet, ancient things that seemed to move with the wind, and that lived in the hollows of trees and rocky ravines, and in the mountains themselves, somewhere deep in the core. Rarely, the feel of these things gave me visions, and suddenly I could see what had happened there, or who had walked where I stood.

When I was fourteen years old an outbreak of yellow fever hit Charlestown that spring, and we moved to the du Pont plantation on the Santee weeks earlier than usual. I spent most of my days at the neighboring plantation, playing with Elizabeth Gadsden, the daughter of the house.

I'd been standing at the edge of the swamp when I saw as clearly as though it was happening at that precise moment, a black man—a slave—pulled into the murk by an alligator, its great scaly tail beating the brackish water like a paddle. When I came to I was sitting on the dock of the Gadsden's rice plantation, my feet brushing the calm river, not a ripple to be found.

Whatever filled this cave along the Cullasaja was old—older perhaps than the river it guarded. Though I sensed no animosity from the spirit here, as the wind continued to brush past my face, and water dripped from somewhere in the dark depths, I felt its curiosity.

I lifted my chin, looking defiantly into the shadows with narrowed eyes. "I'm naught but a crazy white woman," I whispered.

Feet shuffled against stone and a dark figure filled the mouth of the cave, the rushing falls its backdrop. Jack stepped into the light. Slung over his shoulder was the satchel of food we'd carried with us since making purchases at a trading post on the North Carolina border, near the Jocassee village. He dropped the bag, moving to crouch in front of me.

"Hello," he said simply, reaching out and tucking a strand of hair behind my ear. He took the torch from me and set it on the old coals, taking my hands in his and rubbing them for warmth. He brought them to his bare belly, and I yelped when they hit skin. He was hot to the touch. "Better?" he asked, chuckling.

It occurred to me then—as I realized that I had no sudden urge to jerk back my hands, no need to chide him for his familiarity—that something between us had irrevocably changed. I looked up at him and swallowed, praying it wasn't audible. "Quite," I murmured.

He cocked his head at me, studying my face for a moment. Then he picked up the torch and handed it to me again. "Hold this aloft, lass, so I can see to light the fire."

I stood, taking the torch as he moved to gather wood from the stack of kindling and lay it in the coals. He pulled a clump of dried moss from the pocket of his leggings, stuffing it beneath the pyramid of sticks. When he gestured for the torch I handed it over, watching shadows shift on the wet granite behind him as he lit the fire. The moss crackled as the fire spit for a moment, then caught on the bigger pieces of wood. As it grew the cave seemed to shrink with encroaching light, and I went to Jack's pack in search of food.

"Do we have any of the bread left, or did we consume it all yesterday in our famished state?" I asked.

"We've a bit left. There's some cheese and biscuits, and a handful of dried strawberries. No meat, though I could leave you and hunt a bit, fetch a rabbit or squirrel for a stew, mayhap."

He took the pack from me, reaching inside and pulling out the last of the bread, wrapped in a thin cloth. He offered it with a grin. "Not much of the waiting in you, is there, Mac?"

I shook my head, opening the cloth and tearing off a piece of the bread, handing him the rest. Our meals had grown incrementally more casual. I'd given up on attempting to prepare any sort of proper supper on the trail, usually out of sheer exhaustion. Climbing into bed—though one of hardpacked dirt and rough blankets—had been more of a priority than sating my growling stomach. "Patience is surely not my virtue—just ask my grandfather," I said, shrugging. "I fear that the lack thereof runs rampant through the MacFadden bloodline, though my cousin may have been bypassed. Owen used to drive me mad at chess. He'd ponder each move for days."

Jack tucked the bread back into the sack without taking any for himself, set it on the ground. Methodically, he began removing his weapons and laying them in a pile near the fire: first the musket, then the tomahawk, the knife at his belt, and lastly the dagger tucked in his right boot.

"It's normally I'm a patient man," he said quietly, his brogue deepening. "But maybe you'll nay think me as such, seeing as how I've been with you these past months."

I swallowed a bite of bread, working it and a growing ball of thrilling fear down my esophagus. Firelight flashed against the sculpted panes of his bare chest, casting him in bronze. In the dark and the rush, I'd nearly forgotten that he was half-naked. My polite Charlestown upbringing came swiftly to the surface, and I looked away quickly. "Would you mind donning a shirt?" I asked, my voice coming out unconsciously stiff.

He chuckled, bending and tossing another limb on the fire. "Aye, lass, I would. Mind, that is."

"Fine," I muttered, moving to the other side of the fire, putting distance between us. I sat as gracefully as one could in a pair of men's breeches, folding my legs neatly beneath me and stretching out my hands to the flames. "It's surprisingly cold in here, isn't it?" I asked.

"It's the spring," he said. "The heart lies at the deep of this cave, keeps the water and the air cool. We're also higher up in these mountains than back home, which adds to the chill, even in the dead of summer. Do you need a blanket then, lass?"

He moved before I could protest, picking the quilt from where it had fallen earlier and coming to me, pulling me to stand and draping it about my shoulders. He tugged the fabric together at my chest, resting the backs of his knuckles against my breastbone and looking me in the eye, his face inches from mine. I made a move to step back, but he pulled lightly on the quilt, bringing me closer.

"'Tis true I am a patient man, but you've tested me mightily," he said softly, his green eyes black in the shadowed cave. "I want you," he said, quite simply. "God help me, I want your body, but I'll have none of it if I can't have your mind as well. I want us to marry in Chota, Mac. Will you have me?"

I could not break from his emerald gaze as the flush of lust and excitement moved hotly up into my face, and my heart began to beat so loudly that all I could hear was its pounding in my ears, reverberating off the delicate walls of my eardrums. I lifted my hands and set them over his, and in a rush of heat and sound I saw his thoughts as clearly as though they were my own. *Say something, you blockheaded, stubborn woman!*

I closed my eyes as his thoughts ran to Cherokee, shaking my head against the frustratingly foreign language. "Jack," I whispered, my throat as raw as though I'd gulped boiling water. "I'll have twenty-six years this October—I never meant to marry."

"Mac, surely you must know by now I'd never take your land," he said roughly, the mix of Irish and Scottish in his voice emerging the more fervently he spoke, making him difficult to understand. "I'll nay be a dandy of the Lowcountry, and I'll never see you as naught but a frivolous woman." He laid his forehead against mine; his warm breath blew softly against my lips. And it was if the sheer strength of him was bottled, held tightly in check by his will. "I'll not beg you, but I will ask you once more, and only once. *Will you have me?*"

What did I know of him? Merely that he was a man my grandfather would never have chosen for me, a man literally caught between the white world and the Indian. For heaven's sake, he could move without sound, I thought frantically.

He brought you a book, said the voice in my head. *He is unlike any other.*

"Jack," I whispered, licking dry lips. "I do want you. But what of love? We've not known each other long enough to be certain."

He released me suddenly, and when his skin left mine the ground shifted beneath my feet, and the world began to swirl in black patches before my eyes.

Would you risk losing him, for the knowing?

The voice came clearly through the chaos of my thoughts, and I reached out, grabbing Jack by the waist of his deerskin leggings, my fingers burning against his bare skin.

"I'll have you."

Chapter 21

The Cullasaja River Gorge

When I awoke in the hours before dawn, it was with the certain knowledge that I was about to get wet. I opened my eyes and looked up into the cavernous roof of the cave, and a fat, silver drop of water hit me directly on the bridge of my nose, splattering into my eyes. I flung out a belated arm, wiping the sleeve of my man's shirt across my face. The big, warm body next to me shifted at my movement, and a large hand—the palm rough with calluses—slid across my stomach beneath the shirt, gripping my side and pulling me closer.

"*Hi'lunnu,*" he muttered, tucking my head firmly beneath his chin.

We lay on the cold ground, the blanket wrapped snugly around us, as close as two spoons layered in a silver drawer. I squirmed, impatient and awake. "Jack? What does that mean?"

"Hmm?" he murmured, blinking at me like an owl. "Oh, *hi'lunnu?* Means 'go to sleep,' Mac." He grinned at me sleepily, then sighed deeply. Moments later he was snoring.

I stared up at the roof of the cave, on the lookout for more falling water and completely unable to return to slumber. It had never been easy for me, waking and then sleeping again. At times my mind raced with a million minute details, and the remaining flecks of disturbing dreams left me wide awake. In my cabin, I'd light the lamp and read. I glanced down at the brown arm across my belly and sniffed. That old habit obviously wasn't an option this morning.

At some point in the night I'd become used to Jack's arm across my waist, comfortable with—but never unaware of—the length of him pressed closely against me. I'd not given him my body, in the Biblical sense of it, but

158

we'd been as close as I supposed a man and woman could be, without. On this, Jack had stood his ground. *We'll wait until we're married,* he'd said.

Married. The notion, so unthinkable to me merely months ago, now sent a thrill of fear and happiness coursing through my blood—like one of Mr. Franklin's kites whipping about in the wind, both terrified of and yearning for the sparking contact of lightning.

I'd been a woman of the wilderness for a full year now, I thought. And I lay in a compromising position with a large, green-eyed, fair-haired Indian. I'd known, certainly, upon making my decision to retreat to the frontier, that my life would be utterly different than the one I'd lead in Charlestown. But for all my gift of Sight, I had never foreseen Jack. He'd come into my world unbidden, a steady, muscled disturbance that had charmed his way onto my land and into my heart.

"Quincy, lovely," he said, the timber of his voice a low growl that moved from his chest and into my back. "You're thinking so hard I can almost hear you aloud. You can tell me, you know."

"I abhor that name," I muttered, settling back against him.

"Sure, and your golden-tongued cousin calls you by it, now."

"He's the only one who calls me 'Quincy,'" I said, craning my neck to look back at him. "I'd rather have you use that infernal man's name than my given one."

"And I'd rather you reserve 'Mister Wolf' for occasions when you're spittin' mad, and none other. Agreed, lass?"

"Agreed," I answered, smiling. He reached out, pressing a soft kiss to my brow. I turned back around, scooting closer to him and watching the dark.

Though the steady rush of the falls blocked most light from the outside world, pale shards of it were beginning to splinter out around the mouth of the cave. Whether they were moonlight or daylight, I did not know. The thought of scrambling around the rim of the roaring Cullasaja for another full day had me closing my eyes, seeking sleep. Heaven knows I'd need my strength, I thought.

My eyes flew open. "Jack?" I asked, remembering. "What about your friend? What favor do you owe? And how far are we from finding him?"

"Just a wee longer. But it's nay a him, lass—it's a her." I made a move to sit up, and the arm tightened around my stomach again. I felt the gentle bite of his teeth against the tender nape of my neck.

"*Hi'lunnu,* my *unahu',*" he whispered.

In the daylight there seemed something in the air between us that had not been there before last night, and I moved hesitantly around him, unsure how to proceed. How did one act once one was betrothed, I wondered? I'd never even had a suitor before Jack. Certainly I'd never spent the night in a man's arms.

I sat tenderly in the saddle, my sore hips moving gently to the rhythm of Fire Eater's gait as we made our way, single-file, through the forest. Even though we'd left the rocky cliffs of the Cullasaja to trek deeper into the woods, Jack had assured me that the river was still nearby, that we were simply moving parallel to it on a less treacherous trail.

The North Carolina wilderness, though it claimed steeper mountains, was much like that of South Carolina: lush with summer, so green and growing that it seemed endless, an untamed Eden. There were giant ferns here, just as there were in the forest surrounding the Keowee Valley, and hawks and eagles claimed the rock outcroppings and cliff-sides, the great kings of the air. I wondered when we would ever again see a human soul, and if we did, would I recognize my own kind? We'd spent so long alone in the woods that I thought I might begin uttering an animal tongue—something born in the mountains—should we encounter anyone else on the trail.

Ahead, Jack walked beside Murdoch, his eyes scanning the underbrush of elm, glossy rhododendron, and hemlock. He'd tucked the paint's lead into its hemp harness, and the horse followed obediently, faithful as a dog.

Suddenly he turned, muttering a command to Murdoch and walking back towards me as the horses continued to move forward. "Watch for my signal," he said softly. "If you see me wave my hand, I want you to move Fire Eater into the brush and dismount, take cover behind him."

Startled, I nodded. He reached out and touched my thigh, squeezed. Then he turned and ran quickly through the trees beside the trail, pulling the tomahawk from his back in one dangerously graceful movement.

A high, sharp whistle came from the woods, and Jack stopped in the space of a mere heartbeat, crouching low. He returned the whistle and waited. About twenty yards before him two black heads broke from a wild mess of rhododendron. Jack slid the tomahawk back into its sheath on his back and stood, a smile lighting his face. "*Sala'lani'ta! Tuksi!*" he called affectionately.

Two Cherokee boys emerged from the underbrush, grinning sheepishly. Both were tall, though opposites in shape. One was skinny with oncoming manhood and wore his hair in a long braid down his back. The other, perhaps a mite shorter, was chubby with youth, his cheeks round as apples. He wore his hair in a swathe of black down his skull, like many of the older men at Keowee Town. When they neared Jack he pulled them swiftly to him, pounding on their backs and speaking rapidly in Cherokee. They watched me with dark, curious eyes over his shoulders. He saw and said something that had both their mouths falling open, their eyes widening like saucers.

"Mac, these are friends from Kituhwa. Meet Young Squirrel and Turtle, *Yun'wiya* of the *Ani'wa'ya* and *Ani'Tsa'guhi*." He cuffed the skinny one on the head, had the boy ducking and swatting half-heartedly at him with his arm. "Squirrel here is a cousin of Ridge Runner's, on his mother's side."

The one aptly called Turtle couldn't seem to take his eyes from me. He gestured at me with one arm, talking excitedly. Jack answered in Cherokee, and the boy nodded, apparently satisfied.

"He's never seen *gitsu'*—hair—like yours," Jack told me. "He wondered if you were an *ada'wehi*—a conjurer, or a magician, you might call it."

"But all the Cherokee women have long hair," I said.

"No, Mac, he's never seen yellow hair on a woman," he returned, grinning at me. "The only hair like that he's seen is mine, and it's a mite darker than yours."

"What did you tell him?" I asked. The boys were looking back and forth at us as we spoke, as though we were players in a tennis match.

"I told him you'd surely bewitched me, as I'd promised to marry you. And I've managed to avoid joining with a woman in *that* way"—his eyes twinkled merrily at this—"for some time now. Nay, I told him you're no conjurer, lass, but that you are unlike any other."

I blinked at him, a bit stunned, as a blush came to my cheeks. "You continue to surprise me," I said softly.

Young Squirrel chuckled, patting his cheeks with his hands, and Turtle giggled. Jack smiled at them and placed a hand on Turtle's shoulder, telling them something in their language. The conversation continued for a while, and though frustrated at my lack of understanding, I thought I caught the words for "friend," "horse," and "come." The boys nodded, glanced at me again, and trotted off into the woods from the direction they'd appeared.

"They'll meet up with us," Jack said, walking up to Murdoch and making a clicking sound. The horse started forward, and Fire Eater followed suit, his heavy hooves thumping down onto dirt. I hurried alongside, catching up with Jack, forced to follow behind him on the narrow trail.

"Where are they going?"

"For their horse."

"And where are *we* going, exactly?" I asked, hurriedly retying my braid. I'd taken off my planter's hat and stuffed it into my saddlebag long ago, taking full advantage of being able to travel bareheaded.

He didn't answer, but as we rounded the side of a ridge our destination no longer mattered to me. We came to a break in the mountain laurel, and the view was startling: again the rolling mountains, green here but purple in the infinite distance, some high and jutting, others rounded like waves. I caught my breath, a knot at my throat. How many ranges there were, I thought, my eyes engulfing the blue sky and sheer expanse like a woman who'd been starving but had never known it until now.

The sun burned above it all, perfectly round and yellow, in a cloudless cerulean sky. The mountains were so defined against the blue that I felt as though I could reach out and trace the crest of one with my fingertip. Though despite my own intellectual questioning I had long believed in God, I'd never felt so surely in His presence as I did at that moment.

I looked away from the mountains and back to the trail ahead, where sunlight came down through the thick canopy in Michelangelo-like beams, brightening patches of pine needles and ferns, dust motes flickering in midair.

I was a castaway now, I thought, washed ashore like Miranda, dazed and all at once changed.

"Mac, are you all right?"

I shook my head, clearing it. Jack had stopped Murdoch and was looking back at me expectantly.

"I gave you a while, but we need go on. We've got some length to travel before nightfall," he said. "Have you had another vision, then?"

"Yes," I answered, breathing in deeply through my nose and smiling. I ran a quick hand beneath my eyes, wiping away the moisture that had formed there. "But not the kind that you think."

He gave me a half-smile and inclined his head. "Aye. Let's be off, then."

The fire crackled and smoke shifted in the breeze, snaking up into the night sky, a long, white kite tail in the infinite, starry dark. Young Squirrel and Turtle sat across the fire from me, looking quickly down at the ground when I'd catch them staring. Squirrel held Jack's rifle in his hands, studying the barrel with squinted eyes.

The boys had dried venison in their saddlebag, and we chewed on pieces of it, as no one seemed willing to hunt in the dark, tired as we all were. We'd traveled long hours that day, making camp in the dusk-light near the Tuckaseegee River Valley, a vale between two long ranges of mountains. Here had obviously been a Cherokee settlement of some kind: a small pasture had been cleared but was now rough and overgrown, much like the Keowee Valley had been before the cabins had been built and fields planted. We were camped alongside a small creek at the edge of the pasture, and looking up could see a sky spattered across with stars. A long, wide strip—the gauzy pale green of the Milky Way—hovered in the sky above us, the stars thicker along its meandering path.

A branch shifted in the fire and fell down hissing into red coals, and the sound made me think of a stop we'd made—Owen, Grandfather, and I—on our Grand Tour of Europe, when I was a mere twelve years old. We'd been in Italy, on the ancient stone *appia* from Florence to Rome, when one of the horses driving the carriage fell lame.

Being between towns, and Grandfather too frugal to send our driver out in search of another horse, we'd decided to pull off in an olive grove and make camp for the night. The driver had protested fervently, worried we'd be set upon by Gypsies or highwaymen, but Grandfather had shaken his head at the man, his Scottish temper building upon his red-cheeked face like a storm cloud. The driver relented, and Owen fetched wood for a fire while I lay down on the flat stones of the road, still warm from the sun, and stared at up the sky.

"Get off the ground, ye wee urchin," Grandfather growled at me.

I blinked, eyes moving from the starry sky to the large form standing above me, his hands in his pockets. "How many do you think there are, Grandfather?" I asked, impervious at this point in our relationship to the obvious ire in his voice. I heard the affection beneath, and ignored the rest. "There must be thousands, at least. Perhaps millions."

He looked up, blowing air out of his nose in a huff, giving in. It was just beginning to get cold. We'd crossed the French Alps into Italy before the first snowfall, and had been long in Florence—bewitched with the Boboli Gardens, the curved bridges above the River Arno, and the green and pink carrera marble of the Duomo.

"Ye mean the stars, do ye? There's more than millions, lassie—of a number we'll never know. Man has been bewitched by the sky for thousands of years," he said, rocking back on his heels. "Sailors, shepherds, scientists . . . it's still a mighty mystery, best known by God Himself."

He nudged me with the toe of his boot. "Now get up from the ground, Quincy, ye're a young lady, not a hermit crab."

Owen dumped a load of branches by the fire and scoffed, brushing off his hands. "She's no lady," he said. "The only way you can tell she's a girl is by her long hair."

I sat up and sniffed, used to my cousin's teasing but unable to not let it nettle me. "Fine, I'll get up," I said, taking Grandfather's outstretched hand and holding onto it as I glared at Owen in the dark. "And I'll be a girl as long as I'm allowed to keep reading all I want. My Greek is better than yours," I muttered finally, the fight gone out of me.

"Only because it's all you do, pour over Grandfather's books and ride your horse," Owen said, plopping down, trying to light the fire. He rested his hands on his knees and then looked up at me, smiling with sudden kindness. "Not that I mind, of course. I'd much rather have you be a bookworm than act the ninny like the girls at your school, always

flapping those ugly fans about."

Grandfather chuckled at our exchange and let go of my hand, walking over to assist Owen. He bent down and gave me a look over his shoulder, eyes gleaming in the moonlight. "Well, boy, that's only because they're sweet on ye, those friends of Quincy's," he said, winking at me. "They're thinking that if they bat their eyes, they'll get ye to take them for a stroll through White Park."

Owen blanched, rolling his eyes. At seventeen he thought himself far too manly to be thinking of thirteen year-old girls. Grandfather managed a spark and hurried over to the kindling pile, gathering leaves and stuffing them between sticks. Owen looked at me over the fire.

"Promise me you'll never be a daft female," he said, in perfect teenaged solemnity.

Someone tapped my shoulder, and I jumped. Turtle was crouched beside me, holding out a skin of water. I took it and smiled at him.

"*Wado,*" I said, taking a large gulp, wiping my mouth with the back of my hand. I handed it back to him and glanced around for Jack. He stood across the fire beside Squirrel, holding his musket out from his body. He was pointing into the barrel, making a swirling motion with his finger in the air and talking animatedly.

I got to my feet, inquisitive, and skirted the fire, stopping next to them. Jack reached over without looking, and tugged gently on my loosely plaited hair, still talking to Squirrel. "What is it you're telling him?" I interrupted, unable to stifle my curiosity.

They turned and looked at me, and Jack set the stock of the musket on the ground, resting both hands lightly on the tip of the barrel. "He's asking about me gun," he said, smiling, the lilt in his voice deepening. "It's not the average musket, lass. It weighs about the same, mayhap a bit less than a stone, and it's as long, about five feet or so. But a Pennsylvania man made this for me up at Fort Wilderness. I'd got him out of a tough spot."

"What's different about it?" I asked, scratching at a mosquito bite on the side of my neck.

"Well, it's near right-on when fired, can hit a mark at two hundred and fifty yards or more, the normal musket hitting at about one-fifty," he said. "The inside of the barrel's been cut in grooves, in a spiral, so the ball comes out spinning." He grinned suddenly, and I caught a glimpse of what he must have looked like as a boy. "It's a fine, bonny weapon, lass, and as far as I ken I'm the only man below Virginia who owns one."

He handed the musket back to Squirrel and turned to me, bending and kissing the side of my neck. My skin rippled with gooseflesh, and I swatted at him. "Not here," I whispered, cutting my eyes at the boys.

He cocked an eyebrow, a feat that still bothered me, since I'd never been able to do it.

"Come on, Mac," he said, placing his hand at the small of my back and leading me toward the horses, down by the creek. "Let's go make up our pallet for the night. You can pick the spot, since you've a touch of the shyness, now."

I stopped in my tracks. "We are not sleeping side by side with children about," I said sharply.

"Children?" He chuckled, running a hand through his long hair, flicking the eagle's feather with a finger. "Those two have seen more than you think. The Cherokee don't practice monogamy, such as it is. Men and women, though they don't always follow on it, are free to be with whomever they choose—even after marriage."

For a moment I was completely unable to respond. He watched me silently, his eyes hooded and impenetrable in the dark. I crossed my arms over my chest, finding my voice. "And you'll want a marriage like that, won't you? Well, I won't have it," I said angrily. "I never agreed to that. It took enough for me to say 'yes' when you asked me. Do you honestly believe I'll let you play the rake, frolicking in whomever's bed you wish?" I took a breath, glaring at him. "It'll be the two of us and no others, or I'm leaving you now, I swear it."

"And you a fine lady, swearing," he said softly, grinning.

"Jackson Wolf—" I spit out the words, stepping towards him, intent on maiming him permanently.

He took my shoulders in his big hands and squeezed tightly, hard enough for me to catch my breath. "Listen now, for you surely are *ada'wehi*. I told you, I saw you by the creek that day and I knew. If you were to consort with another man I'd rip his bollocks from his body and feed them to a wolf."

"Well, now, that's a lovely declaration." I looked away into the trees across the river, still seething.

"Mac," he said sharply, tightening his grip until I looked at him again. "I saw you there, and I knew I'd never want another. Never, do you hear me? Only you, until the rivers dry up and sun ceases burning, and we're naught but dust."

I stared back at him, struck mute yet again, my anger dissipating like heat leaving a hot iron brand.

"Do you understand?" he asked me, unblinking.

He was so tall, I thought as he stood before me, energy rolling off his body in invisible waves. I reached up and laid my hands on each side of his face, pulling him down to me. Our lips met, and I memorized the contours of his mouth, giving his upper lip a gentle tug with my teeth. He inhaled sharply, and I stepped back, attempting an awkward eyebrow lift. "One day I'll manage it," I said.

He laughed and pulled me to him, hugging me tightly. My heart sped up, and warmth filled my chest, and I wondered if I'd ever become used to his easy affection, given so freely and honestly. "Mac?" he asked quietly.

"I understand," I answered, wrapping my arms around his waist.

I lay with my head against his chest, and in the dark his heartbeat resounded against my eardrum, as if it came from the center of the earth. His breath was steady, but he was not yet asleep.

"What did you do for him, the Pennsylvania man?" I asked quietly. "It must have been quite a kind deed, for him to offer you such a reward." There was no answer, and for a moment I thought I'd been mistaken. Maybe he was sleeping. "Jack?" I whispered.

"I revenged a wrong done him," he said softly.

"Oh." I waited a heartbeat. "What had happened to him?"

"His daughter had been raped and left for dead by a group of French soldiers. I made a vow to him they'd not see morning."

I raised my head from his chest. He was staring up at the sky, his eyes dark and unblinking. Owen's words ran through my mind like a warning: *Can you live with what he tells you, if he tells you of his darkest secrets—of the lives that may have been taken with the tomahawk he wears on his back?*

"Get you to sleep, lass," Jack said. "Morning will come soon enough."

Deep in the night I lay in the crook of Jack's arm, wide awake. I'd been woken out of a restless slumber by the nagging memory of that stop on the Grand Tour, halfway between Florence and Rome. There had been more to that night than Owen's teasing. The rest of the memory had stayed buried for so long in the dark recesses of my mind I'd almost believed it a fantasy. But as I shifted in the humid dark, my body flush with Jack's, I remembered.

I awoke, frantic, forgetting where I was. I sat up and clocked my head against the handle of the carriage door. I rubbed my forehead, memory rushing to the forefront: we were in Italy, camped alongside the highway, and I'd been made to sleep in the carriage. Grandfather and Owen, being men, were sleeping outside by the fire on the ground, the true adventurers. I pushed aside the lace curtain, peering out into the dark. There was a man speaking, his voice strange and high. That must have been what had woken me.

The fire had dwindled, but the coals were still red at the bottom. I scanned the ground, searching for Owen and Grandfather. A horse neighed loudly, and I saw Owen then, standing across the fire, his face white in the moonlight. A strange man stood behind him, dark and pockmarked, holding a knife to my cousin's throat. A wet stain formed at the front of Owen's trousers as he trembled, clutching the man's forearm.

I wanted to cry out, but fear made me halt: where was Grandfather? Had he been killed?

Something was wrong. The highwayman was nervous. Sweat beaded on his forehead, shining in the firelight. His eyes moved frantically from side to side, and he shuffled backwards, pulling Owen with him.

Suddenly I saw something the stranger did not: appearing out of the darkness behind him as though he'd materialized from thin air was Campbell MacFadden, the expression on his face one I'd never seen before. He looked nothing of the austere grandfather I knew. His eyes were strangely lifeless, and he moved without sound, and in both hands—hands that I'd once seen calm a kicking stallion—he held a tremendous broadsword.

He swung the sword down in an arc, moonlight glinting on the blade. At the sound the highwayman's eyes went wide with a sort of animal knowledge. He dropped the knife, pushing Owen to the ground. And my grandfather continued the wide circle of his swing, bringing the blade down onto the man's skull and splitting it in two.

Chapter 22

The Middle Towns
June, 1769

We reached Kituhwa on the night of the summer solstice, and though on any other date it should have been dark, we came upon the village in dusk light. We entered first through long fields of squash, then corn and beans, growing together in a plaited mix of green and yellow vines. On one side, the fields were guarded by low, smoke-colored hills, and on the other the dark water of the Tuckaseegee, curving slowly through fertile bottomland. As we walked our horses down the path between crops, my shoulder brushed a hollow gourd hanging from an upright wooden pole and a purple martin zipped out, flying off into the protection of tall, green stalks of corn.

Though laid out much like Keowee Town—with the Council House in the center, built upon an enormous earthen mound, the summer council house next to it, and other dwellings spread along the river—it seemed different, the air surrounding it peaceful, unhurried, not as scarred by day to day dealings with encroaching Europeans as were the villages of the Lower Towns. Situated along the curling river, in the midst of a stretch of long valley, Kituhwa seemed a world away from civilization, thriving and green. The light hung low over the brown river, casting open-sided huts and buildings in a pumpkin-colored glow, their edges wavering and unfocused.

Jack and I rode side-by-side. Squirrel and Turtle galloped ahead, riding their horse in tandem, as skillfully as one being. When they reached the communal fire pit at the center of the village they slid from the horse, greeted by a gathering crowd. The boys gestured excitedly, pointing back at us. More than two dozen sets of curious brown eyes turned our way, and I sat straighter in my saddle, swallowing.

"Don't fret, Mac, I won't leave you," Jack said from beside me, somehow intercepting my unspoken plea.

We rode into the middle of the village plaza, where the crowd had formed around the boys. Two little girls, their eyes bright, ran alongside Fire Eater, touching my leg and shouting. Jack said something to them in Cherokee and they scampered off, squealing. "They've given you a compliment, Mac," he told me, grinning. "They said you were the prettiest little man they'd ever seen."

I yanked the slouching farmer's hat from my head and stuffed it into one of my saddlebags, and Jack chuckled. I glared at him, and he straightened his face, coughing delicately into a fist. He halted Murdoch, and I followed suit, watching as he slid to the ground. Several women—of various ages and sizes—reached out as they greeted him, touching his arms and shoulders, and he smiled at them, answering obligingly. He was at home here, I thought as he bent, speaking to a young boy who tugged on his beaded belt.

Then he stood, separating himself from the group that had formed around him, and reached back for me, holding an outstretched hand. I hooked a leg over my saddle and hopped to the ground, refusing the help. I needed to find balance on my own, I decided quickly, brushing off the front of my man's breeches, tucking a strand of blond hair behind my left ear.

An old man approached, and the crowd gave for him, parting seamlessly. He wore his gray hair in a swath down the center of the back of his skull; at the collar of his linen shirt hung an engraved silver plate, curved like a half-moon on its side. His deerskin leggings were beaded brightly down the seams. When he saw Jack his eyes widened, and he reached out for the younger man's arm, clasping it at the elbow.

The two men, obviously friends, spoke in quick cadence until the old man looked over at me, black eyes knowing above a long, once-broken nose. "*Wa'ya, tu'tsahyesi'*," he said to me, in a voice gruff with age.

I looked to Jack for help, but he was watching the old man. "*Hayu'*," Jack said to him, reaching out and taking my hand in a firm grip.

"*Astu*," the old man replied, looking me up and down in stately appraisal.

"What did he say?" I asked quietly, feeling more and more like the main attraction of a traveling medicine show.

"Bear Killer says Silent Wolf will marry you," said a woman's voice, low, in broken English.

I turned quickly, releasing Jack's hand. Beside me stood a tall, strikingly beautiful woman, her hair hanging in a fall of black—silky as a seal's—around a chiseled face. She wore a fringed, deerskin skirt, her long, shapely legs ending in standard moccasins. Settled against the front of her white, European-style shirt were two long strands of blue and white beads. I blinked, startled. "Silent Wolf answers yes, and Bear Killer tells him it is good."

"Thank you," I said slowly. I glanced at Jack; he was still talking to the man she'd called Bear Killer. "What is your name?" I asked her.

"The English call me Isabella, but I am also Wise-for-Years. You are Walks Between's woman?"

She looked at me with such a burning intensity that my stomach turned over with the cruel knowledge of a woman's instinct. *This woman has been with him*, I thought. *Had she wanted to marry him? Had he loved her?* I heard a roaring in the inner reaches of my eardrums, and I shook my head to clear it, making an immediate decision.

I offered my hand like a man to the woman who had been Jack's lover. "Yes, I am," I answered her. "My name is Quinn, but I am also called Rides-Like-a-Man, by my friend Ridge Runner, of the *Ani'waya*."

It seemed as though a bubble had settled around the two of us as we stood there in the crowd, the outside world forgotten. The solstice moon began to rise in a hushed, violet sky, and it sat just above the trees, staring down the sun. Wise-for-Years took my hand, her grasp surprisingly gentle. "It is good that I know you," she said.

"I have questions to ask you," I told her, letting go.

A myriad of feelings shot through me as I looked at her, this stately, gorgeous creature who seemed as though she belonged as a goddess in an ancient myth, a curved drawing on a cave wall. I was jealous, of course—for tall women always made me feel as though I was still a girl, lacking the height of true womanhood. But also I was curious, for perhaps she could tell me the things that Jack wouldn't, the things I'd yet to ask him, and perhaps never would.

She stared back at me, black eyes revealing nothing, and then nodded, breaking the bubble and slipping away through the crowd.

I stood by the river beneath the solstice moon, watching starlight waver on the water, white and quick, like the ghosts of water beetles. Behind me someone was singing, and there was music—beating drums and something that sounded almost like a flute. I let it wash over and down my back, a salve.

Footsteps crunched in the grass, and I turned, crossing arms defensively over my chest, knowing instinctively that Jack had come to look for me.

"There you are," he said, stepping close, his face awash in moonlight, eyes hooded. "Did you not like the turkey, then, Mac? I turned at supper and you'd gone." He reached out, cupping the side of my cheek, and I drew in breath through my nose, resisting the urge to rub my face against his calloused palm like a cat.

"I met Isabella," I said, watching him.

"Oh, aye? When?"

"Today, when you were speaking with the old man, Bear Killer. She translated for me."

He took back his hand, running it through his loose hair and giving the eagle's feather a flick. Interesting. It had never occurred to me to wonder if that habit was a nervous one. Until now it seemed utterly impossible that a man like Jack could ever be nervous. "Well, that was kind of her. Wise-for-Years is a good woman. I've known her since I was a lad."

I narrowed my eyes at him in the darkness, wondering how he'd choose to respond. He shifted his feet in the dry grass, folding his arms over his chest. We stood together, our stances mirrored. I looked away, back to the river, now a shapeless movement of black, like a necklace of melted onyx making its way down a jeweler's mold.

Jack chuckled quietly, moved to stand beside me, his arm brushing mine. "How did you know, lass?"

I looked up at him, pursing my lips. "I'm no fool."

"No, you're not," he said. "And 'tis good and well I've never thought that, nor said it. I met Wise-for-Years when we were both children. Back then my mother and father traveled often from the Overhill Towns to the Middle and Lower, visiting relatives and trading beaver pelts—then it was all beaver, they weren't so wiped out as they are now."

I kicked the toe of one moccasin into the dirt at my feet, sending a rock scuttling into the water. *Lord, grant me patience*, I thought.

"We were friends for a long time. We didn't become . . . more . . . until I was a man, running messages back and forth between Fort Prince George and Fort Loudon, for the British." He reached out awkwardly, tugging on my braid. "But it's been done with for nigh over two years now, Mac. And she's had a husband since, though he was killed last winter by the river—got swept down in a big storm."

"Why didn't you tell me? You should have. I felt like an idiot."

"And would you have me know of all your past loves?" he demanded, frustration and embarrassment making him angry. "I didn't see how the knowing of what was once between her and me could have any bearing on today."

"I've no past loves, and you well know it," I said, voice rising. "There would be none to tell you about—we'd certainly never be in a situation like this. You'd never be met by a man I'd shared my body with, and God only knows what else."

He watched me, eerily still. When he spoke it was quietly. "She's naught to me now but a friend, lass."

"I know," I spat out, furious with myself for acting the irrational female, and with him for keeping his past under lock and key. "I'm surprised you ever let her go—she's the Amazon queen, truly."

"Aye, she's a big one," he murmured, laughter in his voice.

I whipped around, unable yet to let go of my anger, of the insidious twinge of betrayal. "You share nothing," I said forcefully. "Nothing of your family, of yourself, your past. I may have consented to marry you, Jack, but I still do not know who you are." I turned on my heel, stalking away towards the light and drumbeats, and the shadows of men dancing wildly around the communal fire. "I will not marry a man I know nothing about," I called defiantly over my shoulder as I stumbled through the darkness towards the center of town.

I slipped into the crowd watching the dancers, moving to sit on a long wooden bench occupied by three old women. They turned to stare at me as I plopped down beside them, but I kept my eyes on the bodies rounding the fire, and the feathers gathered on their backs, moving with them like giant wings.

Across the flames and through the smoke I spotted Wise-for-Years. She took a glass bottle from a teenaged boy, its amber contents sloshing, and patted his arm as he turned from her. Then her eyes met mine, and she gestured with a crook of her head towards the other end of the village. I squinted, not quite sure she wasn't a mirage. But then she lifted a hand, waving me to her. I nodded and stood quickly, and the old women beside me raised their eyebrows, white heads bending closely together, twittering like magpies as I turned away.

Wise-for-Years moved sure-footed through the moonlit village, the bottle tucked beneath her left arm. I hurried after her, almost running, my short stride making me take two steps for each of hers. At a summerhouse near the western end of the village she stopped, motioning for me to stay where I was, and ducked inside. Moments later she appeared with two blankets; she handed them to me and took off again. I glanced back over my shoulder as we followed a skinny trail into the woods, for a fleeting moment wondering if I should find Jack, if this woman was going to murder me in the forest. But the thought of him got my ire up, so I kept trailing behind, holding out a hand to block branches, pushing sweaty strands of my hair back from my forehead.

She stopped at a bramble of rhododendron bushes, the shape an inky mound in the darkness. She looked back at me, motioned for me to follow and ducked, disappearing. I went to the place where she'd been, crouched low and shuffled blindly into a hole in the undergrowth, ending up on the other side at the edge of a large pool tucked in a grove of tall trees. The moon shone down in an untouched beam from above, a yellow orb painted on still water.

Wise-for-Years set the bottle down on a boulder and slipped off her moccasins, wading into the pool up to her thighs. I stood, dumbfounded, until she turned back, rolling her eyes impatiently. "Rides-Like-a-Man, come," she ordered, stripping off her shirt and tossing it onto the bank. She pulled her skirt up over her head and raised an eyebrow at me, the beads swinging between her bare breasts. Then she tossed the skirt—it landed softly on top of the discarded white shirt—and turned, diving shallowly into the pool, her brown body an amphibious form beneath the dark water.

"'O brave new world/ That has such people in't!'" I murmured, bending to slip off my moccasins. I took a breath and unfastened my breeches; they pooled at my feet and I stood there, suddenly frozen, the man's shirt brushing my kneecaps. *What am I doing here?* I thought frantically.

Wise-for-Years splashed water at me, laughing, and the sound was like that of a young girl. "Wolf's woman is frightened?" she teased, and there seemed to be no malice in her voice.

I reached up and began unlacing the shirt before I lost my nerve. "Yes," I answered honestly, tugging it over my head.

At the sight of my makeshift corset she yelped, swimming quickly to the side and hurrying over to me, completely unabashed, her naked body dripping. She reached out, touching the whalebone stays and the fabric cups that had kept my breasts from bouncing painfully on the trail. Finally, she looked up at me, the question gone from her eyes.

"They are *iya'-iyu'sti*," she said grinning, cupping her own breasts and lifting them. I lifted my eyebrows, confused, and she shook her head impatiently. "Like pumpkins," she managed, pointing at me, "but smaller. Pumpkins."

"I'd prefer not to discuss the size of my endowments, generous though they are," I muttered, slapping at her curious hands. "This contraption keeps them from being sore, when I ride my horse."

"Contraption?" She looked at me quizzically, crossing her arms over her chest.

"Oh, for heaven's sake," I said, exasperated, unhooking the corset and letting it fall. "Let's swim, then, since you're so insistent on it." I brushed past her, wanting to cover my naked body as quickly as possible, and did as she had, diving shallowly into the pool.

The water was surprisingly cool, but it felt amazing to the touch, washing away the sweat of the ride and the heat of the day. Even my mosquito bites seemed sated, the infernal itchiness stayed, at least for the moment. I ran my hands along the bottom of the pool, threading my fingers through the mud and grass at the bottom.

God bless Owen, I thought as I surfaced, flipping long hair over my head and staying low, wanting to keep my body below the water. He'd taught me to swim when we were children. In those days he'd raced a small, makeshift sailboat in the Charlestown Harbor, and I'd insisted on joining him. Anything that Owen had done, I'd wanted to do too. Fearing that I would drown and Grandfather would have his head, he had given me lessons from a dock at the mouth of the Ashley River. We'd come home wet every afternoon that July, my dress dripping, and Naji would merely shake his head at us. But he never revealed our secret. To this day Grandfather still did not know of the lengths Owen would go to please him.

Wise-for-Years was sloshing towards me, the bottle held high above her head. She sunk to her waist and stroked through the water with one arm, passing me. At the other side of the pool she set the bottle on the rocky embankment and pulled herself up slightly, turning and sitting, the water splashing against the tops of her breasts.

"Come," she said again. "There is chair here."

I stroked over to her and pulled myself up onto an underwater ledge; it was a long, flat rock, slick with algae. We faced the far end of the pool and the Stygian forest at its edges, infinitely still. I looked up at the sky, counting the stars, cool water lapping at my collarbone.

"Good," she said, sighing, and I looked at her. She swiped the back of her hand across her mouth and held the bottle to me. "Rum—you want?"

"Why not?" I answered brazenly, grasping the neck of the bottle and lifting it to my lips. I took a gulp and immediately gasped for air, coughing and shoving the bottle back towards her. I'd never before partaken of the spirituous drink, and now I knew why: it hurt.

Wise-for-Years giggled, took another swig, and passed it back to me. "You drink and we talk," she said, quite comfortable with ordering me about.

"Hmm," I answered, but I took the bottle, sipping more cautiously this time. I felt the liquor hot in the back of my throat, then warm as it slid down my esophagus to settle in the pit of my empty stomach. "Oh," I murmured appreciatively, surprised. "That's quite good."

We'd passed the bottle back and forth between us several times before she spoke of Jack. She cleared her throat, eyes ahead. "You will marry Walks Between, yes?"

"Perhaps," I answered, thinking disgruntledly of the last words we'd shared by the river.

"You will marry him, even though he is Indian?"

"He is half white, too," I said. "But it does not matter to me. His skin does not matter."

"To others it will." I turned sharply toward her and she held up a hand. "I do not want him, no longer," she said softly. "I have had husband. I loved him. Walks Between, there was no love between us. You are his mate, Rides-Like-a-Man. Bear Killer can see it. I see it."

She paused, looking over at me down her long nose. "Why do you not see it?"

I ran a flat hand over my wet hair, smoothing it down over my shoulder and wringing it out there. My hands shook slightly, and it bothered me. "I do not know him," I said.

She scoffed, trailing a hand through the water. "You know him. He is what he is. He is *wa'ya*, like his name."

I reached behind my head for the bottle, taking another gulp. "Well, forgive me for saying so, but that doesn't tell me anything."

When I passed the bottle back to her she raised her eyebrows playfully, her eyes twinkling. "He is good lover, Silent Wolf."

I snorted, covering my mouth with a hand and blushing violently. She shrugged, giggling, and we burst into laughter, the sound breaking the silence. My whole body was warm now, and I felt free as bird on the wind. I rolled my eyes and hiccupped, which made us laugh even harder.

"Give me that," I ordered, reaching again for the bottle.

Hours later, when the moon had sunk low into the trees, we made our way back to Kituhwa. Wise-for-Years marched ahead of me, wrapped in one of the blankets, singing off-key to a song I could not understand. I hummed along with the beat as I walked behind her, clutching the empty bottle in one hand and her shoulder in my other.

Suddenly she stopped in her tracks, and I bumped into her back, giggling. "What is it?" I whispered, peering around her.

Jack stood on the path at the western entrance to the village, arms crossed over his chest. His face was shadowed; he stood still as a boulder, unspeaking. I dropped the bottle and it rolled away, clinking into the darkness. Wise-for-Years patted my hand and stumbled past Jack, humming softly as she disappeared into an open hut.

"Traitor," I muttered, pulling at the top of my blanket.

"You are drunk, woman," he said sharply, walking towards me. I backed up, tottering, and clutched at the blanket near my collarbone.

"I am not," I denied, then hiccupped, the words strange on my woolly tongue. "I've never touched the demon drink, never in my life."

"Well, lass, you touched it tonight." He reached out, his hands hot on my damp shoulders. "I knew you were a wee bit perturbed with me, but I didn't expect you to run off with Wise-for-Years. What in God's name possessed you, Mac?"

"Don't you 'Mac' me, you daft Irishman," I ordered, poking him in the chest with my pointer finger. "We talked, woman to woman." I stopped suddenly and hiccupped again, covering my mouth with a hand. "You're a good lover," I told him.

"Oh, Christ Jaysus," he murmured, his accent thickening as he jerked back, running a hand through his long hair.

"Jackson Wolf, the Lord will hear you," I said primly, still clutching the blanket.

He moved swiftly, grabbing me by the waist and hauling me over his shoulder. I let out an "oomph" as my gurgling stomach made contact with the side of his neck. "That's it," he growled. "You're to bed."

I bounced on his shoulder as he strode purposely through the sleeping village, the contents of my stomach sloshing about. I spent the trip looking up at the sky, identifying each constellation and stating their names in very loud, very obnoxious Greek.

"Hush, you wee *datsi*," he ordered, ducking into a hut near the river and depositing me on a small platform topped with pelts. I sat up crookedly, bracing my hands at my sides.

"I feel a bit unbalanced," I said, surprised.

He crouched down before me and reached out, running his fingers down the long tail of my still-wet hair. "God, you are lovely," he murmured. "Stupid, but lovely. Now get you to bed, lass. If you feel your gorge rise, just lean over the side, aye?" He stood quickly and went to the open doorway.

"Where are you going?" I asked, turning to snuggle down into the pelts.

"For a cold dip in the river," he answered shortly, disappearing into the dark.

I rolled onto my stomach and yanked the blanket from beneath me, the fur soft against my bare skin. I stretched my arms over my head and pushed my feet down as far as they could go, curling my toes. For some time I watched the doorway for Jack, but soon the world wavered before my eyes. As I closed them I saw in my mind his piercing gaze, green and glittering.

"Wolf," I mumbled, giggling drunkenly. Then, like a dog: "Woof, woof."

In the night I turned to him, my mind sober but my body still loose and yearning from the rum, and ran my hand across his bare chest, setting my lips against the side of his hot neck. "Jack," I whispered, trailing kisses up to his jaw, heedless of consequence and propriety. "Are you awake?"

He moved like a panther, snatching my hand and bringing it down to the square of his breechclout—the only piece of clothing he wore on summer nights. Beneath the thin deerskin he was long and rigid, and I curled my fingers instinctively, exhaling a sigh. He stopped my movements, bringing my hand back to his chest. "Is that awake enough for you?" he asked, his voice raspy.

"Jack, I want . . . ." I murmured, sliding my lips along his cheekbone to the temple that held the jagged, white scar.

He caught my arms, rolling over me and bracing himself on his elbows, the muscles in his forearms sinewy and locked. He ran a rough hand through my hair, clasping the back of my head. He dipped his head, lips wet on my collarbone as he kissed me there, leaving a trail of goose bumps in his wake. "Jack," I whispered, "please."

He took my mouth then, and his lips were deft and firm as he caught my full bottom lip softly in his teeth, and I felt the heat of him pressed against my belly beneath the leather. He bent and took one of my nipples in his mouth, suckled it gently and then released, blowing soft air on it as it peaked. I watched him, eyes widening as my chest rose and fell, my heart erratically beating. He saw me looking at him and pulled away from me, rolling onto his back and tucking me firmly into his side. "Woman, you will surely be the death of me," he said, the words a rumble in his chest.

Suddenly ashamed of myself, I turned from him. "I'm sorry," I murmured. For twenty-six years I'd kept a tight hold on my maidenhood, and now I was willing to give it away in the blink of eye, like some common trollop, I thought hastily and miserably.

"Sorry?" Jack chuckled. "There's naught to be sorry over, lass. It's happy I am to know you want me as much as I want you. But I'll never forgive myself if we do this while you're sotted. I've no control tonight, lass, not with you naked and under me for the first time. I won't have you regretting it on the morrow."

At his words I felt suddenly bereft and ridiculous. He loves me, I thought, though he hasn't yet said the words aloud. *We are meant*, he had said, and at that moment I knew it to be true. All else fled from my mind as I stared out into the darkness of the rude hut. *I am on the wild frontier, with the man who is to be my husband*, I thought. *This truly is a new world, and I can make it my own, live on my own terms.*

"I won't," I said suddenly, and the sureness of my words calmed my beating heart like a promise. "I won't regret it. I want you, Jack." I turned over on my side so that I was facing him again and reached, sliding my hand into his where it rested against the pelts at his side. "Will you have me?" I asked him, my heart in the words.

He rolled over, running a big hand down my arm. "You're certain, Mac? It's sure to hurt a bit, in the beginning."

"I don't care."

"We will be married," he said roughly, watching me intently.

"Aye," I answered, grinning up at him.

His nostrils flared and his eyes widened, and he was above me in the span of a heartbeat, his lean, muscled body flush with mine, his hands in my hair and at my breasts, warm breath on my stomach. I gasped as he kissed his way up my neck, heat building between my legs. I moved restlessly, lifting my hips.

He murmured foreign words as he moved down my body, Cherokee endearments that I could not understand. Something was gathering in me, a thrilling, building feeling, like the rushing of a storm as it picks up speed across the ocean. He took the insides of my thighs in his hands and pressed outward, opening me to him. Then he touched me there, cupping the heat of me in his palm, and I pressed against him, moaning. "God, you are slick as molten silver," he murmured.

I spread my fingers out against the pelts and lifted my head to look at him, and the sight of him there between my legs—the breadth of his shoulders stretching out across my white knees and his muscles bunched and tensed, his eyes liquid emerald—almost stopped my heart. He lowered his head between my knees, and as his tongue touched me my head fell back, and the storm inside me peaked, the unrelenting bashing of the sea against a rocky shore.

"Jack, you can't—" I gasped, and he lifted his head—his eyes bright—then bent again to his work. I called out his name and closed my eyes, and light flickered on the undersides of my eyelids.

He moved up the length of me, poised at the opening of my body, his hardness pushing against the slick folds there. My eyelids fluttered open and he touched his lips gently to mine, his breathing labored. "*Ada'wehi'yu*," he whispered. "You are mine. Say it."

I raised my hips and lifted my arms, running my hands down the planes of his stomach. "I am yours."

He touched his forehead to mine and thrust deeply, and I felt a stab of pain as he filled me, stretching my virgin skin. "Are you all right?" he asked, hovering over me, deep inside, his body still and tight as a drawn arrow.

I swallowed and nodded, the pain slowly ebbing. "Yes."

When he moved inside me I was certain that I would die then and there, and that I'd be found in ashes, still smoldering in the daylight. I pressed my hips to match his movements and we rocked together until the world went white. "Jack," I begged, clutching at his shoulders.

He thrust again, and again, and as energy climbed my body like a fire-fever I let go, and the world turned a deep blue behind my eyelids. "I love you," he uttered roughly. Then he threw back his head and clenched his jaw, and I felt heat pulsing into me.

When it was over, Jack wrapped his arms around me and rolled over onto his back, taking me with him, evidence of him silky and wet between my thighs. I settled my head against his chest, woozy and satiated.

"God help me," he muttered. "Even if you are drunk as a sailor—the devil take me, and be done with it."

Chapter 23

Kituhwa

So this was what it meant to mate. I touched a hand gingerly between my legs and grimaced. I was still sore from the night before, but it was a satisfying feeling, almost as if I'd worked hard at something worthy, and my body knew it.

I slipped from the hut before Jack woke, unbearably shy of him, and went down to the river, following a trail along its edges until I'd found a sandy spot far enough to be hidden from the prying eyes of the village. I waded into the shallow water, naked, and washed with a bar of lye soap I'd tucked in the furthest corner of my saddlebags. The sun had not yet made its quick ascent over the mountains, but the sky was pink around the edges, and so daylight could not be far. Crickets chirped in the reeds along the bank, their music a steady humming that enveloped this part of the river; across the water a doe came to the edge, bending its graceful brown neck and drinking.

I didn't move a muscle as I watched the deer. It raised its head and looked directly at me. Then its eyes shifted behind me and to my left, and it bolted, disappearing into the forest.

"They sing songs of women like you," Jack said quietly.

I crossed my arms over my chest self-consciously, turning my hips to hide my body. "Oh, good morning," I said, my cheeks hot.

"And a fine one it is, at that." He grinned at my attempt at covering myself. "I've seen all of you now, lass—there's no hiding it."

He'd walked to the river in only his breechclout, and he shed it swiftly and ploughed through the water towards me, completely unabashed. His hair, gilded and streaked, hung down over his collarbone, the silver stud in his ear glinting in the sun off the river. As he walked the muscles in his thighs and stomach clenched and released, and I felt myself draw a quick breath, my pulse quickening. "What are you about?" I asked, looking down at the water curling around my hips, avoiding his eyes.

"Well, and I should think that's obvious."

He caught me up in his arms and fell gracelessly, dunking us both beneath the river. I tried to kick away but his grip was sure, and we surfaced, sputtering and laughing. He kept one hand wrapped around my waist and brushed my hair back from my face with the other. His body pressed against mine, hard and seeking. I smiled at him, my hands splayed on his hairless chest.

"You are a child, Jack," I told him, brushing water droplets from his body.

"As of this moment, it's sure I'm a man," he answered, glancing down at the evidence between us. He raised his head and regarded me with a crook of his mouth. "Last night—you don't regret it, do you? You're not hurt?"

"No."

"Well then, would you be willing to make another go of it?" he asked, almost shyly. "For I've found I want you even more, now that I've had you but the once."

"I've had you as well," I countered, embarrassment fled.

"That you have, lass. Again?"

"Aye. Again." I grinned, brushing a hand against the trail of fine hair just below his navel. "And again and again and—"

He silenced me with a kiss, then pulled me down into the shallows until I lay beneath him, my back against the sand. In an instant he was inside me.

It was astonishing, the way he filled me to completeness, and how my body—tender and new—accepted willingly, muscles clenching around him as he began to move, bending and taking one of my breasts in his mouth. "From the first day we met I wanted you beneath me," he whispered as his hands moved over me, slippery and dangerous. "From the next I knew I'd have none but all of you."

My buttocks pushed back against the rough sand at each thrust, and the water lapped against us, splashing up around our hips. Pressure built at my core, and when he bent and laid his mouth against the side of my neck I felt it splinter, and I cried out. The muscles in his arms clenched tightly, his shoulders rounded and tense, and he buried himself inside me to the hilt. His eyes opened on mine, glittering and green, and I clutched at the sand beneath my hands as he pulsed into me. Then the pressure ebbed, and I felt my heart beating there where our bodies joined.

Jack wrapped his arms behind my back and scooted us farther up onto the bank in one motion, staying inside me. He braced himself on his elbows and I hooked my heels around his big calves beneath the water. He watched me, silent.

"The others, was it like this with them?" I asked, unable to stay my racing brain.

He cocked his head to the side, studying me with a wry half-smile. Wet strands of his hair hung down his face, dripping onto my chest. "No," he answered honestly, his eyes clear. "There's something powerful between us, and it frightens me, because I feel I might lose my soul to it, and to you, if I'm not careful. But then I know that you hold me with you, and that if we burn, lass, we burn together."

Chapter 24

The Overhill Towns

We started for Chota at dawn, crossing into the deepest section of the Cherokee Mountains, past ranges the Cherokee called the Unaka and Chilhowee, following alongside a tributary of the Little Tennessee River. We'd stayed three days in Kituhwa, and as we left the village—our saddlebags heavy with corncakes, dried venison, squash, and fresh clothes—I felt as though I'd left a piece of me there by the Tuckaseegee River, a shard of my childhood, of the woman I'd been before and never could be again. I lifted a hand from Fire Eater's reins, touching the necklace of blue beads at my throat. Wise-for-Years had tossed them to me as we'd ridden out of town. She'd jogged alongside our horses, waving a hand at Jack and nodding at me. At the western edge of the village she'd stopped, and when I looked over my shoulder I saw her turn away from the crowd, her regal shoulders slumped.

To Squirrel and Turtle we'd not had to bid farewell. They were our new traveling companions, riding with us to Chota to visit and gather news of their respective clans. Jack had revealed, earlier that morning, that Bear Killer had another purpose in sending them. He hoped that in Chota they'd have better training as young warriors, out on the edge of enemy lands. There, the threat of raids by the Creek from the south, the Iroquois, Shawnee, and Illinois from the north, and the Choctaw and Chickasaw from the west kept the young men busy, watchful of war. Many had already left the Lower and Middle towns for their spiritual capitol, in search of the old ways—of life before the influx of Europeans.

I glanced over at Turtle, who now rode his own horse—a spotted, brown and white mare—at my side. He swatted at a buzzing insect, wrinkling his nose, color high on his round cheeks. I wondered what it would take to turn such a boy into a warrior, battle-ready and hardened. Ahead of us, Jack and Squirrel rode side by side, talking. Squirrel seemed as excited about the journey as his horse, a black gelding who stepped high as his rider bounced up and down in his saddle, waving an arm as he asked questions. They were questions, I knew, because Jack would answer back with a lifted eyebrow and a dry tone, occasionally looking over his shoulder at me and winking.

I was content to listen to them talk, the rapid-fire, guttural language a sound I was now accustomed to. It had been the background music of our time at Kituhwa, like the low hum of an orchestra, hidden in the pit below a stage as the actors go about their business, unaware. Jack's voice was very much altered when he spoke in Cherokee: his lyrical, distinctive mix of accents was suddenly raspy and strange, all traces of the Celt in him vanished.

As I studied the back of his head, sunstreaked hair caught in a hemp cord, I wondered for the thousandth time about this man I was to marry. How did he exist between two such disparate worlds? I was eager to meet his parents, to spend time with the people who'd raised a man capable of both dangerous precision and roguish charm.

Ahead of us, four big deer came flying out of the forest, crossing our trail and bounding into the woods on the other side. Their tails were a flash of white, vanishing in green undergrowth. A sudden thought came to me, and I nudged Fire-Eater with my heels, trotting up to Murdoch.

"Jack," I said sharply, interrupting his conversation with Squirrel. He turned in the saddle, expectant. "The favor?" I asked pointedly.

He grinned at me, Squirrel watching curiously. "Ah, well, the favor was for Wise-for-Years. I promised her, long ago, that I'd bring her the woman I was to marry, should I ever. She wanted to be certain I'd bound myself to a worthy lass."

"Worthy!" I said, temper flaring. I kicked Fire Eater into a canter and moved ahead of the pack, unwilling to argue within hearing of the boys.

"She gave you the beads, so I'd say she finds you fit," he called after me, voice tinged with satisfied amusement.

I raised up in my saddle and turned, glaring back at him. "I don't care a whit what she thinks," I shouted, propriety forgotten. "Arrogant woman."

Jack trotted up next to Fire Eater, and we rode side by side through the tall grass that lined the river. He looked over at me, eyes hooded. "Aye, arrogant she is. And you'll know nothing of that, will you?"

I sniffed indignantly, and he rode Murdoch closer, snatching the reins from me and stopping both horses. He took the back of my neck in one hand and jerked me towards him, kissing me hard. Squirrel and Turtle snickered behind us. "I love you," he said, staring me down. "I've never loved another. So cease fretting about Wise-for-Years, aye? She's keeping the bed warm of a trapper over in Tuckaleechee town, and thinks none of us. And I surely think none of her."

He sounded so frustrated that I nodded silently, and he released me, sitting back into his saddle. I'd never been jealous before, not like this. Mentally, I swore to sweep any notion of Wise-for-Years from my mind, and to think only of the future, stretched out before us wide-open and new.

I cleared my throat. "Saint Augustine once said that 'faith is to believe what you do not yet see,' and that 'the reward for this faith is to see what you believe.'"

He looked over at me and quirked an eyebrow, scratching the top of his head with one hand. "If by that you mean that you have faith in me, all right then. But it seems to me that having faith oftimes means believing in things you're most likely never to witness with your eyes. And that the reward is in the believing itself, not in the seeing."

I do not know when we passed from the westernmost border of the colony of North Carolina into the unfathomably remote reaches of Cherokee country. There were no blazed trees like those that marked the Boundary Line in South Carolina, nothing to tell us where this colony ended and where sheer wilderness began. Here was nothing of backcountry or frontier—terms I'd always heard used by men in Charlestown, to categorize the great unknown. Here the earth shifted, the mountains moved and rolled, flattening into fertile river bottom and rising again, shifting from blue and purple to gray and green and brown in the sunlight. It seemed limitless and wild, and if a lumbering fairy-tale dragon appeared on the path before us—briny scales flashing, with Saint George at his heels—I did not think I'd be at all surprised.

The valleys here were vast, the land between mountains sprawling and flat, perfect for farming. As we followed the Little Tennessee River, winding and muddy with summer rain, I felt as though we'd been transformed, taken into another world. Certainly we'd come from the dark forests, rocky rivers, and steep mountains of the Blue Ridge, and out into the light. Up ahead, fields of cultivated crops appeared in large squares like the rice fields of a huge plantation, only these were filled with pumpkins, corn, beans, and sunflowers—so tall that when I rose on my toes in my stirrups, I could reach up as we passed, brushing one tremendous flower's soft black center.

"The land—it's enormous," I murmured, sitting back down into my saddle, the sun hot on my flushed face. I loosed the neck of my shirt, flapping it against my chest to cool the sweat that beaded there. Jack glanced over at me and grinned, a flash of white in a face already tawny, tanned even more so by the late June sunlight.

"There're three hundred acres or more, or such was the case last I visited," he said. "Since Chota is a white town—a peace town—no blood can be spilled here, and so the women take to the fields with a fury. Have you had a pie made from a pumpkin, Mac?"

"No," I answered, amused at the energy radiating from him as he rolled his shoulders, then patted his flat stomach with one hand.

"Well, 'tis a treat to be sure."

Turtle shouted something from behind us, and Jack's eyes flew to the front. He shaded his face with a hand, leaning forward in his saddle.

"What is it?" I asked, straining my own eyes. There seemed to be two riders approaching far ahead along the riverbank, but I couldn't make out much more than their blurred outlines.

Jack tucked his tongue between his teeth and whistled, high and sharp. He glanced back at Turtle. "Damn fine *dikta*," he said. Then he looked over at me and shrugged, and his eyes flashed—a blink of pure green. "Well, lass, it's Ridge Runner coming for us now. And I hope you're ready, because my Mum's with him and riding fast."

Nerves fluttered in my belly, and I swiped the hat from my head and tucked it in my saddlebag, then wet the tips of my fingers with my tongue, smoothing back the hairs at my temples. I looked back at Jack, but he'd taken no notice of me. He was shaking his head in affectionate exasperation, chuckling as the riders neared.

"Riding like a warwoman, and with Herself turning a half-century old, no more than a week ago."

Fire Eater pawed at the dirt, and I leaned down and patted the side of his neck. "Lord, give me strength," I whispered into his slick coat.

Jack slid from Murdoch and reached for my hand, and I took it as he helped me to the ground. We stood together as the horses pounded up, halting on the riverbank ahead of us.

Ridge Runner—like Jack, clad only in a breechclout, his tomahawk and musket strapped across his back—jumped from his horse and turned to help Jack's mother dismount. She took his outstretched hand like a queen and landed softly on her feet.

I studied her earnestly from beneath my lashes as they approached. Surprisingly—for I'd almost expected her to be clothed like an Indian woman—she wore a light cotton dress, the lace faded a dull yellow at the collar and wrists. Her hair, the color of aged brandy run through with silver, was tied back in a bun. She was tall for a woman, buxom and plump. She moved with an energy and quickness that I recognized well in her son.

When they stopped in the grass before us, her hand light on Ridge

Runner's muscled forearm, she smiled broadly at Jack, and then her eyes settled on me. Wrinkles webbed out from the sides, and when she blinked the color was hazel, green-gold, like that of a cat. She reached out for Jack, and he hugged her tightly, lifting her off the ground. Suddenly Ridge Runner stood before me, smiling down, and I moved impulsively, taking his hands in mine.

"*Ha'siyu*?" I asked quietly, eager to show him what I'd learned since we'd last spoken.

He squeezed my hands gently, his dark eyes warm. "*Ga'siyu*," he answered. "And you, Rides-Like-a-Man, your journey has been long." He bent suddenly, looking intently at my face, then over at Jack, who stood silently with his mother, watching us. He straightened and nodded imperceptibly at his half-brother before reaching out and cupping my cheek. His hand was rough and warm, and when he stepped back from me he chuckled. "You look well, Sister," he said.

"Oh, now, don't you be teasing the lass overmuch, you big Indian." Jack's mother pushed past Ridge Runner and laid her hands on my shoulders, her smile wide. "These two are nothing if not wicked," she said, her eyes pinning mine. "Sure, and you've the golden look of an angel about you. But you'll need have more than pretty to stand next to Jackson."

Jack cleared his throat. "Quinn, may I present my dear, sweet mother, Nora Elizabeth O'Shaunessey Wolf."

I kept my eyes on her and shifted my feet, squaring my shoulders beneath her grip. "Yes madam, I believe I do have more."

"Well then," she said shortly, hooking her arm through my elbow and leading me away from the men along the riverbank, towards Chota town. "'Tis the Lord's own truth I am the lad's mother, though there are times I don't at all claim him. It's a fine, wild life, loving a Cherokee man. I've lived with me own for over thirty years now—since he took me from me own father, down along the banks of the Savannah."

I glanced back over my shoulder at Jack; he stood side by side with Ridge Runner, both of them grinning like loons. He raised a hand and waved. I narrowed my eyes at them.

"So, lass, you'd best be preparing yourself for a wedding. You've the look of a well-loved woman about you, which means we've not much time. I knew the lad was fair tough to resist, but he should've been a wee bit more thoughtful, what with you being a maid untouched."

I coughed and clutched a fist to my chest, my cheeks flaming. The woman was a force of nature, I thought, as relentless as a tidal surge. "But how—" I began, mortified.

She stopped in her tracks and turned to me, patting my hot cheek with a gentle hand. "Do you ken that we're the only white women for hundreds of miles around?" she asked softly. Then she smiled, and it lit her face with a maternal warmth I'd not known I'd been missing. "I can see it in your face, dear one. And, Lord, if I don't know me own son—the way he watches you says it all. Have you not seen a wolf stand o'er its prey? No? Well, the beast's eyes glitter, and the poor animal it's captured is surely done for."

The Council House of the mother town of the Cherokee Nation sat atop a massive earthen mound, perhaps forty feet high. Around it spread familial dwellings. Each of the more than seventy families living here kept both a winter house—a rough, rounded hut—and a summer house, rectangular and half-open, with small outbuildings for storing crops. While the winter huts were dark and closed-in, the summer houses were often two stories high, with sleeping space for parents, children, grandparents, and assorted husbands and cousins. The beds in each were built exactly as the bed we'd slept on in Kituhwa: made of wood and constructed like a platform, they sat two feet above the ground, draped in bear, deer and beaver pelts.

I stood in the summer house we'd been offered by one of the many members of the Wolf clan, setting the few things I'd kept in my saddlebags on a small shelf. I placed them in a row: my pearl inlaid brush, *The Turkish Embassy Letters*, worn from handling, my rapidly diminishing bar of soap, a crumbling corncake and a small piece of cheese, and the druid's rock. I shook out the one dress I'd brought and folded it over my forearm before laying it on the edge of the bed. When I heard footsteps outside I snatched the rock, slipping it into the pocket of my breeches.

A tall Cherokee man ducked beneath the low doorframe. When he raised his head I knew him at once. I'd seen that imposing stance, the sharp cheekbones and flinty jaw, and the flashing dark eyes stamped on both his sons. He approached me silently, his shoulders held back like a soldier, his hands hanging loosely at his sides. He wore deerskin leggings beneath a leather breechclout, a beaded belt with a long knife at his waist, and short moccasins. His head was plucked bare but for a patch of long hair, mostly gray, which was gathered with a leather thong and one black feather, and hung down his back.

I knew that he had to be more than fifty years old, but he was still long and lean, his chest muscled and strong. A line of tiny black dots was tattooed in a curving pattern across his cheekbones and nose, out to the hairline at each temple. Though in appearance utterly different than my grandfather, both men radiated with the same intimidating effect: they were imposing, kingly, possibly without meaning to be either.

I dropped automatically into a curtsy, my knees a bit wobbly. He reached out a hand, clearing his throat. "Please, there is no need," he said in rough English.

I looked up into deep brown eyes, so much like Ridge Runner's that I blinked. I took his hand and stood straight, tilting my chin up to meet his impenetrable gaze. "Your sons look much like you, sir," I said. "I am honored to meet you."

"And I you, Rides-Like-a-Man. My first son has told me much about you. I have never in my life heard him speak of an *un'ega* woman or man with such esteem. Walks Between, he has long needed a wife. For many years I have wondered which he would choose, a *Yun'wiya* woman or a white one."

I cleared my throat. "According to Jack, he didn't have a choice. It seems he had a dream, and that was that."

Jack's father nodded, his lips a line, expression stoic. I could not picture him—so tall and savagely elegant—beside a woman so seemingly earthy as Jack's mother. I could not imagine the events that led them to be married in the Cherokee tradition, could not fathom the fact that the man before me had literally stolen his wife away from a riverbank, and that she'd come to love him and bear him a son.

"Dreams are omens. If my second son saw you in a dream, you were meant to be his." He crossed his arms over his chest then, in an action so like Jack that I bit my lip to stifle a smile. "I know how the *un'ega* view men of two races. They believe them to be less than a man, like a mongrel dog, because their blood is not pure. What do you think, Rides-Like-a-Man?"

The druid rock felt warm in my pocket as I closed my fingers over it. "The men who believe such things are small-minded. They cannot see the world outside of their own." Again, the man was silent, and he stared at me, regal and proud. "I love your son, sir," I said in a rush. "I've never known another like him."

"My name is Walks-With-Hawks," he said. "I am the *uku* of Chota. I am also to be your good-father. I want to welcome you, that is all." He nodded sharply at me, eyes flashing, and turned swiftly, ducking back under the door of the summer house before I could say another word. I put both hands to my flushed cheeks and felt dirt there from the trail. I rubbed at it roughly with my knuckles, walking to the bed and sitting abruptly, my legs perilously close to buckling.

I'd just met my future father-in-law, and he was as stonily enigmatic a man as I'd ever encountered. Images of Owen and Grandfather—red-haired and laughing, arguing over a game of chess—flashed in my mind. Struck with a wave of loneliness, I bent over my knees, resting my forehead against the bones. For the second time since I'd left Charlestown, I felt unbearably strange and out-of-place, a white

Pocahontas in the Indian court of King James. A wave of homesickness washed over me, pain beginning to spread in knifing pangs between my eyes. I rubbed a hand against my forehead and lay back on top of the pelts.

When the vision came I fought against it, but there was naught that I could do.

She folds a letter in white hands, the ruby on her ring finger flashing in candlelight. Her hair is brown, and it falls in soft ringlets around a heart-shaped face, her small nose sprinkled with freckles. She blinks, and her brown eyes spill over with desperate, angry tears.

Her heart aches in her chest, so much so that she feels it would easily break inside her if she let it. He is leaving, sending her away to a savage place where no one will know her and she'll die of longing for him.

"We will leave in the morning," says the man standing behind her in the shadows. "I'll ride with you as far as I can. Saul will accompany you the rest of the way."

"You don't love me at all if you do this," she tells him, looking directly into an oval mirror, framed in ornate silver.

"I do this because I love you more than my own life," he says. "Take the letter to my cousin. Be sure she reads it well." He reaches out from Morphean darkness, but she looks up and directly into the mirror so that her gaze meets his in the reflection, her eyes blazing.

"I hate you."

"Mac, wake up. Come back to me, lass."

The girl slipped away from me like a firefly fading into the night. I felt Jack's hands on my shoulders, heard the fear in his voice. When my eyes finally focused, I found him kneeling before me beside the sleeping platform, his mouth a thin line.

"I'm fine," I muttered, blinking.

He sat back on his heels, sliding his palms down my arms and holding my hands tightly in his. "You didn't seem fine a moment ago, when you were thrashing about on the bed, staring up at the ceiling like a blind woman. It scared me."

"I'm sorry," I said, and at his look I shrugged. "I know, you don't want me to be sorry. But I am, because I know that this is what you'll have to live with for the rest of our lives—your wife having fits like a patient in Bedlam."

"Sure and I've no idea what Bedlam is, but you'll be my wife, fits or no." He studied me, unblinking. "What happened? You cried out a name at the end."

My chin came up sharply, and a face flashed in my mind, frightened and pale. "I did? What did I say?"

"Rebekah," he said softly. "Isn't that Scott's wife?"

I stood quickly, letting go of his hands. I walked out of the summer house into the fading afternoon sunlight, sucking in gulps of air. When I felt

Jack behind me I turned, running a hand harshly over my forehead, back through my unbound hair. *Please, not yet,* I thought frantically. *I'm not ready.*

"Mac?" He stepped up to me, cupping my cheek and laying his forehead to mine, quelling my shuddering. His breath was warm on my mouth.

"Yes, it's Owen's wife," I said wearily. "She's coming."

Chapter 25

Chota

Smoke shifted in the breeze above the Council House. I watched it spiral up into the night, disappearing in a sky void of stars. Earlier that day clouds had built over the Unaka Mountains, threatening a storm that had yet to break. I paced in the dirt, glancing at the open doorway and frowning. Though I was to be the wife of Walks Between, I had yet to be accepted by his people. They'd barred me from their meeting tonight.

I kicked at a rock, sending it rolling over the side of the mound. In Charlestown, I'd heard friends of my grandfather scorn the Cherokee, calling theirs a "petticoat government." But Jack had been telling me for fortnights about the egalitarian nature of his people, how they allowed women to govern side by side with men. So I was desperately curious about what was going on inside the Council House, and uneasy—for I was certain that they must be talking about me.

"Be still, Rides-Like-a-Man," Ridge Runner said from his seat on a wooden bench nearby. "You make me dizzy with your pacing."

I turned on him sharply, squelching the urge to stick out my tongue like a petulant child; he couldn't help that he was my guard for the evening. "I don't understand. They're discussing whether I would be a suitable wife for Jack, are they not? Why can't I attend?"

He looked up, the whites of his eyes bright in the faint light of the fire that burned nearby. "You are white. While you are welcome here, you are still not to be trusted."

I crossed my arms over my chest. "Jack's mother is white."

"Nora was adopted by the *Ani-Yun'wiya*. She has lived here for more than thirty years."

"This is no different than in Charlestown," I said angrily. "My life is being decided for me by those who do not even know who I am."

Ridge Runner shook his head and stretched his long legs out before him in the dirt. "Nothing is being decided tonight. Jack chose you, and that is all."

I narrowed my eyes at him in the dark, wondering if he knew how much he sounded like his own father. "That is *not* all. They are still in there"—I stabbed a finger toward the huge, rotund building—"casting doubt on my intentions, deciding whether or not I am fit to marry one of their own."

"Your people do not do this when a son or daughter wishes to marry?" he asked wryly. "No questions are asked about intention, or about the family of the person they are to marry? Is every mate suitable, then?"

I gritted my teeth, knowing he was right but still frustrated with my own helplessness. I sat beside him with a thump, curling my feet beneath me. Under my breath, I counted slowly to ten, willing patience. Finally, I turned my head, looking up at him. "Do you believe that I am suitable?"

"You are his mate," he said simply. "He has seen it. I have seen it. I welcomed you long ago, little Sister."

"Thank you," I murmured, the weight on my chest easing.

We sat in silence for several minutes, watching the fire. I cleared my throat, folding my hands in my lap. "How old were you when your father married Jack's mother?"

"Perhaps four summers. I barely remember my mother. She passed to the otherworld giving birth to another brother, one who did not live. I do remember when Nora came to Chota." He chuckled, the sound deep and familiar. "I could not understand anything she said. No one could, except for *eda'ta*—my father—who learned English as a boy, from a priest the *Ani-Yun'wiya* took from the Iroquois. But even he had difficulty. You have heard her talk."

I nodded. "I can't imagine how she came to marry him, your father."

"You marry my brother."

"That's different—I do so of my own free will," I said. "Nora was stolen from her family and brought here, was she not?"

"Yes. She was not happy at the first, of course. But she is a rare woman, my second mother. For weeks she screamed, then one day she demanded that my father teach her our language. I do not remember when things changed—when she changed—only that she became *Ani-Yun'wiya*."

I stared out into the dark, considering his words. "I care for the *Yun'wiya*," I said quietly. "But I will never be one of you. I am white, and I am Scottish—an American, I suppose. I will never be Cherokee."

"Perhaps not," he said. "But when you become Silent Wolf's wife you become part of the *Ani'Waya*. You do not have a choice."

The fire popped, sending a bright orange ember onto the dirt near my feet. I watched it fade, thinking of home.

"He will come to live with you," Ridge Runner said suddenly. "That is what we do, we go to the wife's house. He will be restless, but you must remember that he walks between two worlds, and his path is not easy."

"I will remember," I said slowly. A thought occurred to me, and I studied him for a moment. "Will you come to live in Keowee Valley, when we return? Please know that you are welcome."

Ridge Runner shook his head. "No. I will travel back with you to the Lower Towns, but after a time I must leave to return here. The young warriors must be taught. Oconostota has asked me to do this."

"Oconostota?" I asked, the name unfamiliar.

"He is our war chief, the *un'ega* would say. You have not yet met him."

"Jack will not want you to leave," I said, watching his dark eyes. He glanced at the door to the Council House and gave me a half-smile.

"Yes, this I know."

"We would both have you stay, Ridge Runner. The Valley is your home."

He smiled at me warmly, but shook his dark head. "No, even the Lower Towns are not home to me. Trouble comes quickly. Our *uku* has seen it. This is my only home now."

I twisted to look at him. "What is that word, *uku*? That's what your father called himself."

He looked at me sharply, his black brows crooked in question. "You have spoken to Walks-With-Hawks?"

"This morning, in the summer house. He came to see me."

Ridge Runner shook his head. "I had thought he was still in prayer, far away in the woods. An *uku* is the most important priest-chief. The *un'ega* call him shaman, or medicine man."

There was activity at the door of the Council House, and Ridge Runner moved to stand beside me. Two old women exited, talking excitedly to one another. As they passed us they reached out, touching my face and arms and smiling. Others came pouring out now into the night: three middle-aged women and several men—ranging in ages from what seemed to me to be the boyish to the elderly. I watched for Jack, but Nora emerged, dressed in a deerskin sheath, her hair a thick plait down her back. She stopped just before the doorway and Walks-With-Hawks appeared behind her. He put a hand on her shoulder and said something in a low voice, his eyes on Ridge Runner and me. "What is happening?" I whispered.

Ridge Runner moved closer, flanking my right side. He bent to my ear. "I believe you are to be married, Rides-Like-a-Man. Are you ready?"

The couple walked toward us, a study in dark and light, in foreign and familiar. Jack ducked out of the Council House and jogged past them, stopping before us. He reached out, and he and his half-brother clasped arms, gripping near the elbows.

"*Utset'sti*," Ridge Runner said. "This must be good."

Jack nodded, his smile wide and boyish. "Aye. We marry on the morrow."

"Tomorrow?" I asked, a now familiar jolt of fear and anticipation shooting through my bloodstream.

"Tomorrow," he repeated, bending down and taking my face in his hands, kissing me soundly. I squirmed and pushed at his chest, but couldn't keep the smile from my face. "Aye, lass. I told them we must marry soon, for we'll be making the journey back to the Lower Towns the day after. You'll be wanting to get back to the Valley, especially with your cousin coming."

"Yes, I will," I said softly. "Thank you."

"Enough of that, you wee love bugs." Nora came up beside us, taking my arm and tugging me away from her sons. "On the eve of your wedding you'll be staying at me own house, far from the wicked bridegroom. The women have some preparing to do."

I looked up at Jack, speechless, grinning like an idiot. He winked at me.

"Come now, darling girl. You'll see the lad soon enough."

As she pulled me away I watched Walks-With-Hawks step up to his sons, one dark and solemn, the other flaming and bright. He crossed his arms over his chest, and as Nora led me down the incline of the sacred mound I saw the three men turn into each other, their similar copper faces tightly drawn.

"Do you know anything of a Cherokee wedding, then?" Nora asked me gently as she rummaged through a trunk sitting on the dirt floor of her summer house. She lifted out a blanket tied in a square with a piece of thin hemp rope—like a parcel—and shut the trunk, fastening the latches. She laid the blanket on top.

"No, I can't say that I do," I said.

"Well, it's sure to be fair different from what you do know," she said, rising and coming to sit beside me on the edge of her sleeping platform.

I looked around the room. Though Jack's mother had certainly left the English world far behind, she had still managed to hold onto traces of her first life. There was a rough, square table and two spindly-backed chairs in the corner, and a Bible sat on top next to a chipped china pitcher. A wood framed mirror hung from the far wall, lovely but for a long, thin crack down the middle.

"Jack and Ridge Runner gave that to me on me fortieth birthday," she offered. "They bought it off a trader in Nik'wasi. They almost brought it back to me whole, but they were boys and got caught up in a tussle, and so it's cracked. But don't you know I love it anyway."

I folded my hands in my lap. "What will happen tomorrow?"

"The women will take you to the river before dawn. Jack will do the same, but upstream, with the men. Before any celebration, any meeting of importance, any war—the Cherokee go to water to be cleansed. They'll wash you and play up your face, much the same as if you married an Englishman. Then you'll meet alongside the river, where me own dear husband will talk over you. And you'll give Jack a basket of corn, and he a hank of venison to you."

She smiled at me, reaching out and patting my hand. "And then you'll be married, lass. Sure and we'll all dance and sing, then."

"Why do we give each other those things?" I asked. "What do they mean?"

"The corn means that you'll keep him in bread, and the venison that he'll keep you in meat. That you'll take care of each other." She paused. "You will, won't you Quinn? You must take care of me boy, for he's a rare, special man. Sure, and his path has not been an easy one, what with the face he carries."

I put my hand over hers and nodded, feeling foolishly close to tears. "I will, I promise you."

She nodded and stood, reaching for the wrapped blanket and handing it to me. "Then you'll wear this tomorrow, when you wed me only son."

I took the parcel from her, staring down at it in my hands.

"Go on, dear," she said.

I pulled at the hemp rope, letting it drop to the floor. I turned and set the fabric package on the sleeping platform, bending over it as I pulled back the folds. Inside was a white deerskin dress, fringed in blue, green, and yellow beads along the neck, wrists, and hem of the skirt. A pair of white moccasins sat with the dress, faded at their stitched edges.

Nora cleared her throat. "'Twas me own wedding gown, when I married Walks-With-Hawks. I think it will fit you, for I was slim as a sapling in those days—though not quite as curvy in the chest as you are, least not then. When Ridge Runner told me of you I had some of the women help me to clean it." She smiled, her eyes flashing with memory. "The shoes couldn't much be spared—though I wanted Walks-With-Hawks by then, I got spooked when the old *uku* led off wailing in that banshee voice of his, and I made a go for it across the creek. But I think they'll still do, faded as they are."

I sat on the bed and ran a hand over the snow-white fabric, tears gathering along the insides of my bottom lids. "They will most certainly do," I said. "I'll be honored to wear both."

"Good." She stood abruptly, brushing her hands together and walking to the doorway. "Now, wee Singing Bird was supposed to leave some of your things with your satchel. Ah—here it is." When she came back she held one of my saddlebags. "You've a brush in here, I'm sure. Those golden locks are kept too pretty to be without." I nodded, and she set the bag to the side. "Now, you settle into bed. I've still things to do. We've an early morning ahead of us."

She walked over to me and bent down, pressing a kiss to my forehead. "I know you're frightened," she said softly. "But you'll be fine, just fine. When a man of the *Ani-waya* loves, he loves like no other. So be sure that you're ready, because there's no going back after. Know that if you left him, he'd come for you, wherever you are."

She walked to the doorway and stopped, looking back at me with kind eyes. "Thank you for wearing the gown, child. Though he knows you're tied to your own people, he'll surely lose his heart when he sees you in it on the morrow. Sleep well."

Chapter 26

The Little Tennessee River
July, 1769

Fog hung low over the bottomlands, steaming above the river, gray and thick as pea soup. The ground was rough in places but soft and grassy in others, and I felt every stone beneath my bare feet as I walked toward the river. The women of the Wolf clan surrounded me, and though I felt strange and hollow, they buoyed me with care and safety, a moving fortress of combined female consciousness.

On my right walked Nora, clad in a pale blue dress and bonnet, astonishingly English among the Cherokee women, who wore deerskin skirts and sheaths, many in linen trade shirts and their best beaded and silver jewelry. At my left elbow, a woman my age—a cousin of Jack's and Ridge Runner's, called Alice by her trapper husband—led me into the water. Nora stopped at the edge, and I looked back at her as an elderly woman took her place, wrapping my left elbow in her dry hand. Nora nodded at me as the river climbed my calves, her cat eyes shadowed in the fog.

When the women stopped me I stood still as a statue, the Little Tennessee lapping coolly against my hips. The old woman smiled, revealing a full set of teeth, then reached out, taking the top of my shift and pulling it over my head. She folded it gently in her arms as I stood there, naked and white, the sun breaking the morning with pale beams. As the fog began to dissipate the younger women scooped water in clay-fired bowls, dousing my head, chest, and back. As they washed me with handfuls of sand and sweet-smelling soap they talked and sang in low voices, none of which I could understand. I felt both utterly ridiculous and oddly worshipped, all at the same time. I looked upriver, where the mist had split over dark water and the land curved slowly towards the village, and I thought of Jack.

As I was led back to the riverbank I looked down at my body, clean and pink from scrubbing. Water beaded on my breasts and at my nipples; they were peaked and rose-colored, round as coins. My torso was curved and strong from frontier life; water dripped from the dark blond hairs at the juncture of my legs. As I walked, the river broke over my thighs; I lifted them high with each step, the muscles long and prominent. I'd never felt so aware of myself, of my own body, of my place in the natural order of the world. I'd never in my life felt so much like a woman.

On the shore, Alice and the others dried me with a blanket and slipped the shift back over my head; it stuck to my skin in the wet spots at my chest and stomach. As the sun made its way up the backs of the trees it shot yellow beams through the canopy, and on the fields dew shimmered on cornstalks and pumpkin vines. The village seemed peculiar and empty. As we entered the summer house of Jack's parents I saw a young boy scamper across the village plaza, a string of feathers in his hands.

Only four of the women entered the summer house with Nora and me: Alice, the old woman, and two others who seemed to be about Nora's age. They were all of the Wolf clan, but Alice was the only name I knew. I opened my mouth to ask them, but then found that I didn't want to speak at all—I just wanted to be, to allow this ritual to continue without language.

Nora came to my side and led me to a chair she'd placed in the middle of the room. When I sat she brushed my hair, mostly dry now, in long waves down my back. Alice and one of the middle-aged women leaned over me, running their hands over the strands, talking in low voices. Nora shooed them away with a smile. I looked past her to the mirror on the far wall, and when she moved to reach for the wedding dress I saw my face there in the cracked glass, my eyes wide and luminous, color high on the tops of my cheeks, my lips puffy from sunburn.

"Here we go, child. Lift your arms, now, and I'll slip the gown over."

I held up my arms like a little girl, and the aged deerskin slid over me, luxuriously soft. The fringed beading bumped against my shins as Nora brushed at the front of the dress with her hands, eyeing me critically. She said something in Cherokee to the women, and they jumped up, chattering, and moved to a small basket beside the bed. The old woman watched me seriously, her eyes webbed with wrinkles, white hair hanging into her lap. Then the younger women were suddenly before me, and Alice bent down, studying my face. She dipped a finger into a small pot, rubbing a natural rouge on my cheeks and lips. Satisfied, she smiled and stepped back, her dark eyes friendly in a brown face. One of the women stayed her with a hand and dropped a pair of silver ear bobs into her palm. When Alice realized that I'd no holes in my ears she frowned and handed them back.

The old woman spoke gruffly, and we all turned towards her, surprised. She pushed up the sleeves of her shirt, her thin forearms spotted and weathered with age, and slipped off two wide silver cuffs that hung there. She took one of my hands in hers and slid the cuff onto my wrist. After doing the same to other wrist she nodded at me, smiling.

"*Wado*," I said softly, taking her bony hands in mine and squeezing gently.

"Now, let's have you a gander," Nora said, taking my shoulders and ushering me over to the mirror. "My, you look bonny."

At first glance I did not recognize myself. The supple, white deerskin brushed boldly across my chest and down over my hips, the blue beading at the neck making my own eyes look even brighter. My hair fell softly to my waist, and my lips seemed as red as if I'd just been kissed—and kissed roughly. The skin at my arms, chest, and face was ruddy from the sun, a color like heavily creamed coffee, but still much lighter than the tawny faces of the women behind me. I blinked, recognizing myself in the glass.

The old woman said something, and Nora clucked her tongue. "Sure, and she's ready. Can't you see the look in her eyes?" She bent and looked at me in the mirror, her face wavering in the cracked glass. "It's time, dear. Let's be off, then."

The people of the village stood in two long lines in a meadow beside the river, forming a human path that ended at the edge of the water. Jack waited for me at the front. At the sight of him, my pulse quickened and my mouth went dry. He was beautiful, Apollo in the wilderness, so utterly different from anything I'd ever known. He was dressed in full Cherokee regalia: pristine deerskin leggings and breechclout, a white linen shirt opened at the neck. Beaded straps crossed his chest, the colors bold blues and reds. He wore a brilliant sash at his waist, and hooked to it at each hip were his knife and tomahawk, sharpened and flashing in the pale beams of sunlight that broke from the woods, just below the tree line. His hair was tied back in a tail, and from it hung two large feathers, one black and one white. Silver cuffs gleamed at his brawny wrists. He wore a gorget around his neck, the silver engraved with royal markings and symbols.

Across his cheekbones he'd been tattooed with tiny blue dots, the color of lapis, which made curving lines up the bridge of his nose and into the crown of his blond-streaked hair. He reached for my hand and smiled, and when I looked into his green eyes I felt—despite the clutch of fear in my belly—a sense of reassurance and calm. *I feel safe with him*, I thought, gripping tightly to his hand, the silver cuffs clinking together at our wrists.

"How are you, lass? Do I terrify you so that you feel the need to run?" He led me down the path between the villagers, and though I knew that they stood there—each clan represented, their faces dark and strange—I saw nothing but Jack.

We stopped before Walks-With-Hawks, who stood with his back to the river, his wrists and ankles covered in rattles made from turtle shells. He wore a ceremonial robe, his face painted in a slash of colors. He eyed us seriously, a long wooden pipe in his hand. The pipe was much like the one I'd watched Attakullakulla share with Laughing Crow in Keowee Town. Though the mouthpiece was made of stone, the long shaft was carved poplar wood, and from it hung leather tassels, beaded and feathered. I looked up at Jack.

"I won't run," I answered him.

Walks-With-Hawks spoke loudly, in a sonorous voice that carried over the crowd. He lifted his hands in the air, turning to face each of the four sacred directions and blowing smoke towards them with the pipe. When he moved, the rattles at his ankles shook rhythmically. Jack bent his head slightly as smoke was blown towards his chest and then to mine, whispering whenever his father paused. "He blesses the earth and gives thanks to the Creator, and to the four directions," he said. "He welcomes you as a member of the Wolf clan, and as his white daughter."

I kept my eyes pinned on Walks-With-Hawks. He was a powerful figure. Suddenly I understood why he held the highest spiritual position of Chota—when he spoke, those near him could not help but listen, drawn in by the fervor of his words. I was enraptured, despite my fear and despite the fact that without Jack, I could not understand a word he said.

Jack released my hand and turned away from me, and someone touched my shoulder. I broke from a trance and looked up at Nora, who held out a cane-woven basket full of several ears of corn. "Take them, lass," she said, smiling.

I reached out and took the basket from her, the braided river cane handle still warm from her hands. When I turned to Jack, he held a slab of cooked venison set on a wooden plank. We exchanged gifts, and Walks-With-Hawks chanted something that Jack did not explain, and as the villagers cheered and whooped the sun broke over the mountains, heating the fields and flashing on the river before us.

Our wedding meant that the day would be spent feasting and celebrating, with many Cherokee traveling from neighboring villages to meet up with old friends and to speak with Walks-With-Hawks, who was to perform three other marriages before sundown. Jack and I walked along the village plaza hand in hand, winding through the crowd. Squirrel and Turtle caught up with us at the communal fire, where a group of women were laying out clay pots to dry before firing. The boys patted Jack's shoulders in hearty congratulations, grinning widely at me. I curtsied to them like they were English gentlemen, making them laugh. Squirrel—lanky with height—bent towards me shyly. "Happy for you," he said awkwardly in English.

I clapped my hands in delight, rising on my toes to kiss his cheek. "*Wado, Sala'lani'ta,*" I said as he put a hand to his cheek, blushing beneath his brown skin. Turtle nudged him teasingly.

Jack said something in Cherokee to the two boys, and we moved away. "He's been asking me to teach him English since we left Kituhwa," he told me.

"That was kind of you."

He laughed wryly, tucking me into his side as a group of adolescent boys raced past, *anesta* rackets bouncing on their shoulders. "Sure and there was nothing kind about it," he said. "He was driving me batty with the begging."

Suddenly I thought of Meg Wheeler, and how before we'd left for the Overhill Towns, she'd asked me to teach her to ride. The Valley came into my mind then, sloping and long, with the Blue Ridge behind, majestic and familiar. I stopped and turned to him, swallowing back a wave of anxious homesickness. "Do you think that the settlement has fared the summer well?" I asked. "What if the Regulators have returned? You haven't heard of any Creek raids in the Lower Towns, have you?"

He looked down at me, his green eyes solemn. "No, I've not heard talk of any raids. The frontier is no place for the faint o' heart, but you've good people there. Try not to worry overmuch, Mac. We'll be home soon enough."

"I'm ready," I said quickly, the need to be back on Fire Eater and across the South Carolina border buzzing just beneath my skin.

"Don't I know you are," he said. "You look ready to jump out of your skin. We'll leave at dawn, aye? For now, how about the pie I've promised you?"

I laughed as we turned back to the dirt plaza. "I don't see how you eat as much as you do and stay as lean as you are. You must have a bottomless stomach."

"I've always room for pumpkin pie, especially when me mother's made it," he said. Then he waggled his eyebrows at me. "And it's hoping I am that you'll help me burn away the pie, later. I've been seeing your fine, white arse in my hands since Walks-With-Hawks blessed us this morning."

My cheeks flamed and I jerked my hand from his, giving him a shove and grinning despite myself. "Only you could mention something like that and your own father in the same breath," I muttered.

"Aye, 'tis a gift of mine," he said seriously, his eyes twinkling.

On the dirt path ahead stood Jack's father, talking to a white-haired man and a younger woman, their backs to us. A crowd formed nearby; villagers seemed eager to speak with the trio. From the back, the white-haired man seemed so familiar that I squinted, trying to place him.

"Attakullakulla," Jack said shortly, moving faster and pulling me along.

When we stopped before them Walks-With-Hawks nodded at us curtly, and Jack reached out, grasping the forearm and elbow of the older chief in what I'd come to think of as a Cherokee handshake. Attakullakulla, still slight and spry—his dark eyes flashing with youth—exchanged greetings in Cherokee with the younger man. He nodded at the two of us, motioning with his arms. Jack inclined his head, winking at me so subtly that I almost missed it.

"You are Rides-Like-a-Man," Attakullakulla said to me in English, his voice kind. "It has been a long time since we last met. Laughing Crow says you are well."

"Yes," I answered softly, awed by him still and remembering the hot night when I'd asked him for the impossible. "*Wado.*"

He turned to the woman next to him, placing a hand on her shoulder. She was perhaps thirty years old, and of average height. Intelligent dark eyes stared back at me from a face carved in the Cherokee tradition: high cheekbones and prominent nose, her black hair straight and long. She wore a homespun calico dress, but Indian beads hung down over her chest and on her feet were moccasins. I blinked, startled. Pinned to her collar was my grandmother's opal brooch. Attakullakulla looked back at Jack and me. "*Nanye-hi*, daughter of my sister," he said. He glanced at Walks-With-Hawks. "How do you say it?"

"Niece," the *uku* replied.

The woman glanced at me and nodded at Jack, speaking in near-perfect English. "Jack, you have married," she said. "This is good, I can see it in your eyes. This woman is your wife?"

"Quinn MacFadden Wolf, meet Nancy Ward, *Ghighau* of Chota town. She too married an *un'ega*."

The woman laughed, smiling at me. "After my first husband died, I married a white trapper. Before I was *Nanye-hi,* and now I am Nancy. But you were first Quinn, and are now Rides-Like-a-Man. I welcome you to Chota."

A bit disconcerted after hearing my married name spoken aloud for the first time—and to a woman wearing a piece of my own jewelry—I looked at Jack. "*Ghighau?*" I asked.

"Beloved Woman," he said. "Nancy is also a warwoman. When her first husband died in a raid with the *Ani-Kusa* she took up his musket and fought alongside the warriors. Now she makes peace, like her uncle."

"I try, but the task becomes greater day by day," she said modestly, looking back and forth between the two of us.

I cleared my throat delicately, offering a slight curtsy. "It's lovely to meet you, Madam Ward. I owe your family a great debt—without your uncle I would have never met Jack, nor settled in the mountains. He was trusting of me when he had no reason to be."

Attakullakulla clapped his hands together suddenly and turned to Walks-With-Hawks, who had been watching our exchange in silence. He spoke rapidly in Cherokee. Jack took my elbow and smiled at Nancy Ward. "It is good to see you again, *Nanye-hi*," he told her.

"And you," she said. "It was been a long time since you were home, Walks Between. We have all missed you."

As we turned to go the growing crowd descended on the three Cherokee leaders, clamoring for attention. Jack jerked me back suddenly. A naked toddler wobbled past us on chunky legs, squealing, and in her wake waddled a fat old woman, clapping her hands in admonishment.

"Pie," he said succinctly, directing me towards his mother's fire.

That evening, alone in the summer house, we faced each other awkwardly. Outside, the sounds of revelers around the fire—of drums and singing, and feet brushing against dirt in wild dancing—were faint, and it was as if the room had shrunk in comparison, all focus centered on the man before me. On my husband.

Though I'd given him my innocence weeks before, this night—our wedding night—held a weighted meaning that made me as shy and fumbling as if we'd only just met.

He reached back behind his neck, unclasping the engraved gorget and setting it on the table. When he took the hem of his shirt and pulled it up over his head, the muscles at his brown belly clenching, I turned away and faced the sleeping platform, sliding the silver cuffs from my wrists. I slipped out of the moccasins one by one, catching toe to heel as I stepped from them. As I bent, reaching for the hem of the wedding dress, his forearms curled around my waist, drawing me back against his bare chest. I jumped, startled. He pressed a kiss to the side of my neck. "Hello, wife."

I looked down at his forearms, dusky with blond hairs, and ran my hands over them, feeling the vein that rose beneath the skin there. "Hello, husband."

He moved his hands to my shoulders and turned me to him. He wore only the thin leggings, and they hung at his hips, the laces undone at the waist. I pulled my eyes from the faint trail of hair there and looked up into his face, so strangely savage and beautiful. His eyes, so lively and amused for most of the day, were now hooded and sleepy, though the color was intense, a deep black-green.

"I've been wanting you since the sun came up," he said hoarsely, moving his hands to his sides and clenching his fists. "I don't know if I can be gentle."

At his words a low heat simmered at the juncture of my thighs, and I felt the pressure begin to throb there and at my breasts. If he touched me then I knew I'd splinter. I reached again for the hem of the dress, pulling it over my head and laying it carefully over the back of a chair nearby. Then I turned to him and licked my dry lips, and as his hands reached out and curled over my breasts I took his face in my hands, pulling him down to me.

Chapter 27

The North Georgia Mountains
August, 1769

Fire Eater stepped carefully through the rocky waters of Warwoman Creek, his hooves scraping intermittently against stone, thumping down into the shallows. Jack rode Murdoch ahead of us; the paint found his footing and charged up the grassy embankment onto the other side. Behind me, Ridge Runner sat motionless on his horse in the middle of the creek, watching the land with dark eyes that missed nothing. Night was quickly falling, and we had yet to find a place to make camp.

Since we had wanted the journey back to the Lower Towns to be quick, we'd taken a route different from the one we'd used to get to Chota, and the Overhill Towns. Instead of retracing our path along the Cullasaja River trail and back into the northwest end of Keowee Valley, we had skirted several of the southernmost Middle Towns and followed an easier trail into Georgia. We'd soon be upon the Chattooga River, and would ride alongside it into South Carolina, where we'd eventually come into the southwestern edge of the Valley, near Tomassee Knob. And though this well-worn path had certainly been faster and safer for all of us than the rockier trail we'd forged weeks before, the danger lay now in the fact that we were traveling through country claimed by both the Cherokee and the Creek—a stretch of land in northern Georgia the two nations had shed blood over for centuries.

I clucked my tongue and kicked my heels lightly into Fire Eater's sides, lifting my backside from the saddle and taking a swathe of his mane in my fist. He bounded up the bank and onto the other side of the creek. When we reached Jack, the two horses bent their heads in unison, munching on rivercane. But Ridge Runner motioned us onward with a quick wave, his eyes still scanning the creek. Darkness fell much more rapidly in the woods than in the open, and while the thick underbrush around the river made for good cover, it was difficult to navigate. We moved our horses into the trees, silent.

We did not speak for what had to have been at least another hour, moving along the small creek until it opened up into a curling, black river, the tops of its boulders blanketed in moonlight. Finally, Jack turned in the saddle, his face cast in shadows, outlined by the light of a waning moon. "It'll have to be here," he said quietly. "It's the Chattooga."

"Where is Ridge Runner?" I whispered, sliding from Fire Eater's back, my moccasins crunching lightly on fern and pine needles.

Jack looked past me into the dark. "He'll be about soon enough. He's checking our trail." He reached into his saddlebags, pulling out a blanket and stash of food. I followed suit, moving with him away from the horses and farther into the woods. He stopped and dropped the blanket on the ground, sitting upon it with his legs crossed, munching on something that seemed to be a dried venison stick. I folded my blanket into a pallet-shape and laid it beside him. When I moved to sit he suddenly looked up and past me. I whipped my head around, a scream in my throat.

Ridge Runner emerged from the trees, walking silently toward us on the mulchy ground. I gulped back the sound, a hand at my windpipe.

"Anything?" Jack asked, his voice low.

"No—but they are near," Ridge Runner said. Jack nodded, reached up and tugged on my hand until I sat next to him.

"No fire tonight, Mac. Eat something. We're needing sleep."

He said something in quiet Cherokee to Ridge Runner as he stood, finishing off the last of the venison. The two brothers talked for a moment, and then Jack bent and pressed a quick kiss to the top of my head and walked off into the woods, sliding the musket from his back into his deft hands. Ridge Runner took another blanket from his own saddlebag and placed it on the ground across from me. He did not speak to me, just lay on his back and shut his eyes, his arms folded over his chest.

I stared into the shadowed woods after Jack. An owl hooted nearby, and one of the horses snorted, pawing at the ground. Finally I lay back, curling on my side, the pistol at my waist pressing rudely into my hipbone. I slipped it from its hold, setting it inches from my hands.

Though I'd become much more used to the stillness of night in the mountains, I was antsy as a small child, unable to sleep. It was uncanny, I thought, the way that Jack and Ridge Runner could fall asleep in the space of a heartbeat, only to awake alert and ready. When I'd asked him about that particular talent, Jack had told me that such was a trick Cherokee warriors learned as young men. Sleep, though oftimes few hours of it, meant survival. A warrior's body had to find rest if he was to be ready for what could come.

I moved my arms restlessly, repositioning them behind my head. Through the canopy of giant pine, walnut and oak above I could see the moon and stars, utterly clear, as though if I reached out I could pluck one from the sky. I began to count them one by one, as a child counts sheep in her bed.

Hours later I heard Ridge Runner stir. Out of the opened slit of my eyes I watched him stand and pick up his musket, disappearing into the woods like a ghost. In the next moment Jack settled down against me, curling into my back. I reached an arm behind me until I felt him there.

"Sleep, lass," he murmured, his breath warm on the nape of my neck.

The forest exploded with wild screams, the flash of musket fire and bodies racing through moonlight only to disappear into shadow again. I sat up in a rush—my heart in my throat— pulling my knees to my chest and scrambling for the pistol at my side. A hand wrapped around a hank of my hair and my head was whipped back. Pain burst at my skull, and a strange Indian face, painted red, filled my vision. He tilted his head to the sky and shouted something, his Adam's apple convulsing. My fingers found the handle of the pistol, but when I turned the man yanked it away from me with ease and tucked it into his leggings. He jerked my head again, and when the pain cleared from my eyes I watched a knife rip across the man's throat in the dark. My face was splattered suddenly with hot blood.

Jack crouched over me, and at the sight of him I jerked back. Blood streaked across his face and into his hair. His eyes were black with banked rage, the tattoo a live thing that moved across his nose and forehead. He grabbed my arm, yanking me to my feet. "Get to the river. Swim 'til you find cover along the bank and stay there. Take this." He folded my hands around the leather hilt of his knife. "I'll find you—go!"

I stood there dumbly as he sprinted into the fray. Bodies moved across my vision in the dark. A pair of unfamiliar eyes met mine, and I took off towards the river, stumbling through undergrowth. A horse raced across the clearing in front of me, riderless. I caught the sheen of moonlight on water and shoved my way through a bramble.

I went into the Chattooga River at full run, scrambling over boulders, slipping and soaking my legs up to the knee. The knife scraped against granite as I pulled myself up. Ahead I saw moonlight hit a swirling mess of whitewater.

Someone breathed deeply behind me, and I turned. His face was in half-shadow but I recognized it well—it was the Creek man from Tomassee Knob, the one who'd dragged me along the ground like a leashed dog. He grabbed my ankle, yanking me off the rock. I tumbled down on top of him, keeping my grip on the knife. He pinned me against the boulder, and when his hand closed around my throat I took the knife hilt in both hands, shoving it awkwardly into his stomach. The shock of hitting human skin jarred my arms. There was the sickening sound of blade against bone. The man looked at me in something akin to astonishment, the whites of his eyes blazingly bright, and curled his hands around the blade protruding from his belly, black blood surfacing in the crooks of his knuckles.

He gurgled something unintelligible and fell forward, crashing into me. I pushed at his sweat-slick shoulders—my breath wild, nausea and fear rising in my throat—and he crumpled to the rocky shallows, a still hump in the dark, water lapping at his lifeless body. I stepped away, my moccasins soaked, and felt my face and neck go hot as I heaved the contents of my stomach into the water. I wiped my mouth with the back of my hand, the sick, steely taste of bile on my tongue.

The sounds of fighting still clamored in the woods by the river, and I spit into the dark, tears running down my cheeks. I'd started to turn away when I remembered the knife. I bent down to the body and pushed at it with my foot. The dead man rolled over. I avoided looking at his face and reached for the knife at his belly, and when I gripped the handle and pulled, it made a ghastly, sucking sound. Choking on my own tears, I tied the hilt of the knife to my belt, hooking it against a loop there. I took one last look at the forest—hoping for a glimpse of my companions, but seeing only the yellow flash of musket fire in the underbrush—then sloshed into the river, cool water swirling up around my waist and over my chest. I stroked with my arms and kicked my legs like a pair of scissors, keeping myself afloat as the rush took me downstream.

Water sloshed into my ears and mouth. I heard only the dull roar of the swift-moving river and my own desperate breathing. Each time I blinked the water from my eyes I saw nothing but blackness before me, and at times a flash of silver light against boulders and tree trunks along the bank. Broken tree branches and logs bumped against me; the rapids threw me into a boulder, pain splintering out through my right shoulder. I grappled for a hold on the stone with my other arm, but my fingers slid through the slime along its underbelly.

Exhausted, my head sank under the water and I closed my eyes. When the burning started in my lungs I surfaced with a hard kick, inhaling air in deep gulps. Above the river the moon emerged from a cloud and cast in wide, pale light an eddy, a spot near the bank, away from the current, where the water lay stagnant. I swam towards it with the last bit of my strength, and when my feet felt the pebbled bottom and my hands a downed tree dragging its end in the water, I wrapped my arms around the roots, hugging them tightly.

Something solid bumped against my legs. I looked down to find the man I'd killed staring up at me, his mouth slack and bubbling with river water. I screamed and kicked out, sending the body back towards the rapids. He bobbed away, disappearing into whitewater, and I pressed my face against a root, the wet bark imprinting its rough design into my cold cheek.

I pulled my legs up beneath me and braced them against the ground, half of my body still submerged. As exhaustion overtook me and my eyes drooped with weight, I wound my arms through the maze of roots, anchoring myself to the dead tree. Underwater, the knife blade bumped lightly against my hip in the murk.

"There now, dearie, lay your head down and let me care for you."

A short, plump woman in a country dress—of middle age, the hair springing from the sides of her bonnet sprinkled with strands of gray—leaned over him, pressing something cool to his forehead. He blinked eyes that felt swollen and dry, but managed to reach up and hold onto her wrist with the last bit of his strength. She looked down at him, pity deepening brown eyes.

"Please, mum, where am I?" He asked, his throat hoarse. "What's happened to me?"

"You've been shot, a clean musket ball through the side." She took his hand from her wrist and laid it gently on his chest. "You're at my home, near King's Mountain. Do you know who you are, dearie?"

He closed his eyes tightly though they stung, and when he opened them he stared out over the end of the bed and the tops of his grungy black boots, focusing on the painting that hung above a rough, wooden hearth. It was of a toddling boy, in white baptismal dress. "I'm Arthur Covington, mum. I'm a soldier of His Majesty's army."

The woman leaned over him again, this time with a tin mug. She pressed it to his lips, and he drank, cool water coating his parched throat. "That you are, and if my husband finds you here he'll have us both tarred and feathered. So lie still. You're welcome to shelter 'til you're well enough to sit a horse."

"You're a rebel, mum?" he asked in a high voice, clenching his fingers against the soft down of the bed quilt.

"I am."

He cleared his throat, and despite the fear he found his voice. "Why do you help me?"

She looked up at the painting, and it was if a ghost of her reached out, touching the face of the chubby-cheeked babe.

"Because you've red hair, like my sweet Henry."

My nose pressed against something cold, and I woke in a woozy rush. I opened my eyes to the square underside of Jack's jaw. I reached up a hand to my nose, feeling the beaded strap that lay beneath my face. The sight of Tomassee Knob in the distance, rising above weedy fields, passed before my eyes. It was several moments before I realized that I was tucked in front of Jack on Murdoch's back, that we were riding along the trail, headed home.

Jack's face was bruised along the side I could see, and beneath his right eye bloomed a round swell, a dried cut slashed in a thin, dark red line through the middle of it. When I reached up to touch him there, hot pain shot through my shoulder, and I sucked in air. He jerked his head toward me, and in the split second before it vanished I saw fear and relief flash in his green eyes.

Then he smiled. "Well, now—look who's come back to us," he said.

"How is she?" Ridge Runner rode up beside, craning his neck to look at me.

I swallowed, my mouth as dry as if I'd not spoken in days. Ridge Runner's chest was covered in green and black bruises, as if someone had pummeled him repeatedly with a mallet. I blinked back the tears that stung the backs of my eyes. "You're wounded, both of you," I croaked.

"Aye, but we're not so bad as you, lass," Jack said. "Your shoulder was rent from its socket—that whole side of you is a nasty yellow. Though I set the arm, you'll feel it for a while now."

"How long have I been asleep?" I asked, a rush of weariness settling over me like a blanket.

"We didn't find you 'til dawn, and you've been with the spirits since then, so we've no way of knowing." He cleared his throat, looking up at the trail ahead. "I thought you'd drowned, Mac. I sent you to the river unknowing if you could even swim."

I lay my head against his warm chest, sleep settling over me. "I can swim," I murmured.

"You must swim as an otter does, Rides-Like-a-Man," I heard Ridge Runner say, and his voice sounded as though it came from a great distance. "You held to that tree for hours. Surely the spirits were with you. You made it through the Drowning Hole."

"I can swim," I repeated, as welcoming blackness engulfed me.

Lush green enveloped our small party as we rode the skinny trail into the south end of Keowee Valley. It was August now, the deep of summer, and trees hung heavy with growth, blocking the sun. I was fully awake, sitting upright on Fire Eater—I'd insisted that I could ride alone—and though my shoulder throbbed incessantly, I kept my eyes trained to the trail ahead.

My face was flushed, anticipation fizzing beneath my skin. I felt much the same as I had that day over a year ago, when I'd laid eyes on the Valley for the first time. Today, though, there was more than the joy—there was peace, a sense of utter rightness that I'd never felt before, not even in Charlestown. This was home.

The horses stepped carefully down the embankment and out of the forest, a rutted path there where a year before had been only a solid carpet of slippery pine needles. Green hills rolled before us, long and rising, and I silently counted the cabins by name: O'Hare, Simons, Brown, Harris. I swallowed against the knot that formed in my throat at the sight of the Wheeler's finished cabin among the others. The great blue hills, the Blue Ridge, rose from behind my own cabin, mystical and seemingly distant, smoky as aged sapphire.

We crossed the lower pastures, skirting patches of corn, and passed by the smoldering communal fire pit. Murdoch snorted, and Jack shifted in his saddle. I strained forward, eyes seeking any sign of the homesteaders. When we moved through the cluster of cabins in the middle pasture and started up the hill to my own I shut my eyes tightly, fear a dull ache in my bones. "They're gone," I said.

"Nay, look. They're just at your own house."

A crowd of people stood in the dirt yard before my cabin. Zeke and Hosa were perched on my porch step, and though I couldn't make out the expressions on their faces, I saw that they hung back from the action, leaning against the posts there. At the sound of our approach the crowd turned almost in unison, and Meg broke from her father's hand, bounding down the hill.

"You're back!" she yelled, head bare, brown hair flying out wildly behind her. "You're finally back!"

"Meg, wait a moment," her father ordered, and she stopped, looking back at him pleadingly.

"Mac, you've company." At Jack's low words I looked up and past the child, watching as the tall, barrel-chested figure of my grandfather stepped to the front, the tails of his burgundy coat flapping against the backs of his knees in the breeze. Behind him, Naji stood formally, his driving dress pristine among the crowd of weathered farming clothes. Beside Naji was a stranger, a short, olive-skinned man in European dress. My gaze shifted past him, focusing on the gray-haired man moving down the hill.

I blinked. "God's eyeballs, it's Grandfather."

Jack stiffened. "Your grandfather? The one who raised you?"

"Yes," I whispered. Campbell was moving down the hill toward us, his walking cane punching the ground at each step. His expression was oddly banked, and I wondered that he wasn't yelling.

"He'll not know we've married, then."

Jack's tone was odd, a mixture of confusion and—could it be nerves? I turned, raising my eyebrows. "Jack, he hasn't a fathom you even exist. How could he?"

He looked down at me, his mouth a line. "Owen."

"Elspeth Quincy MacFadden!" Grandfather bellowed, chugging down the slope. I slid my right leg across Fire Eater's back, slipping to the ground.

Ridge Runner snorted. "Elspeth?"

I shot him an evil look but squared my shoulders, awaiting my fate. Grandfather stopped in the grass before me, a Clydesdale coming to sudden halt. He stamped his cane into the ground inches from my feet, both gnarled hands on the silver handle. I dropped into an unconscious curtsy, eyes on the brass buckles of his shoes. "Good God, ye are a boy!"

Startled, I remembered what I wore: men's breeches, ripped and stained, a dirty trade shirt, the arm missing from my injured shoulder—Jack had had to cut it away to set the bone— and Indian moccasins. I stood and scratched my head, at a complete loss.

"And with a bare head, like a heathen," he growled, the tip of his round nose bright pink.

"Hello, Grandfather," I managed. "I'd no idea you'd be coming for a visit."

Without warning, he stepped forward and crushed me to him, hugging me tightly. I wrapped my arms around his generous belly, love coursing through me. "More than a year it's been," he grumbled, his chin against the top of my head. Then he pushed me away from him, grasping my upper arms. "A year," he repeated, his voice rising. "And no word from ye, not a one—from the girl with ink stains down her fingers, who kept a dozen diaries."

He tightened his grip, and I yelped, pain at my sore shoulder. He jerked back his hand and leaned forward, and at the sight of my bare arm, the bruises an ugly yellow, his face went alarmingly white. "Who is responsible for this?" he roared.

Jack, who had been standing silently by with Ridge Runner, dropped Murdoch's lead and stepped to my side. Though Grandfather was well above the average height of a man, Jack towered over him, stoic and strange.

"I am," he said.

Chapter 28

The MacFadden Settlement

"So ye are the Wolf, aye?"

The three of us—Grandfather, Jack and I—gathered on the porch of my cabin, the sun sinking behind the Blue Ridge in a melting ball of orange. I sat primly in one of the rockers that Hosa had built for me, clad now in one of my best dresses. The silk ruffle at my collar itched my neck, but I squelched the urge to scratch. My hair, clean from a quick dunk in Tomassee Creek, was plaited and tied with a pale pink bow, not a hair out of place. Jack faced me, his back to the mountains as he leaned against a post, the picture of perfect ease. I studied his face, searching for any sign of anger. Grandfather paced across the porch between us, the wooden planks groaning with each step.

"I am, sir," Jack answered him, crossing one moccasined ankle neatly over the other. If not for that face he could've been a young English lord, waiting indolently for his turn at the whist tables. Though he'd need a glass of sherry and a change of clothes, I thought absently.

"My grandson spoke of ye," Grandfather said. "Said ye'd been sniffing 'round my granddaughter."

"Grandfather!" I rocked forward, planting my neat boots on the floor. "Owen said nothing of the sort."

"You be silent, child," he ordered. "Ye are in enough hot water as it is. I'm talking to the mannie here."

Jack glanced at me, and in a heartbeat I caught his thoughts. *Let him be, lass, he's had a shock of it.* He uncrossed his arms, dropping his hands. "Aye, sir, I suppose that would be true."

Grandfather turned to me, pausing in his interrogation of Jack. "You'll know Owen's married? To a sweet lassie named Rebekah?"

"I do," I said. And at the question in his eyes I cleared my throat. "He told me he would, but I saw it, too. I didn't know it'd happened so soon. I hate to have missed it."

"Aye. Well. Ye know your cousin. He's working as secretary to the girl's father now, moved to Boston, of all places. Pah." Grandfather waved a hand through the air and turned abruptly to Jack, niceties finished. "That big savage who travels with ye, he's your brother? So you're an Indian, are ye?"

"I am. And I'm half-Irish, as my mother's an O'Shaunessy of Cork. My father is Walks-With-Hawks, priest-chief of Chota town. I'm descended from six generations of priest-chiefs, though I'm afraid that the Irish in me has a far less noble history. My great grandfather was a gambler and a wanderer—but not an unsuccessful one. He once won a Spanish cutlass off a Gypsy king."

Grandfather's head shot up, a smile threatening the corners of his mouth. "A Gypsy king, posh," he muttered. Then his eyes clouded. "You've been called half-breed, I'd wager."

"Aye."

"That will hurt my Quincy," he said, shaking his head. I began to rise, and he held out a hand to stay me, palm down. "It will, and there's nothing the either of ye can do about it. As for me, lad, I care not what ye look like, only that ye see her well-cared for. Do ye even have a pound to your name?"

"Oh, we're about discussing the dowry now, are we?" Jack said, remaining expressionless, though his eyes sparked. My eyes widened, and I whipped my head towards Grandfather. He'd stopped his pacing and watched the younger man in awe. When he found his voice he threw a hand up in dismissal. "We'll get to that soon enough."

"Well, then," Jack uncrossed his legs, straightening and looking out over the mountains. He nodded at them. "I've no great load of money to speak of, seeing as how we don't use coin that way. We trade instead. But I do own most of the land from the western border of Quinn's to the North Carolina boundary, and several miles across. It's rich earth, and I've had more than a fair share of offers for bits of it."

"You own that land—all of it?" This time I stood, my hands at my cheeks. "Why did you never tell me?"

"I was hoping you'd want me for my other charms," he grinned.

"My heavens," I murmured, finding that I needed to sit again.

"Well," Grandfather cleared his throat. "Why have ye not started a plantation, lad? Ye could be rich in fruits and even cotton, should ye wish it. Ye'd surely be the wealthiest landowner in the whole of the backcountry."

"Mayhap, but I've no interest in forcing slaves to do my bidding."

Grandfather rolled his eyes and looked over at me. I shrugged helplessly. "Ye'd best get to changing his mind about that, lass." He brushed his hands together. "The dowry. Hmph. If I consent to your taking Quincy's hand, ye'd be offered a dowry of fifty thousand pounds a year. That suit ye, Wolf?"

I glanced at Jack and swallowed. "Grandfather, we've already married," I said in a rush.

The old man looked back and forth between us, his eyes narrowing. I cringed, anticipating the explosion to come. But he leaned over, shaking his head and muttering beneath his breath. When he rose his face was red as a cherry, and I got to my feet, walking to him. He waved me away and backed into one of the other chairs, sitting with a thump. When he looked up, sound burst from him in an uncontrollable guffaw. He slapped his knees, continuing to shake his head, laughing so hard that he wheezed. I looked frantically at Jack, and he shrugged, the corner of his mouth crooking up.

"Grandfather, are you quite all right?" I crouched before him, my hand on his knee. He wiped the back of one hand across his nose, his eyes watering, and patted my hand with the other.

"Of course ye've married," he managed. "Why in the world would ye have asked me? Ye've never asked me to do a thing in your life—ye've just gone and done it."

"Grandfather," I murmured, worried.

"Well, lass, it's true. Ye are as stubborn as your father was, and I gave up trying to change ye long ago. Married," he said, standing. He reached out and ruffled my hair, as if I were a young boy. Then he stood and went to Jack, holding out his hand. "Good luck to ye, man. She's a trial."

They shook hands and Jack grinned, and Grandfather lumbered off the porch. "I'm to bed," he called, waving a hand behind him.

"But you're to have the cabin," I called, starting after him. He turned, shaking his head.

"No, I'll sleep in the barn with Naji. I'd rather be with the horses anyhow."

Stupefied, I watched him start away. But he stopped suddenly and turned back to us, stuffing his hands in his pockets. "One more stipulation to the dowry, Wolf," he said loudly. "Within six months ye must to Charlestown to be married good and proper, by a Catholic priest. I dinna think a journey to the Town of Lies would kill ye."

Then he walked away, the back of his gray head bobbing over the crest of the hill.

"The Town of Lies?" I asked Jack, moving to stand beside him. He reached out and tugged at my plait.

"That's the name the Cherokee gave your Charlestown, long ago." He watched as my grandfather disappeared into the barn. "Your wily grandsire knows more than he lets on."

I walked softly down the run in the middle of the barn, looking for Grandfather and Naji, who I hadn't even had a chance to greet properly in all of the madness of the day before. Morning light pierced the cracks in the rough boards, paling the ground near the open doors. I reached up and took a crabapple from the ledge there, and when I turned back I saw the strange man from yesterday at the end of the long hallway, peering over Fire Eater's stall door. I cleared my throat. "Good morning, sir. I'm afraid I was remiss yesterday—I am Madam Wolf."

The man jumped at the sound of my voice, staring at me for a moment before swiping the feathered cap from his head and bending a leg in a courtly bow. His rich brown hair was tied back with a piece of gold string. He wore striped pantaloons and red hose, his feet encased in buckled leather shoes. When he spoke it was heavily accented, the syllables rolling extravagantly off his tongue.

"*Signora* Wolf, allow me to introduce myself. I am Paulo Di Pietro, servant to her Highness Maria Therese, the Duchess of Tuscany and mother of Grand Duke Leopold III. Your grandpapa tells me that this is your horse. He is *bellisimo*."

I walked to the stall door and dropped my hand over the side. Fire Eater loped over, taking the fruit from my palm with a slap of his lips. As he crunched away I reached out my other hand, rubbing his velvet nose. "Mr. Di Pietro—" I began.

"Please, I am Paulo," he insisted, interrupting.

I nodded politely. "Paulo, if I may ask, how did you come to be acquainted with my grandfather?"

The man smiled. "I came upon him in Charlestown, *signora*. We attended the same dinner party, at the house of a man named Drayton. You know of him, *sì?*"

I nodded, wondering why on earth my grandfather—an ardent Whig—would be supping at the table of one the most powerful Tories in the colony.

"I was sent by Her Highness to purchase foreign treasures for the *Palazzo Pitti*—the royal palace. She has great appreciation for the work of an artist called Rembrandt, and it seems that *Signor* Drayton has several paintings in his possession."

"Her Highness must lead quite a life, to be able to send you all the way across the ocean," I said.

Paulo nodded solemnly, as if taking the statement to heart. "Ah, yes, it is 'quite a life,' as you say. Since the end of the Medici reign the Duchy has been the most powerful family in all of *Italia*; they, too, are great patrons of the arts." He clapped his hands suddenly. "But you know this—*Signor* MacFadden told me of your travels in my country."

"I know but a little," I said, unable to suppress the smile. "But tell me sir, how did you arrive in Cherokee country?"

"When I told *Signor* MacFadden of my wish to see the great frontier, he offered me a place on his journey. I could not dismiss an opportunity to report to my patroness all the bounties of South Carolina. She has a great interest in your wild savages, especially."

I grinned now, picturing my robust Scottish grandfather making a deal with the spry little European before me. Paulo walked to Fire Eater's stall, rising on his toes to look over at the stallion.

"He surely cannot be of English blood, *no*? His head and neck, they are curved like that of an Arabian stallion. What is his lineage?"

I stood beside him, watching Fire Eater pace the stall, shaking his head and snorting. "He's showing off for you, sir," I said, smiling. "His lineage? According to my Cherokee good-brother, he is of Spanish descent—he comes from a line of horses stolen from De Soto and his men when they traveled through Georgia more than two hundred years ago."

Paulo cocked his head, studying Fire Eater with lively brown eyes. "If this is true, he could still be of an Arabian line. In those days the Spanish king bought many of his horses from an Arabian shah. They arrived on ships, just as they did in Italy, when the Medici family did the same." He looked up at me suddenly. "How does he ride? He is fast, *no*?"

I nodded. "The fastest I've ridden."

Paulo considered me with a look I can only describe as intensely Italian: a steady warming of the eyes, masculine and appreciative. "Your *nonno* told me of your skills at horsemanship. If you say that he is fast, *signora*, I must believe you."

He backed away from the stall and offered another bow, taking my hand and kissing the back of it. Startled, I merely stared. "Perhaps I will see you and your Fire Eater race before I am to leave this place. *Ciao, Signora* Wolf."

As Paulo walked out of the barn Jack entered, nodding politely as he passed the shorter man. The Italian stared after him, obviously stumped by Jack's size and arresting looks. Then he saw me watching and offered a jaunty wave before exiting out into the sunlight.

Jack bent down, cupping the back of my head with his hand and pressing his lips solidly to mine. I leaned into him, unable to resist. "I'm wondering if the dandy Italian has an eye for my wife?"

I chuckled, shaking my head. "No, but he's quite smitten with Fire Eater. He seems to think that the horse has royal Arabian bloodlines. I believe he'd like to see him ridden, to gauge how fast he can be. Interesting, hmm?"

Jack grinned suddenly, taking my hand in his. "Well, he's to get his chance, lass. Your grandsire's bet five pounds on Fire Eater, on a race to be held the day after next, down at the English fort. Settlers all the way from the Long Canes to Estatoe will be gathering for food and drink, to watch the horses run."

"He's made a bet on Fire Eater?" I said sharply, irritated. "That's just like him, to use another without asking, the old tyrant. And whom does he propose to ride *my* horse?"

Jack chuckled, and there was something in the sound that made me snatch my hand from him.

"Why you, Mac, of course."

Chapter 29

Fort Prince George

The grounds around the abandoned English fort were packed with people. It was such an utterly different view from the one I'd seen on my arrival to the frontier over a year ago that I had to blink my eyes in the mid-morning sunlight, certain that red-coated soldiers would emerge from the barracks, carrying sacks of provisions on their shoulders. But now a variety of shades colored the faces of the people gathered here: there were the copper tones of the Cherokee, who had come by canoe across the river and from upper towns on the Keowee to watch the race and to trade deerskins and pottery; the leathery browns of local trappers, faces permanently dirty from years in the bush, harvesting pelts; and the startlingly white faces of colonial settlers—including my own—who had traveled long distances to do some trading of their own and to interact with other Englishmen, perhaps desperate for the sight of something familiar in a still-strange land.

I watched a family from a settlement near Seneca pick a spot near the water. Two young boys dug birch fishing poles from the back of a packed wagon while a mother and daughter—both clad in green bonnets and checkered, muslin dresses—draped a blanket on the grass, the father passing over a basket which I knew would be filled with picnicking food.

And over beneath the Treaty Oak stood the gambling men, spitting tobacco into the dirt and placing wagers on the race to come with an old man—a wizened sort of master of ceremony—who kept the coins in a faded leather pouch. The old man heckled the others, daring them to bet more of their hard-earned money and needling them into raising the stakes. Nearby, tied to several posts were the racehorses. Their riders stood beside their mounts: two rough backcountrymen, an upcountry planter, and two

Indians who talked quietly, ignoring the *un'ega* participants.

Our canoe slid to a stop in the rocky sand. I hiked up my skirts and stepped out, glaring over my shoulder at my grandfather. "I simply cannot believe that you have wagered on *my* horse," I said forcefully but quietly, heat and nerves heightening the color on my cheeks. "And just what do you think they'll all do when they find that Quincy MacFadden is a woman, Grandfather? They will not permit me to ride."

"Faith and coin, lassie," he answered, stepping out behind me and nearly toppling over into the water. Naji caught his elbow, pulling him away from the river. He looked at me from behind the old man, crooking an eyebrow.

"He's grown into quite the codger since I've been away, hasn't he?" I asked the black man impertinently, fuming. Grandfather spun around to look at his servant, and Naji shook his head, his voice low, smooth and dark as warm molasses.

"Miss Quinn, you know better than to ask me somethin' like that," he said.

Grandfather patted Naji on the shoulder. "Good man," he said, then took his tricorn from the canoe and moved past me. "Move on, girl—I'm off to convince the lads to let ye race."

"If he wants to win so fearsomely, why does he not ride the bloody horse himself?" I muttered.

Behind us, Jack and Hosa emptied supplies from the canoe—stacks of deerskin pelts, two bearskin blankets and several muskets brought from Chota to be sold. Another canoe pulled up beside in a flurry of giggling and shouting. Paulo, Lord Harris, the entire Simons clan, both Wheelers, and Zeke and Eliza had made the trip. Micah and Sam stepped from the boat early, rocking it, and tumbled off into the shallow water, soaking themselves. Abigail threw up her hands but kept the smile on her face. A day at the race was like a day at the fair in a more populated part of the colony. Surely it was the most interaction with outsiders that any of us had had all year.

Naji took my elbow, helping me up the bank. "You know why he doesn't ride that horse," he whispered. "He knows you're faster than he is."

I blew air out through my nose, looking up at the man who doubtless knew my grandfather better than he knew himself, despite the labyrinthine boundaries of slavery. "He's an ogre," I said.

"No, Miss Quinn—he just likes to win," Naji said, chuckling.

"Naji?" I asked suddenly, "would you like for me to talk to him again of your freedom? You and Elsa should not have to cater to such a doddering old fool."

"He gave us our freedom when you left last year," he said quietly, chocolate-colored eyes revealing nothing. "We earn more than most Negroes anywhere near Charlestown. Bein' house slaves for so long, neither one of us knows how to work the fields."

"I did not realize he'd done such a thing," I said, surprised.

My grandfather's views on slavery had long been a mystery to me. He railed against the injustices of it, but kept slaves himself. And though he most likely valued Naji's opinion more than his own law clerk's, he could not see past the dreadful institution to a society where white and black men were accepted on equal terms.

"Miss Quinn, he's been payin' us for years," Naji said. "He keeps it all in an account at the firm, pays it out when we ask for it and holds what we want saved."

There was a flurry of movement along the riverbank. People stopped whatever they were doing to turn and gawk at the other side. I abandoned the conversation for the moment, craning my neck.

"Ah, here's Ridge Runner," Jack said from behind us.

Across the river Ridge Runner sat barebacked atop his own horse, holding Fire Eater's lead rope and coaxing the stallion into the calm water. Fire Eater reared up, hooves slicing near the other horse's face. The crowd gasped, and I moved around several onlookers until I found good footing on the bank. By then Ridge Runner had both horses swimming. Fire Eater's great head bobbed above the surface; he jerked at the lead for spite. I cupped my hands around my mouth.

"Easy, boy," I called, keeping my voice calm. His ears perked up, and his gaze shifted. I met his big brown eyes and made a low, clicking sound in the back of my throat.

When they reached the other side the horses broke the surface like giant water monsters, dripping onto the grass as the crowd backed away, talking excitedly amongst themselves. Some of the gamblers had come to watch. They stood in a group, eyes on my horse. I stopped before the animals as Ridge Runner dismounted smoothly. He handed the lead rope to me and came as close to rolling his eyes as I'd ever seen him.

"You take the *sa'gwali digu'lanahi'ta*—I'm done with him," he said. He led his horse away, and I turned to Jack, who watched his brother with a wide grin, enjoying his annoyance.

"What did he say?" I asked.

"He called your horse a mule, Mac."

I rubbed Fire Eater's nose with my knuckles. He was as calm now as a kitten, sniffing at my lace collar. "Well, it is true he can be a stubborn mount. I do hope Ridge Runner's not angry with me. I'd have brought him myself if Grandfather hadn't insisted I ride in the canoe."

"Don't think on it overmuch, lass. Ridge Runner's a hardy sort. He'll nurse his wounds elsewhere." Jack reached out, fingered the ruffle at my neck. "I hardly recognize you in your lady's dress," he said. "You look bonny. If anyone makes a grab for you, just give a yelp, and I'll come to you."

I smiled. That he worried over my safety seemed in complete opposition to the confident energy he exuded. Like many of the Cherokee in attendance, he'd worn thin deerskin leggings, short moccasins, and a trade shirt, merely for the mixed company—at home he'd be bare-chested. He wore musket and tomahawk strapped to his back, his knife at its usual position at his hip, looped through the beaded belt. He'd taken care to comb out his hair, and it hung down onto his shoulders in a fall of dark gold, the tips the whitest I'd ever seen them from time in the sun. His green eyes were startlingly brilliant in a face that still could take my breath. If not for the hooded emerald eyes, the cedar-burnt skin and the arresting lines of his nose, cheekbones and jaw marked him as Indian.

Many of the Indians from Keowee Town had approached him as we stood on the bank. He'd greeted them with affection, transitioning easily from Cherokee to English when several trappers did the same, inquiring after what he thought of the summer's lagging fur cache.

Though he seemed to me to be truly the epitome of a rugged frontiersman, he moved deftly through conversation, able to talk just as easily with an Upcountry planter who had journeyed north from the Waxhaws to a nearly unintelligible beaver trapper from Jocassee who lacked most of his upper teeth.

"That's it, Quincy, they're going to let ye ride," said Grandfather, who'd walked up behind me and patted Fire Eater on the neck. The stallion eyed him suspiciously, and I clucked my tongue quietly in warning. I looked over at the group of men about whom he spoke. They watched me with amusement, one man doffing his hat and winking.

"Well, when is the race to begin?" I asked, giving in.

"At noon, which canna be long." He dug in the pocket of his shirt, producing the gold timepiece he'd carried as far back as I could remember. "Ye've five minutes, lass, best get the beast to the starting line."

I tugged on Fire Eater's lead, but Jack caught my free hand, pulling me to him. He grinned, a flash of white, and bent, kissing me soundly. There were some hoots from the crowd around us as I blushed. "You're sure to surprise the lot of them, Mac," he said. "But keep an eye on the fancy man there."

I made my way to the fence posts where the other riders stood with their horses. They watched me warily as I approached. The better-dressed upcountryman—the one Jack had called 'fancy'—shook his head, shouting at the gambling master. "You can't be serious, Gunther—we can't ride against a woman!"

"And why not?" The old German man, now perched on a tree stump with the heavy leather pouch at his feet, waved a hand at the disgruntled racer. "She's paid good money. You're not afraid of a little woman like that, are you, Brian? She'd barely reach your belt buckle."

Someone from the crowd called out, "What if she's hurt?"

"Then she gets hurt," Gunther shrugged, his accent rough. "There's no law against it. Now make your last wagers, folks. Riders to the start!"

We moved the horses to the starting place, literally a rough line drawn in the dry dirt. Far down the riverbank I could see a man in a white shirt, holding something red in his hands.

"The race is a mile long," Gunther said. "John O' Banyon's down at the end with a red flag. He's going to plant it in the dirt. The riders will round the flag and head back. Whoever crosses the finish line first wins the pool, and it's up to fifty pounds."

"What does a lady need with fifty pounds?" The same man who'd protested my arrival earlier grumbled as he swung up onto his horse, shooting me an angry look.

"You are wife to Walks Between?" one of the Indian racers mounted beside me asked quietly, inclining his head. I nodded, and he turned to the other man. They spoke rapidly in Cherokee, and I thought I heard one say "Rides-Like-a-Man," but with the crowd growing louder I could not be certain.

I made a quick study of the other riders. The white men rode sturdy but smaller horses, and they were larger men, certain to be harder on their mounts. The two Cherokee men rode Indian ponies, which were sure to be quick, especially at the start. I walked over to Fire Eater's orange neck, rubbing the coat beneath his black tuft of mane. He was by far the biggest horse in the group, and only I knew how much he loved to run, how he'd strain to bursting even on a trail ride, just to pass the lead horse. I whispered endearments into his neck, trying to calm my own breathing. "There now, beautiful boy," I murmured. "You're to run soon, won't you enjoy that?"

"Riders, to your mounts!"

The crowd gathered around the starting line. I saw Jack, his bright head above the others, standing next to my grandfather, who clapped his hands in delight. I narrowed my eyes at the old man before scanning the rest. Abigail held the boys back by the cuffs of their wet shirts, and Lord Harris stood with Paulo, talking to a well-dressed stranger, most likely another landowner from settlements to the south. I put a foot in the stirrup and swung up onto Fire Eater's back without help, shoving my skirts to each side and tucking them before me, sitting astride.

"She's even to ride like a man?" The affronted man growled, obviously well past patience.

"Aw, shut your trap, Brian," Gunther ordered. He raised the pistol above his head, and the riders shifted in their saddles, ready. I rose in mine, tucking my knees into Fire Eater's sides. I could feel him humming beneath me, all energy gathering at his core. I focused on the sight of the red flag flapping in the breeze far down the riverbank, positioning it between the horse's ears in my line of vision. I breathed in deeply through my nose, exhaling slowly from my mouth. I let the sounds of the crowd fade to silence, the riders beside me disappearing in a fog, the whole of my attention on the horse beneath me and the race ahead.

The pistol fired, and Fire Eater burst from the starting line, muscles heaving. As I crouched inches above his back—reins loose but clutched in one hand, the other in the black tuft of his mane—I remembered *The Anatomy of the Horse*, a book in Grandfather's library whose drawings I'd studied only a few years ago, and in my mind's eye I saw Fire Eater's bones in motion, his tendons and ligaments stretching and curling, muscles red and bunching on his skeleton. The sun shone brightly on the river. Across the water at Keowee Town the villagers ran from their work and headed toward the rocky bank, watching us with hands at their foreheads, shading their eyes.

Fire Eater whipped his head to the side, grunting, and bared his teeth. The horse beside me came into focus, nipping at Fire Eater's flanks. My eyes met the rider's—the man named Brian, the angry one—and I looked ahead toward the nearing flag, kicking my heels and leaning further over Fire Eater's neck.

One of the Cherokee men rounded the flag first, but we were close behind, enough to catch a patch of sand flung up from the horse's hooves. I blinked my eyes and swiped a hand across them, crouching lower. I knew that Fire Eater had yet to even let go—I'd held him back, knowing that he would have a better chance of outpacing the smaller horses in the last stretch of the race.

I could hear the other horses pounding up behind us. The Indian who was leading glanced back over his shoulder at me, his swathe of black hair flapping across gritted teeth. The crowd began to grow larger, and soon I could make out the faces of those cheering and jumping up and down. I bent over Fire Eater's neck.

"Go!" I said loudly into his ear, and he leapt ahead, neck and head stretching, chest heaving, his hooves beating the dirt. We passed the lead horse easily, and I felt the pins in my hair come loose. As we crossed the finish line and rumbled to a walk I lifted my face to the sun and laughed, my heart full to bursting.

Grandfather reached up to me, a grin splitting his grizzled face, and I took his hand, sliding to the ground. "Fine race, lass—you're a braw horsewoman, that ye are."

"Step away, folks," Hosa said from nearby. We turned as he dumped a pail of river water over Fire Eater's sweat-soaked back. I let go of Grandfather's hand and went to my fearless mount, kissing him on his long nose. "He's no dog," Hosa said, pursing his lips at me and shaking his head.

"Kiss me, Mistress MacFadden, I'm the one with the coin." Gunther hefted the pouch into his arms and held it out to me. But Jack reached from behind, taking the heavy winnings. He winked at me, green eyes dancing, and inclined his head at the shorter man.

"Sure, and that would be Madam Wolf, old man," he said, his brogue deep. "Don't you be making cow eyes at me wife, now—for I know the one you've at home will tan your hide, should she find out."

"Good luck to you, madam," Gunther reached out, shaking Jack's hand. "If this wild man is truly your *guidmann*, you will need it."

The two Cherokee from the race approached Ridge Runner, questioning him excitedly. He shook his head and glanced over at us. They nodded at me politely. Jack chuckled. "Your legend is growing, Mac," he said. "Before they'd but heard tales of Rides-Like-a-Man, and then only from sad-mouthed Laughing Crow. But now they've seen for themselves."

"Lovely," I said. "Now they truly will believe that I'm a sorcerer."

"No, I think Ridge Runner's attempting to quell that way of thinking," he said. "He'll tell them he's seen you sleep, and that you snore like an old man."

"Hush," I muttered, pushing half-heartedly at his arm.

"Wolf, you'll want to hear this—there's news from Boston." Lord Harris pushed his way through the crowd. He stopped before Jack, his face flushed as he looked at us both. "Madam Wolf, where is your grandfather?"

"Most likely placing my horse in another race—without my permission, of course." But the smile disappeared from my face. Lord Harris did look serious, much more so than usual. "What's amiss?"

He hesitated, looking questioningly at Jack. He obviously felt uncomfortable speaking in front of me. Jack raised an eyebrow, expressionless. "Go on, Harris," he said.

"The days between letters here are countless," the Englishman muttered, agitated. "God knows what could have occurred more than a month ago."

"What's this about letters?" Grandfather stepped up beside me, a jug of spirits hooked around his pointer finger. He looked at the three of us and set it on the ground, brushing off his hands. "Spit it out, man."

"His Excellency Francis Bernard, the governor of Massachusetts, has been recalled to London," he said, removing the gray tricorn from his head and running a hand through his dull, blond hair. "This occurred in the latter part of June, I believe. English soldiers aimed a cannon at the House chambers of the legislature and refused to move it."

"Has Boston gone mad, then?" Grandfather asked.

"The members of the House refused to conduct any business, and Bernard forced them to move to Harvard College. If what's being said is true, someone cut the heart out of Bernard's portrait there. John Adams and Henry Otis ordered a resolution to be drawn, and it passed—Bernard's to be recalled to London. This can speak of nothing but ill, sirs."

"War's been broiling since the redcoats arrived in Boston last year to enforce the blasted Customs Law," Grandfather said, his Scottish burr making his voice a low growl. "Parliament's certainly going to protest having a man they appointed sent back to them in shame."

"Boston is surely the first of many," I said quietly, and Harris turned, surprised to hear me speak.

"Aye," Jack said. "It's but the beginning." He inclined his head at Lord Harris. "Where did you learn of this?"

"It was printed in the *South Carolina Gazette*. Simon King, from the Waxhaws, brought a newspaper with him to the race. I spoke with him just before I revealed as much to you."

Grandfather eyed Harris warily, and he placed a hand on my shoulder, warm. "How do ye feel about this, man? It's sure your own loyalties are tempered."

Harris bowed his head. When he raised it his brown eyes were filled with a mixture of honesty and angst. "I came to this land stripped of my title, seeking a new life. That I've found, and far from England. Though I do believe the colonies intemperate in dealing with Parliament, I've no love of the wigged fools. But if it does come to war, they will send all armies here as punishment and stop at nothing to reclaim what they believe they own." He replaced his tricorn and nodded at us. "Perhaps we are safe here, so removed from the coast. I wish to God it were so."

As Harris walked away the three of us stood in momentary silence. It was the most impassioned I had ever heard the English lord, and I wondered that he felt perhaps split in two, unable to choose between his old homeland and the new. I reached up and clutched Grandfather's hand at my shoulder. "Owen—when he quit Charlestown for Boston, did he say anything of this?"

Grandfather shook his head. "Nay, lass. He spoke only of his new wife. But the lad's a patriot, I know it. As his good-father is employed by the Crown, this puts him in a grave quandary. I pray he is well," he said, tapering off into quiet at the end.

"He sends Rebekah here from Boston as we speak," I whispered, the enormity of the situation sending a chill through my bones. Grandfather looked up, surprised.

"Have ye seen something, lass?" he asked cautiously, glancing around. I nodded, unspeaking, and Jack took my hand.

"Aye, sir, she's seen," he said. "And the girl could arrive at any time, so let's be off."

We loaded the canoe in silence, a morose group in the midst of celebration. People had been drinking heavily. There was a quick scuffle over a trade of deerskins, and the men involved sat apart, nursing bloody noses. Jack bent his head to Ridge Runner's, whispering something in his ear. The Cherokee man nodded, then waited for Jack to be seated in the boat with paddle in hand before pushing us into the Keowee. As we left the bank I watched the revelers, the women laughing together in groups, bonnets bobbing in the dust. Someone somewhere struck up a song, and a fiddle rang out, a zip of light music on the hot air. But the merriment soon faded, and all that I could hear was the *swoosh* of Jack's paddle as he dipped it into the cool river, sending us home.

Chapter 30

The MacFadden Settlement
September, 1769

The room was dark and still. The oil lamp flickered, sending odd patterns of light across the roof of the cabin. I glanced over at Jack, who was sprawled atop the quilt, a forearm thrown over his eyes. I flipped the page of my book slowly, my eyes racing over the words. I'd only just begun *A Sentimental Journey*, and I was entranced, eager to see what other tales the engaging Mr. Yorick had to tell of his sojourns through France and Italy.

"Jaysus, Mac—blow out the lamp. It must be nigh on three in the morning."

I jerked, startled, and set the slim book in my lap. "I thought you'd long been asleep," I said accusingly. He moved his arm, opening one green eye.

"You have wee conversations with yourself when you read, lass. It's a bit disconcerting."

"I do not," I retorted, raising my chin. I leaned over the side of the bed and put a hand to the glass, blowing out the lamp. In the darkness I snuggled down beneath the muslin cover, pulling it to my collarbone.

"Aye, you do," he growled, reaching out an arm and pulling me against his chest. "You say things like, 'Oh, how lovely,' and 'Isn't that wonderful?' Sure, and if someone passed by our window they'd think you mad."

"It's just that the story is so thoroughly entertaining," I said, unable to stifle my enthusiasm. "It's a new book, published in London only last year. Grandfather was able to secure a copy from a bookseller in Charlestown before he left."

"I'll have to thank him, then."

"The author, a Laurence Stern, has such a zeal for travel and for the people that he meets. His writing is refreshing. A bit foolish at times, but truly enchanting."

"If you say so, lass."

I pulled back from him, rising up on an elbow. In the moonlight from the open window I could see the outline of his face, long lashes resting against the sharp edge of his cheekbones. His hair was scattered about the pillow like wild threads of dark gold. Though he still wasn't used to spending his nights in a bed, he looked almost like a sleeping Achilles, restless at peace. "Do you ever have want to travel abroad?" I asked.

Reluctantly he opened both eyes, turning on his side to face me. "Not especially, no. I've all I want here. And could you see me in Paris or Rome, lass? They'd surely run screaming from a face like mine."

I reached out and traced the blue tattoo across his forehead, my touch soft.

"You are quite fearsome," I admitted, smiling. "But you're very striking to look at, as well. I'd be worried that the European ladies would snatch you from me for the rareness of your hide."

"Not a chance," he said, reaching up and taking my hand, tucking it against his chest. "Harris says the lasses wear perfume in Europe. I don't think I'd want my woman smelling like a field of weeds."

I laughed, closing my eyes. The draught of sleep settled over me, and I relaxed into Jack. "Is that so? Well, then, we'll certainly never journey to Europe."

"I'd go if you asked me, Mac," he said, his voice drowsy. "But I'll nay wear a wig."

Darkness settled over me as my thoughts calmed, and I sank back into the bed, turning to him.

In the hour just before dawn I awoke in a sweat, shaking and confused. I wiped the hair back from my forehead, the strands wet and my face clammy. *It was a dream*, I thought, *only a dream*. I sat up against the window at my back and pulled my knees to my chest beneath the muslin cover. Breathing raggedly, I rested my head there, wrapping my arms around my shins.

In my dream, the man from Tomassee Knob had returned, and he'd stalked me in a dark wood, his eyes red and glowing. "He's dead," I whispered. "You killed him."

"What is it?" Jack sat up beside me, tense and alert. He slid a hand beneath his pillow for the knife there, but saw the look on my face and stopped. "Are you all right?"

I nodded, my forehead rubbing against the bones in my knees. But there was a catch in my throat, and I couldn't speak, and I felt the flood of tears just waiting to choke me.

"Mac, I don't believe you," he said, running a soft hand over my hair. "Tell me."

"I killed a man," I said, looking up at him with stinging eyes. "That night, at the river."

His eyes widened fractionally, and he nodded slowly. "All right, then. Why did you not tell me after?"

"I don't know," I muttered, feeling hot tears run down my cheeks. I swiped at them, swallowing roughly. "When I woke we were almost home. I suppose I simply forgot."

"You don't forget killing a man for the first time. Come now, love—why have you said nothing since?"

At his soft words the tears came in full force, and I buried my face again, wetting the blanket that lay over my bent knees. He took his hand away, and I sucked in breath, trying to control myself. "It was one of the Creek men from that day on the Knob," I said. "He tried to choke me. I used the knife you gave me."

"You had to do it, Mac. He would've killed you."

I hiccupped loudly, trying to catch my breath, and tightened my grip on my knees. Though I knew that he was right, I could not get past the horrible truth: I had taken a man's life.

I'd shoved a knife into his belly and watched as he died.

"Quinn," Jack said sharply. I jerked up at the sound, looking at him as I ran the back of my hand across wet cheeks. "He would have killed you, there's no doubt there. And afterwards, he'd have taken your scalp. Do you ken? You had no choice."

"I understand, I do," I said, gulping against the knot. "But it haunts me."

He scooted over to me and wrapped his arms around my back and beneath my knees, lifting me onto his lap. I turned my head into the hollow of his warm neck, and when he spoke his Adam's apple moved up and down against the bridge of my nose. "I forget, sometimes, that you know little of life here—of how it can be," he said, running a hand soothingly along my trembling thigh. "You seem so brave, and you are. But you'll know nothing of the harshness of it, being raised from a child in a place such as Charlestown." He paused, rubbing his chin into the top of my head.

"The truth of it is, you'll kill again."

I pulled back from him, shocked. "I will not!"

"You will, if you are to live out your life here, in the wilderness with me. There's nothing to be done about it, save do what you can to avoid it. But at times, you have no choice but to kill for your home and family." He sighed deeply. "I wish it were different than it is, but it's been the way of the *Yun'wiya'* for hundreds of years."

"I don't understand," I whispered.

"No, you couldn't." He wrapped his arms around me again and lay back on the bed, and with one hand he pulled the quilt over us. We lay in silence, the minutes stretching out into morning. My eyes were still open as the sun rose far from us, away over the ocean, and I watched it as it came in through an east-facing window, climbing the foot of the bed and warming my dry, salty face.

"Quinn, you must wake." I felt Jack's hands on my shoulders, shaking me gently. I opened my eyes, yawning widely. His face came into focus above me. He was fully dressed, standing beside our bed. September sunlight, crisp and free from summer humidity, poured in through the windows.

"I've overslept," I murmured, covering my mouth. "What time is it?"

"I'd say about nine of the clock," he said, pushing a strand of hair from my cheek and tucking it behind my ear. "You need get dressed. Hosa's on the porch with a letter from your grandsire."

"What?" I threw back the blanket and set my feet on the wood floor, shaking my head to clear it. "Why would he write a letter when—"

Suddenly I stopped, realization dawning. "He's left, hasn't he?"

"Aye, and he may have his reasons for not telling you. Get dressed, lass."

When I opened the door Hosa stood; he'd been sitting on the stoop. He held out a folded piece of paper, avoiding the sight of bare toes peeking out from the hem of my skirts. "Here you go, Miss Quinn," he said. "Mr. MacFadden gave dis to me before he lef' las' night. He wan' be sure I put it in yo' own two hands."

"Thank you," I said, taking the letter and moving to a rocker, sitting. When he turned to go I held out a hand. "Wait, Hosa—did he say anything at all? Was he well?"

He took the rough farmer's hat from his head and held it against his worn shirt, crumpling the brim in his fingers, their tips rough and squared off from years of manual labor. "He didn't say nothing," he replied, then ran a hand across his face, scratching the black stubble at his jaw. "But de man called Naji said to tell you dat yo' grandfather's meetin' wid dat group o' patriots more and more, an' dat he come home most nights an' sit in his library 'til de morning hours. Dis man Naji, he thinks dere might be trouble in Charlestown soon, between de Tories and de Whigs, an' he thinks your grandfather be part of it."

I spread the letter across my knee, smoothing it with my fingers so I wouldn't crumple it anxiously in my fist. "Did he say what the name of the group was?"

"De sons o' something."

"The Sons of Liberty?"

Hosa replaced his hat, tucking his hands in the pockets of his breeches. "Dat's it." He nodded at me and turned, stepping off the porch.

"Thank you, Hosa," I murmured, turning the letter over and smoothing out the edges. In the back of my mind I heard the cabin door open and close behind me.

MacFadden Settlement

2 September, 1769

Dearest Quincy,

> *I write this letter the night before I am to return to our home in Charlestown, and Signor Di Pietro with me. I am sorry that I have no time to tell you myself, but there are Things which I feel are not ready to be said aloud.*

> *When he was home Owen revealed far more than what I told you at the Race. I have long been wary of the way that the two of you see Ahead—it goes against all that I know of Man's timorous place in this World, and of the Reason that I raised you both with, for I do believe fervently in Man's Reason. You will know that I put more stock in that than in any show of false faith in the benevolence of an angry God.*

> *I know not whether your Cousin has told of what he has seen to you and your Man. Though you have not revealed as such to me, I know that you too have seen Things of the Future. I will tell you only that I work now with a Group fervent in the Cause of Liberty, who believe that War will come and that we must do all we can to create for this Country a new Age. I fear that with this fight will come much Death and Sorrow, though for a greater good. So, I leave for you both a box in Naji's safekeeping—made of Scottish oak, adorned with our family crest in gold inscribed on its Cover. If any Ill should befall me, you Must open it straightaway.*

> *I am now to Charlestown, to continue in my Work. Remember your promise to come to me within six months time, to be married as a good woman should.*

I find favor in your choice of Husband.
Your Grandfather,
Campbell Ian Murphry MacFadden, Esquire
MacFadden Barn, Keowee Valley

Post Script:
I've left you a gift in the smithy room of the barn. Call it a
Housewarming, if you will.

Cocking my head, I wondered what he could've left for me, but left it
for later. At his choice of adieu I smiled despite myself, folding the top of
the letter over the bottom and resting my hands on it on my thighs, looking
up and out at the mountains. In the piercingly blue September sky their
curving edges seemed etched in purple ink, rolling against a cloudless
backdrop. The Valley was quiet. At the crest of the upper pasture I watched
a hawk land in a cluster of trees there, disappearing among still-green leaves.
The gurgle and flow of Tomassee Creek was a soothing reminder of
blankets and clothes to be washed, of fish to be caught and cleaned, and of
the ceaseless influx of these needful things—things necessary to life here, in
these mountains.

Jack stepped up beside me, his moccasins silent on the wood. He, too,
watched the hawk, and I knew that he could see it still, despite its
camouflage. "She seeks a rabbit," he said.

I nodded and looked up at him, my eyes bright. "There's much to be
done," I said, the letter in my hands. "Owen's wife will need a place of her
own, don't you think?"

He nodded. "Sure, and I'm not quite ready to share the bridal
chamber, are you?"

I smiled. "Not at all." I looked back toward the Blue Ridge, then down
at the letter. "You were right about Grandfather. He knows more than he
reveals. He's involved with the Sons of Liberty—have you knowledge of
them?"

"Aye. They're much in the Boston and Philadelphia papers, for
rabbling against the King."

"Yes," I answered quietly. I stood and went to him, wrapping my arm
around his waist and pressing my face against his side. He curled an arm
around me, and we stood as one, surveying the land that we loved. The
voice came from somewhere in the flow of thought that hummed between
us: *Change is coming.*

"Are you ready, Mac?" he asked, and though I could not be sure
whether he spoke of taking on the day and its many chores, or of facing the

madness building in New England, stretching its fevered fingers south over the Appalachians, I answered him.

"I am."

He squeezed my waist and took my hand, and with the other reached for the musket nearby, propped up against the rail. We stepped off the porch together, ready to work.

Wednesday, a little less than two fortnights since my Grandfather had abandoned the backcountry for the drama and secret backroom meetings of Charlestown, was a day of letters. For Keowee Valley, a place so far removed from English civilization—perhaps but twice a year receiving a real newspaper, and then only by the passing down of worn parchment from settler to settler—a visit from the post-rider was a true event, and all work stopped for several hours upon the man's arrival.

I dislodged my foot from between downed branches in Tomassee Creek, wincing as bark dug into the tender skin at my heel. I dropped the small boulder I'd been carrying into the wall of others in the weir, the Cherokee fish trap that Ridge Runner, Samuel and I had been repairing. It was a stone dam built across a wide, deep part of the creek—a place where the bottom was sandy and where the water rushed quickly—starting at each bank and forming a vee towards the middle, the top of the vee open and a crail, a hemp net and trap, attached there to catch trout and bass. The weir had been built long ago, perhaps by the former residents of the Tomassee village, but it had fallen to ruin in the years since the Cherokee Wars.

I moved the boulder firmly into place, brushing dirt from my hands as I straightened. Ridge Runner stood in waist-deep water at the point of the dam, mending a break in the net. His long, black braid fell over a rounded brown shoulder, the muscle there clenching as he worked at the rope. Across his chest the bruises from our ambush on the Chattooga had dulled. Samuel sloshed into the water from the pasture-side bank, face red with exertion as he heaved a huge stone into a gap in that side of the wall. The water splashed up, soaking the knees of his breeches; he stretched his shoulders, closing his eyes and rubbing the small of his back.

I glanced back and forth between the two men because they made such a startling picture of utter physical differences: middle-aged Samuel with his graying hair and the quiet, unassuming face of a farmer, and Ridge Runner, shirtless, lean and brown, the very picture of Cherokee manhood, his deerskin leggings rolled up over his knees. He felt me looking at him and met my eyes. "We will soon become *ama'yine'hi* if we work much longer," he said. "Shall we rest?"

"Sounds good to me, Miss Quinn," Samuel said quietly, the wrinkles at the corners of his eyes deepening as he gazed at me across the creek, the sun in his eyes.

"I thought I heard Abigail say that she'd made corn cakes for lunch, with cream for dessert," I said, smiling at the older man.

"She did," he answered, looking back and forth between Ridge Runner and me. "I suppose the work will still be here when we return."

We left the wheelbarrow filled to the brim with boulders we'd gathered from other places in the creek and in the forest, and made our way across the lower pastures. Hosa and Zeke were walking in a field nearby, through the rows of apple trees, inspecting the fruit-bearing branches. Zeke pulled a branch down and plucked off an apple. He handed it to Hosa, and the older man held the apple to his nose and sniffed, saying something to the boy that we were too far away to hear.

As we neared the communal fire pit we could see Lord Harris beyond in the pen, working with a horse he'd purchased only a few days ago from Fort Prince George. Jack sat on the railing nearby, offering advice and encouragement, the farmer's hat that he rarely wore pulled low to shade his eyes. An upcountry planter, the same Simon King who had informed us of the recent occurrences in Massachusetts, had met Harris at the abandoned fort. They'd settled on the purchase back at the race in August.

The horse was a sleek, black mare, a two year-old thoroughbred with a sweet temperament and strong legs. We'd given her the stall far down the run from Fire Eater's as he'd acted a bit jealous on her arrival, kicking out a board in his door.

Samuel slid onto the bench and removed his hat as Abigail walked out of their house with a basket in her arms. She smiled at us—all of us, including Ridge Runner, which was something new—in welcome. Ridge Runner and I took our places with care.

"Thank you, Madam Simons," I said. "This is so kind of you."

Suddenly a long, high whistle pierced the air, and Ridge Runner jumped immediately to his feet, snatching the tomahawk from his back. Samuel leapt up, knocking his knees against the table. "What is it?" I asked.

"Someone's coming," Ridge Runner said, shading his eyes as he looked across the middle pasture for Jack, who had mounted Murdoch and was riding toward us, musket in hand. He pointed the long gun as he rode, like an arrow down towards the south end of the Valley.

"I'll get my musket," Samuel muttered. As he passed Abigail he gripped her shoulders and turned her towards the cabin. "Get inside—I'll watch for the boys."

Jack called out something in Cherokee as he neared. I watched in awe as Ridge Runner jogged toward him, reached out and took Jack's free hand, leaping up behind him on the horse. "Wait here," Jack called out to me as they thundered past.

I couldn't wait. I ran after them, holding my skirts as I rushed through the orchard, stumbling in the ruts. I could see a horse and rider emerging from the woods, at the head of the Keowee Path. At Jack and Ridge Runner's approach the rider threw up his arms, shouting something. They stopped in the dirt before him and dismounted. As I neared I saw that the stranger had walked back to his horse and carried a saddlebag over his shoulders. I recognized the shape at once.

I turned back to the settlement, breathing hard. Samuel stood with musket in hand, his face white, beside Lord Harris, who held his own gun. Abigail emerged from her porch, the basket of corn cakes still clutched in her arms.

"All is well!" I shouted, resting my hands on my knees. "It's the post-rider!"

Thomas Tanner sat hunched over Abigail's table, inhaling corn cakes and chewing with his mouth open. Crumbs fell onto his plate as he talked, the words muffled.

"I'm new, see," he said, eating like a starving man. "The old post-rider got the gout. I been working his routes since early summer. These parts ain't had no news since then." He stopped suddenly and swallowed, his Adam's apple bobbing in a scrawny neck. He couldn't have been more than fifteen years old, I thought, as he stared up at the crowd that had gathered around the table.

"Sorry to give you folks a scare," he said, belatedly. I took the pitcher and poured water into a mug, sliding it to him. "Thank you, madam," he said, swallowing in huge gulps. He set the mug down with a thump and looked over at Abigail, his brown eyes innocent as a puppy's. "Is there any ale?"

"Mr. Tanner, forgive me, but have you news for us?" I asked.

As it was common frontier custom to feed a post-rider before he handed out the mail, except in cases of dire emergency, we'd waited to ask. But impatience sparked in the air around our small company of settlers. We'd not had mail in months. Micah and Sam leaned over the end of the table, chins resting on their arms. They'd been playing in the barn when the post-rider arrived. Micah scratched at a mosquito bite on his forearm, biting his lip in concentration as he looked at Tanner.

"I do," the boy answered, setting down his fork. He scratched his head, the look on his freckled, homely face one of befuddlement. "Now, where's my mail bags?"

Jack stepped forward and hefted the weathered saddlebag onto the table, clipping the edge of the wooden plate. It flipped over, dumping out the last crumbs of corn cake. Tanner looked up, and at the bigger man's expression swallowed audibly. He pushed aside the plate and reached for the bags, unlatching the buckle and pulling out a mound of parchment and envelopes, some tied together with string.

"I got three for Mr. O' Hare, from Virginia," he said. Zeke, who'd been standing behind Jack, reached out an arm and snatched the bundle. He and Eliza, who'd waited silently beside him, rushed off together, their heads bent. "Here's one for Madam Simons, from a Madam Zane of Savannah."

"My sister," Abigail whispered, taking the envelope with careful hands.

"Can't hardly read the writing on this one," Tanner murmured, holding up a thin sheet and squinting his eyes. "It's chicken scratch lettering, but it looks like it's for a Mr. Brown. You got anybody here by that name?"

Those of us still standing there looked around in surprise. Hosa had not received a post the entire time we'd lived in the Valley. "That's Mr. Jehosaphat Brown," I said, reaching to take the letter. "I don't know where he is—most likely in the barn." I looked over at the boys. "Micah," I said, and he perked up. "Could you take this to Hosa? Check the barn and the out buildings first."

"Yes, Miss Quinn," he said, taking the folded parchment as carefully as if he'd been entrusted with gold coin. He and Sam scampered away, dust at their heels.

Tanner flipped through more of the papers; he set two to the side. "That seems to be it, besides these. These are for you, Madam Wolf." He held each aloft, reading aloud before handing them over. I groaned inwardly, wiping sweaty palms on my skirts. "There's one from Boston—from a Mr. Scott, Esquire. This one's from Charlestown, from a Mr. Paulo Di Pietro—what kind of name is that? French?"

I snatched the letters, patience lost, and hurried away toward the log seating around the fire pit. Meg scampered past me with a letter in hand, her father at her heels. I acknowledged them with a vague nod, those still crowding the table disappearing from my mind. I sat, opening the letter from Owen first, my hands shaking. Jack stepped behind me and set his hands lightly on my shoulders. "It's dated the fifth of July," I murmured, reading aloud.

Boston, Massachusetts

Dear Quincy,

> *Boston abounds with rumors, and Whig and Tory alike chastise one another in the streets, as though they are nothing more than rabble. It is a place unsafe for me now,*

*especially with my placement as Secretary to Mr.
Bradstreet, and he so close to the abdicated Governor. You
will have heard of Gov. Bernard's expulsion to London, I
presume—even in your Removal. All here exist in a state of
anticipation, awaiting the Crown's response to such
"Continental impertinence."*

*I cannot reveal what I presume to do, even to you, dear
Cousin. The post is an unsafe vessel for such secrets. I am
sending to you my new wife, Rebekah, as I told you I would.
She leaves tomorrow. With her travel two servants and a
hired driver—they have been paid in advance for the
service of the journey. You should expect Rebekah by early
September, depending on weather and river crossings. I
cannot express in mere words my gratitude for such an
undertaking. Though I am certain in her love of me, her
anger at my leaving is still ripe. I pray that she finds relief in
your good Company.*

*There is much that I would reveal to you, but cannot.
Know that I am doing all in my power for Freedom and
Country. Know that I would not regret any action I have
taken, or will take in the Future.*

Here ink slashed across his next words, blotting out their message, as
though Owen had written something he'd decided was too revealing for my
eyes. I looked quickly past them to the rest of the letter.

*Please remain in the safety of the Mountains for as
long as you can. Be wary of the Cherokee—though I know
that you have new reason to love them, their loyalties are
hitherto unknown to us. Tell Jack that I trust him to keep you
both in good care.*

*I will write again when I am able.
With great affection, Your Cousin,
Owen MacFadden Scott, Esq.*

"Well," I said, folding the letter and slipping it beneath the other one
on my lap. "He tells me less than Grandfather. If his wife left Boston in
July, should she not have arrived already? It frightens me to think of her
alone and in the wilds, with but a servant as companion. And Owen—what

can he be thinking? Why the secrecy?"

I ran a rough hand across my forehead, rubbing the ache that I could just feel beginning. "I know Owen is convinced that if she remains in Boston, Rebekah's safety will be in jeopardy. Why, I don't know. But he believes sending her here is the safest course, despite the dangers." I took a breath, anxiety returning. "But they're not always true, the visions. Most of the time I never learn what becomes of them—his could merely be dreams. Why does he put such trust in them? Why now?"

Jack squeezed my shoulder, his voice low. "What of the other, lass?"

"It's from Mr. Di Pietro. He must have posted it before leaving for Italy." I slid a finger beneath the parchment, ripping the top. My hands were steadier this time, and I held the letter up to my face, the English writing large and swirling. "This one is recent—I cannot imagine how it made it to the post in time."

The first of September, 1769

Charleston, The Royal Colony of South Carolina

My dear Signora *Wolf,*

> *I am writing to you to express much gratitude at your kind Hospitality of the past weeks. You took a stranger into your Homeplace and offered him respite, and for that I am immensely grateful. I took the opportunity to request that* Signor *MacFadden send this letter with his Post, before I take my leave of your Country. I will soon return to* Firenze *and report to Her Grace the Duchess of my findings on these lands, which are most Marvelous. I can only hope that you and your good Husband will allow me to return the compliment, should you ever travel to* Italia. *Know that you both are forever welcome.*

> *The other reason for this post is to express to you,* Signora, *my wish to relay the Specifications of your horse to my Liege lady. I feel that if you should choose to breed the stallion, the Duchess would have want of a foal. I have not seen in my lifetime a mount as rare and quick as your Fire Eater. These Qualities are as prized as gold by the horsemen of* Firenze. *When the time comes, you will be paid well. I would ask that you continue a Correspondence with me about this important matter. I, and all the Duchy of Tuscany, look forward with great happiness to your post.*

My kindest regards to your Husband. I am, always—

Your humble Servant,

Paulo Di Pietro

Chapter 31

October, 1769

When the leaves changed colors on this, my second autumn in Cherokee country and first as a frontier wife, they did so with the youthful fervor of an impatient lover, the mountains exploding overnight in bursts of reds and golds—so brilliant that it hurt the eyes to look upon them, spreading across ridges like wildfire. When Owen had first traveled to Pennsylvania in the War he'd written of the leaf-changing there, claiming that the streets of Philadelphia and the trees of the surrounding countryside seemed covered in a patchwork quilt. Lovely as it sounded, I thought our season here quite different. If anything, the vibrant blanket draped over the Blue Ridge was a living thing, emblazoned and visceral, consuming all green in its path.

The air itself seemed to change personality on a whim. During the day it was often warm as summer, even sweat-inducing, but at night it pierced the cabins with a distinct chill, forcing us to pull wool blankets out of storage, to clean and brush them much earlier than usual. Even so, I loved October. It was my favorite month in the mountains, and I cherished the sight of the Blue Ridge from my porch as I rocked in a chair there in late afternoons, a worn quilt around my shoulders and a book forever in hand.

Jack and Ridge Runner were due back to the settlement any day now. They'd been out in the mountains for well over a week, trapping bear, deer, and the ever-elusive beaver. Jack wanted to get a head start on our stores before winter set in. Standing here on the porch, the sun still burning in the afternoon sky, I could not yet fathom the roar of winter—I pictured it far away from us, a snow monster hibernating in a frozen cave.

My beloved cache of books was swiftly dwindling. I'd read most of them over again until I knew each line by heart. Though I never tired of my

Shakespeare, Johnson, Petrarch and Pope—and the fiercely independent Lady Montagu—I yearned for my Grandfather's library, for the bookseller on Meeting Street in Charlestown, where I'd once had an account. I wished also for pamphlets and newspapers, and especially the writings of political essayists that had been delivered directly to our door on Tradd Street. When I'd left the city, an anonymous journalist had been writing of political vanity in the *South Carolina Gazette*. I missed the excitement of such news—the rare, thrilling touch of a world outside my own. Though Grandfather regularly brought the *Gazette* home, stained and wrinkled from his visits to the coffeehouse, he had never failed to offer the newspaper up to me, to sit with me as though I were equal to a man and tell me of the conversations he'd had with friends and colleagues.

Here, though we often shared coffee around the communal fire pit, my homesteaders—and now, friends—were much more interested in discussing life on the farm: what crops should be planted for the coming year, how to keep pests out of the corn, the difficulties of frontier weather, and the constant threat of Regulator or Indian raids. As much as I tried desperately to focus on these pertinent domestic issues, whenever talk shifted to knitting or baking recipes, or even the deerskin trade, my right knee would begin to twitch, bouncing up and down with impatience.

Certainly I was not weary of frontier life, not at all. I just could not help but want to know more of the world outside the forested boundaries of Keowee Valley. This hunger for knowledge beyond my own, such an innate restlessness, had long been a part of my nature. As a child, Grandfather had called this unique and often bothersome aspect of my personality my "itchy feet," and would claim that—had I been a Buddhist of China and believed in reincarnation—I would have surely been a pirate in a former life, watching always for a strange, new shore to appear in my sights.

I smiled at the thought and paused with the straw broom in my hands. I'd been brushing dirt and dust from our porch. A flash of light in the woods caught my eye and I squinted, but it was only the sun reflecting off a curve in the creek. For a moment I'd thought it could be the men, home from hunting.

Never in my sheltered life had I truly missed the sight of someone, the mere physical nearness of him, as much as I did Jack. I woke in the mornings sprawled uncharacteristically across the bed, my arm flung over the spot where his chest would normally be, coming up empty-handed. For the first time since I'd read her poems did I truly recognize what the Puritan poet Anne Bradstreet meant when she wrote of her husband, "Where ever, ever stay, and go not thence,/ Till nature's sad decree shall call thee hence."

As a child, I'd thought the poem overly sentimental and even a bit morbid. Why did she want him to stay always with her, and never leave until he died? Would he not feel imprisoned by his own wife? But now, my bed cold and my small cabin so seemingly huge with its emptiness, I understood such longing. I wanted Jack to return that instant, and to never again take his leave of me.

"Quinn!"

I dropped the broom, startled, and it clapped against the wood floor.

Micah scrambled over the crest of the hill, auburn hair ablaze in the late afternoon sun, his cheeks red with exertion. "Quinn!" he shouted again, his little chest heaving.

I picked up my skirts and hurried down the step and out into the grass. When he reached me I caught his thin shoulders in my hands, bending down to meet his eyes. "What is it? What's happened?"

"There's a wagon what's come up the trail, and it's got a lady in it. Mama asked me to tell you come quick—the lady's got blood in her hair and a crazed look. There ain't nobody with her, just her alone. I never seen anything like it—" he trailed off in a rush.

Rebekah, the voice hissed in my ear.

"Wait here," I told him, and sprinted back up the step and into the cabin, my heart pounding in my throat. My mind raced. *Why is she alone? Why is she bleeding?* I grabbed the quilt from the bed and the box of bandages and liniment from the bottom of the armoire. At the door I paused, then rushed back inside and jerked open the drawer of the cherry side table, snatching the pistol and sliding it into the pocket in my skirts.

I caught Micah's elbow in full run, and we hurried down through the orchard, skirting the pen and racing along the rutted wagon trail there, crossing the middle pasture and flying over the crest, our boots trampling old corn. "There she is!" Micah cried, pointing to the south edge of the forest. I stopped in full stride and grabbed his arm, jerking him back.

"You must wait here."

"But, Quinn—"

"Micah, do as I say," I ordered roughly. His freckled face paled, and he nodded, and before I could feel sorry Abigail called up to me.

"Madam Wolf! Come quickly!"

Just below the pine embankment, where the Keowee Path emptied out into our lower fields, sat a wagon with a woman at the helm, gripping the reins of a horse that foamed at the mouth. I lifted the sides of my skirts and hurried toward them, not taking my eyes from her. She wore no bonnet. Her brown hair was tangled and long, and a patch of dried blood crusted the top of her head, another above her left ear. Her dress, once a garment of fine silk, was ripped down one side from knee to foot, and beneath her skirts the whalebone of her hoop stuck out, jagged and broken. Abigail took my forearm in her hand when I neared, the touch startling me.

"She asks only for you," the older woman whispered. "I don't know where Samuel's run off to. I asked Hosa and Lord Harris to help."

"Thank you, Madam Simons," I said, stepping away from her and toward the wagon.

Hosa stood by the horse, his calming hand on its sweaty neck.

"Needs water, Miss Quinn," he said softly. "But she be out o' her mind, won' let me give it none."

Harris had one hand on the wagon bench, poised to step up to her. He kept his tricorn in hand, pressed against his chest. "Please, madam, you must alight. Take my hand," he pleaded in a low voice, as if not to frighten her. For a heartbeat I stared at him, caught by the look of knowing grief in his pale blue eyes.

"Stay back," the woman said hoarsely, and I saw beneath the grit and fear the heart-shaped face, brown eyes, and the freckles sprinkled lightly across her nose, just as Owen had described.

"Rebekah," I said slowly. "Are you well?"

"They killed Saul, and the driver," she answered dully, staring past me. "They took my things, all the food."

"Rebekah, did they hurt you?" I asked, and Lord Harris whipped his head around, shock filling his eyes. She did not look at me, and I spoke again. "Rebekah—"

"They beat me," she said, and Abigail gasped behind me. I stepped forward and took a breath.

"Did they hurt you elsewhere?" I asked awkwardly. "Did they touch you—"

"Quinn!" Lord Harris said sharply, and it was the first time he'd called me by my given name. "That is quite enough. Can you not see what the poor woman has been through?"

Suddenly Rebekah stood, and the wagon teetered to one side. She looked straight at me, fists clenched at her sides. Everyone started, and Harris stepped towards her to catch her should she fall. "Quincy?" she asked in a little girl's voice. "Is that you?"

Tears threatened, burning the backs of my eyes, and I smiled up at her. "Yes, Rebekah, it's Quincy. Owen has told me much of you. Welcome to your new home."

"I never wanted a sister," she said, her eyes rolling back into her head as she toppled off the wagon.

I shut the door to my cabin softly behind me, keeping my hand on the handle. A lamp sat on the railing, casting the porch and the people there in a soft light. Insects buzzed at it, bouncing against the glass. Beyond was blackness, and a wolf called in the Southern woods, somewhere in the direction of Tomassee Knob. Harris leapt to his feet, hands clasped as if to prevent him from taking my shoulders. "Is she well?"

"She's sleeping, but she's fevered," I said. I looked at Abigail, who sat in a rocking chair with little Sam on her lap. "Abigail, I'd be grateful if you'd assist me tonight. I'll make up a pallet near the hearth."

"Let me, I'll stay," Harris said suddenly, a note of desperation in his voice. But before I could answer Abigail had deposited Sam on the floor next to Micah, who sat in the corner, head propped against a post.

"Have a care, my lord," she said quietly. "She needs a woman, now. I'll be glad to help," she told me, the sleeve of her dress brushing against mine as she passed. She slipped into the cabin behind us, the door creaking as it opened and closed.

"Who is she, Miz Quinn?" Zeke asked. He stood with Eliza at the foot of the stoop, his hand tucked in hers.

"We didn't know you had a sister," she added quietly, pulling the blanket she wore closer around her thin shoulders.

"She's not my sister—I have no siblings," I said, wiping the hair back from my face with a restless hand. "She is Owen's wife. Her name is Rebekah—Rebekah Scott."

I paused, looking up into the darkness beyond the porch as Hosa emerged there, his hands in his pockets. "Thank you for caring for her horse," I said, and he nodded. "She has come to live with us," I told them all, the enormity of the situation bearing down on me like a hand heavy on the back of my neck. I shrugged, trying to loosen the feeling. "My cousin has sent her, and asked that she stay here until he is able to take her home, which could be months from now—perhaps even a year. I am sorry that I did not tell any of you this. I should have discussed it with you long before tonight."

"It is not for us to decide, Madam Wolf," Mr. Wheeler said, in his sonorous minister's voice. He stood at the other end of the short porch from the Simons children, his big hands on his daughter's shoulders before him. "The Valley is yours. You may welcome whomever you wish. We know this."

"Be that as it may, I would've hoped to have had each person's opinion on the matter," I answered. "This is your home, all of you. Any decision concerning us all should be a matter of public discussion." I clasped my hands together at my waist, watching them tentatively. "You do feel that you can speak with me?"

"Madam, she is your family," Mr. Wheeler intoned, and Meg looked up at me with big eyes. "We welcome her gladly."

"She didn't get scalped, did she?" Meg asked. "Micah said her head was bloody as a wrung rooster's."

I put a hand to my mouth, half to stifle laughter and half to stifle tears. Samuel glared at his sleeping son, but I took away my hand and pressed it to my chest. "No, she wasn't scalped, but she was struck on the head, and so we must be watchful of her through the night." I smiled at Meg and looked up, seeking out Zeke and Hosa. "Would you gentlemen mind stabling the horses?" I asked. "I'm afraid that I left Fire Eater in the upper pasture while I cleaned and forgot all about him. You might try luring him with an apple," I added when Hosa raised an eyebrow at me, the whites of his eyes bright in the dark.

"You will ask if there is anything at all that you require?" Lord Harris had been so quiet since Abigail had admonished him that I started when he spoke, but turned to him and nodded.

"Yes, I will ask. But for now I'd have you all to your homes. The hour is growing late, and you'll be safer there."

"Watch for panthers," Samuel advised, hefting the sleeping Micah into his arms and taking Sam's hand in his. The younger boy rubbed his eyes and yawned. Samuel nodded at Hosa, his expression solemn. "Hosa saw one this morning near the Knob, eating off an elk."

"Bigger dan' a wolf," Hosa muttered, "so keep yo' guns about." He looked at Zeke. "You ready?"

When Eliza gripped Zeke's arm he turned to Lord Harris. "Sir, if you wouldn't mind walking Eliza to our cabin—it's closest to yours."

"Of course," Harris murmured, taking off his hat and offering his arm to the girl. She parted from Zeke reluctantly but slid her arm through the older man's, offering a grateful smile.

"Well, then," I said, backing towards my door, wanting to be inside with Rebekah, to learn more of the troubles that had befallen her on her journey south. "Goodnight, everyone. Sleep well."

"And you, Madam Wolf."

"Goodnight, Quinn." Meg picked up the lamp and handed it to her father, and the light shifted on the dark porch as I slipped back into the cabin.

Inside, Abigail had stoked the fire I'd haphazardly begun hours before, when we'd first brought an unconscious Rebekah into the cabin. It roared now, warming the chilly room and providing more light than even the two lamps she'd lit on each side of the bed. Rebekah lay there, a wet cloth across her forehead. She looked up at me with red-rimmed eyes as I crossed to her.

"How goes it, coz?" I asked with a smile, hoping that she'd respond to the familiar title as Owen always had, with a grin and a laugh. But she closed her eyes briefly, licking dry lips. When she opened them she turned her head towards the opposite wall, unanswering. I sat beside her on the bed, my hands folded in my lap though I wanted to reach for her hand. Abigail brought over a china cup filled with water.

"Drink now, Madam Scott, you need get some water in you," she said softly. She lifted Rebekah's head with one arm, tipping the cup to the younger woman's lips. Rebekah drank slowly, her eyes—bottomless and walnut-colored—still watching me.

I took a deep breath. "I cannot imagine the ordeal you have suffered these past weeks," I said quietly. "I hope that you know, despite all this, how glad I am to have you here with me. When Owen was visiting I begged him incessantly for more word of you. Now that you're finally here we can come to know one another on our own."

She blinked and raised a weak hand, pushing at the cup. Abigail stood back, glanced at me and walked over to the fire to stir a broth she'd started. Rebekah cleared her throat. "I am not mad," she said, in a patrician New England accent, the syllables clipped and formal.

"Well, you did marry my cousin, whom I do profess to love like a brother, so I can only believe that you are quite sane," I assured her.

"What did he say of me?"

"That you were possessed of beautiful brown eyes and that you enjoy the theatre."

"Well, that is true," she answered, and finally something real flashed in her eyes. "I have heard much of you, too."

"Oh? I can't imagine what." I rolled my eyes dramatically, and she smiled faintly.

"Owen assured me that though on the surface you seem a lovely woman, you are indeed the most stubborn person he's ever known. He said that you tend to dress much as a man, and that if you had your way you'd do naught but ride horses all day and read novels at night." She caught her breath. Though she spoke with a quickness I wasn't accustomed to she seemed still weary from her journey. "I've been thinking of you in breeches, but you wear a dress."

"You'll see her in her mannish clothes soon enough," Abigail said suddenly from the other side of the room. "It's most like naught but her dresses are clean this week."

I raised my eyebrows at the woman, keeping a straight face. "Why, Abigail, you've been keeping that wit all to yourself." She sniffed and turned back to the fire. I reached out now, taking Rebekah's cold hand in mine. "Please, cousin—tell me what happened to you."

The smile vanished from her pale face, and she blinked at sudden tears. "I can't," she answered, shaking her head. Then she looked over at Abigail, flushed. I stood and walked to the hearth, leaning over the older woman as she stoked the fire.

"Abigail, would you mind stepping onto the porch for a moment? I'd like to speak privately with Rebekah."

Abigail straightened and leaned the poker against the wall. She met my eyes and nodded, then walked to the door, slipping outside. I went back to the bed, sitting and taking Rebekah's hand once more. "You can tell me," I said softly. "It's naught but the two of us now."

"They came upon us at night," she said. "They were terrible men. Their language was so rough that I was barely able to understand. One of the men had a patch over his eye. He shot Saul through the back of the head." She wiped a hand over her eyes, choking on the words. "Saul has been with my family since he was a boy. He has a wife and children in Boston."

"Were they Indians?" I asked quickly, and she shook her head.

"No, two of them were white. One was a Negro. He slit the driver's throat and held me down while the other two emptied our wagon of trunks and supplies. Then one of the men—he smelled of fish, rotten fish—told the Negro to hold me tightly, and he put his hands on me."

She started to cry softly, and my heart ached for her. I leaned forward and pushed her hair gently back from her face. "How, Rebekah?"

"He groped me like a common trollop," she sobbed. "I kicked at him with my knee, as Owen taught me. He was so angry he beat me on the head with the butt of his pistol until I bled. I could barely see, then. Once they'd loaded up their own wagon with my things the other man told the Negro to keep restraining me, that he deserved a turn. He ripped my skirts and put his hand between my legs, and I screamed. But the Negro told him that he didn't hold with rape, and when he said that the man shot him between the eyes.

"He fell into me before he hit the ground," she cried, her hands now covering her face, her voice muffled. "I touched a dead man."

"Rebekah, were you raped?" I asked shortly, terrified of her answer.

"Yes," she said, and she lowered her hands to the blanket, her voice hard. "He put himself inside me, and did not cease, though I beat at him with my fists. Then he held me as the other man used me, too. When they were finished they slapped me and pushed me into the woods. I don't know why they left the horse." She laughed harshly and her eyes burned brightly as she looked up at me. "They could have sold the horse."

"I am so sorry," I said, knowing the words were utterly inadequate.

She spoke again as if she hadn't heard me. "When I awoke there were flies buzzing about the blood at my head. I climbed into the wagon and drove. For days and nights I drove. An old Indian man helped me to cross the Keowee River. He gave me water and bread and told me how to get here." She paused, and her eyes glittered. "I didn't have the strength to be scared."

I couldn't stop myself. I leaned forward and took her in my arms, clasping her to my chest. I pressed my cheek against her hair, the hair that Abigail had wiped clean of dried blood. I rocked her gently, rubbing my hand up and down her back. "You have more courage than any man I've ever met," I told her.

When she'd fallen asleep, I laid her back against the pillows and took one of the lamps in hand, then draped a blanket over my arm and slipped out onto the porch. Abigail rocked in one of the chairs, humming a low tune. When she saw me she stood. "Was she abused?" she asked.

I nodded, unable to speak. Abigail walked to me and took my shoulder in a warm hand, then patted me gently. "She will heal," she said.

She moved past me and into the cabin, closing the door behind her. I sat in the chair, still warm with her presence, and set the lamp on the floor at my feet. Then I pressed the blanket into my face and let the tears finally come.

Around the cabin and in the fields and woods, crickets chirped in loud chorus, incognizant of human sorrow.

In my dream Jack and Ridge Runner emerged from the dark like ghosts. Ridge Runner bent before me, his black eyes fathomless, mud painted on his cheeks, and wiped a finger across the salt on my face. He spoke to Jack in Cherokee, and Jack answered, lifting me from the chair as though I was lighter than air, the silver of his earring cold on my face.

Something's happened, he said, and though he too spoke in Cherokee, in my dream I understood every word.

There's another inside with the Simons woman. Ridge Runner's voice was deep and soothing, and in my mind I moved toward it, wanting to wake—to tell them of all that had occurred while they were away.

We'll sleep in the barn, then. A hand brushed my hair, cupping the back of my head.

Wolf—she has been weeping.

Warm breath puffed across my face. I pushed at it with a hand, connecting with something soft and velvety. I wiggled my thumb. Definitely a nostril, I thought. My eyes flew open, and I scooted backwards. When I blinked I saw Fire Eater's long neck stretched over the side of the next stall. He whinnied loudly, showing his teeth.

"Good heavens," I murmured, blinking. "What are you doing in my bed?" He kicked at the wooden divider, the sound echoing through the barn. "Stop that," I ordered, scrambling to my feet.

Hay stuck in random patches all over my gown. I brushed at it, looking back at where I'd slept. Someone had placed me in an empty stall. There was a blanket and pillow strewn across the floor. My eyes lit on the musket propped up in the corner; the tip of the barrel skimmed a water bucket hanging from a beam above, it was so long. I shoved open the stall door, slipping on pine needles, and raced down the barn run, clay cold against my bare feet. "Jack!" I yelled, "Jack!"

I burst from the dark barn and into bright sunlight, almost tripping on the hem of my dress. Jack and Ridge Runner stood at the edge of the pen, talking to Hosa and Zeke. There were furs of every shade of brown draped over the fence line. Ridge Runner gestured at them, saying something I couldn't make out, the others nodding in agreement. I picked up my skirts and ran towards them. "Jack!" I shouted again, my voice hitching.

All four men turned to me, but I saw nothing but Jack's white smile as I leapt into his arms like a child. He laughed loudly, spinning me in a circle. When my feet touched the ground the words flew from my mouth ahead of thought. "You're home—I thought you'd never return! So much has happened. Rebekah—my cousin is here, she's had a horrible journey. On the way she was accosted—"

Jack stopped me with a kiss. He took my face in his hands and his lips covered mine, warm and firm, and wonderfully familiar. His tongue traced the inside of my mouth. My eyes closed as I felt myself sinking into him. Nearby, a throat was cleared, and I drew back from him, flushed. "Welcome home," I said, unable to stifle the grin.

"I'll say," Zeke chuckled, nudging Hosa, who took the teenager's elbow and dragged him away towards the barn.

"Come on, we bes' let them alone," he said wryly.

Though I tried again to pull away, Jack kept a firm grip on my forearms. Behind him, Ridge Runner smiled—a rare show of teeth—and gave me a quick wink, such an English gesture that my eyes widened. When I opened my mouth to welcome him home, he turned on his heel and headed off towards the forest. "Now where's he going?" I asked.

Jack shook me gently, and I raised my face to him. His eyes burned a true green, flashing with humor and lust. He blew a strand of dark blond hair from his face, the tip sun-bleached with white, and ran his hands up to my shoulders. "I've missed you, Mac," he said quietly. "How long has it been?"

"Nine days and this morning," I answered pertly. "You lied—you told me you'd be gone but one week."

"Sure, and we're only a day or so over." He pulled me to him and nuzzled the side of my neck, his lips tickling the tender spot as his hand roamed around my back, curling over my bottom. His brogue deepened.

"Have you missed me, then, lass? Or have your wee books given you all the company you need?"

"I missed you," I murmured, pressing my lips to the warm, bare skin at the opening of his shirtfront. I laughed softly against his chest. "I've read all my books."

He chuckled, and it rumbled through him as he held me. I tilted my head back to look up at him. "I love you."

Jack cocked his head, lowering his chin and pinning me with hooded, cat eyes. "And I you." He cupped a hand to my cheek, rubbing his palm against my jaw. "We've a visitor now, don't we?"

"Oh, my heavens," I said, breaking from him and starting up the hill for our cabin. "Rebekah."

He reached out, catching my hand in his. I pulled at it, impatient. "Quinn, love—your shoes," he said dryly.

"But I must go to her. She's been alone all morning."

"Madam Simons is at the cabin caring for your good-cousin. Eliza's with her as well, keeping them both in water and fresh towels—though the girl's up and eating. Ridge Runner and I figured to wait for an introduction from you. We worried she might think savages had come to do her harm."

"Yes, hm," I murmured, thinking. To introduce Rebekah to my big, half-Indian husband and his brother—both tattooed and fierce—might return her to a state of shock. But she would have to meet them at some juncture, I considered.

"All right, I suppose I do need my shoes," I said, starting for the barn. I looked over my shoulder at him. His face was lined with dirt, his trade shirt grimy and spotted, and there was a tear where it hung at his shoulder, exposing an expanse of brown chest. His earring flashed in the sun. "You, sir, are in need of a bath. The smell alone will send Rebekah into a state of distress."

He grinned again, gave an English soldier's jaunty salute and jogged off in the direction of the creek. "And Ridge Runner, too!" I called after him.

"Aye, Mac, I'll hold his face beneath the water 'til all the war paint washes off," he shouted in answer.

Chapter 32

The MacFadden Settlement

Though the afternoon sun was warm, a cool breeze swept down over the hills, rustling old corn stalks and flapping the muslin curtains at my windows. The oaks near our cabin had turned a brilliant shade of red. They guarded the humble house like flaming giants, stout and perdurable. Near the edge of the upper pasture, an eagle slowly beat its enormous wings, coming to rest in the crook of a dead pine tree. It turned twice on a bough silver with age and ruffled its feathers before tucking chin in and staring out towards the mountains, surveying its kingdom.

The settlement's horses stood in the yellowing field nearby as if painted there, heads bent, munching on the last of the summer grass. Plato and Mutt, older and wiser than Lord Harris's young mount, stayed far from Fire Eater. The black mare wandered over to the stallion and tried for some of his grass, but Fire Eater snorted and kicked out a back leg in warning, and the smaller horse pranced off unharmed, stepping high, her midnight mane whipping out like a banner behind her.

Rebekah sat in one of the rocking chairs on the porch, looking towards the mountains. I approached her quietly, a silver tray in my hands with two porcelain cups of tea balanced on it. Though of not much real use on the frontier, I'd brought the ornate tray because I'd thought it might be useful to trade at some point. It had been my grandmother's, and I thought Rebekah might warm to the sight of something that may have been much like what she used in her own home in the city.

She turned when I set the tray on a rudimentary wooden table between rocking chairs. "A bit different landscape than Boston, I'm certain," I said, sitting beside her.

Both chairs faced the mountains; they creaked pleasantly as we rocked them to and fro.

She turned her head. Her hair had been combed and plaited, and she wore a gown of Abigail's. Unfortunately, mine had not fit as my new cousin was taller than I by several inches. A thin blanket draped her shoulders, and she held the edges together at her collarbone, her fingers long and pale. "It is quite lovely," she said. "I've never seen anything like it. I had never traveled outside of the New England colonies before this."

"I had expected these mountains to look much like the Alps," I admitted, smiling. "Those were some of the only mountains I'd seen before, but they're nothing like this. These seem more rounded and ancient, unexplored."

"And they're a strange blue color for most of the year, are they not? Owen was fascinated with them—that and some Cherokee ball game."

I laughed softly, remembering. "Yes, Owen truly enjoyed the Cherokee stickball. I think he may have even bargained with one of the players for a racquet to take home with him, but I do not think he succeeded—*anesta* racquets are highly valued by warriors."

"What does that mean, *anesta?*"

"It's the Cherokee name for the game that means 'little brother of war.' I suppose it's their way of practicing for warfare, much as English soldiers learn to march and form columns." I cleared my throat and kept my eyes on her as she turned her gaze back to the mountains.

"Rebekah, you'll be meeting my husband and his brother soon. Owen may have told you a bit of them. Jack is of both Cherokee and Irish blood, and Ridge Runner is a Cherokee—they share the same father. Jack's mother was kidnapped by the Indians when she was a young woman, though she does share a loving relationship with Jack's father, now." I ran my fingers along the arms of the chair, tapping my right hand nervously.

"The simple truth of it is that they will seem quite savage to you in their looks, and I don't want you to fear them. They are good men—they will care for you and protect you as though you are kin."

I heard her swallow before answering, but she still did not look at me. "Owen spoke of them . . . he said the same," she said. "I've a friend whose family moved to the western frontier when we were children. She was captured by the Iroquois—her parents and brothers were murdered. She's not been seen since."

"Rebekah," I began, wanting to reassure her.

"Please, Quinn. I trust in my husband's word. But I see his similar temperament in you. Owen rarely sees the bad in any face he meets, nor the color of skin. Would that I could be as undiscerning."

I made a move to speak, and she turned then, her brown eyes pleading.

"I will try," she said.

Down in the middle of the valley Lord Harris emerged from the barn, a bucket of oats in hand. He walked up the hill towards the horses, shaking it. When he noticed us he immediately removed his hat, pausing to bow slightly. I raised a hand in greeting. When I glanced at Rebekah I saw that she'd not even moved her head to look at the Englishman.

"Did you have enough of the supper?" I asked, worried that she wasn't eating properly, or even at all, since she'd arrived.

"Yes—the fish was quite adequate. I'd never had it prepared over fire before."

"You will eat more fish than you can stand while living here," I said. "It truly is a staple of frontier life. Though I've grown accustomed to it I cannot say in all sincerity that I like it. I quite tire of it after a while. But Jack and Ridge Runner have surely provided us with enough venison and bear to last the first of winter. And we do have wild turkey, rabbit, deer and grouse."

"I should hope to never encounter a bear in the wild," she said, shuddering. "A man kept one locked in a cage on the corner of Queen and George streets and charged three shillings for a look. The beast terrified me, always throwing itself against the bars, swiping its claws at us. I am not fond of such creatures. I do believe they lust after human blood." She sat forward suddenly, her leather boots flat on the porch planks. "Is that your husband?" she asked, a note of fear in her voice.

Jack and Ridge Runner approached over the hill. They matched each other stride for stride, their expressions stoic. Jack's dark gold hair was loose and gleaming from a good brushing, the feather at the end of his one skinny braid bumping against a shoulder. He'd changed into farmer's breeches and a fresh shirt, and though he'd tied up the laces he wore the silver gorget around his tawny neck, and it flashed in the sun. Ridge Runner wore a pair of black leggings I'd not seen before and a clean white shirt, a beaded belt at his waist. His hair he'd let hang long and loose, and it fell down to the center of his back, black and shiny with bear grease.

At their feet were short moccasins, and neither had donned weapons—at least not visibly—most likely figuring that the sight of muskets and tomahawks could send the fragile Rebekah into a fit of hysteria. Inwardly, I prayed for fortitude. Though they'd obviously made an attempt to appear civilized, their warrior tattoos seemed even more pronounced on their freshly scrubbed faces.

"They're huge," she whispered, clutching the arms of her chair.

I smiled faintly, remembering my first meeting with Jack. "Yes, they are. I do believe it's the air."

"What?"

"Nothing," I murmured, standing.

They stopped in the dirt at the bottom of the stoop. I bent to Rebekah and took her elbow lightly, urging her to rise. She did, staring at the brothers with a complete lack of her usual polite New England aplomb. When the tips of my moccasins hung over the porch step I stopped. Jack smiled, his green eyes friendly, and Ridge Runner kept his sculpted face blank, his dark gaze intent on Rebekah. Though we stood more than a foot above them, they met our eyes.

"May I introduce my husband, Jackson Wolf, and his brother Ridge Runner, both Cherokee of the Wolf clan. Gentlemen, this is Rebekah Scott, wife of my cousin Owen. She is to make a home with us here in the Valley for the time being."

Jack bowed slightly at the waist, his voice soft and lilting. "'Tis a fine thing to see two lovely ladies watching the sun go down. We're happy to have you with us, Madam Scott. Though it's sorry I am for your troubles, I am glad to meet another of Quinn's family."

Rebekah seemed to break from her surprise. She curtsied quickly and cleared her throat. "And I you, Mr. Wolf."

He flashed white teeth and Irish charm, and I raised an eyebrow at him. "Oh, no—you must call me Jack, for we're to be cousins now with no formalities between us."

"Jack," she said softly, folding her hands at her waist.

Ridge Runner broke the calm exchange by turning sharply to Jack and speaking low in Cherokee, agitation filling his face and the timbre of his voice. Rebekah started, reaching over to grip my forearm. Jack nodded at him as he responded, and the two argued in that language for a few minutes. Then Jack looked up at us, and he smiled again, though not as brightly, avoiding the question in my eyes.

Ridge Runner cleared his throat as if remembering himself, and crossed his arms over his chest, a gesture unfitting of the moment and only causing him to seem more severe. He nodded curtly at Rebekah. "Welcome, Madam Scott. It is an honor to meet you."

The four of us stood in awkward silence, and a chill wind wafted across the upper pasture as the sun made its descent behind the mountains. Down in the middle of the Valley Meg and Micah raced across the orchard with rivercane fishing poles in hand, Sam lagging behind, his cane trailing in the dirt. Abigail emerged from her cabin and called for the boys to come inside.

I clapped my hands together, the sound startling the others. "Coffee," I said suddenly. "Let's inside and enjoy a cup by the fire." Without giving them time to protest I hurried to the cabin door and took the latch in hand, smiling brightly as I pulled it open. Rebekah watched me with wide, fawn-like eyes.

Jack stepped up onto the porch beside her and made a gesture toward the cabin, not touching her. "After you, Madam Scott."

"But he cannot come inside," she said in a rush, paling, and I knew that she spoke of Ridge Runner.

I left the door standing open and walked to her, taking her elbow firmly in hand and raising my chin to meet her eyes. "Don't be silly," I said shortly, patience evaporating. "This is my good-brother—of course he can come inside."

"But he is a savage," she whispered furtively, glancing back at the two men, who stood silently behind us. I tightened my grip on her arm, and she pulled at it, but I held. A hot flash of indignation and shame filled my face: indignation at her prejudice, shame for her ignorance. *So much for trying,* I thought. I opened my mouth to speak, but Jack cleared his throat, stopping me.

"Sure, and we're not at all savage," he said lightly, his brogue thick, making the problem about them both. This time he reached out and took her elbow in hand, tugged her gently from me. "The truth of it is that I can dance a waltz just as an English gent, and I'll be happy to show you if you'll just step inside, Cousin. Of course, the cabin is a wee bit smaller than a ballroom, so you cannot laugh when I bang my knees against a chair or two."

She looked up at him, and the panicked expression on her face vanished in an instant, color returning to her cheeks. She let him lead her inside, unspeaking. I turned to Ridge Runner, who stepped up onto the porch, watching the scene with unreadable eyes. "I suppose you do catch more bees with honey," I said wryly. He didn't move his gaze from the door, and I cocked my head at him, curious. "What's amiss?"

He blinked and looked down at me, shaking his head. "Nothing. But I do not think I should be part of this coffee drinking."

"Nonsense. You are Jack's brother, and mine too. I want you here." I made an arm towards the open door as Jack had done with Rebekah. "After you, Mister Runner."

He offered a half-smile and looked down at me, amusement warming his dark eyes. "Will you be this stubborn as an old woman, I wonder?"

"Well, I should hope so."

Though Rebekah had protested, we'd decided that Jack should stay the night in the barn so that she could share the cabin with me. She was still unsettled on the frontier, scared to be alone. And the small cabin we'd begun building for her after receiving Owen's post was only in its early stages, a foundation settled and the beginnings of log and clay walls rested in the same shape—a square—now but a few feet high. Her cabin had been cleared in a spot near the middle pastures and the other homes there, but closer to Jack's and mine than they were, at the bottom of the upper pasture where the land just began to slope upward.

Faced with the lonely prospect of spending several nights away from each other after a still longer absence, Jack and I lingered on the step, the night sky a dark, starry canopy above our heads. A mosquito buzzed near my face, and I backed away quickly, swatting at it. He jerked back from our embrace, narrowly missing a smack on the nose.

"First you keep me from our bed and now you aim to break my nose, Mac," he said, smiling good-naturedly despite the truth of the statement. He stepped forward and took my arms again. I wrapped mine around his waist, looking up.

"My apologies—I was trying for the mosquito. Should they not be gone by now?"

"Aye, but so long as there's fresh blood about, like yours, they'll bite." He bent and pressed his mouth to the side of my neck, opening his teeth lightly against the skin. I shivered.

"It's been so long," I said shyly. "I don't want to spend another night without you."

"Well, now—the girl doesn't need watching the whole night through. You could away to the barn for a while, could you not?"

"I could," I nodded. "Especially since there's been such trouble between Fire Eater and Lord Harris's mare. Surely I'll be needed to calm him."

He pulled me to him, pressing our bodies close, and I felt him through the fabric of my skirts, hard in the crook of my thighs. "You're needed for other reasons too, lass, but if such is the faerie's tale you choose, I'll go with it."

I laughed, the sound echoing easily across the hills in the otherwise silent night. Inside the cabin I heard a thump, as if something had been dropped onto the wood floor. I pulled back from him reluctantly. He reached out and cupped the side of my face in one big hand, rubbing his thumb across my cheek and staring down into my eyes. "For the sake of all holy saints, Mac, don't wait too long," he said, then smiled and took away his hand, turning and disappearing in the direction of the barn.

Inside, Rebekah sat primly at the edge of the bed. She wore a thin sheath of mine, goosebumps trailing down her arms, her brown hair loose and curling onto her chest. The fire crackled at the hearth. When I shut the door behind me she cleared her throat expectantly.

"I did not know which side of the bed you preferred," she said formally, and I thought suddenly of how privileged we both were, never having to share a bed with someone else. Since each of us was of relative wealth and with no female siblings, we'd always had quarters of our own. But in most frontier cabins, like those in the Valley, whole families often shared the same bed for lack of space.

"I sleep on the side nearest the hearth, but both sides have lamps for reading. You're welcome to borrow a book, or blow out the lamp, whichever you prefer. It's been a long day."

"You have stacks of them," she said, indicating the trunk at the foot of the bed and the books piled upon it. "Have you read them all?"

I went to the armoire, pulling my dress over my head without untying the laces—a trick I'd learned here on the frontier, with no hand maid to help—and hung it inside on a latch.

"Sadly, yes," I said, standing on one foot as I shed my moccasins and stockings. I slid both arms into my shift and tugged at the makeshift whalebone corset. Rebekah watched in surprise as I bent and tugged it down over my knees until it dropped onto the floor.

"Whatever is that?" She asked, her patrician accent losing some of its formality.

I picked up the contraption and smiled as I put it away, thinking of Wise-for-Years. "I made it from an old stomacher," I told her. "I found that I could not ride in comfort without something to support this ungainly chest of mine."

She blushed a sudden, florid pink, covering her mouth with a hand.

I put a hand to my forehead and grimaced. "Oh, forgive me—I've become quite mouthy from time in the wilderness. Please, don't be offended."

"At least you are well-endowed," she answered, setting her hand in her lap and smiling. "I feel as though I'd not fill out a boy's dress shirt."

I walked to the fire and took the poker, pushing ashes over the flames until it died. I set it back against the stone hearth and turned to her, dusting off my hands. "Well, if it eases your mind I've bemoaned my figure since childhood—it's not easy to ride horses when you're buxom. I used to bind my chest with strips of old cloth, at least until Elsa—one of Grandfather's house slaves—caught me at it and helped me fashion something from one of my old corsets." I cocked my head, remembering. "I do believe that the French have developed something like this, and sell it on the clothing market. How I wish I still had access to the traders on King Street—though I don't know how I would request such an odd and unseemly item."

She stood and walked to the other side of the bed, waiting as I held back the sheets. We climbed in at the same time, settling down against our pillows as our sides touched, shyness fading. She sat suddenly and blew out the lamp at her side table, then scooted back down, pulling the sheets to her chin and resting her knuckles against her chest. I resisted the urge to pick up a book at the side table and studied the roof of the cabin for a moment before turning on my side.

"What is it like, in Boston?" I asked softly.

"Much like Charlestown, I suppose, as they are both seafaring ports," she answered, her eyes ahead. "It's a bustling city. The streets are filled with carriages at all hours of the day and night. From my father's house I could see the ships in the harbor, bringing in trade goods. Now they are British ships, and they hover there as though they'd fire a cannon at any moment should they choose—and at their own subjects." She shook her head slightly as if clearing it, took a breath. "In the winter the wind blows in from the ocean, so desperately cold that it feels as though your bones will freeze. The wind whips through the streets, and people sometimes must walk almost sideways against it, just to stay upright."

"Owen wrote me of the troubles after merchants protested the Stamp Act," I said. "It must have made for a frightening scene."

"It was. Suddenly, those who had known each other for years and had been cordial—despite whether they were Tory or Whig—no longer spoke in the street. Redcoat soldiers were sent to guard most businesses. Some were spit upon, tossed rotten food at. It's been horrible for both sides." She turned then on her pillow and looked at me, her face shadowed. "Owen believes that war will come. He says that he sees it."

"Yes," I whispered, wondering how much he'd told her of my own peculiar sense of sight.

"He should not have sent me here," she said, her expression closing in on itself. "I am his wife, and I should be at his side, no matter the danger."

"I don't think Owen would agree. He loves you, Rebekah. He wants you safe."

She scoffed, her voice suddenly hard. "Safe? Among the savages? In the wild mountains? Well, he was wrong about that, wasn't he."

"It would kill him to know what you have suffered," I said. "He would never have sent you here, had he believed that you would be misused as you were. You must know that. He loves you," I repeated firmly.

She turned to the opposite wall, her back to me. When she spoke her words seemed hollow and far away. "He loves liberty more than his own wife."

I thought to protest but instead rolled onto my back, staring again at the beams and clay of the roof. The lamp cast flickering shadows against the wood, making everything in the room seem wavering and unreal, as though it all sat imprisoned in some underwater vault. I leaned over, cupped my hand at the back of the glass and blew out the lamp.

I waited until Rebekah breathed deeply and steadily and then slipped from the bed, sliding quietly into my moccasins, a thin blanket in hand as I pulled open the door, vanishing into the dark. The Valley was hushed but for the sound of wind in the trees. It made a human moan as it rushed through the boughs of hemlocks and oaks, swaying heavy trunks. I hurried over the hill, my eyes on the pale yellow light leaking from beneath the doors of the barn. My hands found the latch there and I pulled them open, cringing at the creak they made. I glanced back over my shoulder—nothing but darkness—and stepped into the barn.

Plato snorted when I passed, walking towards the light coming from an empty stall at the middle of the dirt run. But hay and pine needles crunched, and a few doors down Fire Eater lifted his great head over the side, whinnying softly. I hurried towards him, my moccasined feet making no sound, passing the stall with the light. The stallion put his muzzle into my hands, blowing warm air on my palms. When I'd quieted him I turned, feeling the tiny hairs at the back of my neck stand at attention, prickling down along my spine.

Jack stood at the door of the lighted stall, leaned up against the frame. He wore only the farmer's breeches from earlier, and the planes of his torso were shadowed, his hooded eyes dark. I walked to him, the familiar buzz starting beneath my skin. He reached out and took my hand, pulling me into the empty stall. He shut the door behind us, latching the board. On the floor was a pallet of blankets. The lamp hung from a nail, casting the tiny space in a muted glow.

"You've been a while," he said quietly. "I thought you wouldn't come."

I took the blanket from my shoulders, dropping it onto the pallet. "I waited until she slept. I worried she'd be frightened with me gone."

I stepped forward, and he met me there in the center of the room. He took my shoulders in his hands and I laid my hands against his chest, the skin hot to the touch. Between us he was hard and urgent; he pressed himself against me, and it felt as though all my body's blood pulsed at the spot. His eyes were sea-bottom green, shadowed and languid. I reached out, tracing the clenched line of his jaw. The raw need between us was heavy in the cool air.

"Do not be gentle," I murmured.

His hands were at the straps of my shift and mine at the laces of his breeches. We both fumbled, laughing together as we worked. Suddenly my shift was gone and the air hit my erect nipples. His breeches fell to the ground and he tried to kick them away, but I was being lifted into his arms, my legs around his waist. The touch of my breasts against his smooth chest was startling. I caught my breath when he set his lips to my tender neck.

"You are beautiful, Quinn," he said, the words muffled. I let my head fall back, abandoning myself to the feeling. "I've thought of naught but you, of this, night and day."

"I dreamed of you so much that I felt you there beside me," I whispered. "I've wanted your hands on me so badly I thought I felt you in my sleep."

He moved with me still about his waist, stumbling toward the wall. My naked back hit the boards there and he shifted me in his arms, his hands gripping my waist. "I can't wait," he said on a breath, and thrust roughly, so deeply I thought he'd touch the other side. He thrust again, and again, long and smooth, sliding in and out of my slippery cache, the flesh of my inner walls tingling. He cupped his hands around my bare buttocks and lifted me against him; I moaned at the contact. My breasts were covered in a sheen of sweat, crushed against his chest as we moved together, the taut muscles of his stomach sliding against my slick belly. There was a roar in my ears, and I felt myself hovering near release. I closed my eyes tightly and watched colors spark behind dark lids.

"Quinn," he said as he continued to thrust harder. "Look at me."

"Jack," I whispered hoarsely, the wood planks rough at my back. "Please—"

He pressed his forehead against mine, long hair falling onto his collarbone, meeting my own where it hung in a tangle over my breasts. He lifted me again and moved into me one last time, going so deep I cried out. Then he too, found release, and he braced me there against the wall, one arm at my waist and one around my neck, pressing me to him. We trembled together as he bent his head, kissing my shoulder.

"I can't stand much longer," he said, and he shifted me in his arms and turned, carrying me to the pallet, where he laid us down on top of the blankets, still inside me. Our bodies hot and our breathing shallow, we lay entangled, my leg hooked over his thigh. I slid my foot down his calf, but it was caught in a bundle of clothes. I buried my face in his chest, laughing.

"Jack—you're not even out of your breeches."

He rose up on an elbow and looked down. "Aye," he chuckled. "When I said couldn't wait, I meant it." He lifted a heavy arm, brushed a damp strand of hair back from my face, tucking it behind my ear. "I hope you're unhurt."

I stretched my arms above my head luxuriously, my fingers brushing pine needles. "I feel wanton," I said, grinning.

"Good—then I've done right by you." He rolled onto his back, hooking an arm around my shoulders and pulling me with him, and the feel of him going soft inside me, still connected, was comforting and right.

I propped my chin on my hands at his chest, watching him as his eyes drifted closed. I studied the lines of his face, usually so hard and unflinching but now almost boyish in sleep. When his breathing went deep I leaned forward to kiss the bottom of his jaw. His hand slid from the small of my back and down along my hip, cupping one buttock possessively, squeezing. He smiled in sleep, and I lay my cheek against his chest, listening to his heart.

Chapter 33

November, 1769

Cold rain pelted the roof, whipping the sides of the cabin in whooshing bursts of wind. Water fell from the edges of the porch in a downpour, heavy and sheet-like. I breathed silent thanks to Mother Nature that the storm brought but bone-chilling rain. The only thing worse would be a destructively early snowfall.

The fire crackling in the stone fireplace put out a good bit of heat, in spite of the drops that splattered down the chimney, hissing in the coals. I leaned back, feeling a bit shameless, and let the base of my skull rest against the rim of the huge whiskey barrel, filled with warm water, that sat a few feet before the hearth—and with me in it. We'd hauled it from Fort Prince George on the back of a wagon—two traders there had been using it as a card table—and though I had intended on using it to wash clothes during the winter when the creek froze over, I could not resist the chance for a hot bath.

When Zeke, Jack and Hosa had hauled it up to our cabin yesterday the women had watched in bewilderment, Abigail stating aloud that I was silly to be bathing in the cold weather, that I'd surely catch a fever from it. Thankfully, Jack had rolled the barrel across the porch and into our cabin on its side, paying them no mind. The Cherokee bathed daily, despite foul weather and in frigid rivers and creeks, something the English—who washed sometimes no more than once a fortnight—could never understand.

I'd spent the afternoon catching rainwater in my pitcher and transferring it to the makeshift tub. The torrential downpour had kept us all away from work, tightly ensconced in our own homes. Rebekah had been trapped down at the Wheeler's cabin since morning. Meg had made a mad, wet dash up the hillside to tell us that she'd be staying the night with them, that they were drinking tea and playing tiddlywinks.

I shifted my legs beneath the water, watching it lap gently against the tops of my bare knees, poking up like rounded, white islands.

"If you were an Indian lass you'd be out in the creek, washing despite the cold," Jack said as he took the kettle from the spit above the fire. He moved to the barrel and poured water near my feet, careful not to scald.

"Well, I'm not. I'm a woman who adores a hot bath, and nothing is going to change that."

"Can I get you a book, Lady Quinn?"

I tipped my chin, smiling up at him. "No, it's rude to read in the company of others. But you can fill the pitcher again and put more water in the kettle, if you don't mind."

"Certainly, Your Highness." He bowed slightly at the waist, long hair falling over his shoulders. When he straightened he gave me a wink and walked to the door, leaving it open as he moved about on the porch. The rain made a steady roar until he closed the door behind him.

He pulled a chair beside the makeshift tub and settled down with legs outstretched, hooking one ankle over the other. I felt the bottom of the barrel for the bar of lye soap, grasping it between slick fingers and bringing it to the surface to rub it against a cloth I'd draped over the rim. He watched me with lazy eyes as I moved the cloth across my collarbone.

"Tell me again of the Roman baths," he said conversationally. "Did the Italian women really bathe together, naked as newly born babes?"

"Yes, they really did. The water flows through the aqueducts—large piping systems built by the ancients that run all the way from the mountains into the city. I'm not sure how they heat it, though—I suppose with some sort of fire." I reached back, coiling a damp, stray strand of hair up around my topknot. "Most of the Roman baths were destroyed when churches were built over them during the sixteenth century. The one I visited in Rome was small, but relatively clean. It was the only day that Grandfather let me go off without him or Owen, though not for long, and with a servant from the palazzo where we'd rented. It was heaven."

"Aye, sounds like," he said, grinning.

I flipped my hand lightly, splashing his outstretched legs. He pulled them back quickly. "Jack Wolf. Don't even *think* of imagining those women without their clothes."

"If you'd stand up and let me dry you I'll be incapable of thinking of any other naked women."

"Tempting," I answered, sliding down until the water reached my chin, "but this feels far too lovely to abandon just yet. Besides, I think the water in the kettle's ready. Could you?"

He cocked an eyebrow at me but rose and took the kettle, this time pouring it onto my knees. I yelped and sat up, legs disappearing beneath the water. "Beast," I told him, but couldn't keep the smile from my face. He bent and set the kettle on the hearth.

"Just trying to be of use, Mac. I don't want you to turn scaly as a lizard." He sat back in the chair and crossed his arms over his chest, tilting back so that the two front legs left the floor. He smiled at me, but his eyes clouded suddenly, moving to the window beside the door where the rain splattered against the rough curtain.

"He didn't reveal where he was going?" I asked quietly.

The chair legs returned to the wood floor with a bump. "You mean Ridge Runner?" I nodded. "No, he didn't tell me anything but that he'd something to settle northeast of here, at the North Carolina border."

"Why did you not ask him?"

"Because I'm his brother, not his nursemaid." He stood abruptly, walking to the window. "He said he'd return before the month's out, that's all I can tell you."

The water had turned suddenly cold. When I stood it sluiced down my body as I reached out for a blanket draped over a chair back nearby. "I just don't understand the secrecy," I said. "Does it not seem strange to you that suddenly and for seemingly no reason Ridge Runner has something 'to settle' so far from here, something we know nothing about?"

"I told you, I did not ask him. You're the one with the Sight—you find out why he's gone."

I stepped out of the barrel, my feet making wet prints on the wood floor. I wrapped the blanket around me, my color high. "I can't control what I see, Jack," I said, stung by his tone.

He turned from the window, his eyes shadowed. The outside world had gone dark, but lamp and firelight flickered in the room. Thunder rumbled across the ridges, rattling the teacups in the chifferobe. Jack looked as though he was about to speak, but his gaze moved to my feet and he stepped forward. "Mac, love—you're bleeding."

I looked down. A rivulet of red ran down the side of my calf and across the top of my foot. I put a hand to my stomach, my cheeks burning. "My menses," I murmured. "I've some rags in the chifferobe."

He was across the cabin in a few steps; after a moment I felt a hand on my shoulder. "Here, lass."

"Please, could you turn away?" I asked, embarrassed.

"Mac," he said softly, and I heard his thoughts: *for God's sake, you are my wife*.

"Please."

He blew out a sigh and turned around, folding his arms across his chest. I quickly dried myself with the blanket, draping it over the chair again. I folded the clean rags and pressed them between my legs, holding them with one hand as I walked naked to the trunk at the foot of the bed, slipping into the leggings I'd left there. Covering my breasts, I moved quickly to the chifferobe and took a dress, pulling it over my head.

"All right," I said, and he turned, crossing to me.

"Does it pain you?" He took my shoulders in big hands and bent so that we met at eye level.

It occurred to me suddenly that with the flux of my menses came again the realization that I was not yet with child. I walked away from him, sitting on the edge of our bed. Relief rushed through me, and I ran a hand back over my hair, unsure how to deal with the feeling.

"No, there's no pain but an occasional griping of the stomach," I assured him. He crouched before me, reaching out and taking my hand where it rested on my knee.

"Are you sad that there's no babe?"

"Are you?" I asked sharply, watching him.

He rocked back on his heels, studying me with those intense emerald eyes of his. When I looked away he reached out and cupped my jaw, turning my face back to him.

"The thought of you with my child in your belly makes my heart feel like it's been squeezed by a giant," he said slowly. "I can see you in my mind, round and flushed, and I lose my words. But then I watch your face, and I see that you're happy that it's not happened yet. And I wonder if it's because our babe will be part Indian—that our son or daughter could look as savage as my father."

"Jack, no." I leaned forward and took his face in my hands, tears pooling hotly at the corners of my eyes. My heart ached at his words. "No, you must not think that. When we have a child I'll love it, no matter what it looks like—I'll love that child even more so because it's part of you. Please believe me."

He reached up and took my right hand from his face, kissing the palm. "Aye, I believe you. But I still wonder what you're not telling me."

"I'm not ready yet to be a mother," I whispered in a rush, before I could stop myself. "I want to bear your children someday—I do—but not now, not while there's still so much to be done with the settlement, and our marriage still so new." I took my hands back, wiping beneath my eyes. I blinked, attempting a smile. "I'm ashamed that I want this time with you, that I want you alone. I'm a horrible excuse for a woman, to feel this way. It must surely be unnatural."

He stood, pulling me to my feet. His eyes were dark and unreadable, but he wrapped his arms around my waist and tugged me to him, resting his chin on the top of my head. When he spoke I felt the movement against my skull. "Mayhap you can't get with child," he said, and I started to pull back, but he held me firmly. "Mayhap it's something to do with me, and not you—but surely 'tis a decision for the Creator, lass. I want you happy, and if you're not ready, I'll abide by that."

"I don't know how I will sleep at your side and not want you to touch me," I muttered into his shirtfront, my cheeks flaming. He chuckled, and I stepped back freely.

"Why do you laugh?" I asked accusingly. "I'm not the only one who will find chastity difficult. And from you, the man who once claimed a woman in every village on the frontier." I moved past him, shrugging off his hand, and stopped before the fire, crossing my arms over my chest.

The nerve of that man, I thought, infuriated. It was difficult enough to admit something so untoward, and he made it worse by finding it all amusing. The mattress creaked, and I spun around. He'd sat there as though ready for bed, his back against the wall. I narrowed my eyes at him as he watched me, his mouth twitching.

"Oh, I'm not planning to keep my hands off you, Mac—I'll share your bed when I please, as I'm your husband, and it's my right, not to mention part of your own English law."

Fuming, I turned back and grabbed the poker, jabbing at the fire. "So you were lying when you told me you'd abide by my wishes—you with your slick Irish charm."

"Sure, and I've not told a falsehood since I was a wee lad," he said. "I'll abide by your wishes, I said I would. But we'll not have to forgo lovemaking, that's what I'm trying to tell you, you maddening woman."

"And how will we keep from having a child if we don't?" I asked, my voice rising along with my temper.

"*Cicuta maculata*," he said simply, watching me.

"What on earth are you saying? It sounds like Latin."

"Aye, it's the Latin name for spotted cowbane, a plant the Cherokee use to prevent a babe from taking root in the womb." He shrugged as he watched me, using the toes of one foot to slip off the moccasin on the other. "The use of it's frowned upon, but I'm told it works. If the storm lets up by morning, we'll take a stroll in the woods and get you some. I'm sure I can find an old woman from Keowee Town who can show you how to use it, without chastising you too harshly."

"How in the world do you know the Latin name for such a plant? No matter," I muttered, walking to my side of our bed and pulling the dress over my head. I reached into the chifferobe and took out one of my shifts, yanking it over me before shucking the leggings. I pulled a makeshift undergarment I'd cut from another pair of leggings and tugged it up over my thighs, keeping the cloth in place between my legs. I flung back the quilt and scooted in beside him, shutting my eyes, still frustrated and mortified with the situation, all of it made worse by the cramping starting in my belly.

"It shouldn't keep you from getting with child, when you are ready," he said softly. "And I do hope that someday you will want my child."

I rolled onto my side and looked at him, my eyes filling again with the tears I couldn't seem to quell. "I will, I promise you. I am sorry that I feel this way—there must be something wrong with me. I must be an even queerer woman than I'd thought."

In one move he'd wrapped an arm around my shoulders, pulling me to rest against his chest. "Your queer qualities are part of the reason why I had to have you. You're a rare woman, Mac. You've so much life and yearning in you. And for now, if you want more than motherhood, I'm willing to stand by your side, to go wherever ye go."

I lifted my head, moving so that I lay along his side, my hands braced on his chest. I leaned forward, pressing my lips to his, hard. When I pulled back I sniffed and smiled. "I love you, Jack."

"And I you. Just do me the one favor, love. Don't make me a father when I'm a doddering old man—I'd like the wee ones to understand me when I order them to fetch me wooden teeth."

I laughed, touching my forehead against his chest. He shifted so that I lay completely on top of him, and reached his arms down to cup my buttocks. I moved again, folding my arms and resting my chin in my hands as I looked at him, his green eyes bright. "I promise," I said, smiling. "And I don't know why I'm crying—it must be the menses."

"When a Cherokee woman goes through this time she's sent away to a house by herself, and is forbidden to make contact with any others in the tribe while she bleeds, unless they are women who suffer as she does. A bleeding woman is a powerful one, dangerous even." He smiled, the hard line of his jaw softening. "Mayhap I'll build a hut for you in the woods, make you stay in it 'til you are yourself again."

I curled an arm around his side and pinched him. When he yelped, I grinned. "Be careful I don't use my powers on you, husband."

He grinned back, flinging his arms out to the sides like a sacrifice. "Use them at will, lass—I'm at your mercy."

"One last go 'round, Meg, and then we'll need give Plato a rest," I called over my shoulder, walking across the pen to unlatch the gate. I'd finally—after hours of cajoling—convinced Father Wheeler to allow me to teach Meg to ride, and it was all worth it to see the sheer joy in her face whenever Plato made a slow circle around the inside of the pen. Meg sat stiffly on his back, boots tucked firmly in the stirrups. She held herself straight, as I'd showed her, and was doing a right good job of keeping her heels down. Watching her, I felt a burst of warm pride, and I remembered just how good it felt to teach.

I lifted the heavy rail and moved it aside. From where I stood I could see Abigail and Eliza at the fire pit, bonnets pulled up over their heads and coats on, to keep warm. Samuel turned a spit, roasting fish for supper as Rebekah looked on, holding a blanket over her shoulders. I glanced up at the mountains. The sun lay low on the leafless ridges, which meant it must be near to five of the clock. We ate earlier in the late autumn, each of us preferring to retreat to our cabins in the cold.

"Ridge Runner! Look at me!" Meg shouted.

My eyes flew to the girl. She kicked her heels into Plato's sides, trying unsuccessfully to make the old horse trot. I followed her line of vision, shading my eyes.

Ridge Runner stood at the edge of the settlement, where the middle pasture met dark forest. He stood so unmoving that he seemed a part of the trees, the brown of his deerskin leggings and jacket melding into bare branches and dead undergrowth. Behind him the creek gurgled. I lifted an arm to wave to him, but stopped in mid-reach. He hands were loose by his sides, and in one he held something unfamiliar. I squinted, focusing on it. When he stepped into the open I gasped, turning back and running towards Meg. I pulled her from the old horse and grabbed her hand, snatching the lead and closing her fingers over it. "Take Plato to the barn," I said shortly. "Put him in his stall and fill his trough."

"But—"

I bent to her eye level, placing a hand on her shoulder. She trembled slightly beneath it. "This is important, Meg. Remember, you promised to do whatever I asked. Go now."

I waited until she nodded and tugged on the lead, the horse following obligingly. Then I picked up my skirts, running across the dirt pen and towards my good-brother, winter grass slapping at my legs. I climbed through the fence and stopped several yards from him, and when I did his black eyes met mine, unblinking. "Whose are they?" I asked, my voice shaking.

He held two scalps by their dirty brown hair, the slabs of skin connected to each encrusted with dried blood. From the same hand that held the scalps hung a black leather strap; sewed to it was an eye patch.

"Ridge Runner," I said softly. "What have you done?"

"Where is your cousin?"

"Ridge Runner, talk to me, for—"

"Your cousin, where is she? And your husband?"

"Rebekah is down by the fire pit. I don't know where Jack is—he could be at the cabin. Please," I begged. "You must tell me what happened."

He walked past me and crossed the field in long strides. I took my skirts in hand again, hurrying after him. As we neared the fire pit I saw that Jack had joined the group there and had set his musket against a log, warming his hands by the fire. When he saw us he straightened, smiling. But when his gaze lit on his brother he stilled. He watched Ridge Runner approach Rebekah soundlessly.

Abigail and Eliza stopped what they were doing, and Samuel stayed where he was, as if a magic powder had been dropped on them all, causing them to freeze in place. I ran to Jack, gripping his forearm. "What's he doing?" I asked, but he shook his head at me, his eyes hard.

"Wait," he said shortly.

"Rebekah Scott," Ridge Runner said, his voice low. She turned on her heel and put a hand to her throat, startled. He walked to her and she backed away, almost stumbling in the dirt. He held out the scalps, dropping them at her feet. "The men who took your honor no longer walk this earth. This is your proof."

As I watched my cousin—this privileged, genteel young woman who had lived her entire life in a world of comfort and elegance—I was sure she'd scream at the sight of that bloody mess of hair in the dirt. Instead, she bent over and lifted the strap with the eye patch, crumpling it in her white fist. Eyes blazing, she looked at the Indian who stood hushed, asking nothing of her.

"Thank you," she said.

Looking between them, I felt a flicker of fear. Heat seemed to emanate from Ridge Runner's still form, and he and Rebekah had not moved. *Owen,* I thought, *I hope whatever you are embroiled in is worth it.*

Chapter 34

December, 1769

Quincy. It nears.

I dropped the bucket, and it landed hard on the floor of Fire Eater's stall, the frozen water within cracking and breaking, sending chunks of ice into the hay at my feet. The stallion bent his great neck, breath puffing out in clouds from his nostrils into the frigid air; he nosed at the bucket, licking at the handle. I backed over to the smithy's bench I kept in his stall and sat on the cold wood, my stomach clenching. "What does that mean?" I whispered, pressing a fist to my navel.

It had been quite some time since I'd heard the voice, and I'd become easy in my mind because of its absence, lured into believing in normalcy. I shut my eyes tightly, feeling the ache begin to throb at my eyebrows, faint but building. I willed it back, knowing I'd not get an answer.

I got to my feet, steadier now, and picked the bucket from the floor, twisting to set it back on the bench. Fire Eater pawed at the ice in the straw with one hoof. I wrapped my fingers around his hemp halter and dragged his nose down to mine, staring into intelligent brown eyes.

"Stop that, you monster," I said. He clicked his teeth and pulled back, testing me. I released the halter and moved to the side of the stall, lifting a blanket from the wall. He stilled as I draped it over his broad, tall back, watching me. "Oh, you're ever the sweetheart now that I'm keeping you warm, aren't you?" I murmured. Bending, I tied the corners of the blanket together at his chest, giving him a pat there before rising. Fire Eater's coat stayed short throughout the year, for some reason not bushing up in winter, never growing as wooly as the other horses'.

"You be treating dat hoss like a king." Hosa's deep voice came from the run. I walked to the door and stood on my tip-toes, looking over.

"Yes, I know," I admitted. Hosa carried a long plank of wood beneath one arm, an iron chisel in his free hand. He set the end of the plank on the ground. "What are you building?"

"A book shelf for de priest. Man's got almost as many books as you."

He picked up the plank and started to walk away, and the sight of his curly black head—his face dark and rich as chocolate crème, the look of another land forever stamped there—I stopped him. "Hosa?" I asked. "Are you content?"

He turned. "What you mean, Miz Quinn?"

I glanced back at Fire Eater and dismissed the water bucket for the moment, unlatching the stall door and closing it behind me. I crossed my arms over my chest tightly, rubbing my upper arms for warmth. "I mean what I mean," I said, approaching him. "Are you happy here, in the settlement? Are you ever lonely?"

He rolled his eyes, the whites bright, and hefted the plank in his arms, crooking his head towards the other end of the barn. "I guess you mus' come on down to de workshop, you wan' talk about loneliness."

Hosa's workshop was an area the size of several barn stalls, open and high, with a loft above. Here he welded shoes for the horses, stored tools and wood for carpentry. The rocking chair he'd been building for Meg Wheeler sat pale and unfinished in the corner, next to four planes of glass that leaned against the wall: the gift from my grandfather, to be installed in our cabin when Hosa could find the time. Several rough chestnut planks, similar to the one he held under his arm, leaned against the wall near them. He set the one he carried on top of two sawhorses in the middle of the room. "You go ahead and talk, 'cause I can' stop you. I'll jes work here."

"Hosa, you haven't answered my question," I said dryly, perching on a bench. My breath filled the air in front of my face, white, then disappeared.

He looked up, his eyes flashed. "You lonely? You de one always talking to someone dat's not dere."

"I asked you first."

He took the chisel, began scraping away a layer of dried chestnut. "You wan' know do I miss having folks about who are black as me. To be honest, Miz Quinn, I don' care what dem folks look like, I like de company, black or white. De only black folks I'd wan' 'round me be my wife and son, and dey be long gone."

"I've never asked you about your life in Virginia," I said softly. "I'm sorry."

"Don' you be sorry." He set the chisel down for a heartbeat and bent over the wood, his face hidden from my view. He shook his head. "I swear, you de only white woman I know wan' make friends wid a Negro."

"Well, then—you've never met the Grimble sisters," I said shortly.

He turned his head, and I saw the look of question in his eyes. "They are ladies from Charlestown, fiercely against slavery. Most think they're an oddity, but Catherine Grimble caught me once, at a meeting of the Charlestown Library Society. I was eleven years old, and Grandfather had taken Owen but not me, so I'd snuck away and slipped in behind Mr. Lawton's coattails—quite a large man, actually. She found me under a table that held a stack of scientific essays, reading a scandalous copy of some science book about the human body." Hosa sniffed, the corner of his mouth crooking up, and I grinned in response.

"From then on she gave me leave to borrow from her personal library." I paused before continuing. "Grandfather is a slave owner, of course, but he claims to abhor the institution. I learned much of my disdain for it from him. But my belief in the equality of all men *and* women, no matter their race—that came from the Grimbles."

"Das an ugly name for good women," Hosa said, and I nodded.

"Oh, yes—a horrible one, and unfortunately they lack a bit of grace in their looks. But they quite make up for it in passion and intellect. I hope they are well . . ." I trailed off, thinking of Charlestown.

"Now who's de lonely one?"

"You are changing the subject," I told him. He went back to chiseling, and I watched a smooth, curled shaving drop to the dirt floor.

"'Course I get lonely. Dis wilderness, it takes a bit o' getting used to. But I be happier here dan in Virginia, bein' a slave."

"What happened to your family?"

"My wife died, birthing our second son. My older son was sold to de highest bidder, when de master gone broke gambling in Harrisburg." He moved the chisel harder, thinning the end of the plank. The shavings began to pile at his feet. "I tried, when Zeke and I first left, to find him. But he be gone, and don' nobody know where."

We were silent for a while, and I watched him work, my mind whirling with thoughts of the future—wondering what would happen to him, to all of us, when war came, as I knew it would. I did not want to leave Keowee Valley and the life we had made. The thought of doing so felt like a cold hand clutching my throat, like a weight I could not lift on my own. When Hosa spoke it startled me.

"You see things, don' you? You see de future." He'd stopped working but was still bent over the plank of wood, his back to me.

I watched the line of his shoulders, the old fear that came with admitting it aloud welling up inside. I stood, gulped back the knot in my throat and nodded, the word whispered: "Yes."

He said nothing but went still as a marble statue, the chisel in hand. I turned and left the room before he could speak again.

Wind wailed like an old woman as it rushed down from the Blue Ridge, whipping through the settlement. A light dusting of snow had fallen last night, and it encrusted the ground, freezing the grass that poked up from the dirt, brown and unmoving. In the orchard the apple trees stood in rows, the younger trees sheened with ice. The others at the back of the orchard—the original trees we'd found when we'd arrived—were like old men, gnarled and bare, limbs curled inward, arthritic. A single piece of rotted fruit lay on the ground, white as an apple offered from the fist of a witch.

I poured broth made from the bones of a bear that Ridge Runner had shot last week into three bowls, handing one to Jack. "Ridge Runner, please sit."

He stood by the window of the cabin, arms crossed, staring out through the frosted glass. At my words he turned and joined Jack in front of the hearth, sitting in a chair. I handed him a bowl and he raised an eyebrow at me, his tattoo arching into his hairline. "It's only broth," I muttered, offended. "It won't kill you."

He sniffed at the bowl and Jack chuckled, watching him. "How can you be certain, Rides-Like-a-Man?" he asked. "You have not been cooking long."

Jack slurped theatrically at his soup, and I gave up my ire. I took a bowl for myself and sat in a rocking chair between them. We ate in silence, the men methodically eating. After a moment I set my bowl down, not used to the lack of dinner conversation.

"How are things at Keowee Town?" I asked them. They'd been away for one night, only arriving home that afternoon. Jack took a last sip and set his bowl on the floor near his feet. He planted his hands on his thighs, rocking forward.

"A wee bit strange, to be honest," he answered. "The British were there recently, plying folks with jewelry and clothes. Kicking Horse is getting old, and with Attakullakulla staying for the most part in Chota, there's no one in the Lower Towns who knows the British as well, who can barter with them."

"What do they want?"

"They're trying to make up for the loss of the fort," Ridge Runner said, resting the bowl in his lap. "They've been doing so since the summer. But they visit for other reasons, too."

Jack stood and went to the hearth, taking the poker and stoking the fire. He crouched low, the deerskin stretching across his muscular thighs, and blew into the coals. Orange flame flickered up, catching on the white underside of a log. "They're testing the Cherokee, lass," he said shortly. "They want to know if we're sympathetic to the colonial cause, or if we're for them."

I looked back and forth between the two brothers, my mind racing. "Well, how do you think the Cherokee will side, should there be war?"

"There will be war," Ridge Runner said. "You had a vision."

"Yes, but they're not always to be trusted," I answered, frustrated. Though I knew deep within me that war would come, I was anxious at the thought of others trusting in my often capricious "gift."

"Your cousin, he is like you. He also had this vision." Ridge Runner watched me, but his black eyes grew solemn. "If you were *Ani'Yun'wiya*, your dream would be treated as prophecy."

"Besides, Mac—look what's happening in the port cities, with British ships guarding the harbors, and soldiers in the streets. Something's coming."

It nears, the voice had said. I sighed deeply, wanting to clear my head, wishing for word from Owen and worried that none had come. I raised my eyes suddenly to meet Jack's. "Which will the Cherokee choose?" I repeated, fear of his answer gnawing at me. I remembered Owen's words—*you do not know how the Cherokee will side*—and I wondered.

He glanced at Ridge Runner, shrugged. "I'm no lover of the English—none of us are."

"But?" I asked sharply, hearing the hesitation. Ridge Runner stood, walking back to the window.

"But they have made the only effort to keep settlers from encroaching on our lands," he said, peering through the glass. He looked back over his shoulder at me. "It's been seven years since your King made his proclamation, but his subjects here do not listen."

"The Cherokee cannot take the side of a people who will banish them from their homeland, Mac." Jack watched me carefully, concern filling his hooded green eyes. "I know you love liberty. It is a cause worth fighting for, to be sure. But what liberty will the colonials give the Cherokee?"

"I'm a patriot, Jack." I looked up at him, meeting his eyes. "I could never side with the British—I won't. I believe that we should govern ourselves, that we need no self-proclaimed King to rule us. The people deserve freedom, not subjugation."

"Aye, they do," he said, his expression hardening. "But do the *Yun'wiya* not deserve their freedom, to be left alone from thieves and vagrants, from white men taking their women only out of land lust? As each year passes more settlers cross the Boundary Line. Are we to give up all lands, let them take as they please?" He shook his head. "Other settlers will not be as kindhearted as you, lass. They think of us all as godless savages, something to be rid of. They see our lands like a pirate sees gold, and they'll steal them, just as sure."

"You are an American, Jack—just as I am. And you, too," I said to Ridge Runner. "Or do you truly consider yourself subjects of the Crown?"

Jack laughed shortly, and Ridge Runner made a sound in his throat. They looked at each other silently, passing some sort of secret brother-speak between them through the air.

"Well, do you?" I asked again, growing more vexed by the moment.

Ridge Runner turned from the window and said something in Cherokee to Jack, then nodded quickly at me before opening the door. "*Wadan'*, little sister," he said. "The meal was good."

The door shut behind him, sending a bracing chill through the warm cabin. I shivered, rubbing the wool sleeves of my upper arms for warmth and looking up at Jack. He leaned against the stone hearth, watching at the door as if Ridge Runner still stood there. "I hope I did not offend," I said stiltedly at Ridge Runner's unexpected exit. Jack turned, looking down at me intensely.

"We do not consider ourselves subject to anyone but the earth, and the Creator who made it," he said. "I will not turn against my own people, Mac."

"What about the thousands of Irish who have come to this country, who now live in every colony—especially the Southern ones. They too want liberty. Are they not your people?"

"No, they aren't," he said roughly. "I know nothing of them, save for what my mother's told me and for the way that I speak. I am Silent Wolf, of the *Ani'waya*, more than I'll ever be Jack Wolf, whose mother once lived in County Cork. You'd best be deciding if you're willing to be wife to the man that I am."

I stood and walked from chair to chair, stacking the bowls in my hands. When I brushed past him he stopped me with a clamped hand over my forearm. "I'm no Irishman, Quinn. Look at the marks on my face. Can you live with that?"

"Yes, I can," I said, enunciating angrily. "I married you in a Cherokee dress, in a Cherokee village, by a Cherokee medicine man. Do not doubt that I am your wife." I tugged my arm from his grasp, and he let me go. I stacked the bowls on the table, braced my hands against the edge. "We will deal with the other when the time comes."

"The time's come." He dropped a letter onto the table in front of me. On the flap was a red wax seal, broken at the fold: the seal of the British army. I took the letter in hand but could not bring myself to open it.

"What is it?" I asked, cold rushing through me—having nothing to do with the snow outside—causing all the tiny hairs from my fingers to my shoulders to stand at attention.

"It's a summons. From General Cornwallis of the King's army. My services as translator have been required by the Crown. I'm to be in Charlestown by the first of February."

"Why you?" My throat felt as if it were closing up. The letter slipped through my fingers, fluttering to rest beneath the table. Jack walked past me, around to his side of the bed. He sat on the edge and started to lift the hem of his shirt. "Jack?" I asked, fighting to keep the desperation from my voice.

He dropped his elbows onto his knees, hands hanging between. Then he blew out a breath, bent his head and ran his fingers through his long hair. He looked over his shoulder, his face shadowed by lamp and firelight. "The other translator got himself burned to death at a Mohawk stake, so I'm to sail with a group of his Majesty's finest to New York. It seems that the King is in need of someone who speaks Iroquois."

"But you speak Cherokee." My voice hitched. I knew I sounded near hysteria.

"Cherokee and Iroquois are fair similar. As it happens, I speak both."

"But they can't know that. You have to tell them that the two are completely unalike, that you cannot translate for them—they must find someone else."

"I can't, Mac."

He sighed, and I rushed to his side of the bed, crouching before him, laying my hands over his where they rested on his knees. *We can't leave,* I thought frantically. *We must not leave our home—I'm not ready.* "Why not? I don't understand—surely they can find another translator."

He raised his head, and the corner of his mouth crooked up in a bittersweet smile, his green eyes full of resignation and regret.

"It's too late," he said. "I've done it before."

Chapter 35

The MacFadden Settlement
Christmas Eve 1769

Every Christmas Eve when I'd lived with Grandfather, I'd stood outside, alone, on the veranda of his house in Charlestown. No matter how cold that December night, I stood looking at the sky, listening to the wind, to the call of the lamplighter as he moved down Tradd Street, announcing the hour. There was something unearthly, preternatural, about that witching time. The minutes moved in infinitesimal increments until the hands of all clocks struck midnight. And something in the air changed. The sky became blacker, the stars more luminous, the wind a living thing, thrown like a magic cloak over the city.

One Christmas Eve, when I was sixteen years old, a pirate managed to escape the swinging oaks in White Point Park and made his way through the sewers, hoping to exit the peninsula without anyone noticing. He'd been caught near our house, and the soldiers had dragged him down our street, his boots scraping the cobblestones. I had witnessed it all from the second story piazza. The man had fingernails longer than mine, a yellow caste to his eyes, and several piercings in the stretched lobe of his left ear that glinted in the light of the torch one of the soldiers held aloft. He had been neither old nor young, but his fate had been sealed. He went back to the noose, and swung that night.

"Poor sod," Grandfather said, walking up behind me. We watched the soldiers drag the pirate down the street until oak boughs blocked our view. "To be hung on Christmas Eve." He shook his head, and I looked up at him.

"He's got a knife tucked in his boot," I said quietly. "He's going to stab a lieutenant in the neck."

Grandfather's eyes widened, and he took my shoulders in his hands, squeezing tightly. "You're certain?"

"Yes," I whispered. He turned me toward the glass doors marking the entrance to my dressing rooms and gave me a nudge.

"Get ye inside," he said sharply. "I'll try and catch them."

He hurried across the veranda to another door, his boots sounding on the wood. I went back to the railing, disobeying him, and crouched low, watching through the slats for breathless minutes until he burst from the stable, his horse's hooves clattering on the cobblestones.

Tonight, I stood at the crest of the highest pasture watching the stars. The moon was brilliant: I could see the shadowy hollows where one ridge broke from another in the mountains. My way to this spot had been so clear I'd not even brought a torch. I rubbed my hands together, blowing warm air into cupped palms. I crossed my arms over my chest, tucking my hands into the heated area between breast and upper arm.

Something large and dark walked from the trees and into the pasture, red eyes blinking. I moved a hand slowly to the pocket of my skirts, fingering the pistol there, fearful it was a panther. But then the creature moved into brighter moonlight, and I saw then it was a wolf, its belly heavy with pregnancy. It raised its head, sniffing the air. There was more movement in the shadows and another stepped out. In all my time in the Keowee Valley I had heard several wolves call to one another on the ridges, but I'd never actually seen more than one at a time. The male turned his head in my direction, then the female, and the three of us stood completely still, studying each other for what seemed like hours. *I take this for granted,* I thought suddenly, *this everyday connection between the wild and the human, this feeling that we're not at all so different. Will it be lost with leaving?*

The cold began to sting my eyes, and I blinked, and at the separation the wolves moved in perfect concord, trotting off towards the other side of the forest, disappearing into the trees. I let out a long, frosty breath and shifted my feet, reluctant to go. I took one last look at the sky, and then made my way back to the cabin.

Tugging the sleeve of Grandfather's old greatcoat over my wrist, I leaned forward, rubbing a circle on the window before me with the heel of my hand. The glass was frosted over, and the circle revealed an outside world of hushed wilderness: still mountains and glassy, ice-coated trees. It felt as though if I could reach a finger into it all, touch it like the canvas of a painting, the whole thing would crack.

I sat back into the chair, an elbow on the desk. The ink in the inkpot had dried. I forced the quill into it, swirling it like a batter until it liquefied again. Signor Di Pietro's letter sat before me, propped up against the bottom of the windowsill. My eyes flew over the lines as they had done hundreds of times before. That the Grand Duchess of Tuscany would want one of Fire Eater's foals was something I had difficulty accepting. However, if there was one thing I'd learned from my short time in Italy, it was that the Florentines were an eclectic, curious lot—surely their monarch would be no different.

What I knew of the Grand Duchy came from Grandfather during our Grand Tour, and a history lesson he'd given after a walk along the Ponte Vecchio had been interrupted by the Duke's royal carriage. Two riders had galloped across the bridge, their mounts emblazoned with the royal crest, shouting for the way to be cleared. The shopkeepers had packed their goods hastily, eyes flittering about for signs of jewel thieves. Grandfather had reached his stout arms around Owen's and my shoulders, pulling us back from the fray. When the carriage sped past, surrounded by Florentine guards, someone—the gender unrevealed—had reached a white, bejeweled hand from the draped window, waving lazily. Around us, the crowd cheered.

"Who was that?" I asked, straining against Grandfather's grip. I tugged at the collar of my dress, feeling foolish and gangly, my twelve year-old body already beginning to blossom uncomfortably into womanhood.

He released Owen but kept a hand on my shoulder, light. "That's one of the Grand Duchy of Tuscany, lass. They're rulers here. I couldn't make out if it was a man or woman, though—could you, Owen?"

"Had to be a woman," Owen said, blue eyes dancing beneath a mop of shocking red hair. He wore it pulled back into a tail at the nape of his neck, rebelliously unpowdered. At seventeen, he'd finally reached the same height as Grandfather, and had stopped being awkward with it. He cut a striking picture: he wore finely cut gentlemen's pantaloons and jacket, black hose and shiny, buckled shoes. The size of him—standing at least a half foot above the Italian men—and the fact that he refused to wear a wig, had people staring at him freely, the women from behind dark eyelashes and elaborate fans.

"Not necessarily, lad," Grandfather answered, directing us across the Arno, toward the Uffizi Museum, just opened for the public only recently. "The royals tend to bejewel themselves, man or no. It very well could've been Leopold II—the Grand Duke—or his wife, Maria Louisa."

He reached up, adjusted his gray wig. His silver-blue eyes narrowed as he watched the crowd ahead; he tugged me back from being squashed by a passing cart. "Mayhap it was the Grand Duchess Maria Therese, Leopold's mother."

"But what of the Medicis?" I asked, disappointed. I'd spent the weeks before the trip pouring over books in Grandfather's library, entranced with the Medici's lengthy and fascinating rule of Florence. I was astounded that the family who had commissioned the artists Michelangelo, Raphael and Bernini no longer reigned.

"The last of their line died not long ago, and the crown—or the Tuscan version of it— went to Leopold. It's a long, complicated process, lass, mired in bloodlines and scandal," he said. "Even moreso than the English monarchy. But the Grand Duchess, now—the current Duke's mother—is purported to be a woman of fine intellect, and a lover of the arts. She wields much power here, I'd say."

"A Duke overpowered by a woman," Owen scoffed, tucking his hands in the pockets of his jacket and raising a rust-colored eyebrow. "Why does he allow his own mother to rule over him?"

Grandfather reached out, popped him lightly on the back of the head. "We're all ruled by women, boy—you're just too much the bantam rooster to recognize it."

Owen rubbed the back of his head, scowling at me when I giggled.

I smiled, but it was bittersweet memory, one that made me blink back emotion. Missing both of them was sometimes a physical feeling, a pain in the chest near my heart. I settled a piece of blank parchment on the desk in front of me and dipped the quill, thinking.

The twenty-fifth of December, 1769

MacFadden Settlement, South Carolina

Dear Signor Di Pietro,

I wish a Happy Christmas to you and your family, though it will be well into the New Year when you receive this letter. I apologize for the tardiness of my response to your last Post. It has been my own reticence and not the lengthiness of travel between letters that is to blame. I am happy that you found the Keowee Valley to be worth a trip into the dangerous Frontier. I am glad to say that we are all well, but ready to welcome Spring. It has been a cold Winter, and we have many months of it remaining.

As you must know by now, the Colonies are facing much turmoil, though mostly in New England. You may have seen Protesting in Charlestown, and in your time with my Grandfather. As we are so Removed on the Frontier, we do not feel the upheaval as do the Cities. In fact, the threat of it seems far away, as if it cannot touch us—though I know this to be a dangerous way of thinking.

Pausing, I wondered if I should reveal personal fears to a man I barely knew. Yet there was something immensely relieving in the writing down of such thoughts, and so I picked up the quill again, picturing the Italian's friendly countenance in my mind.

*As for the Cherokees, they are in constant danger of
facing Removal by settlers, and may in fact decide to seek
British favor, should the skirmishes begin in the South. This
I fear intensely, because of my own Political leanings, and
my Husband's love of his family. I worry that when the time
comes, such an Issue will divide us. I do not know why I feel
Free to write of such things to You, but your Openness
during your Time in Keowee Valley, and your Friendship
with my Grandfather seem to allow me to do so. Also, you
are thousands of Miles across the Ocean, certainly
untouched by the fetters of English law.*

*Soon, my Husband and I must travel to Charlestown,
as he has been ordered by His Majesty's army to report for
service as an Indian translator. We are to arrive on the
coast by the first of February. From there, we are to sail to
New York, a journey that I cannot help but dread.*

*Please know that I appreciate the interest of the Grand
Duchess in my horse. However, I am sad to Report that
because of this sudden and perilous change in our
circumstances, I do not feel that I can risk the
Complications of breeding him. Should future Events alter,
I will be happy to once again discuss this Topic. It is my
hope that we may Continue to correspond in spite of these
recent occurrences. I am curious about Florentine life, and
have many questions to ask of you.*

*Please give my warmest regards to the Grand Duchess,
and thank her for considering an offspring of Fire Eater to
be worthy of the Royal Stables. I look forward to our
Continuing post.*

Sincerely,

Quincy M. Wolf

Presently of Keowee Valley

A warm hand snaked up my thigh beneath the heavy quilt. I smiled
sleepily, turning my head on the pillow and lifting heavy eyelids. The air
inside the cabin was cold, and all instinct warned me to stay under cover, to
burrow and hibernate like a bear. I blinked slowly, focusing on the gold
flecks in Jack's green eyes. The hand continued its upward journey, and I
shifted, stretching languidly. "Good morning," I murmured, sliding an arm

across his lower stomach, spreading my fingers against the down of tawny hair there. "How did you sleep?"

The green gaze disappeared, and he moved on top of me beneath the quilt, pressing a trail with his lips across my collarbone. He took the straps of my shift in hand, tugging upward. I lifted my hips and then shoulders obligingly, and the garment slipped over my head.

"Jack?" His response was mumbled against my stomach, and I laughed when he blew air into my navel. "I can't understand a word you're saying," I murmured, reaching my arms over my head and stretching again until my fingertips touched cold glass. He drew his teeth gently across the protrusion of my right hipbone, and all the muscles below my waist tensed in pleasure.

When he buried his face between my legs I arched up, the shock a heated thing that had me moaning softly. I ran my hands through his long hair, cupping the back of his skull. For several minutes all thought vanished from my mind, and I gripped the windowsill between the tips of my fingers and thumbs, incognizant of time and place.

He raised his head and settled forward on his elbows, bending to kiss my navel. "Good morning, Mac. And how did you fare the night?"

I reached down and gripped his shoulders, tugging him up to me. He followed agreeably, sinking into me in one smooth, long thrust. "I asked you first," I said, catching my breath as he went deeper.

"Slept like a babe," he whispered, his muscular buttocks clenching as he moved in slow rhythm. Sweat beaded across my forehead, and I moved my hands to grip his shoulders. We both panted at the end, and when he tensed above me I closed my eyes, running my palms down his broad back. He sank into me, his mouth at my throat. When he licked at the sweat there I sighed, satisfied and cat-like.

"Jack! Quinn!" Someone shouted, pounding on the door. "There's Indians crossing Tomassee Creek!" It was Zeke, his voice cracking like a boy's.

Jack leapt from the bed, and his sudden exit from me was a quick, hollowing shock. He took his tomahawk from the trunk at the foot, yanking on the deerskin leggings he'd left there the night before. I swung my feet over the side of the mattress, my thighs slick as I rushed to the chest, reaching in and tugging a dress over my head, shunning need of a shift.

"Jack!" Zeke called again, knocking so hard against the oak door that the cabin shook.

Jack had thrown a shirt haphazardly over his head. In one breathless move he wrapped a bearskin around his shoulders and took his musket from the wall. He stepped quickly into his moccasins, snatching his knife from my desk and tossing it onto the bed. "Take that. Stay in the cabin 'til I return."

He was out the door before I'd laced my own boots. When he pulled it open there was a flash of cold air and gray sky, and Zeke's white face, then it closed again. I stood, shoved my arms into the wool coat and took the planter's hat from its hook on the wall, hefting open the door.

"Quinn, what's happening?" Rebekah grabbed my hands, her brown eyes wide and frightened, freckles standing out across her white cheeks. Eliza and Meg stood on my porch. Abigail puffed across the field and up the step, a musket in her arms. Sam and Micah followed at her heels. She looked up at me, her lips a line.

"We're to stay here until there's word," she said shortly, setting the musket against the railing. She glanced at Meg. "Young miss, you and the boys should be inside where it's warm."

"It's not—I've not started a fire," I murmured, my eyes on the crest of the hill. There was no one else to be seen. The men must already be gathered at the creek, I thought.

"Quinn!" Rebekah cried, squeezing my hands. "Is it a raid?"

"The men have gone to the creek," Eliza whispered, her hands on Meg's shoulders.

"They're all armed. What will we do? What if they get past?"

"I don't want to be scalped," Sam cried, wrapping his arms around his mother's knees.

"The chief looks an awful lot like Ridge Runner," Meg said suddenly, looking up at me in question. I broke from Rebekah's grip, reaching down and taking the girl's hands in mine.

"How much?" I asked quickly. "How much does he look like Ridge Runner?"

"Quinn, what does it matter? They all look alike," Abigail said sharply. She drew Sam back from her and met Micah's eyes. "Take your brother inside," she ordered.

"Meg, you too," I said, and Abigail ushered them into the cabin. When she shut the door behind her I looked around at the women on my porch. "It could be Jack's and Ridge Runner's father—he may have come from Chota."

"We can't know for certain," Abigail said. "For now we must do as told and stay here where it's safe."

"We're not safe," Eliza moaned, covering her face with her hands. "They'll kill us all."

"Hush, child." Abigail took the girl's skinny shoulders in hand, opened the cabin door and pushed her inside. "Help with the children—they need you now." She turned to me, and the hair spiraling out from her calico bonnet was streaked with white, making her seem suddenly older. "I hope to God you're right," she said.

At that moment a *whoop* came from the southern edge of the woods, and from behind the barn walked a group of men. There were several Indians that I did not recognize. I counted seven in total, and the men from the settlement hung around the edges of the band, seemingly nervous. I looked for Jack, finding him in the middle of the pack. He walked beside his father, who looked as fierce as I'd ever seen him. A trio of black and white feathers capped his dark swathe of hair, and he wore a brown bearskin around his shoulders, fastened with a leather loop at his chest. A musket was strapped to his back; from a beaded belt at his waist hung a small bag, and at the other hip a tomahawk. His face was expressionless, the sharp lines of his cheekbones, nose and jaw mirroring Jack's. Ridge Runner hung back at the edge of the group, talking with another of the strangers.

I turned to Abigail, exhaling with relief. "It's him—it's Walks-With-Hawks. It's all right." I walked to the edge of the porch and waited, nerves flittering about in my stomach. I wondered how Jack's father would greet me. Our time together in Chota had been brief, and I still had no knowledge of how he felt about a white woman joining with his youngest son. From Nora Wolf I'd received nothing but affection, but Walks-With-Hawks was a different story. Though he'd certainly welcomed me into his family, he'd remained a mystery to me, keeping conversations between us succinct.

The group stopped in the dirt before the cabin. It was then that I noticed that one of the Indian men had a deer draped over his shoulders. He bent, setting it on the ground. When he rose I recognized him at once. "Squirrel!" I said aloud, smiling instantly. He had grown so, gotten taller and more muscular, his body filled out to its man-shape. He smiled back at me and inclined his head.

"Rides-Like-a-Man." Walks-With-Hawks stepped forward, and he reached out. Surprised, I put my hand in his. His dark eyes met mine and something flashed in their depths. He reached out his other hand, placing it over the top of our joined ones and leaning in. "I have dreamed of you," he said, his voice low, the English rough. "We must speak of this."

Suddenly Jack was at there at his side. "We can talk inside the cabin." He turned, finding Zeke and Hosa, who stood together at the edge of the porch. Zeke held Eliza's hand over the rail: she'd rushed out when the men had approached. Three of the Indians from Chota stood together near Hosa, watching him and talking amongst themselves, and I wondered if they'd ever before seen a black man.

"Zeke, Hosa," Jack said, stopping all conversation. "Could you help these men to the barn, give them a place to tie their horses?" When they nodded he sought Lord Harris, who had found a spot near the other side of the porch, and was talking in fervent whispers with Samuel. They both looked up at him. "My wife and I need some time, alone, with my father. If it's not too much to ask, I'd prefer that everyone go back to their work. When we meet for supper I'll do my best to explain what's about. We'll have proper introductions then."

We waited until the others left. "You will leave this place," Walks-With-Hawks said to the both of us. "I have dreamed of it." He turned to me then, his eyes softening. "What have you seen, *agwe'tsi age'hya?*"

"He calls you his daughter," Jack said.

As Walks-With-Hawks waited for my answer—this formidable, honorable man, so unknown to me still—I wanted desperately to be able to say that I'd pictured it in my dreams, that his son would return to the Valley, and perhaps even to him, after he'd served at the whim of the English king. But I could not lie.

"Nothing," I said, helpless. "I have seen nothing."

Chapter 36

The Keowee Valley

Frozen leaves crackled beneath my moccasins, and I shifted the skin of water at my hip, adjusting the leather strap that held it there, crossing my chest at a diagonal. I wore deerskin leggings, a heavy, cotton shirt and a wool coat, a farmer's hat pulled low at my eyebrows and over the tips of my red ears for warmth. I'd tied my hair in one long braid, and it swung back and forth across my shoulders as I followed Walks-With-Hawks through the forest, hiking up and over trees felled from heavy ice, crossing rivulets of creeks and scrambling up and down steep ridges, making our way towards Tomassee Knob.

My good-father had spoken only once to me since we'd left the cabin that morning in the dark, the stars still bright in the sky, no sign yet of dawn. But now pale light skimmed low over the treetops, glinting on icicles that hung from wet boulders and branches. Earlier, when we crossed through overgrown fields and approached the burned-out village at the foot of the mountain he'd stopped, bending and taking something from the bag at his waist. As the first beams of sun made long ghost-shadows out of rotting fence posts and ruined huts he scratched at the ground, mixing a clump of dirt with whatever he held in his other hand. He blew the commingled earth in the four directions, said something in Cherokee I could not translate. His face looked suddenly old as his eyes skimmed the dead village, but he nodded to it—such a subtle gesture I almost believed I'd not really seen it—and looked over his shoulder without meeting my eyes.

"We go," he said quietly, walking away.

Before we entered into the forest again I looked up at the Knob looming there in front of us, cone-shaped and lonely, covered in bare trees. I had never been to the top. My only experience on the solitary mountain had been that near-capture by a band of Creek hunters, the year before.

We scrambled up steep ridges, and I clung to roots and young trees, my lungs burning as Walks-With-Hawks climbed easily, agile as a mountain lion. We followed a skinny trail along the side of the Knob and up along the ridgeline. I kept to the inside of the footpath, brushing against undergrowth and avoiding looking at the overhang to my right. If I slipped, I'd fall hundreds of yards, surely bashing against trees and rocks on the way down.

After moving steadily along the trail we came to a granite outcropping, and the view from it stretched out into the distant horizon. Jack had once told me that from the top of Tomassee Knob one could see into the colonies of Georgia and North Carolina, and even the far, western reaches of Cherokee country. The sun hung low in the gray winter sky, and I narrowed my eyes to slits as I made out the curling Keowee River to the south and the settlement to the west, pastureland cut like a yellow square from the dark forest.

Smoke from some of the settlers' chimneys puffed steadily up into the air, making curling, white tails that emptied out into silver sky. And farther, to the northwest, the Blue Ridge swelled—a wave of deepest blue—and from it we could see huge mountains, isolated balds of sheer rock that interrupted the horizon, sun reflecting off trails of water that striped the granite. At that moment, the view before us was the whole world.

Walks-With-Hawks unhooked a skin of water from his belt, setting it on the rock at his feet. He walked to the undergrowth and pulled out several twigs and branches. As I stood silent, watching, he made a small fire. When he sat beside it, facing the overlook, I did the same.

"The first time I came to this place, I was a boy," he said. "The village below was filled with families. The women worked the land and men hunted. It was a good place. The Beloved Man there, he brought me here one night, and I saw *atsil'-tluntu'tsi*."

When I shook my head, not understanding, he cleared his throat. "I do not know the English word for this. We call it 'fire panther'—a star that falls to earth with a tail behind it."

"Oh, a comet? Or meteorite, perhaps?"

"It passed over our heads, and it looked to fall in the trees below. I wanted to search for it, but the Beloved Man told me to leave it, that it was a sign. You know of signs, Rides-Like-a-Man?" He took a drink from the skin beside him, setting it in his lap.

"Yes," I answered. When he didn't speak again I swallowed. "Why did you bring me here?"

"I dreamt of my white daughter on a ship in the middle of the ocean. *Waya* was at your side. You were far from the land of the *Ani'yun'wiya*." He turned to me then, looking down his long nose, his back as straight as if he sat in an English chair. "What will become of my youngest son?"

"You must have dreamed of us on a ship bound for New York," I murmured. "Jack has been ordered by the British army to serve as a translator there, to help them make treaty with the Iroquois. We leave for Charlestown soon." I looked up at him, raising my chin. "How did you know that I have the Sight?"

"My oldest son told me this, when you came to be married at Chota town. I had not before met a *un'ega* woman who could dream. I worried that you were dangerous, that you would bring darkness to my son and my family. But I was wrong."

The sun warmed our backs as it poured in through bare branches, and I pulled my knees into my chest, resting my chin there. Below us, a group of hawks spiraled down beneath the granite outcropping, disappearing into the trees. When Walks-With-Hawks spoke again his deep voice pierced the quiet, sending out a soft echo. "The French who trade from the south warn us against making treaty with the English, but I do not trust them. I do not trust the English, but their king has agreed to keep his children from hunting and living on our lands. Yet he seems powerless to do this." He rested his hands on his thighs, tapping his fingers lightly. "I asked you to come to this place so that you could tell me what you have seen."

"I have seen war," I said honestly, "but I have not seen the Cherokee warring. I see the red coats of the British, and when I do they are fighting other white men—the men who seek liberty from their king, like my grandfather." I reached up and took the hat from my head, running a hand through my hair, impatient. "But this does not mean that the Cherokee will not fight—it may just be I have not seen everything. I don't know what to tell you, sir. All I am certain of is something is coming, something that will change everything." I shook my head, frustrated. "I just don't know what."

"You must not go to New York," he said suddenly, and I turned my head sharply, studying him.

"But how can we not? Jack has been ordered by the Crown."

He picked up the skin again, taking a long gulp of water, his Adam's apple bobbing in his brown neck, moving a scar at his throat I'd not noticed before. He took the skin from his lips, spilling some of the water purposely on the rock.

"You will think of something," he said.

The sun was close to setting, and the upper curve of it was all that showed—astonishingly orange—just above the rolling line of the mountains. As clouds hovered in the air over the ridgeline their underbellies were cast in pink light, the sky around a cool indigo. I marveled at the change in the scene before me. Though I'd witnessed hundreds of sunsets from where I now stood, the ones in winter seemed sharper, more realized, coldly brilliant. Behind me and high above my head the moon was almost full, and it hung there suspended, waiting its turn to shine.

I released a long sigh, the air crystallizing in front of my face in a tiny cloud. I rolled my shoulders beneath the bearskin blanket, shifted Fire Eater's reins in my gloved hands. He tossed his head, wanting to run. "Not tonight," I murmured. "Tonight we watch."

Tomorrow morning we were leaving, headed back down the Cherokee Path—a road I'd not taken in over a year and a half. "It hasn't been long enough," I whispered, and Fire Eater's ears twitched at the sound.

And it hadn't. I had a home here, one I had once thought none could take from me. It was a place of my own making, and the thought of leaving it was an emptiness in my gut that climbed its way into my chest, clawing at my throat. I blinked back against the bracing air. The sun had sunk behind the mountains, taking most of the light with it. I watched, silent, until the clouds lost their color and moonlight traced my shadow on the grass before me, the odd outline of a woman on a horse, looking more like some kind of mythological beast, only half human.

The wagons were already loaded, piled with pelts to sell in Ninety-Six and filled with the necessities of a three weeks' journey down the middle of the colony, literally from mountains to sea. I'd taken my trunk—had stuffed it today with clothing, blankets, random objects—as if the quicker I did so, the sooner I'd squelch the pain. But I left several books for Meg and had hope that she'd teach Micah and little Sam to read while we were away. Though I appeased myself with the notion that we'd certainly return to the Valley, the truth was that once commandeered by the King, we could be years away from ever coming home. And with war looming, there was always the possibility that anything could happen, could go wrong, and that we'd be torn forever from these mountains. I'd had dreams of it the night before, corybantic and strange, and in them war had nipped at our heels, bleeding from its fangs like a feral dog.

But tomorrow the day would be clear, as tonight's sky attested, and we'd exit the settlement and Keowee Valley with our friends looking on. I dreaded that leave-taking, dreaded saying goodbye to the rag-tag group that had become my family. Though I had no doubt that they'd keep the Valley well, I worried without us here, time and the precariousness of everyday life on the frontier could drive them away.

"I ken that you need time alone, Mac, but you've been rooted to this spot for hours. Come to bed."

I whipped my head around, startled despite the low tone of Jack's voice. He stood in the darkness at my side, a hand resting lightly on Fire

Eater's right flank. "I spoke with Harris about maintaining trade with the Middle and Overhill towns," he continued. "He seems the best to do so, as he doesn't have as many qualms about dealing with the Cherokee as some of the others. My father will do much to make certain the Valley's unharmed."

I nodded in the dark, but couldn't staunch the words that had lain unspoken between us since the arrival of His Majesty's summons. "We're never coming back, are we?"

Jack moved his hand from the horse, stepping up and taking mine where it lay on my thigh, my pointer and middle fingers tapping. He stilled them, his palm warm and heavy. Before he answered I saw his words in my mind, written like silver letters across the black of my thoughts. *We will return—we must. I won't forsake my family for the whim of a un'ega king. I won't make a life away from these mountains.*

But when he spoke his voice was flat, edged with reluctant honesty. "I don't know."

Micah stood on the bank of Tomassee Creek, his scuffed boots sinking into the sand, and hurled a rock towards the water. It skipped across, sinking near the point of the weir. His burnished red hair stuck out from his head in spikes. He'd shorn it the other day with a kitchen knife before Abigail could catch him. I came upon him quietly, tucking my hands into the pockets of my trousers, and watched as he snatched up another rock, his young face set in anger, and flung it recklessly. It pinged into a tree on the other bank, dropping into a thicket of molted, yellow ferns.

"Hello, Micah," I said quietly. He spun around, guilt flashing across his red-cheeked face. It disappeared just as quickly, and he turned away, crossing his arms over his chest in a stubborn stance that seemed so like a man's. "I have a favor to ask of you."

He hunched knobby shoulders, refusing to acknowledge me, and dug his rough heels deeper into the flecked sand.

"I know you're angry with me for leaving, but you must know that I'd never go unless it was necessary," I tried again, moving closer. I leaned over his shoulder, smiling, and lay a hand there. "Come now, talk to me. I won't ask you the favor if you don't. And it's a special one—it involves a magic stone that came all the way across the sea, from Scotland."

"I don't care." He jerked away, moving a few feet closer to the water. The sunlight filtering down through the bare branches dappled us both; at his movement a startled snake slid into the creek with a rustle of leaves. I crossed my arms over my chest and rolled my eyes, not caring that I mimicked the boy.

"Yes, you do," I said dryly. "You do care, just as I care about you and do not want to leave. But the truth of it is that I've no choice in the matter. And I thought you'd like to watch over the stone for me, especially seeing as how it's been charmed by a wizard. But I suppose we're not true friends, as I'd always assumed."

I turned on my heel and started into the lower pasture, and managed to keep the smile from showing on my face when I heard him running across the frozen ground behind me.

"Wait! I'm sorry, Quinn." He wrapped skinny arms around my waist from the back, and I patted them gently, turning and bending to his eye level. I brushed at the cowlick at his crown, then reached into my pocket.

"I know you are," I said. "Here is the stone." I reached out and took his little hand, turned it palm up and dropped the druid's rock into it.

He looked down at it, then back up at me. "Why's it so special?"

"It comes from the top of a magical hill in Scotland. The hill is called Arthur's Seat. Do you remember what I told you about King Arthur?"

"He had a round table and a sword that he pulled out of a big rock. He had the best knights."

"Exactly. Well, Arthur's Seat is the place where it is believed that he met with those very same knights, where his round table stood. I found this stone there when I was only a little older than you, and I've had it ever since. It's always helped me be brave when I've been afraid." I straightened, tucking a strand of hair behind my ear. "Now it's yours. I want you to take good care of it until I return."

He sniffed, turning the stone over in his palm. "I can do that."

"Good. Well, shall you escort me to my wagon, Master Simons? It's time for me to take my leave." I reached out a hand, and because he was still a young boy he took it, slipping the druid's rock into his pocket. We walked together through the field. Below us stood one wagon and every single soul in the settlement, waiting at the entrance to the Keowee Path. Jack looked up, and his eyes met mine.

I know, he seemed to say with the look.

"What about the wizard?" Micah said suddenly, tugging on my hand. I choked back emotion, grateful for a reason to laugh.

"Of course, the wizard. Remember Merlin? He put a spell on Arthur's Seat, and so anything that comes from it has special power. So use it wisely."

"Can it make you stay?"

I wiped quickly at my eyes, grinning at him, at the bittersweet tenor of the question. "No, my friend. I'm afraid it cannot. Even Merlin can't make people stay."

He nodded, solemn. But then he caught sight of Sam and let go of my hand, sprinting towards the crowd. "Sam, look what I got!" he shouted, digging for the stone in his pocket and waving it above his head. "It's a wizard rock!"

I stopped briefly and pressed a hand hard against my chest, shut my eyes for a heartbeat. Though they stung, I opened them against the sun.

When I reached Jack he pulled me to him gently, pressed a soft kiss against my hair. "It's time," he murmured.

No one spoke as we mounted our horses. Rebekah already sat at the helm of our wagon, knuckles white as she clutched Plato's reins. It had not taken much for her to agree to come with us and to live with Grandfather while we were in New York. When we'd spoken of it she'd been relieved, eager to leave the frontier behind. Lord Harris stood beside her, his tricorn in hand, speaking quietly to her. Ridge Runner waited at the top of the pine embankment, seated silently atop his horse. I took a breath, letting it out on a long sigh. Though we'd made our adieus earlier, I still couldn't fathom that I had to say goodbye.

Abigail and Samuel stood together, the boys before them, still talking excitedly over the druid's rock. Hosa walked over from inspecting the wagon. He'd done so at least four different times, and I knew it was his way of showing concern for our safety. His brown eyes met mine, and he nodded slowly. I smiled through a sheen of tears.

"You be safe, Miz Quinn," Zeke said roughly, an arm holding Eliza stiffly at his side. "Don't you worry none about us, we'll keep the land well 'til you return." Eliza turned her head into his shoulder, hiding her face, and I moved my gaze to Mr. Wheeler, standing alone.

He smiled regretfully and shook his head. "She refuses to leave the cabin," he said.

Abigail cleared her throat, and everyone turned towards the sound. "I packed a dozen corncakes in the wagon with Rebekah," she said. "And I'll be happy to keep up your home while you're away."

"Thank you, Madam Simons," Jack said, and he wheeled Murdoch around, his voice kind. "Thank you all. Be well and safe until we see you again."

Before I could speak the priest stepped forward, clasping his hands together at his belly. "If I may, a word of prayer for the safety of your journey." Heads bowed in unison. Jack glanced over at me and winked. I smiled at him, and some of the sadness abated.

Mr. Wheeler lifted his arms out from his sides, his long fingers open to the sky. Even as he spoke, my eyes followed the sloping Valley, past the settlers' cabins, the fire pit, and the barn, gray from weathering. They lit on our cabin—Jack's and mine—and stilled, and the sun hit the glass in one of the windows, blinding me for an instant. I blinked, and when my vision cleared all I could see were mountains, blue and infinite.

Chapter 37

Charlestown
Late January, 1770

Jack and Ridge Runner stood in the imposing foyer of my grandfather's home, tall and stiff, mirroring each other with arms crossed over their chests as they studied the servants rushing about, carrying our things in from the wagon. One of the maids, a young Negro girl who looked to be about sixteen years old, backed past Ridge Runner with a stack of my books in her hands. The whites of her eyes went wide with fear. Ridge Runner gestured sharply, speaking so succinctly to Jack in Cherokee that I understood. "They think we are animals," he said.

A moment later the girl rammed into the curved post at the bottom of the stairs and books went flying, scattering across the gleaming wood floor. She gasped and crouched low, scrambling to retrieve them. I hurried over and laid a hand on her shoulder.

"Please, let me help," I said. At my touch she stilled, and I bent low. "It's all right, not to worry. Books are hardy things."

When I felt her tremble I pulled back my hand. Suddenly Naji was there, taking the girl's elbow and helping her to her feet. "I got this," he told her softly. "You go on now, help Dina with the beds."

She rushed off, and I looked up at him, confused. "I don't understand—I think she was frightened of me."

Naji bent and gathered the books in his arms. When he stood he tucked in his chin and breathed in sharply through his nose. As always, his clothing was finely pressed, and the swell of a white, ruffled collar brushed his dusky jawline. "You don't touch no slave, Miss Quinn. You get her into trouble if you do."

"But—" I protested, and he shook his head, the movement sharp enough to make me hush.

"This is Charlestown, not the frontier. Things are different." Then he bowed his head, his eyes to the floor. "If you don't mind me sayin' so."

"No, of course not," I murmured, and he walked past me to chastise two boys carrying in one of my trunks. They'd wedged it in the doorframe.

I had forgotten, I realized, my cheeks hot. While the frontier was certainly a lawless place in so many ways, there was still such freedom there—freedom unheard of in the Lowcountry. I'd become so easy with the luxury of an everyday adherence to my own will that I'd forgotten what it meant to have my most minute actions governed by social custom. Suddenly I was ashamed for having scared the poor girl, and sick in my stomach that such an innocent gesture could do so.

"Are you all right, Mac?" Jack asked, though he didn't approach me. He and his brother stood close together, a unit of almost primitive strength. They could've been statues, their eyes hooded, arms still folded tightly over broad chests. I glanced down at the floor, my gaze following their moccasined feet and deerskin leggings, up to the black pelts wrapped around their shoulders. On each side of them the silk-papered walls of the foyer were filled with European paintings—Scottish ancestors mounted on horseback, pastoral scenes of a tamed sort of land they knew nothing of. Above our heads gleamed a candle chandelier, lit as though it were midnight instead of early afternoon.

I let out a sigh, started to run a hand through my hair before I realized that it was plaited carefully, tied tightly with a silk ribbon. "Yes, I'm fine," I said. "But you two look utterly uncomfortable. If I didn't know you so well I'd worry that you'd try for escape."

"Without a wagon we could make Keowee Town in two weeks," Ridge Runner said dryly.

"Less, with good *sa'gwali'*," Jack returned. He nodded toward the open door. "Sure, and there's a lass who seems right at home."

Grandfather and Rebekah were headed inside. Rebekah had her arm tucked through the old man's, and she looked happy and bright, her cotton skirts flouncing—not at all pale and skittish, as she so often had on the journey. Grandfather set his cane against the mahogany coat rack by the door, grimacing when one of the boys dropped the end of my trunk with a loud *thunk* on the wide staircase. "Have a care, lads," he rumbled, waving a hand. "You'll put a hole through the floor soon enough."

Jack glanced at Ridge Runner, and the two men moved in unison, jogging up the curving stairs and taking the trunk from the boys. They hefted it onto their shoulders, the boys agog as they pressed themselves against the railing and wall, letting the men pass.

"It's the second door on the right, Wolf," Grandfather called after them.

I tugged at the collar of my dress, uncomfortable with the stiff fabric and thinking longingly of the softly-worn deerskin leggings and coat that were packed with my things. Even my feet felt foreign in the leather boots I wore; I walked awkwardly in now unfamiliar heels, my gait stiff. Just as soon as Grandfather gave us leave to settle in our rooms I was determined to immediately shed them and the whalebone corset that was digging into my waist.

"Quincy," Grandfather said, approaching with Rebekah still on his arm. "Why don't ye show your good-cousin about the place? I've a bit of business to tend to before supper." He patted Rebekah's hand and walked into the drawing room, instructing as he went. "I'd suggest ye all taking a stroll, but it's a raw wind coming off the harbor today—besides, your Indian friend would have all of society gawking like idiots."

"Come, coz," I said. "We'll freshen up, and then I'll show you Owen's old quarters. There are a few of his things there you might enjoy seeing."

As we started up the staircase, skirts in hand, I happened to glance into the drawing room. Grandfather's back was to the foyer, and his gray head bobbed as he spoke to a stranger standing by the fireplace. I paused, a hand on the oak banister, and the man glanced up, meeting my eyes.

He was young—perhaps in his early twenties—dressed in a long, fitted black vest, a frill of lace at his wrists and neck. On his feet were heeled, buckled shoes, his slender calves adorned in fashionable, white silk stockings. He dipped his head, acknowledging me, and lashes as long as a girl's brushed down over deeply set brown eyes. I nodded back but kept moving. Rebekah tugged on my sleeve. "Quinn, who is that man?" she whispered, taking a delicate look over her right shoulder. "He looks like a statesman."

My mind was running at its usual speed, and I racked it for answers. The stranger did not seem at all familiar; I did not think I'd ever met him before. Perhaps he was a new clerk in Grandfather's firm, I wondered, or even a member of the Charlestown Sons of Liberty? If so, I'd be desperately curious to listen in on the conversation.

"Quinn?" Rebekah tugged again, and I shook my head.

"No, sorry. I don't know him. He must be a colleague of Grandfather's."

"Perhaps he'll stay for dinner," she said, her eyes unnaturally bright. "It would be lovely to enjoy something of society for a change."

We reached the top of the steps and I nudged her with my elbow, smiling. "What, you've not had enough curtsying and gossip in the wilderness? I'll have you know that Keowee Valley never lacks for polite custom—I did serve you tea on my grandmother's silver tray, did I not?" Rebekah tossed brown curls, eyeing me with a look of affectionate sarcasm.

"Yes, and it was lovely. But I don't see anything 'polite' about wandering around in bearskin all winter. Besides, I've noticed you tugging at your dress. I know you'd rather be garbed as a savage."

I stopped in my tracks, slapping the heel of my right hand against my forehead. "I knew I forgot something," I said dramatically. "I wonder if I could send for a tomahawk?"

"Ha, ha."

Jack stood, his back to me, facing the window of my room and looking down onto Tradd Street. Outside, the light had mellowed into early evening, and leaves rustled in the huge oaks as horses' hooves and carriage wheels clattered on the cobblestones below. He rolled his shoulders and stretched out his arms as if attempting to make more room in the dinner jacket he wore. It was one of Grandfather's, made of burgundy velvet and fashioned with large lapels that turned back at each shoulder, the neck of his shirt and his wrists cuffed with fine lace. When he made a move to cross his arms I cleared my throat. "Oh, no," I said firmly, brush in hand. "You'll split the seam in the back. It's just for one night, do try and stay still."

He ran a hand through his hair, almost dislodging it from the matching ribbon I'd tied it in at the back. When I'd asked earlier if he'd like me to powder his hair he'd almost tripped on the rug, backing away as if I held a lighted cannonball.

"I look a buffoon," he growled.

I lay the silver brush on the gilt vanity I'd used as a young girl and rolled my eyes at my image in the mirror. "If it appeases you, remember that Ridge Runner is dressed the same as you by now, and surely feels just as ridiculous."

I turned my head, studying the line of his back as he watched the window. Grandfather's clothes clung to him—Jack was both broader in the shoulders and taller than the older man, the muscles in his legs more pronounced—but instead of looking like a young boy who'd grown too quickly for the tailor, the snug fit of the short breeches showcased the muscular curve of his buttocks and big thighs. I couldn't imagine how he looked from the front. His calves clenched beneath green hose as he rocked back on booted heels.

"At least the only ladies present at dinner will be related to you," I murmured wryly. "We wouldn't want anyone fainting in the gravy."

He looked over his shoulder and frowned, the tattoo dipping menacingly between his eyebrows. "What was that, lass?"

"Not a thing."

A soft knock sounded on the door, and I pulled the lapels of the silk robe I wore closer to my collarbone, covering my still-unbound corset. "Come in," I called.

A pretty, young Negro woman in a simple gown and hoopskirt entered timidly, her eyes on the floor. "I've come to dress you, Madam," she said, her Gullah accent low and honeyed. "My name be Dina."

"Many thanks, Dina," I said, smiling. "I haven't worn a stomacher in so long I think I've forgotten how it works. My name is Quinn." When her eyes shot to mine, filled with fearful surprise, I cleared my throat. "Er, Madam Wolf, that is."

Jack turned from the window and headed for the door, his heels sounding loudly on the wood floor. When he passed the four-poster bed—piled high with a froth of lavender pillows—he snatched the tomahawk lying there and flipped up one of his velvet coattails, tucking it into the waist of the breeches. Dina's eyes went impossibly wider as she watched. I worried momentarily that she'd keel over.

"I'll be out of your way then," he said shortly. He stopped by the maid. "Do you ken where Ridge Runner is, lassie? The big Indian with the tattoo like mine?"

"Downstairs," she whispered. He nodded at her and met my eyes over her head, his ire not yet faded. He was still perturbed with having to wear English clothes. I lifted my shoulders in apology, and he muttered something under his breath in Cherokee before shutting the door firmly behind him.

At his exit I stood and shed the robe, draping it over the stool I'd been sitting on. Dina hurried to my side, and I turned. She took the laces at my back in deft fingers and began tugging tightly. "Oomph," I said, hugging my stomach. "These things should be banned, no matter how tiny they make a waist seem."

"Too tight?" she asked.

"No, that will do. If you don't mind, the gown is on the bed."

She stepped back, her dark eyes considering. "We needs put on your skirts first, Madam. I'll fetch them."

I held out a hand, my rebellious nature getting the better of me. "Let's forget the hoopskirt and only concern ourselves with the gown."

She looked at me as if I'd suddenly sprouted another head. "Oh, no, Madam. You gots to wear the hoopskirt. It won't look proper without."

I walked stiffly to the bed, lifting the gown myself. Beneath the blue silk overlay were at least four other layers of taffeta and cotton skirts. I eyed the hoopskirt where it hung inside the open Chippendale armoire. The wooden hoop stuck out at least six feet. I shook my head. "No, I truly don't think it's necessary. Besides, no one will be able to tell it's missing."

"I'll be punished."

"No, you will not," I said solidly, tossing the huge dress over my head and shimmying down into it. She hurried to my side, bending and fluffing the skirts beneath. "I promise," I muttered against the smothering cloth. My head popped out, and I smiled reassuringly.

She cocked a black eyebrow at me, the first sign of anything other than subservience, and I wiggled around until my back was to her, looking over my shoulder. "All right, then," I said brightly. "Lace away."

In the light from the French chandelier the cherry dining table gleamed almost black. As children, Owen and I had made horrible faces in it when Grandfather wasn't looking. Servants scurried about with silver trays in hand, balancing decanters of brandy and crystal glasses. A svelte Negro man that I did not recognize set the main course on the table before us, roasted duck glazed in a cranberry sauce. My stomach gurgled, and I pressed a hand to it, feeling my cheeks go pink. The man beside me—the stranger from the sitting room—leaned in conspiratorially.

"I, for one, am famished," he whispered, his accent of the Lowcountry, rolling and smooth. Then he sat back, smiling at my Grandfather at the table's head. "I should apologize, Campbell—I kept you too long at business tonight. Your guests must be starving."

Grandfather set his brandy decanter on the table with a thump and emitted a hearty belch. "Pardon," he said quickly. "Nonsense, lad. We had important issues to discuss. The future of the colony depends on such action." He glanced around the table, his eyes coming to rest on Jack.

"Wolf, did ye know that young Crouch here is the editor of the *South Carolina Gazette and Country Journal*? The most scandalous newspaper in Charlestown, if ye ask me—and that's saying much, considering that the gossip-mongers are rarely sated." Grandfather smiled affectionately at the rather pretty young man, and I coughed delicately into my fist.

"Mr. Crouch, what is it that you print?" I asked, turning to him. He sat back in his chair, crossing a leg. Across the table Jack lifted an eyebrow at me, and Ridge Runner, who sat in the chair next to him, regarded us all with stoic imperiousness. Rebekah, who was seated to my left, leaned forward to offer her full attention and smiled demurely.

"News of the town, mostly. But we also carry articles concerning the nobility back in Europe," he said charmingly. "People seem fascinated with the aristocracy, be they royal or rake."

"As if that's all," Grandfather scoffed. "The *Journal* is the only paper in the Southern colonies brave enough to challenge Britain's ire, to counter how they've covered our shores in redcoat soldiers, forced us to live under martial law, as it is."

"You're no Tory, I'd wager," I said to the young man, and Crouch seemed momentarily shocked at my outspokenness before slipping back into a smile.

"No, Madam Wolf, I'm afraid I am not and never will be."

"The lad's a patriot, lass."

"Are you a fellow member of the Sons of Liberty?" I asked suddenly, and the room went quiet. I could feel Grandfather glaring at me, and didn't need to look at him to know that the color was rising in his cheeks.

"Quincy, ye overstep your place," he said gruffly.

I bowed my head. "My apologies," I said quietly.

"No need," Crouch said graciously, spearing a slice of duck with his fork. "I'm not ashamed of my association—far from it. We're doing good work, aren't we, Campbell? It's due time others sit up and take notice before more British taxes are heaped upon us all and we're forced to bow down to men like Drayton and Montagu."

"So you want war with England, do you?" Jack's words were soft but clear, and suddenly the focus of the entire table shifted to him.

Crouch blotted his lips with a linen napkin. "I do. We are better off out from under the yoke of kingly rule."

"Then who will rule? Will you name your own king?"

"No, absolutely not," Grandfather interrupted, placing both palms on either side of his dinner plate. "We need no monarchy—we'll have the people decide. All free men will decide."

"A glorious goal, certainly," Jack said, the lilt in his voice strong. He scratched his chin thoughtfully, his green eyes sparking. "I'm certainly for not having to come like a dog when the Crown calls, as I do now. But what will be decided about the Cherokee? I'll place a wager now, at this table, that if the time comes, those same free white men will quickly see to it that all red men be banished from the Blue Ridge."

Crouch glanced anxiously at Ridge Runner, who studied him silently, and it was the first time all evening that the young editor seemed without his usual confidence. He looked quickly to Grandfather, I assume not wanting to offend a guest in the man's home—no matter how unusual the guest. Surprisingly, it was Rebekah who spoke next.

"Not all feel for the Cherokee as you do, Jack," she said, keeping her gaze away from Ridge Runner. "They can be quite terrifying, with their pagan rituals and revenge killings. I'm sure that if they began to live properly, as Englishmen, they'd be allowed to keep their lands."

Ridge Runner spoke suddenly in Cherokee, forcing Rebekah to look at him. He lifted his glass calmly, tipping it over Jack's and dumping the brandy there. Rebekah looked around nervously. "I don't understand what he's saying," she said, her voice rising.

"I said, madam, that you didn't seem adverse to revenge killings mere fortnights ago."

Everyone stilled, and Jack said something beneath his breath in Cherokee to his brother. He regarded Rebekah with subtle disappointment, his eyes solemn.

"What are they talking about, Quinn?" Grandfather asked sharply.

Rebekah set her fork down daintily by her plate and pushed back in her chair. A butler hurried to her side but she was up already, her color high. "Please excuse me," she said. "I'm feeling poorly. I believe I'll retire." I reached out a hand to her as she passed, but she jerked back from it, her crinolines rustling as she rushed from the room.

I started to push back my own chair, to go after her, but Ridge Runner stood quickly, and he regarded my Grandfather with impassible dark eyes. He made quite a picture, tall and elegant in brown velvet, his Indian face such a shocking contrast to the gentleman's suit. The top of his black head shone in the candlelight above, shadowing the hollows beneath his cheekbones. "I will see to her," he said softly, before turning and exiting the room in silence.

Jack and I met eyes across the table. It took all my willpower not to drag him from the room, to demand to know if he was thinking what I was thinking: if there was something more between Ridge Runner and Rebekah than friendship? And if so, God help us all.

"Fascinating," Crouch breathed, his eyes on the door. "He speaks English."

"Aye, and I'll wager his French is better than yours, too," Jack said dryly. He leaned back in his chair, and I knew that if I were to look beneath the table I'd see the two front legs lifted off the floor. "I'm curious, Mr. Crouch—what will you do when war comes to your own door? When men are hunting you at will, setting fire to your printing press and anchoring their ships in your harbor? Have you seen death before, man?"

Crouch's cheeks went pink, but he sat up straight and seemed determined despite his apparent youth. "No, the only death I've seen is from sickness. I was too young for the war with the French. But make no mistake, Mr. Wolf, I am willing to go to war with England, if it means that this colony will be free of King and parliament."

"I believe you will," Jack said, considering him. "And I think your reasons honorable, certainly well-founded. I hope you're prepared for what will come."

"I have seen war." Grandfather tugged on his beard thoughtfully, his eyes only on Jack. "And I know the price, lad. But it's already begun—ye know that yourself, else ye wouldn't be here in the first place. Cornwallis has called ye to negotiate with the Iroquois certainly because he wants use of them as an army against the people. He fears the Frenchmen whispering betrayal in their ears."

The old man blinked, and suddenly he seemed as wily as a young man. "So, what will ye do, lad? Sail to New York and my only granddaughter with ye, and help King George subdue the wild savages? Or will ye join our cause, help make this colony free of British overlord?"

Jack shook his head, smiled without showing his teeth. "Oh, no, old man," he said ruefully. "You'd have me join you to force out the Cherokee so more can steal land from under them. I'm a freer man a Cherokee than I ever was an Irishman, and I don't need a group o' raving Whigs to tell me so."

"Is that so?"

"Aye, 'tis. I'll be keeping your granddaughter safe, so don't fear."

Grandfather planted both hands on the table and leaned forward, his beard coming perilously close to dipping into the leftover gravy on his plate. "And just how do ye plan to do that, man? Ye can promise no such thing. You're heading into dangerous territory—New York's no South Carolina frontier, where you're protected because you're a half-breed. There, they're building fires in the street. It's an unholy mess. I won't have ye taking Quinn into that. It's far too dangerous. She must stay here, with me."

I stood immediately, my face burning. "I certainly will not. Jack is my husband—I go where he goes."

Thomas Crouch leaned back in his seat, following the exchange as though watching the ball fly back and forth at a tennis match, his hands clasped before him. *We'll all be in the news tomorrow,* I thought. I looked across at Jack, willing him to meet my eyes. He set his linen napkin politely on the table and pushed back his chair, standing. He emanated such banked energy, and he was so much bigger than the other men that he seemed to take up all the space in the room. "Jack," I said. "You will not leave me here."

"I'm afraid I'll have to, lass," he said, and it felt as if I'd just taken a fist in the stomach, all the air sucked from my lungs.

"What is this?" I folded my arms across my chest, disbelieving.

"Good man," Grandfather said gruffly, but he watched me cautiously.

I moved in a fog to the entryway, wanting to be outside, to escape from this room and those words. I put a hand to the doorframe, to keep my balance, and saw that Ridge Runner was walking down the staircase, his feet silent on the wood. He looked up at me, a question in his eyes.

"Mac," Jack said loudly. I closed my eyes, bowing my head and shaking it in denial. When he came to me he curled a hand around the back of my neck, turning me to him gently. "You'll be safer with your grandsire."

"I can't believe you're saying this," I said roughly. "Why don't you want me in New York with you? We'll be surrounded by British soldiers—safety cannot be the reason."

He looked up then, noticing Ridge Runner on the stairs and speaking to both of us. "We're not for New York," he said quietly. "I can't do what they ask of me. Which means I'll most likely be sentenced to the prison here, or hung for treason. It's either that or make a run for the Overhill towns, hide out in the wilderness." He squeezed my neck lightly, rubbed his thumb against my hairline. "That's no kind of life for you."

"They'd follow you, *Wa'ya*," Ridge Runner said from the stairs. He watched us both.

Jack nodded. "Aye, they would. And I won't have British troops raiding those villages just to hunt me."

"We'll go some other place," I said, wiping my eyes roughly with the back of my hand. "Surely the two of you know of places in the wilderness that the soldiers could never find."

"Then you'll always be running," Grandfather said. He stood behind us, just inside the dining room. He looked over his shoulder, sliding his hands into the pockets of his vest. "Thomas, could ye give us a moment?"

"Certainly, I'll step outside." Crouch stood quickly, almost knocking over his chair. He hurried past us, glancing back only once before closing the front door behind him.

Cold air swept through the foyer. I rubbed my upper arms, watching as Grandfather rocked back on his heels. I recognized the look on his face. There was a wicked shine to his piercingly blue eyes, one that surely mirrored the plans whirling in his head. "It will be some time before the troubles reach our frontier," he said. "The Legislature is not yet willing to declare a break from England, and probably won't be for fortnights—mayhap even years. Politicians never can make up their bloody minds."

"I don't understand," I muttered, impatient. That blue gaze lit on me then, and I swallowed.

"You've seen war, aye—seen it in your mind?" he asked, and I nodded. "Did ye ever see it occurring in the mountains?"

"No," I shook my head slowly. "I saw a swamp, and a woman who spoke of a place called King's Mountain."

Grandfather nodded. "That's not even halfway up the colony, and it's near the border of North Carolina, in Catawba territory . . . nowhere near the Cherokees. Perhaps there will never be a battle in the Indian mountains."

"There will be battle," Ridge Runner said, and Grandfather glanced at him, nodded thoughtfully.

"Yes—some day. But that could be years from now. If war comes, it will happen first on the coast and in the cities."

"What are you getting at, MacFadden?" Jack asked, moving his hand from my neck and squeezing my shoulder before crossing his arms over his chest.

"Would ye fight in this war, lad, should it come?" Grandfather asked, ignoring the question.

"You just said yourself it may be years."

"Aye, but would ye, even years from now?"

Jack's look was grim. "I will fight to protect my land and my family. If that means choosing one evil over another, when the time comes, then aye. I'll do it."

A long shiver went through me at his words. I gripped my hands at my waist, my knuckles going white.

Grandfather seemed oddly delighted at Jack's response. He clapped his hands together, and the sound was startlingly loud. "Well, then—there's no sense in jumping on Geordie's boat to go help with a war that might be years in the making, and just as long 'til it affects your own."

"Grandfather," I said incredulously, unwilling to engage in any more wordplay with the man who'd first introduced me to the writings of Niccolo Machiavelli. "You sound a madman. If we listen to you it seems that we cannot escape into the wilderness, we cannot go to New York, and we certainly cannot stay here, or Jack will surely be hanged for defying the King. Just what do you suggest we do?"

He rocked back on his heels again and grinned like a young boy at my husband. "Well, Wolf. How do ye feel about Italy?"

Hours later, after Thomas Crouch had retreated to the safety of his own home and the dining table had been cleared of crystal and half-eaten food, I found my grandfather alone in his library. He was standing at the window when I entered, and I could see his face reflected in the black pane. It wavered, half-lit with flashes of light from the fire burning on the other side of the dark room. I set my candle down on his desk near the door. At the sound his chin lifted, and his eyes met mine in the glass. "Coming to steal a book, are ye?"

"No. I've come to see you, actually." I went to the fireplace and did as I always had as a young girl in the wintertime, stepping up onto the hearth and stretching my hands behind me for heat.

"Ye're bound to catch fire to your dress, girl," he said gruffly.

I rolled my eyes, unable to stay angry with him for long. "You always say that."

"Aye—and I'm right. Ye ruined a half dozen gowns as a child, made grimy black splotches all down the skirts. Wasted my hard-earned coin."

I smiled prettily, refusing to be goaded. "It was two gowns, not six. And Elsa was able to repair one of them so that I could at least ride in it." He crossed the room to his desk and began fiddling with papers there. I stepped off the hearth. When I did he snatched up something that looked like a map and yanked open the drawer there, stuffing it inside. He did not look at me, despite the teasing, so I let it go. "Grandfather?"

"Aye?"

"Why Italy?" He looked up and met my eyes, and I went to a stuffed chair in the corner of the room—one I used to read in while he worked—and perched on the edge. I clutched my hands in my lap, moving a thumb nervously over my knuckles. "Why not Scotland, where there's family? Or France, where we might be of some use?"

He sat back heavily into the chair behind his desk, rubbed his knees briskly. He chuckled. "Of use, eh? In France? Ye always were too quick, Quincy."

I lowered my voice, even though we were alone. "I only assumed that you—and the Sons of Liberty—would have allies there, rather than anywhere else. Should we not seek favor with France? They're England's oldest enemy. I'd think they'd be happy to fund a war against them."

"Ye speak treason, lass." He leaned forward, paused. "You'll no go to Scotland because Scotland's in a mess as it is, poor and wild, and overgrown with the King's men same as we are here. And France, well . . . ye may get there someday, but it won't be now. First ye must away to Italy, and the Tuscan court, where Di Pietro can watch o'er ye. You'll be safe there."

"For how long?" I was wringing my hands now, my voice hollow, overwhelmed and uncertain of the future more than I had been two years before, when I left Charlestown for the backcountry. "Jack will not stay long away from his people. He can't—I can't."

"Ye can," Grandfather said gruffly, his wild eyebrows meeting between his eyes as he frowned at me. "Ye have no choice. Do ye want to see your man hanged in White Park? And the Indian with him?" He shook his head when I started to speak. "No, I know ye don't. Ye must away to a place where ye won't be of much notice—or if ye are, it won't matter. Italy's a mess, aye. It's a mass of city-states, all feuding with one another. But Tuscany holds the power, and while the Court there's certainly a bed of intrigue and back-door dealings like any other, it's safe. The only English there—if there are any—are mostly poets and painters who care nothing for politics."

"How will we know when to return? You will write, won't you?"

He reached into the drawer of the desk, taking an envelope already sealed and passing it across to me. I wiped my palms on my skirts and then took it, holding it in my lap. I looked down. The MacFadden seal was pressed into green wax at the flap: *Lamh Laidir An nachtar*—the strong hand uppermost. "I'll send my posts through Di Pietro, and you're to do the same," Grandfather said. "He'll see to it that we hear of each other."

I looked back up at him, swiped the back of my hand across my eyes. He smiled then, with some tenderness. "I'll write as soon as it's safe for ye to return, I promise ye."

Standing, I cleared my throat, pressing my fingers against the edges of the envelope. "What is this?"

He stood too, and came around the side of the desk. He reached out and laid a big hand on my shoulder, and his palm was warm. "It's for the Duchess. I'll ask that ye give it to her as soon as ye meet, and that you'll not read it."

I swallowed back the knot in my throat and shook my head, frustrated and sad and scared, already missing him. "Fine, I won't. But I'm not happy about it."

I moved from under his hand before he could stop me and snatched the candle from his desk. At the doorway I stopped and turned, and when I looked back I found him still standing in the center of the room, his hands in the pockets of his vest and his eyes once again on the window. "You will write to me of Owen."

"Aye, as soon as I hear," he answered, but did not look back. He did not look away from that square of black on the far wall, leading out into a world that had become capricious and fleeting for all of us.

Chapter 38

The Sign of Bacchus, on the Charlestown Harbor

The Sign of Bacchus bustled with the business of the Charlestown elite, and they filled the tavern's dining room, enjoying dinner served on gleaming mahogany furniture or meandering through a haze of cheroot smoke, feeding on local gossip. At a table near the door sat a well-heeled man and his wife. She wore a deeply-cut, pale green gown and a towering white wig done in the European fashion. She picked at the glazed hen on the plate before her, the beauty mark at the corner of her top lip disappearing into her cheek with each bite.

At the end of the long room a group of young men stood around a whist table, drinking wine and ale and debating loudly amongst themselves. They were members of the Bachelor's Society, Grandfather told us. Apparently, the tavern was a meeting place for several of Charlestown's many clubs. The Sons of Liberty, the Laughing Club, the Beef-Steak Club, and the Order of Ubiquarians all met here on one night or another, though the South Carolina Society met on Elliott Street, at the home of the politician Joel Poinsett. "Too many secrets to keep," Grandfather said, winking.

We took a table in the dining room and ordered drinks from a slave girl. It was naught but the three of us, Jack, Grandfather and me. Ridge Runner had remained at the house on Tradd Street, claiming he wanted to examine the Scotsman's grand stables and tend to the horses for a while. But as my eyes took in the lay of the tavern I knew it was more that he didn't want to cause a disturbance—and an Indian drinking in a tavern full of white men would have surely incited riot.

As one of only a few women present, I'd garnered my fair share of study. But I kept my head high and my smile appealing, proper as a schoolgirl. Outside, when we'd crossed the piazza to enter the establishment an inebriated patron had stumbled past us, barely managing to make his way down the steps. When he'd leered at me, gripping hat to chest, Jack stepped silently in front and gave the character a courtly bow.

"Needing assistance?" he'd asked, and at the sight of him—strangely tattooed and towering—the other man shook his head quickly and continued into the street, narrowly missing being trampled by a chaise when he craned his head to look back.

When our drinks arrived they were carried by a richly dressed woman in a satin gown, her hoopskirt smaller than the usual frock, though just as fine. Her neckline plunged to reveal a silk petticoat beneath. She set the drinks on the table and smiled at Grandfather. "Welcome, Campbell. You've not been by as much as usual—I've been worried that the Sons had decided to start meeting over at Nightingale's, and that wouldn't have made me happy at all. Who is this with you, now?"

"Catherine, you're looking fine. This is my granddaughter, Quincy, and her husband, Mister Jackson Wolf. They're in town for a bit of a visit, and I thought I'd be remiss if I didn't bring them to the finest establishment in the colony." She preened at him when he smiled, his eyes merry. "Quinn, Jack, allow me to present Catherine Backhouse, owner and operator."

"Oh, and won't Benjamin love hearing you say that," she chuckled.

"A pleasure, madam," Jack inclined his head elegantly, and I smiled politely at her. She'd caught a look at Jack's face, and her eyes appraised him warmly, widening at the sight of the curving, blue tattoo. She cleared her throat.

"Will you be having a meal this evening, Campbell?"

"Nothing but the ale, madam," he said, then lowered his voice. "A favor, too, perhaps. I'm needing to find a certain ship's captain, one with a boat in the harbor that's ready to sail for Europe, and one without any love of the Crown. Could ye help an old friend, lassie?"

She shifted the tray in her hands and bent over his shoulder, displaying ample cleavage. She nodded towards a group of men across the dining room. They sat drinking together and playing cards, and were a bit more humbly dressed than most of the other patrons. "See the short fellow there, with the gray beard and the scar on his cheek? That's Captain Reginald Baker, of the *Queen Anne*. He owns one of the few merchant vessels that makes a direct crossing to England, doesn't head to the Barbados first. He's an odd fellow. Loathes the English, and doesn't believe in running slaves."

She cocked her head thoughtfully. "To be honest with you, I'm not at all certain how he makes his wages, but he may be the man you seek."

Grandfather reached out, patted her on the arm. "Thank ye,

Catherine."

"Enjoy the ale," she said, and walked away.

Jack reached for his mug, took a gulp and wiped his mouth with the back of his hand. He leaned lazily back in his chair, but his green eyes were deep and serious. "Are you planning on telling us what you're about, then?" he asked Grandfather. "I know you're looking for a ship to put us on, but how can we trust that he won't betray us to the British? It's a fair risk, helping a half-breed and his wife run from the Crown."

Grandfather stood slowly, tucking one hand in the pocket of his tailored vest and taking his mug of ale with the other. "If he loathes the redcoats, he'll do it." He cocked an eyebrow wryly. "And I did bring coin with me, lad—I'm no fool. I'm going to have a walk outside with the captain, see what he thinks of our proposition. I'd ask him to the house, but we can't risk it. Enjoy your drinks, bairns—I shall return in a bit."

Jack shot me a pointed look but we watched him go. He made his way across the room, stopping to speak to another group of men before approaching the sailors. When he introduced himself to Baker the shorter man stood, and they clasped hands. After a few moments, Baker nodded, and he and Grandfather exited the dining room side by side.

I shook my head. "This is insanity."

"Aye, but unless you want me locked in the gaol or swinging by a rope I think it's our only choice. Let's hope that your wee Italian friend still feels as warmly towards you when we land on his doorstep."

"Have you ever been on a ship?" I asked, pressing my fingers to my already aching brow.

"Once before, and only up to New England. After that, naught but canoe. I suppose that crossing the great blue sea's a mite different." He smiled then, and I nodded, reaching for my glass.

"A mite." I thought of the one trip across the ocean that I could remember, and how I'd spent the first four nights bent over a chamber pot, Grandfather and Owen taking turns holding my hair back and wiping the sweat from my neck. "In his letters Signor Di Pietro has made several invitations for us to visit Florence, so I'm certain that we'll be welcomed."

"Certain, aye?" Though his lilt held a tinge of sarcasm he smiled at me good-naturedly, and I remembered again why I loved this unusual, enigmatic man.

Across the room men cheered and slapped each other on the shoulders; someone had obviously won at cards. Jack glanced over his shoulder at the doorway. "Mayhap your grandsire's talking the man to death," he said. He took his glass in hand and held it out to me. "Well, Mac, here's to a new life—even if not a one of us speaks the language."

I smiled reluctantly, but took my glass in hand and clinked it to his.

Then my eyes flew past him. Grandfather and the sea captain had entered the tavern. They parted ways in the middle of the room, and the old man returned to the table, his grizzled face revealing nothing.

"Well?" I asked quietly, my nerves humming.

He drew a few coins from his pocket and dropped them on the table. Then he looked from Jack to me, and I could see it in his eyes, shining brightly beneath wild, red brows—success. "We must away home," he said. "There is much to be done."

In my dreams I am on a never-ending ocean of white-capped waves, rolling and swelling with tremendous height. I walk on them as though they are solid as an oak floor, and I can see my feet beneath the blue, the long bones of my toes pale as a skeleton's. Before me, growing closer on the gold line of the horizon is a dock, and as I near it I can see that Jack stands on it dressed in the same clothes he wore on our wedding day. The eagle's feather in his hair blows over his shoulder in a breeze I cannot feel. Beside him is Owen, suntanned and hale.

My cousin lifts a hand at me in greeting, and I smile.

But something causes me to turn in the opposite direction, and when I do the ocean melds into mountains. Walks-With-Hawks sits before my cabin on a black horse, a silver falcon perched on his bare arm. He cups a hand around his mouth, his lips moving without sound, and I strain to hear. Unable, I look back at Jack and Owen for help. Now, both of them are dressed in frontiersmen's clothing, armed for war. They wear blue paint slashed across their solemn faces, muskets strapped to their broad backs.

"Well, come on, coz!" Owen shouts clearly over the water. Then, his face changes, sharp. "Hurry!"

I sat straight up in bed, gasping for air, one hand gripping the bedsheets, the other clutched at my throat. When my vision cleared I recognized my old bedroom. A chill swept through the space, and the door to the veranda bumped lightly against the stop, open to the night. I knew without looking that the other side of the bed was empty—Jack was gone. I slipped from the bed and went to the armoire, wrapping myself in my robe. Without the benefit of the hot water bottle my feet were suddenly freezing. I sat on the floor like a child and tugged on a pair of woolen stockings. I padded across the room, closing the door quietly behind me.

There was a new moon tonight, and it was darker than usual. The wind whipped through the trees, oak boughs creaked—an old woman's low moan—and palmetto branches scraped against the side of the house. The street was empty, the light burning steadily in the lamp near the front walk. I hurried across the veranda to the stairwell, moving quickly. I ran through the dooryard to the stable, hugging the robe to me and bracing against the cold. At the sight of light beneath the stable door I felt relief rush through me. I took the iron latch and pulled, hefting it open.

Inside, the cobblestones were round and smooth against my stockinged feet. I moved along the wall of one of the stalls. When I heard men's voices arguing in a rough language I stopped instantly, pressing a hand against the wood. I knew the sound. It was Jack and Ridge Runner, and they spoke entirely in Cherokee, so quickly that there was no chance of my deciphering a word.

Taking a deep breath, I made a move to step out from behind the wall, but before I could Ridge Runner strode past, tension in every step. Though he moved as silently as usual there was a seeping anger in his body, and his face was closed and hard. He did not see me. For several moments I was frozen to the spot. When Jack spoke I started. "Come out, Mac. I know you're there."

I moved into the light, hurrying down the wide run, each step crackling against the hay on the floor. He stood with stooped shoulders, a lamp sitting on the bench beside him. His eyes were so dark that I couldn't read them, and he looked weary, his mouth a thin line.

"What is it? What's amiss?" I asked quickly, stopping in front of him but making no move to touch him.

"My brother is gone," he said slowly. "I sent him home."

There was a soft neigh from the far end of the barn and the sound of footsteps in the hay. Nearby, Fire Eater snorted, and before I could make a move to quiet him a small figure emerged from the darkness, rubbing his eyes. It was the stable boy, and he blinked at us blearily, the whites of his eyes startlingly bright in his sooty face. He wore a pair of breeches and no shirt, and the lacing at his waist had come undone, hanging to his knees. He pulled at it absently. "Go back to sleep," I told him softly. "All is well."

He nodded slowly and turned as if sleepwalking, disappearing into the shadows, I supposed heading back to his bed. I stepped to Jack then, taking his forearms in my cold hands; he was hot to the touch. "Why did you make him go?"

"It's time," he said. "There's naught for him here but trouble—he's better off back with the *Yun'wiya*, at Chota where he belongs."

I squeezed his arms, lifting my face to his. "I'm sorry that he must go alone," I said. "I know you'd much rather be home than here, having to cross the ocean to a place we know nothing of."

Jack shook his head and backed up a step. My hands fell away. "I'd rather be with you, Mac," he said quietly. "But if we make it—past the soldiers, onto the boat and across the sea, and even into Italy—we will miss it. We'll miss it so much our hearts will surely feel close to breaking from the pain."

I crossed my arms over my chest, partly from the cold and partly in defense of his words. "I know," I answered. "It will be difficult. I certainly don't expect it to be easy."

He took a long breath in through his nose and tipped his head back, his eyes hooded. "If war does come to *Yun'wiya* lands, I will return to this place. Leaving you would be like ripping the heart from my chest, but I'll do it, if war comes."

"I know," I said again, soft. "And I'll be with you."

Jack stepped forward then, reaching out and taking my hand in his bigger one. His grip was warm, and as we walked from the barn together I felt almost as if we were being followed in the dark—but by what, I did not know.

Later, lying in bed he turned to me. I moved a hand from beneath the sheets, cupping his rough-hewn face tenderly in my palm. He blinked, and in the muted glow from the lamp outside his eyes looked almost gold, like a wolf's. When he whispered to me in the quiet room he spoke in Cherokee, but I understood.

"When I close my eyes," he said, "all I see is blue."

I brushed the hair back from his brow. "Jack. I think we should leave tonight."

"Did you see something?" His eyes focused on me, the lines of his face seeming to sharpen somehow.

"Yes, but nothing specific. It was enough to make me feel that we should go now, in the night, while we can."

"Mac, your grandsire has a plan, and I think we should hold strong to it. He knows the city, knows the army here. We're not ready to leave."

I let my head fall back on the pillow, looking up at the ornate molding of the ceiling. "Maybe you're right," I whispered. But unease sat upon me like a dark cloud, and I knew I'd not sleep easy.

British soldiers arrived at the house at mid-morning. I watched from the upstairs window as the stable boys rushed to handle their horses, and the men stepped sharply up the brick walk, white wigs bobbing like cotton in a windy field. When they pounded on the door instead of knocking and called out for my grandfather, I knew that everything had changed.

Jack and I were in my old bedroom, loading our things back into the trunks as quickly as we could. At the continued shouting below I rushed to him, gripping his arm. "What will we do, Jack? We should have left in the night."

"Aye." He grinned quickly, and the ease of it stunned me enough to make me still for a moment. "Next time, I'll listen to you."

"What are you about?" I hissed, squeezing tighter. But footsteps thumped up the stairs and down the hall, nearing. The door swung open and Grandfather stood in the frame, breathing hard, his cheeks red. He, too, wore a wig, though it sat askew on his head, as though he'd donned it haphazardly. In his hands was a sheath of papers, wrapped in twine. He shoved them at Jack, who rolled them like a telescope, flipping up the back of his trade shirt and sliding them into the waistband of his leggings.

What in heaven's name is happening? I wondered, too startled to say it aloud.

"Ye should go, man. Find your way to the wharf," Grandfather said to Jack. "Quincy will meet ye there." Jack stood and made a move for his tomahawk where it sat at the end of the bed, but Grandfather reached it first. He shoved it into Jack's hands and pushed him toward the veranda door. "Go on, now. Remember—use the papers if necessary. And don't let them see you. I'll take care of this." He snatched my hand and pulled me along. "Quincy, come with me."

"Wait!" I tugged back on my arm, turning desperately for Jack. "Jack? What if—"

He moved silently, quickly, to my side, and reached out both hands to cup my face. He leaned in, pressing his forehead to mine. "I'll find you. I always do."

I closed my eyes for one brief moment, and I could feel the pulse of my heartbeat in his hands and his breath warm on my skin. "I won't go without you."

"Best be quick about it, Wolf," Grandfather interjected, releasing my arm.

Jack and I leaned in at the same time, and we kissed firmly, briefly. As we separated he put a finger to his lips, nodded at Grandfather, and backed toward the veranda door. Outside the winter wind moved the palmettos. I could see them sway through the wavy glass of the window.

"Jack?" I whispered again, unable to help myself.

He grinned at me then—a flash of heartbreaking white—winked, and was gone.

"Let's go," Grandfather ordered, gripping my hand as we rushed into the hall. At the top of the stairway he stopped, rolling his neck on his shoulders until it popped. He took a calming breath and let go of my hand, straightening the tails of this coat, fixing the wig. I pinched my cheeks for color and smoothed back flyaway strands of hair around my face. "Don't say a word," he said softly. "Let me do the talking." He looked at me then, nodded gruffly and offered his arm. Before taking it I wiped wet palms on my skirts.

Jack was gone. I hated being separated from him, however momentarily. It made me feel as though I were missing an appendage, like the loss of an arm. But he was safe—would be safe, I knew. I'd seen it, hadn't I? I'd seen him standing there, waiting for me. I had to trust in the feeling, and trust in Jack—no easy feat with possibly the whole of the British army in the foyer.

"Breathe," I ordered myself. I nodded at Grandfather. "I'm ready."

We moved down the steps together, my left hand on Grandfather's arm and my right skimming the banister. When we came in view of Naji, who stood silently in the foyer, Grandfather nodded. "Show them in," he said.

There was an awkward scuffle at the door, and in walked three red-coated officers. They brushed by Naji as if he wasn't even there. I caught sight of others standing outside, straight and still as toys in a boy's army, before the black butler shut the door softly and turned. "Lieutenants Mauberly and Cross, and Major Dunham, of His Majesty's army," he announced.

We made the last step into the foyer, and Grandfather patted my hand, releasing me. I stood back, waiting. He walked to the men and offered a courtly bow. "Gentlemen, I am Campbell MacFadden, and this is my granddaughter, Madam Wolf." I curtsied deeply behind him, and through my lashes watched the two younger lieutenants glance at each other. The older man, the major, bowed sharply. "How may we be of service?"

"Mr. MacFadden, Madam." Major Dunham spoke brusquely. "I have been ordered by General Cornwallis to bring Jackson Wolf to the wharf at once. He was supposed to inform us when he arrived in the city. As you know, his services have been requested by the king, and agitators are multiplying in the New England colonies. The General is anxious that we be on our way."

Grandfather gestured toward the library, smiling politely. "Officers, might I offer ye some tea while ye wait?"

Dunham shook his head, glancing darkly at his subordinates when they began whispering behind him. "No, but our thanks. If you'll send for Mr. Wolf, immediately."

"Well, I'm afraid that's not possible," Grandfather said, innocent as a priest. "It's my own fault he's not here. I've sent him to Georgetown to fetch documents from a colleague there. However, he should return by morning. Where shall I send him when he arrives?"

At this I had to physically restrain myself from looking at Grandfather. Ah—so that explained the papers he'd shoved at Jack. I coughed delicately, to hide an exclamation.

"What sort o' documents?" Lieutenant Cross narrowed his brown eyes at him, his accent flat. A spattering of red freckles stood out along his nose, making him look more boy than man.

"Lieutenant, hold your tongue," Major Dunham ordered.

"Legal documents, pertaining to a case I'm trying. Now," Grandfather said, smiling. "Shall we sit down to tea?"

Dunham looked back and forth between Grandfather and me, studying us with hazel eyes. He pulled lightly on his beard, then shook his head. "No, we must be off. But Mr. Wolf must arrive at the Cooper River wharf tomorrow at dawn. Lord Cornwallis will not suffer a delay." He stopped Grandfather's protest with an outstretched hand. "I don't care how you do it. Dawn, sir. We sail on the *Elizabeth*."

The men bowed almost in unison, and I curtsied again, and when Naji shut the door behind them I backed into the newel post, bracing myself. "My heart is fluttering like a flock of mad seagulls," I whispered. "You knew this would happen, didn't you? You knew someone would report Jack's presence in the city."

Grandfather shook his head, his expression grim. He started up the steps, and I watched him for a heartbeat, dazed, before taking my skirts in hand and hurrying after him. "Aye," he said, taking the steps two at a time like a much younger man. "We worked it out, Wolf and I. But he didn't want to leave ye before the morning." He paused, looked back at me. "Hurry and pack your things, lassie. We've not much time. Ye must be on that boat tonight."

I stood in the shadows between two stalls in Grandfather's stable, my arms outstretched like a heretic being tortured on the rack. In each hand I held the slobbered remnants of a sugar cube, still being munched upon by Ninian and Fire Eater respectively. They hung their heads over the wooden doors, craning for the last bite. Down the run I could see Murdoch's head draped over his own stall. He kicked at the door like a petulant child, and I smiled sadly. I'd given him his treat earlier.

"All right, that's it," I told them, holding dripping hands away from my sides and grimacing before dunking them into the nearest water trough. The water was freezing. I shook them hurriedly, then dried them against my overcoat. Though I did wear a gown, I'd refused to leave the old greatcoat behind.

Fire Eater butted his chest against his door and threw his head back, neighing loudly. I stepped to his stall and reached out, taking his bridle in my hands and pulling him down to me until I could feel the warm breath from his nostrils against my face. "That's the last of it, you great brute," I murmured, hoping to calm him. "I gave you all I had."

But I knew it wasn't more of the sugar cube he was after. He sensed my leaving, instinct making the whites of his eyes flash and his ears fold back with wild knowledge. Despite his snorting I laid my forehead against his velvet nose, and he stopped pulling on the bridle immediately. "It will be like living in a castle, compared to home," I told him. "Look how much larger a stall you have here, with Grandfather and Naji to care for you. By the time we return you'll be pulling a chaise through town, and everyone will admire how beautiful you are." I took a breath. "If we ever return. My God, can we do this? Can we pull off such a feat?"

I pressed the heel of my hand to my forehead, breathing out through my nose. Then I reached up, patting Fire Eater lightly on his curved jaw, shutting my eyes for a heartbeat before releasing him. Tears gathered at the corners; I wiped them roughly and backed away. The ache in my chest rose to my throat, and I took off at a run through the stable and outside, my skirts flapping awkwardly against my legs. Two of Grandfather's horses were hitched to his carriage, and on the back sat our trunk. Naji strapped it down as I approached, the white palms of his hands moving swiftly over the trunk. Grandfather stood beside him, talking quietly. He looked up as I neared, slowing to a walk.

"He'll be fine here," he said.

"Yes," I murmured. In the dusk the hollows of Grandfather's face were shadowed. The wrinkles at the corners of his eyes suddenly seemed deeper and more pronounced, making him look shockingly old. He bent his head for a heartbeat and cleared his throat, stuffing his hands in his pockets. "What is it?" I asked.

He shook his head, gruff. "We'll say our goodbyes here, lass. Naji knows where ye must go to find Baker's boat. I gave Wolf the purse for the captain." He reached out then, patting my head as though I was still the little girl who had fallen off her horse too many times to count. "'Tis better this way. If I'm with ye there will only be questions."

I nodded as I moved forward, pressing my face into his shirt and wrapping my arms as far as they could go around his barrel of a belly. His vest smelled of coffee; the familiarity of it was heartbreaking. He hugged me tightly and then took my shoulders in his hands, pushing me back from him and bending to look me in the face. "We'll be seeing each other again," he said.

"Will we?" I asked him, for I honestly didn't know.

Before Grandfather could speak, Naji emerged from behind him, his hat pulled low over his eyes. "Ready, sir?"

Before Grandfather could answer there was a loud crash from the stables, the sound like a thunderclap in the quiet. One of the grooms came tearing down the drive, his feet bare.

"Mister Campbell, that horse gone crazy!" he yelled. "He broke his stall!"

Hooves clattered on the cobblestones behind him and the boy screamed, diving into one of the hedges that lined the drive. Fire Eater came charging out of the shadowed entryway, flinging his head from side to side, his knees bloodied.

"Oh, my," I breathed. Naji walked calmly toward the stallion, his arms wide. He spoke lowly in a language I didn't recognize, and as he neared Fire Eater kicked up his front legs a last defiant time, then settled.

"Easy, boy. You draw too much attention, and your girl be unhappy with you. Quiet, now." Naji reached a gentle hand along Fire Eater's neck, took the bridle at his jaw. He turned back to us, his movements slow and controlled. "You got to take him with you," he said.

A slave poked his head out the front door of the neighbor's house, looking out onto the street. A carriage clattered past, and the coachmen shouted out a greeting to Naji, who calmly raised a hand. I couldn't believe it—how we were all moving so calmly, packing the carriage as if we were off for a quick visit somewhere. And soon, I'd have to bid farewell to my Grandfather—a man I loved only less than I did Jack—as if I'd see him again in days, when the truth was, we could be separated forever. The painful danger of it all was like ice beneath my skin, and I mentally clamped down on the panic.

Grandfather turned to Naji. "Go to my desk. There's a leather purse in the drawer—bring all the notes there." Naji nodded and hurried into the dooryard, disappearing up the front walk. Grandfather eyed the stallion warily.

"I dinna ken if there's a horse hold on the boat or not," he said. "But I imagine a flash of pound notes will convince Baker to take the beast."

"We'll need hay," I murmured, making a move for the stable. Grandfather grabbed my wrist, looking past me to Naji, who'd returned with a new, square bulge beneath his jacket. "You get the feed, let the lass take the horse."

Fire Eater dipped his head as I approached, then craned it to the side, looking away. I took his bridle in hand, pressing the other against my mouth. "You are mad," I murmured against my fingers, feeling a bit delirious myself. "You'll abhor being at sea."

I walked him toward the carriage. Naji hefted a block of hay on top of the trunk, reaching beneath to unhook a leather strap, tie it down. Then he stepped quickly to me, taking Fire Eater.

"Aye. Up ye go," Grandfather said, glancing at the neighboring mansion. He took my elbow, led me to the carriage and opened the door. I stepped up, turning hesitantly. "Go on, now," he said.

He shut the carriage door; it clicked into place. Naji climbed into the driver's seat, and I scooted as close to the window as I could, my fingers curled over the sides. Grandfather looked toward the front and nodded. The carriage lurched forward, and I leaned out, and Grandfather put his hand over one of mine, his weathered palm calloused and dry.

"I love ye, lassie," he said roughly, then let go.

Chapter 39

Charlestown Harbor

By the time we arrived at the harbor dusk had sunk into night, and the sailors of the *Queen Anne* moved easily aboard the ship, securing lines. There was little movement on the wharf, save for the few people coming in and out of the taverns and bawdy houses across the street, laughter and music spilling out along with the light each time they exited. Not a soul glanced at us. Above us ship masts bobbed in the dark; there was the low squeak of wood sliding on wood, the muffled slap of waves against the seawall.

Lamps swinging from the masts spread light across the ship in arching flashes. The sailors' faces were pale ovals as they lowered the gangplank and carried our trunk aboard, and I watched as the gangplank curved slightly under their weight. There were dozens of ships moored along the wharf, waiting to be loaded, and many more anchored in the harbor. Masts invaded the sky, shooting up into the air like a forest of moving tree trunks. The sea beyond seemed melded with the sky, an endless, inky movement of black.

Naji barely touched my arm. "Goodbye, Miss Quinn. I wish you luck."

I turned and lay a hand on his arm, looking up into the kind brown eyes I'd known since childhood, uncaring if anyone saw. "Be well, my friend. I know you'll take good care of Grandfather."

He nodded shortly and touched a hand to his hat. Then he looked up and past me.

Jack was coming down the dock. He was dressed as a sailor, his hair tied back and a rough tricorn pulled low to shade his face, covering the tattoo. I breathed in, relief cooling and sweet. When I turned back to bid farewell to Naji, he was gone.

Jack reached me and offered his arm, and I took it automatically. "Allow me to escort you aboard, madam," he murmured. When finally we stepped onto the deck I stilled.

Standing in a pool of lamplight and smiling up at the stocky, grizzled captain was my cousin—and Ridge Runner behind her, still as marble.

"What are they doing here?" I muttered to Jack. What are they doing *together?* I wanted to shout. Now I could no longer deny the connection between my good-brother and my cousin's wife. I didn't know what to make of it—only that soon I'd have to decide what to tell Owen. But Owen had kept me purposely in the dark these last months about whatever it was he was plotting, and he'd undoubtedly put his wife in danger. I'd watched her painstaking recovery. Though I knew his cause had to be just, I was angry with him.

Captain Baker turned at our approach, his face flushed, and bowed shortly.

"Madam Wolf. Welcome aboard the *Queen Anne.*"

I forced a smile, wanting nothing more than to get Rebekah alone. "Thank you, Captain."

"Well, Wolf," he continued, eyes on Jack, "I've arranged for Madam Scott to have the cabin next to you and your wife. But I've too many men to put them out of a room for her slave here." Rebekah batted her eyelashes at the man, and he colored even more deeply, clearing his throat. "I suppose he can sleep with the deckhands."

"Slave, eh?" Jack said pointedly, staring at Ridge Runner with rage banked in his green eyes. Then he blinked, and the look was gone, replaced with pure Irish charm. "So, Baker, what will it take to have these two aboard? What poundage do you require?"

Rebekah moved to my side, slipping her arm through mine. I looked over at her warily, realizing with a sort of hollow feeling in my gut that I perhaps did not know her at all.

"It's all been settled," she said, her voice soft as a girl's. "I've paid the captain for the both of us."

"You have, have you?" I murmured. Her arm on mine jerked slightly at the sound.

"Be that as it may, we've one more passenger," Jack cocked an eyebrow at the captain.

"Another—" Captain Baker faltered, his eyes narrowing. "'Zounds, man. We've no room. This is a ship, not a stagecoach. Have you heard nothing I've said?"

I cleared my throat. "It's for my horse, Captain. I must have him with me. Now, what poundage do you require?"

Baker stared at me, stunned at the sound of a woman taking charge, and turned back to Jack. "Wolf, have a word with your wife, please. A horse is a damned inconvenience—certainly a passing fancy. You can buy her a new one in Italy."

Jack merely blinked. "What poundage do you require, Captain?"

As sailors from the *Queen Anne* uncurled the heavy lines of rope from their moorings and tossed them onto the ship I stood at the side, my hands atop the thick railing. I wore my hair tucked beneath a dull, russet-colored bonnet, as much of a disguise as I could muster on short notice. Rebekah stood beside me, silent in the darkness.

"I couldn't stay here, Quinn," she said softly. "Alone, in that big house with your grandfather and his slaves. And Owen's things, sitting there as though he'd walk through the door at any moment. And he won't—we both know that."

"You'd be safer there. It's foolish for you to come with us," I said, turning to her and shaking my head, feeling like I was admonishing a young pupil. "We're running from the Crown, Rebekah. Defying an order from the King himself. If we are caught, it's likely we'll all be hung."

She turned back to the wharf, shaking her head. "Owen asked you to watch over me. You, Quinn—not Grandfather. If he truly wanted me in his care Owen would've sent me from Boston to Charlestown instead of the frontier."

Reluctantly, I nodded. Though I couldn't claim to understand the quicksilver workings of my cousin's mind, I had to admit that he had made the choice not to leave his wife with our grandfather. And in doing so, he must have had a reason. "I still worry that this decision is far too rash."

Letting a long breath out through my nose, I reached out, clamping a hand on her forearm. She looked up at me in surprise, and I squeezed tighter, whispering. "Rebekah, for God's sake, what is going on between you and Ridge Runner?"

She pulled at her arm, but I held it securely. I watched her throat contract as she gulped. "Whatever are you implying?"

"You know what I'm implying. You are married to my cousin."

Rebekah's face softened, and I eased my grip on her arm. She put a hand on top of mine. "I am." She paused as if searching for words. "And I do love him, despite all that's happened since he sent me away. Please, Quinn. Reserve judgment of me, at least for now. I need you, of all people, to do this. Please."

Two sailors jogged up the gangplank, then turned with quick precision to pull at the ropes—thick as a man's thigh—that held the walkway in place and heft it onto the ship. I wanted to believe my good-cousin, for I heard the begging in her voice, despite the iron beneath it.

You, of all people, she'd said. Because I was married to Jack, and he was Cherokee? I shook off the questions and looked her in the eyes. "All right," I said, releasing her arm.

"Thank you," she murmured.

There was a shuffle of movement around us as sailors took their places at the huge oars at the sides. Beneath the lamplight at the captain's deck, Baker stood with a slight man at his side, a small book in his arms. He shouted something down to the sailors, and they heaved together, moving the ship into the harbor.

The wharf was lonely and empty, no one there to bid us farewell as we began to move from the dock. The ship groaned, making a turn, and it rocked in the water, the stern coming perpendicular with the wharf.

The ship moved farther from shore. As we moved into deeper water the waves in the harbor rocked against the hull, and I craned my neck, hoping for a last look at the night-dark city. I moved along the railing towards the stern, my eyes narrowing, searching. In an alley near the wharf, the flash of a familiar face beneath the lamplight there caught my eye, and I stopped, my fingers gripping the wood. All movement and sound around me—sailors rushing to move booms, unrolling huge, white sails, the clatter of feet on the deck—lulled to silence, as if the world had stopped on its axis.

Owen was there, on the wharf, as if in a dream. He stood near the edge of the dock, and when he saw me he lifted the tricorn from his head, making a quick leg. Even from the distance and in the dark, I knew those eyes, gray and serious. But then I blinked, and he was gone, disappeared down the dark alley. My heart beat madly. *Was it a vision? How could he be here?*

"Quinn, are you well?" Rebekah had followed me down the ship; she clutched my arm.

"Did you see him?" I asked frantically, turning to her. "There, on the docks?"

"See who?"

Once at full sail the ship moved rapidly, and the lights of the wharf faded, the buildings and moored ships there melding together in a black, indistinct mass. I shook my head to clear it. "No one," I said. "Sorry."

Chapter 40

The Atlantic Ocean, aboard the Queen Anne

The world beneath me shifted, and I rolled, smashing my forehead against something hard. I opened my eyes, dry from uneasy sleep, to find a wooden wall inches from my face. I pressed a hand to it and pushed back, and found myself tucked against something large and solid, Jack, asleep at my side. His arm was thrown over my stomach, anchoring me to the bunk. I rolled onto my back—his big hand sliding along my bare belly—and rubbed my forehead, wincing. Then I reached up, pressing my palm against the floor of the bunk above, close enough to make the berth feel close as a coffin.

Rising up on my left elbow, I looked out at our cabin. It was certainly tiny. There was a navigator's desk at the wall beneath a small, round porthole. A chamber pot sat beside a spindly-backed chair—empty, I prayed. Our trunk sat open beside it, clothes and books strewn across the floor. Not five feet away, at the room's only door, was a large burlap sack. I sank back onto the bunk and closed my eyes, and Jack shifted.

"How long have you been awake?" he asked quietly, and I turned to him. He was raised up on his elbow, a hand bracing his head. In the morning light coming in through the porthole his eyes were stunningly green, like new growth in the southern forest. A lock of yellow-streaked hair fell across his long nose, and he blew it back with a puff.

"Not long," I answered. "I couldn't remember where I was for a moment." I reached out, touching the sliver of silver that hung from his right ear. "I can't believe they came."

He pulled his other hand from beneath the rough sheet, took mine from his ear and pressed it to his warm chest. He arched an eyebrow. "Your good-cousin must have used the old man's life savings to pay for their passage. I wonder if he knows she's gone."

"He does," I said. "She told me so last night." I paused. "I asked her about Ridge Runner."

"Aye?" He shifted on the mattress.

"I had to know, Jack. She's married to my cousin, and I won't have him cuckolded, no matter what he's done."

"Quinn," Jack's voice was soft and low, admonishing. "Do you really think that's what they're doing?"

"I don't know. Do you?"

"My brother won't speak to me of it," he admitted. "And you know him—the man's as lock-jawed as Walks-With-Hawks. I don't know what they're about, and I don't want my brother hurt. Nor Owen," he added. He squeezed my hand, met my gaze again. "Some things are out of our hands, love. Pitch your prayers to the heavens. That's all we can do."

He moved his left shoulder in a half-hearted shrug, then glanced back at the window. I wanted to say something more, to pick at the issue until we found the truth, but I could see he was done with it . . . at least for now. When he spoke again, the change of subject startled me.

"We must talk of Italy, and of the war, Mac—I know you've had words with your grandfather."

"Not now, I beg of you. We've the whole of the crossing to talk," I said, impatience getting the better of me. "For now we must make the best of this. Will you let me out, please?" A look of reluctance passed over Jack, and his tawny face turned a shade darker than usual. "What?" I asked, drawing out the word.

"Well, you might have a problem with your gown, lass. I may have torn it a bit, helping you to bed last night."

I remembered then, heat rising in my face, how Jack's hands had raced over my body, ripped at my laces. He'd tossed his shirt across the room, and my fists had found purchase in his hair as the planes of his brown stomach gleamed in the lamplight. Through the wall of the cabin next to ours we had heard Rebekah's soft snores. I closed my eyes briefly, mortified. "I cannot believe she didn't wake."

He shook his head, grinning like a large, barely-domesticated cat. "Aye, but she slept like a drunk." He rolled his eyes and paused, cocking his head towards the wall where sure enough, there was a faint, feminine rumble. "She's at it again. And I'm hard as a lad of fourteen. Care to help me with that?"

I scooted back instinctively, pressing my backside against the wall of the berth. I shook my head. "Certainly not," I whispered shortly. "It's morning. Everyone will hear."

He slid towards me, pinned me there. "We'll be quiet about it," he murmured, dipping his head and pressing his lips to my collarbone. He trailed the line of my neck, his mouth hot, and slipped a hand into the sheet that I held clutched to my chest, pushing it down to my waist and cupping my breast lazily.

"Oh, certainly," I said, biting back a moan as his hand slid across my belly and between my legs. "Quiet as church mice, that's the two of us. But I'll try."

Through the wall we could hear the creak of Rebekah shifting in her berth, and the snoring stopped. I stilled instantly, but Jack's deft fingers found their purpose, and I covered his hand with mine and pressed down. Arousal spread through my bloodstream, blinding and quick. The soft snoring resumed, and I choked on a laugh, giving in and reaching down Jack's body, taking the length of him in my fist. He groaned and leaned forward, taking one of my nipples in his mouth and moving the tip lightly between his teeth. When he lifted his head his hair fell forward, covering one eye like a pirate's patch. I moved my hand, gripping the muscular curve of his buttock. "God, you're slick," he said. "I want you too quickly."

I shook my head, my hair fanning out against the mattress beneath. "No, it's the same for me."

"Try and stay quiet, then," he said, moving over me and bracing himself on his outstretched arms, his muscles tense. I leaned up, traced a vein in one arm from wrist to elbow with the pad of my finger. When he sank into me I made a noise in the back of my throat and he pressed his lips against mine, firm. "Hush, now," he murmured, going deeper.

I lifted my hips and curled my ankles around his calves, and we moved together, our breathing quick and shallow. The sound of a cough came from the cabin next door. We stopped, and I giggled, and he touched his forehead to mine, grinning. I moved my hips wickedly, and he raised up, shaking his head and grimacing. "You wee witch," he breathed. "You know I can't stop."

When he moved so that his hipbones touched mine I pressed my mouth against his shoulder, moaning into his skin. When I cried out he fell against me and kissed me deeply, his own cry a thrumming of his tongue against my throat.

Moments later—how long I could not know—he lifted his head and moved to the side, pulling me with him, our bodies still joined. He pressed a quick kiss against the tip of my nose, his eyes dancing like a boy's. I felt the laughter rising in me, and it bubbled out. I clapped a hand over my mouth, and he rolled his eyes, and at the sight I let it come, burying my face in the bed sheet. His body began to shake, rocking the bed. When I looked up at him again I saw that he'd taken the sheet in his mouth like a dog, and his eyes were streaming with tears.

Helpless, we collapsed against each other, laughing like loons.

Epilogue

We stood at the bow in the late morning light.

"I had a dream last night," he said, speaking above the rush of air and water. "My father was there. He was standing at the top of the highest pasture, in Keowee Valley, with the mountains at his back. A fire burned beside him, and the smoke danced around him as if it were alive." He set his chin against the top of my head and I leaned back into him.

"Did he say anything?"

"No. He turned to the mountains and took a piece of them in his hand like he was picking an apple from a tree. Then he turned back and held it out to me, and it was naught but a shard of blue glass. But when I reached for it he shook his head and put it into the bag at his waist." Jack chuckled softly, moving his chin against my skull. "He waved at me, like a white man. And then he disappeared."

"I, too, had a dream," I told him, after a moment.

"A dream, lass, or a vision?"

"Maybe both. I was walking across the ocean as if it were a wood floor. You and Owen stood on one side, and Owen called me to you." I paused. "Walks-With-Hawks stood on the other side, but he didn't say anything. And then I woke."

Jack rubbed his chin against my head, tightened his arms around my waist. We stood in silence, looking out to sea. The white-capped ocean was empty of other ships, and it seemed endless, as if to reach the pale line of the horizon would mean coming up on the other side of the world.

It comes. The voice whispered in my ear, above the cold rush of the wind.

And it was true. Whatever *it* was—revolution and war, danger and intrigue—would come no matter what I or anyone could do about it. We were headed to new life in a new country, at least for the time being.

But we'd be together.

I stepped forward, breaking from Jack, and set my hands against the rail. Then I closed my eyes, banishing the sea. My nostrils flared at the scent of wood smoke, and I leaned into the wind.

I thought then of the settlement, of the way the Blue Ridge went cobalt on winter days like this, becoming an infinite, rolling line that reached up to meet the heavens, separating the wilderness from the tame. The Keowee Valley had been my freedom, and it had brought me Jack. Our children would know it. And we would fight for it no matter how long it took, no matter the cost.

"We'll be back, all of us," I whispered, the words a vow. For the land called to me even now, in an ancient tongue, willing me home.

Katherine Scott Crawford

Acknowledgements

It took me two years to complete this first novel, but it was many more in coming. My writing life has been nourished and celebrated by my family and friends since I was a child. It's impossible to gauge the purely magical affect that sort of love and belief has on a person, and it's just as impossible to properly say "thank you." Still, I'm going to try. My deepest apologies if I've left anyone out.

My heartfelt thanks go to . . .

Henry Morrison, my literary agent and true gentleman of the industry, who took a chance on an unknown writer and her first novel.

Deborah Smith and Debra Dixon at Bell Bridge Books, fellow Southerners, writers, and publishers extraordinaire—able to leap literary hurdles and willing to answer questions with a single, often-hilarious bound. I'm so glad you loved *Keowee Valley*.

Lynn Coddington, my generous and insightful editor, who not only loved the novel, but made it better. And to copyeditor Jeanette Roycraft, for many "catches," but mostly for making sure Quinn didn't sound like Rudyard Kipling.

James Pharr, my talented cousin-in-law, the artist responsible for the gorgeous drawings inside the book.

My early readers: Callie Caldwell, Karen Crawford, Gloria Douglass, Jill Hutchins, Kathleen Kuna, Erin McManus, Paula Bennett Paddick, and Liddell Shannon.

My dear friends Ben Muldrow and Brian Zufall, marketing, copywriting, and design pros, who created my online worlds, offer their advice and time free of charge, and who've stuck with me since we were 14 years-old.

The teachers over the years who challenged me, encouraged me, read my work aloud in class, who made me fall in love with learning: Karen and Newell Crawford (my first teachers), Karen Gaskins (my 1st grade teacher, who let me color outside the lines, and who collected books for me from the upper grades when I read all of hers), Mary McWhorter (my 8th grade history teacher, who ignited my love of South Carolina history, and who let me wear a tricorn hat to class), Jeanne White (who gave me my first alarming C in Honors Freshman English, challenging my writing for the first time) and Sue Wilson (my incomparable AP English teacher, who prepared us for college so utterly well, and who always believed I'd be a writer), for Dr. William F. Steirer (my history professor and Alumni Master Teacher at Clemson University, whose office door was always open, who met with me to discuss *Keowee Valley* when it was just an idea, and who gave me an invaluable list of resources), Dr. Scott Lucas (English professor at The Citadel, who melded history, politics, religion, and literature with energy and fun) and for Dr. Joseph Harrison (my thesis advisor and mentor at the College of Charleston, whose dedication to teaching and love of his students showed me the kind of professor I still want to be, and who gave me Italy).

The North Carolina Arts Council, who awarded me with a 2007-2008 North Carolina Arts Award.

Duncan Murrell, former faculty member at the South Carolina Writer's Workshop, who read the first 10 pages of my novel and gave me the blunt and professional encouragement to get moving.

The South Carolina Room of the Greenville County Public Library, home to countless state resources, and a man named Durham, who poured over old maps with me and tracked down a friend in Ninety-Six, who told me just what it would've been like to travel the Cherokee Path in a wagon.

James Mooney, American ethnographer and great friend to the Cherokee, whose work and insights I could not have done without.

The Eastern Band of Cherokee Indians, whose rich and ancient history, culture, and landscapes have informed so much of the South, and who have fascinated me since childhood.

Louisa May Alcott, Pat Conroy, Harper Lee, Margaret Mitchell, L. M. Montgomery, William Shakespeare, Mark Twain, and all the rest, who opened the doors to the kingdom.

My tribe of friends and family-friends. From the neighborhood of Botany Woods in my hometown of Greenville, South Carolina, to the North Carolina mountains, across the country and the world, who've shared so much of my life, put up with my tall tales and artistic temperament, and loved me despite myself. You are far too many to list here, but you know who you are.

The Dodsons (and the Joyces), the most lovely family a girl could marry into.

My family members gone before and all too soon, especially my beloved Crawford, Kuna, Player, and Tiger grandparents and great-grandparents, and my irreplaceable cousin, Hunter Hudson.

My extended family of aunts, uncles, and cousins on both sides, who always thought of me as a writer, even before I did.

Scout, my favorite trail partner and boon companion.

My sister and fiercest ally, Callie Caldwell, with whom I share a childhood and a sense of humor. And her husband, John David, whom I love like a brother.

My parents, Newell and Karen Crawford, who nurtured my imagination, made our family life an adventure, and who never once—not even for a second—doubted I could do it. Because of the two of you, I'm a writer.

My daughter, Wylie, who wasn't born or even conceived when this book was written, but who has always been in my heart.

Stuart Dodson, my husband, best friend, and most staunch supporter, who has given me a home, a writing life, and my greatest treasure: Wylie. I'm so grateful I get to walk through this world with you.

Glossary of Cherokee Words & Phrases

ada'wehi	magician; supernatural being; *ada'wehi'yu:* very great magician; intensive form of *ada'wehi*
ama'yine'hi	water dwellers
Ani-Kusa	Creek Indians
Ani'waya	wolf clan
Astu	"very good"; *a'stu'tsiki':* very good, best of all
datsi	water monster
eda'ta	my father
Ha	"Now!"
hayu'	"yes, sir!"; affirmative
hi'lahi	"you climb"
hwi'lahi	"you must go"
iya'-iyu'sti	like a pumpkin
ka'gu	crow
sa'gwali'	horse
sa'gwali digu'lanahi'ta	mule
Sala'lani'ta	Young Squirrel
tadeya'statakuhi'	"we will see each other"
T'salagi	Cherokee, to the English
tuksi'	land tortoise
tu'tsahyesi'	"he will marry you"
ya'nu	bear
Yun'wiya	Cherokee; what they call themselves; the Principal People

uku	most important priest-chief; spiritual leader
ulasu'la	moccasin, shoe
unahu'	heart
un'ega	white
utset'st	"he grins"
wadan'	"thanks!"; *wado*: "thank you"
wa'ya	wolf
Yun'wi Gunahi'ta	a river; "the Long Man"

The Cherokee language dialects utilized in the novel are thought to be 18th century dialects used by both the Lower and Overhill Cherokee. These dialects sometimes sound much altered from the ones used by the Eastern and Western bands of Cherokee today.

Compiled using James Mooney's *History, Myths, and Sacred Formulas of the Cherokees*.

Author's Note

Keowee Valley is, above all, a work of fiction. While many of the places, events, and people in the novel are historically accurate, they have been recreated through my imagination. Those familiar with the Southern Appalachians, the Cherokee, and the history of the colonial period in the South may find that a random event or date may vary a bit from the historical record. All of the historical figures and locations have been used fictionally, and I've used 18th century spellings, so those may look differently than they do today. The Cherokee words and phrases utilized are an 18th century dialect taken from James Mooney's *History, Myths, and Sacred Formulas of the Cherokees*; any mistakes with these are unintentional and are mine. Much of what we know about the Southern Frontier during the 18th century comes from British army records: mostly dry accounts of routes, forts, villages, and demographics. This makes the time and place positively rich for fiction, and I've taken a novelist's liberty with all of it.

Anyone wishing to learn more about the history of the period and the places in the novel should look to the many research sources available. Here are some of the works I consulted when writing; they're a great place to start:

Alden, John Richard. *The South in the Revolution: 1763-1789*. Louisiana: Louisiana State University Press, 1957.

Bartram, William. *Travels Through North and South Carolina*. New York: Penguin Books, (1791) 1988.

De Vorsey, Louis. *Indian Boundary in Southern Colonies, 1763-1775*. Chapel Hill: University of North Carolina Press., 1966.

Duncan, Barbara R. and Brett H. Riggs. *Cherokee Heritage Trails Guidebook.*

Chapel Hill: University of North Carolina Press, 2003.

Edgar, Walter. *South Carolina: A History*. Columbia: University of South Carolina Press, 1998.

Hamel, Paul. B and Mary U. Chiltoskey. *Cherokee Plants and Their Uses: A 400 Year History*. Sylva, North Carolina: Herald Publishing Company, 1975.

Hatley, Tom. *The Dividing Paths: Cherokees and South Carolinians Through the Era of Revolution*. New York: Oxford University Press, 1993.

Historic Sites of Oconee County, South Carolina. S.C. Pam Box 71-Historic. (Greenville County Library, South Carolina)

Johnson, George Lloyd. *The Frontier in the Colonial South: South Carolina Backcountry, 1736-1800*. Connecticut: Greenwood Press, 1997.

Logan, John H. *A History of the Upper Country of South Carolina: From the Earliest Periods to the Close of the War of Independence*. Charleston: S. G. Courtenay & Company, and P. B. Glass, Columbia, 1859.

Milling, Chapman J. *Red Carolinians*. Chapel Hill: University of North Carolina Press, 1940.

Mooney, James. *History, Myths, and Sacred Formulas of the Cherokees*. Asheville: Bright Mountain Books, (1891, 1900) 1992.

Perdue, Theda. *Cherokee Women: 1700-1835*. Lincoln: University of Nebraska Press, 1998.

Rozema, Vicki. *Footsteps of the Cherokees: A Guide to the Eastern Homelands of the Cherokee Nation*. Winston-Salem: John F. Blair, Publisher, 1995.

Timberlake, Henry. *The Memoirs of Lieut. Henry Timberlake: 1756-1765*. Marietta, Georgia: Continental Book Company, 1948.

As a happy boon to my research, I also hiked, backpacked, and river paddled throughout the Southern Appalachians, and visited many historic sites. If you've not explored this gorgeous and unique part of the country, it's there waiting for you. Here are some of the places I traveled, and which I highly recommend:

In South Carolina:

Caesar's Head State Park & Jones Gap State Park/Mountain Bridge Wilderness

The Chattooga National Wild & Scenic River

The Horsepasture National Wild & Scenic River

The Jocassee Gorges
Keowee-Toxaway State Natural Area
Oconee Heritage Center
Oconee Station State Historic Site
Sumter National Forest

In North Carolina:
Chimney Rock State Park
The Cullasaja River
Dupont State Forest
The French Broad River
Gorges State Park
Great Smoky Mountains National Park
Museum of the Cherokee Indian
Nantahala National Forest
The Nantahala River
The Nolichucky River
Pisgah National Forest
The Qualla Boundary
The Tuckaseegee River

In Tennessee:
Great Smoky Mountains National Park
The French Broad River
The Holston River
The Nolichucky River
The Pigeon River
The Tennessee River

Other States:
National Museum of the American Indian, Washington, D.C.
Shenandoah National Park, Virginia
Rabun County, Georgia

About Katherine Scott Crawford

Katherine Scott Crawford's writing has appeared in newspapers, magazines, and literary journals. A native South Carolinian, she has  spent most of her life outdoors—hiking, paddling, and backpacking through the Southern Appalachian backcountry. Winner of a North Carolina Arts Award by the N.C. Arts Council, she holds degrees in English and Speech & Communications Studies from Clemson University, the College of Charleston and The Citadel, and is currently working towards a MFA in Writing from the Vermont College of Fine Arts.

An unabashed travel junkie, she's also spent short (and long) stints backpacking, writing, and playing in Alaska, Montana, Costa Rica, Italy, Panama, and Scotland. Despite the call of her far-too-crisp passport, the American South remains her favorite home base. She writes, teaches, and hikes in the mountains of Western North Carolina, where she lives with her husband, young daughter, and favorite trail partner: her 90 lb dog, Scout. Keowee Valley is her first novel.

Visit her web site at www.katherinescottcrawford.com for more information, to connect with Katherine on Facebook, via Twitter, and to find her blog, The Writing Scott.

CPSIA information can be obtained at www.ICGtesting.com
Printed in the USA
LVOW12s1103231213

366559LV00002B/139/P